THUNDER ON THE LAKE

CALLING YOU HOME
BOOK ONE

KARIN MALLARD

To the wolves —
Who aren't as big and bad as they seem

CONTENTS

1

STALKER BOOK CLUB

"Not again!" Ren burst out, glaring at his phone.

"Jeez! Ren, I thought we agreed no jump scares while I'm trying to solder microscopic wires together," Alek reminded from their dining room table, which was currently covered in a variety of tools, gears, a hand-drawn schematic, and a can of Coke that Alek insisted he was not drinking but using as some sort of caustic agent.

"Can you believe he canceled on me *again*?" Ren vocalized his annoyance, though he did gentle his tone, shoving his phone into his scrubs pocket. "The write-up is due Monday, but I can't even start unless I sit down and talk to this freak for at least twenty minutes."

"So corner him after class and follow him," Alek suggested mildly, selecting a miniature screwdriver from the assortment on the table.

"That'd be a great idea," Ren acknowledged, grumpily rearranging the contents of his backpack. "If he ever came to class!"

"Can you talk to the professor? Get an extension or a different partner or something?"

Ren paused, calming down thanks to his roommate's steady voice and practical commentary.

"He says he should be on campus tomorrow," Ren admitted. "I'll give him one more chance." Ren shrugged on his backpack over the bulkiness of his coat sleeves and stood in front of Alek. "Ok, I'm off; you can science in peace," Ren said, changing the subject. "How do I look?"

Alek barely glanced at him.

"Dude, you look like you always do. You're wearing a lab coat like every other tech in the place. If you want to impress her, you're going to have to talk to her."

"I do talk to her!" Ren protested.

"Taking her vitals doesn't count as conversation," Alek pointed out. "Would you just ask her out already? Bring her here; I'll cook. You can have the place to yourselves, but please, if you have ever cared about me, ask her out so I don't have to keep listening to you pining over her."

Ren fought the urge to throw his mittens at Alek's face.

"Yeah, yeah," Ren committed nonchalantly. "Just solder your wires and drink your Coke."

"I'm *not* drinking it," Alek protested. "It's for —"

"Tell me later," Ren interrupted, already on his way out. "I don't want to be late." He just caught a glimpse of Alek shaking his head as Ren closed the door behind him.

He'd only taken five steps outside before he almost slipped on an icy patch. A bit of ungraceful flailing saved him from going down, but it made him question, again, why he'd picked a college so far north. Surely, he could have gotten into a pre-med program somewhere warmer? Like Loma Linda? He wondered if they would have required him to take English 101, do a stupid interview, and write a biography on his emo, absent classmate who kept making plans to meet and then rescheduling.

Come to think of it, Ren hadn't responded after receiving the last text. Checking ahead to make sure the sidewalk was shoveled and ice-free, he pulled out his phone, reading the latest from his partner one more time.

Stuck in meetings, it said. *Tomorrow at 7?* But Ren couldn't do tomorrow at seven; he'd be working until after eight. But did he dare ask for that kind of change? Maybe it'd be easier to ask his supervisor to get off early; this guy's schedule was tighter than the lid on a leaky tube of glue. On the other hand, Ren had already bent over backwards the last ten days whenever a new time was suggested, and he was sick of it. Because really, what kind of meetings could possibly be going on that would require this kind of flaky behavior?

I can do eight-thirty tomorrow, Ren typed. *Meet you at the library by that picture of James Joyce.*

"Last chance, psycho," he said to himself, replacing his phone and mitten. Then he plunged both hands in his pockets, hunched his face deeper into his scarf, and tried to pretend he was home on a beach instead of freezing his way to the plasma donation center on Maryland Avenue.

It wasn't a requirement to be in any kind of med program to work at the center as a phlebotomist, but it certainly helped Ren get the job. Working there gave him good practice, better connections, and enough funding to buy groceries. And it meant that every Wednesday he would see Celeste Lyons.

Celeste didn't come every week because she needed grocery money; she came because she was a humanitarian. Ren was completely fascinated by her. Her dedication to service was just one part of her charm; it didn't hurt at all that she was the most pristine kind of gorgeous he'd ever seen. White-blonde hair, fair skin, and eyes the multi-color of crystals when you try to take pictures of them, a very specific shade of light blue and almost pink, with an impossible-to-describe inner brightness. And even though it had nothing to do with anything, Ren couldn't get over the fact that she wore a perfectly white peacoat.

The first time he met her, she'd dropped her book trying to turn a page. Ren happened to be right there, so he picked it up and helped her find her place again. He couldn't remember the title of that first one, but he looked at them all now. Spied on the title, checked them out at the library, and read them so they could have something to start a conversation over.

Except he never got that far. He'd read so many Jane Austen-esque period romances that he'd started to dream in Regency all without ever saying a word to Celeste about any of them. No wonder Alek teased him. What kind of idiot stayed up until four in the morning reading *Pride and Prejudice* for a girl without ever telling her about it?

"Hey, Ren," one of his coworkers nudged him as they stood washing their hands together, five minutes to six, right on schedule. "Your girl's here."

Everyone who worked with him knew Ren had dibs on Celeste, and his seniority at the center granted him status as her designated tech. Ren dried his hands, grabbed Celeste's chart from the wall, and crossed the floor to where she sat in the waiting area. He hunched a little as he walked as if his racing heart could be seen through his scrubs. It never changed. It never mattered how often he looked at her. It had the same effect on him every single time.

"Must be Wednesday," he said as he approached, hoping his voice sounded casual. "I've got your chair ready, Celeste."

She smiled at him, grabbing her bag and standing — more proof they were made for each other. Celeste stood a model five foot nine inches tall, the perfect complement to his six one. He gestured for her to make herself comfortable in the donation chair as he grabbed a new venipuncture kit and attempted unawkward small talk.

"How was your week?" he began with a safe question as he attached a blood pressure cuff to her arm. She already had her book out, a new one, but it was upside down and under her palm so he couldn't see the title yet.

"Chaotic," she answered vaguely in her beautiful accent. He knew it wasn't British, but it sounded similarly sophisticated, nicely trimmed around the consonants. When he asked her where she was from once, she'd raised her eyebrow and said Oak Brook. He'd had to look it up, disappointed to see it was not in Europe at all. It was on the top ten list of wealthiest suburbs in Chicago. Which explained why she didn't need to donate for the money.

Ren wished she'd elaborate on what chaotic meant, but he didn't ask. Instead, he focused on scrubbing her arm sterile with iodine and peeling bits of medical tape from the roll in his pocket.

"Little sting here," he warned, because no matter how skilled you were, and Ren had been told that he was *very* skilled, he was still piercing through skin with something sharp. He used his thumb to press where he needed to insert, holding her arm still and steady, expertly slipping the point in place and covering the puncture site with a piece of gauze. "And done. All right?"

"Perfect," she assured, and his soul melted as they made eye contact. *Yes, you are.* He hooked up the tubes and pushed the necessary buttons on the centrifuge, starting the first draw. He heard a beeping from another chair in his area. Someone was finished.

"I'll come check you in a few minutes," he promised, allowing himself to brush two fingers against her hand in parting.

The center was getting busy, which was normal for the evening. But it meant that by the time Ren made it back to Celeste, she was over halfway through her cycle. She had her legs drawn up, resting the book against her thighs, hand draped over the top to keep it open. It was larger than the books she usually brought, hardcover, tiny print.

"How are we doing over here?" he alerted her to his presence. "Feeling ok?" He knew she was ok. Her vitals were fine; her color was amazing. She'd done this many times before. She raised her eyes to him and nodded.

"What are you reading?" he asked since he couldn't see from the way she was holding it. He hoped it wasn't more Austen. She twisted her wrist without speaking, allowing him to read the title. It was a biography about a doctor, Paul Farley, who specialized in tuberculosis. Ren felt a little zing of excitement. He'd already read that! Not only that ...

"Oh cool, I met him once," he told her, with perhaps too much enthusiasm, the words coming out of his mouth before he had really planned on whether it would be a good idea. "Dr. Farley, I mean." Celeste's eyes widened in surprise. It was the first time Ren had ever gotten any kind of emotional response from her.

"You did?" she questioned, tone interested and eager. Right? That's what Ren was hearing anyway. Definitely interested. "Where?"

"In the Dominican Republic," he answered, hoping he wouldn't stutter or forget English words. Two things he almost never did anymore, but this was the most interaction they'd ever had so he was in new territory. "Mostly he works in Haiti, but he comes to the Dominican every so often. He gave a lecture near my hometown once when I was in high school."

"That's amazing," Celeste told him, which made his knees feel weird, like they weren't going to hold him anymore. "I'm supposed to do a report about him for my humanities class."

Another beep across the floor. Ren groaned inwardly. He'd have to leave to see what that was, abandoning all the progress they were making. "Be right back," he said. Except it took longer than he thought. He cleared a clotted line, restocked a cart, started a new donor, and walked a finished donor to the cashier. Ren didn't have another minute to spare for Celeste until her machine started beeping.

"Great job," he congratulated, shutting down the machine and beginning the process of disconnecting Celeste from it, gently removing the tape, folding a new patch of gauze into a tight square, and pressing it on top of the needle. In one smooth motion, he pulled it free. "You know what to do," he said, but she was already lifting her arm, pressing hard on the gauze square to stop the bleeding.

"I was thinking," Celeste said slowly as Ren gathered the used tubes for biohazard waste. He paused, unsure what to do. She didn't initiate conversation. "If you had some time, maybe we could get together and talk about your experience with Dr. Paul Farley. It would make an excellent addition to my report to note his influence extended to students at our university, don't you think?"

Ren missed the waste container, dropping the tubes straight onto the floor. He felt heat in his face and ducked down quickly, narrowly missing knocking his head against the corner of the cart holding the centrifuge, gathering up the tubes. Was she asking him out? Is that what was happening?

"Uh, well, yeah, sure," he stammered, hating himself for it. Then hating himself even more when he couldn't seem to shut up. "I mean, if you think it would help. Yeah, we can chat about it. He's an awesome guy. Where should we meet? At my place, maybe? Or yours, or you know, wherever you want." *Jeez, Lorenzo, shut the hell up!* "I mean — when?" he finally finished, turning his head away, wishing he could redo that entire outburst.

She had an amused expression on her lips now, her eyes sparkly. He could only look at her out of the corner of his eye.

"Friday?" she suggested calmly, magnanimously ignoring everything he'd just done. "At seven? I'll already be at the library; do you think you could meet me there?"

"Yeah, cool. Sounds great," Ren replied, drowning in dopamine. "I'll see you then." He nodded, pivoting, ready to make an exit before he did anything else stupid.

"Um, excuse me!" Celeste called after him, and he turned to look over his shoulder, wondering what she could have to add. "Aren't you going to finish my bandage?" It took a lot of effort not to smack himself in the face. She was sitting there with her arm still raised, looking confused.

"Ha," Ren half-laughed, not knowing how he was going to go out with her on Friday since it suddenly seemed a really good idea to go drown himself in Lake Michigan. "Yeah, let's take care of that."

He kept his mouth closed and eyes down, purposefully not looking at her so he could finish what he had to do on autopilot. Even though his insides were trembling, his hands were steady as he carefully lowered her hand and wrapped blue gauze around her elbow. He heard himself tell her the required precautions she should follow after a donation, having said those words so many times already he could do it without any conscious effort. The comfort of the routine relaxed him. He even managed the courage to lightly place his hand on the small of her back as she stood from the chair, and he left it there as he walked her over to the cashier.

Before he moved on to attend to his other donors, she dipped in her bag for a notebook and pen, writing her number for him. "See you Friday," she said, smiling. He didn't trust his brain not to betray him, so he simply nodded.

It was a good thing he was so used to the rhythm of the donation center. By the time he finished the rest of his shift and was once again outside walking home, he realized he couldn't remember doing a single thing after Celeste left. He checked his pocket, making sure that precious slip of paper was still there. Friday. They'd be together in the library; he would figure out a speech by then of what he was going to say because obviously he couldn't be trusted with improv. Oh! And he could finally be wearing clothes for once!

Alek had been busy while Ren was gone; Ren opened the door to a cleared table and the most heavenly scent coming from the kitchen. Alek wasn't taking classes this semester; he was working part-time as a research assistant and waiting to see if some special internship position was going to come through from the Jet Propulsion Laboratory in California. Which meant he had more time and desire for cooking than Ren did.

"Alek, that smells amazing," Ren said gratefully, happy to enjoy the results of Alek's hobby. "What is it?"

"Nothing much," Alek recited as he ladled up what looked like chowder into bowls. There was a fresh loaf of bread on the table, made from Alek's treasured yeast starter. "A dash of chemistry, a pinch of alchemy. Intentional, controlled reactions requiring temperature elevation — just the usual."

"Is this dinner or a Potions assignment?"

"I'll tell you later."

"You two are the biggest dorks."

Oh, so Denny was here. Ren should have known. She joined them from the bathroom, her tone sharp but her hazel eyes affectionate. Ren liked it when she had dinner with them. He also liked it when she and Alek brought all their super-smart, adorably awkward physicist buddies over. It made it feel more like the home he'd left when the apartment was full of people and good food, the atmosphere chatty and warm.

"Hey, Denny," Ren greeted, removing all his winter gear and tossing it on the camp chair near the door that they used as a coat rack. "Any word yet?" He already knew the answer; if they'd heard good news, he would have come home to a party. And if it had been bad, Alek would probably be a sobbing mess of disappointment on the sofa. Denny had applied with Alek for the JPL team internship, the physicist to his engineering.

"No," Alek said, wilting slightly. Every day that went by without a call or letter from California drained hope from Alek. Denny remained undaunted, though.

"Any day, now," she maintained, certain. "For sure we'll know before the end of February."

"Because the positions start on March first?" Ren guessed.

"Precisely," Denny complimented, missing that Ren had been half-teasing her. They automatically took seats at the table as they spoke while Alek set down bowls and spoons. It felt snug and pleasant, Ren's little college family all together on a winter evening.

"So Renzo, did you ask her?" Alek asked, sitting down.

"Oh yeah, it's Wednesday, isn't it?" Denny interjected, cutting into the bread. "What's the newest title in your stalker book club?" Ren looked up from the spoon he'd just put in his mouth, stamping this moment in his emotional memory, the moment right before he dropped the news that even though they'd been laughing at him for over a semester, Ren had Celeste's number in his pocket.

"A biography on Paul Farley," Ren replied, trying to keep his voice smooth. Like this wasn't very exciting. "She's doing a report."

"That's different," Denny said, unconvinced.

"Wait, I know that name. How do we know him?" Alek said slowly, like he was scanning his memory.

"Because I met him once," Ren reminded them. "Went to one of his lectures back home, so I thought I could offer to help her get a little more in-depth material."

"Shame you didn't," Denny lamented, teasing.

"Oh yeah?" Ren shot back, pulling the slip of paper from his pocket and slapping it on the table like a winning poker hand. "Then why are we getting together on Friday to talk about it?"

"Ren, dude!" Alek boomed, congratulatory. Denny snatched up the paper, examining it like a merchant inspecting potentially counterfeit currency. Alek punched him in the arm. "Man, finally."

"You sure this is her number?" Denny had the audacity to ask, tainting the moment. "Did you test it to make sure she didn't give you one to the humane society or something?"

Ren felt a sliver of doubt pierce his heart. It hadn't occurred to him that stuff like that happened. She'd asked him after all. He guessed it could be a set up, but he dismissed it rapidly. People who went to the trouble of donating plasma in the middle of winter every single week were probably above that kind of wickedness.

"Have a little faith," he said, leaning over the table to take the number back. The paper suddenly seemed fragile to him now.

They finished eating, concluding with a brief but intense argument between Alek and Denny about if it was Denny's turn to do the dishes. Ren won the point for Alek with a quiet but clear, "freeloaders clean." He didn't know why he bothered. It was only a few minutes before Alek was standing at the sink with her, both scrubbing, rinsing, and drying while chatting a million miles an hour about the whatever-it-was Alek had been tinkering with earlier, its purpose and functionality, and the upcoming test they were going to conduct to see if it really would do what Alek intended when he made it.

Ren sat relaxed at the table, just watching them, not understanding half of what they were saying. Something about the space station and the legality of broadcasting music. Denny was adamant in the affirmative, but Alek wanted a cited reference. One of them had the music in question playing on their phone as they worked. It sounded familiar, but Ren didn't know the name.

"Hey!"

Ren startled, blinking fast to reorient himself as their conversation melded around him again.

"Huh?" he said, wondering how long and how far he'd strayed from their talking.

"He's all blissed out," Denny noted, smiling indulgently and slipping her arms around his neck, her hands still slightly wet from the dishwater. Denny was the smartest person Ren knew, though Alek came in at a quick second. She didn't express affection physically often, so when she did, he took advantage of it; this time grabbing her tight and pulling her in close. He knew she'd only allow it for five seconds, but it was worth the annoyed squawking when she got tired of it.

"You're so pathetic," she whispered kindly into his ear. "Now let me go."

"So anyway," Alek redirected Ren as he detached himself from Denny. "I wanted to go over some things with Denny. Did you need the table, or can we set our stuff up?"

"Go ahead," Ren told them, standing. It was study time for him anyway. "Try not to stay up all night?" He loved them both dearly, but it always weirded him out when he found them still at it in the morning, the late hours working them into a disheveled frenzy. A little too close to the mad scientists of old movies for his comfort level.

They waved him off; the table quickly disappearing as Alek and Denny began the elaborate set up of whatever they were going to need. Ren had a moment of guilt looking at them. Alek had half-remembered the single time Ren mentioned Paul Farley, but Ren didn't have a clue what was happening with that transmitter. He promised himself that he would have Alek show him sometime tomorrow.

And yet, as with many of his good intentions, he ended up simply running out of time. Denny was missing when he returned to the kitchen shortly after sunrise, and he could hear Alek snoring softly from his bedroom. The table was still cluttered with a little note:

We had to choose — clear the table or not stay up all night. I'll do it later. Promise!

Ren wasn't too worried. He started the coffeemaker, moving quietly so as not to disturb his gentle roommate. By the time he'd finished getting his things together for the day, the pot was ready to transfer to his travel mug. He poured in half the liquid, leaving the rest for Alek. Thursdays were full days — biology lab for the entire morning, a quick lunch, child development, chemistry, and his longest shift at work. Then the library for the English assignment. Maybe.

Ren checked his phone, surprised he hadn't received a cancellation text from his mysterious and flaky-as-hell partner yet. This really might be happening after all. Weird. While he had his phone out, Ren entered Celeste into his contacts, feeling more secure once he had the number in two places.

"Bye Alek," he whispered, simply for the tradition of the thing, pulling the door shut behind him. It was the last thing he did slowly all day.

His mother told him, half fondly and half in exasperation, that Ren had been born with something to prove. Consequently, he moved through his life as though he were always running late. Other children learned to walk at thirteen months? Ren started at nine and was swimming shortly after that. By kindergarten, he could read his native Spanish, and he had a good grasp on English as well. And by the time he was ten, he could mimic just about any of the accents of the one million tourists that flocked to the beaches of Cabarete each year, a trick that earned him trust and tips from visitors who needed a guide or information. Now he spoke English with a Midwestern accent so perfectly that no one ever asked him where he came from — making it an accomplishment that canceled itself out because he'd done it so well that no one knew it was an accomplishment. But that was fine. Because Ren never did anything halfway.

That's why, even though he was only in his second year of pre-med, he already kept a fully stocked emergency medical kit. Why he was already a volunteer EMT. He'd trained himself in first aid and charmed his way into the hearts of the staff at the campus hospital. One of the doctors even allowed Ren to shadow him and gave Ren time on Sunday afternoons to go over case studies. His relentless pace earned him a lot of incredulity and head shaking, but Ren brushed off teasing, competitiveness, and even hostility. All he cared about was the next milestone toward his personal MD finish line. Progress on his checklists, finishing the next thing.

They'd talked about it once — Ren with Alek, Denny, and a behavioral psychology book in front of them, studying about STAR personalities. It had been Ren's homework, but since it had the word "star" in it, the other two put down their astrological charts to listen. They'd figured out immediately that Denny was the T — technical, hungry for knowledge, and logical. Alek was the R — into relationships, empathy, and morality. Then they'd debated back and forth on whether Ren was an action-oriented A or a systems-driven S. In the end, they'd concluded S — citing his passion for spreadsheets as evidence.

"We should find ourselves an A," Alek suggested. "Get a complete set." The structure of that idea sounded good to Ren too, but when Denny said it sounded too much like a boy band, they moved on. Ren sometimes still thought of himself as an A, particularly when his schedule seemed over the top, but then he would find himself contentedly standing in his Stony Island apartment with all his medical accoutrements spilled over the table, structurally ordering and organizing his bag. The ritual of checking each article and putting it into place, restocking things like bandages, tape, and painkillers, confirmed that his friends were right. He was an S.

He couldn't help it, though. He liked it. Thrived on it. Most of the time, it served him well. But then there were times, like now, actually, sitting here fuming under the picture of an equally frustrated-looking James Joyce, where being an S meant that Ren hated it when plans fell through, when things changed too quickly without notice. Ren had a schedule, and he wanted it respected. Why was that so hard?

Ren checked his phone. No sign or word from his partner. Where the hell was he? How come he didn't have the decency to at least say he wasn't coming again? Ren was sitting here still in his scrubs, starving, an ache in his lower back from the hours he'd spent hunched over tubes and monitors. His hands were chapped from washing them constantly at work and from the cold that persistently penetrated his mittens. He didn't want to be here either. He wanted to be at home, eating a late dinner and listening to Alek talk about his transmitter. Maybe Ren should switch and write the biography on Alek instead. How would his teacher even know? Ren checked the phone again. He'd give Justin until close, the last possible second to make good on his promise that they'd meet today.

Not one to waste time and needing a distraction, Ren took his uncomfortable fury and plunged it deep into his coursework, which he had brought with him for this exact reason, somehow knowing in his soul that he was going to be stood up again. He read the next child development chapter, balanced some chemistry equations, and finally started writing the biography assignment based solely on his perception of his partner. It was full of snark and judgment, but it felt so good to bash it all down on paper.

Justin Kittrick is the poster child of irresponsibility, Ren began with the surest of thesis statements and went on about Justin's many, varied, and completely fabricated faults. Why not? It wasn't like he was here to set the record straight. *He's horrible at communication, lacking in integrity, broody, a slacker, and a future drain on the community.* Ren even knew, without a shadow of a doubt, that whenever a loud vehicle screeched past a window in the dead of night, squealing

tires or revving motors, ripping decent people from their sleep —
most assuredly, every time, no matter where in the country he
happened to physically be, it was Justin's fault.

Ren wrote until the library announced closing time, scrawling in
conclusion that he was putting all six of his names on this essay,
because he had never spoken a word to Justin and this was a one-
man effort performed by me, myself, and I. Then he closed the notebook, zipped up his backpack, and headed home. He'd talk to the
professor in the morning, explain how he'd given Justin more
chances than he thought should be required of any patient mortal,
and he simply had to find an alternative. He was unwilling to be held
accountable for Justin's truancy. He was in college, for heaven's sake!
Wasn't it way beyond time to have to do shitty things like picking up
all the slack for group assignments? The stakes were higher now; if
Ren wanted to be a doctor, he had to graduate college. If he wanted
to continue in college, he needed his scholarship. In order to keep his
scholarship, he had to maintain near perfect grades. And while he
didn't exactly know what a missing English 101 biography would do
as far as his overall GPA, it just felt wrong to lose points on something so simple. What if he needed that decimal cushion for something more serious?

Being pissed off kept him warm on the fifteen-minute walk back
to the apartment. At least he hadn't noticed the cold as much as he
normally did. Or maybe he was just too tired to pay any attention.
Thursdays were such long days.

He'd no sooner opened his door when Alek was on top of him.

"Where have you been?" Alek accused. "Since when do you come
home after eleven?" He kept it up as Ren took off his coat, scarf, and
mittens, waiting until Ren finished to motion Ren over to the table.
Ren was too tired to do anything except submit, noticing that Alek
was already in his pajamas. Apparently without Denny around, he
wasn't planning another late night messing with wires.

"I was at the library," Ren reminded him. It wasn't like either of
them needed permission to be anywhere, nor did they really have a

curfew, but out of friendship and for safety's sake they usually kept tabs on each other's schedules.

"I thought your date was tomorrow," Alek challenged, though now he sounded uncertain. Like he'd missed something. Maybe Ren hadn't told him he was going somewhere after work. That made him feel guilty. Especially as Alek was moving around the kitchen, putting together hot tea and buttering toast, continuing to talk as he cooked. "Or wait — was it for your English thing? That guy finally showed?" Ren's guilt magnified. How did Alek remember all this stuff?

"Supposed to be, but no, he didn't," Ren answered both questions, tucking one of his legs under him on the chair before remembering it was still January, which meant the bottom four inches of his pants were always going to be soaked. "But no one can ever say I didn't give him a chance."

"I wonder what's up with that?" Alek mused, absently putting toast, eggs, and tea in front of Ren.

"Um, he's a lazy slacker?" Ren answered, not having thought much about the why of the absences and lack of communication. "He hates me? I have the best roommate ever so the universe is seeking balance by giving me crappy homework partners?"

"I doubt it," Alek dismissed the compliment. "How could he hate you? I mean, you've never talked to the guy. What if something happened to him, you know? Like maybe he had a family emergency out of state? Like a funeral?"

"Or maybe it's January and the skiing is really good in Colorado," Ren shot back, not feeling particularly forgiving. Though the tea was helping.

"I'm just saying you can't hate him before you know what happened," Alek counseled, and Ren knew he was right but didn't want to say it. He rolled his eyes as he chewed.

"I don't even care what happened," Ren said callously. "I'm talking to the professor tomorrow to see if he'll let me do the write-up on you instead."

"Me?" Alek asked, and Ren could tell he'd caught him off guard, but in a good way. Much like Ren's accent, Alek didn't get near enough credit for his accomplishments.

"Yeah, you're endlessly fascinating and infinitely more available. Would you mind?"

"I guess not," Alek pretended to think about it, obviously pleased.

"Thanks, man," Ren sighed, putting down his fork on his empty plate. "Maybe we can start with your transmitter? I'm not sure what you're doing with it."

Alek picked up the dishes and set them in the sink, shaking his head. "We'll get there," he acknowledged. "Later. Get to bed before you fall asleep at the table."

"I really do want to know," Ren protested, trying to be convincing. Alek shooed him away.

"And I want to tell you," Alek returned. "But only once, ok?"

"Ok," Ren gave in. "You need help cleaning up?" He felt completely spoiled.

"Go to bed, Renzo," Alek commanded, knowing Ren didn't do well if he stayed up too late. Ren thought a minute about pushing the issue, but let it go. Alek was right; he was too tired to pay attention. After changing, brushing his teeth, and burrowing under his quilt, he was asleep in seconds.

2

STARTLE REFLEX

When Ren woke the next morning, he was certain it was a mistake. He may be an early riser, but this was too dark even for him. He checked the time, then the weather, and realized what was going on. Chicago had been taken hostage by a change in wind direction. There would be snow later, probably a lot of it. And Ren had been in the city long enough that the idea of a fresh snowfall no longer charmed him. He pulled his quilt off the bed, wrapping himself up as he stood to look out the window, studying the gloom that seemed to be crawling out of Lake Michigan like a horror movie. The only thing separating him from the threatening shore was the two-mile span of the Museum of Science and Industry.

Getting started on his morning routine, he pulled his warmest thermal sweater from his drawer and threw on his maroon college hoodie over it. Then he neatly replaced the quilt and moved toward the kitchen to start the coffee, pausing in the hall to nudge the thermostat higher. Not too much, just a few degrees. Alek was a native Hawaiian, so he also preferred things warm, but they found out quickly that if they wanted to avoid extra electric charges, they needed to set temperature boundaries. It made them both feel victimized and chilly.

Alek surprised him by flopping down on the couch just as the coffee finished. They hardly ever saw each other in the mornings unless Alek had stayed up all the previous night or something kept Ren home late enough. Alek had a notebook with him, also an unusual sight before breakfast.

"Morning, sunshine," Ren greeted, smiling as Alek yawned, still in his pajamas and looking rumpled.

"Where?" Alek asked innocently, glancing around as if to make it clear that there was no sunshine, morning variety or otherwise. Ren patted his shoulder in solidarity as he handed over a brimming coffee mug.

"Sorry if I woke you," Ren apologized, leaning back against the counter with his own steaming cup.

"You didn't, I needed to see you before you go," Alek replied, safely depositing his coffee and opening the notebook. "Looks like it's going to be awful all weekend, so I'm going grocery shopping today instead of tomorrow. Do you need anything?"

"Mangoes," Ren responded immediately, not without bitterness, picturing the fully laden trees in his backyard. The shade of their leaves, the hum of the bees as they crowded around the dropped fruit, the taste of the warm sun.

"Frozen?" Alek clarified, abruptly shaking him away from the memory, reminding him that mangoes were not always so readily available.

"Yeah," Ren replied, resigned. "Frozen mangoes and coconut milk."

"You know you're lying to yourself if you think blending an icy tropical smoothie is going to make it seem in any way close to warm here, right?" Alek said skeptically while Ren hid his face in his mug. "But sure. Smoothie stuff. Anything else?"

"No, just the usual. Spinach, milk, whatever you get that turns into dinner every day. More coffee. How bad is it supposed to snow?"

Ren switched directions so fast he suspected Alek had written half his question as if he were still making a list. Ren grinned as Alek scratched part of what he'd written out.

"Bad enough that Denny wants to stay with us this weekend," Alek said, once he'd processed the question. "The second subject I needed to ask you about."

"You know you don't have to ask about that," Ren returned. "Denny is welcome whenever."

"Yeah, I know, but are you bringing Celeste home with you or anything?" Ren felt his brain tighten around the question, snapping to it with instant focus. He'd almost forgotten about that! It was Friday.

"Oh!" he said, not sure if he was excited or terrified. "Right. No, we're not coming back here; we're meeting at the library, so she probably wouldn't want to ... not if it's snowing. But what if she does? What do I do if she wants to? But then what if she cancels? What if the weather is too bad to meet? Should we reschedule?"

"Ren, chill," Alek commanded, pressing a hand in midair as if lowering a valve. "How about this? I'll plan on yes, make enough food, and wait to put blankets on the couch until we know one way or the other. Deal?"

"But should I ask her, though?" Ren queried again, feeling out of his element. Like he'd made a mistake before he'd even done anything.

"Eh, do what feels right," Alek advised carelessly, which didn't help at all. Ren set down the last few sips of his coffee. He didn't feel like finishing it now.

"Bold of you to assume," Ren muttered, retrieving his coat from the pile near the door.

"Don't worry so much," Alek told him.

"Easy for you to say," Ren said, smiling through his nerves, buttoning his coat and his humor tightly in place. "Sitting there, practically engaged —"

"Don't be late, Ren," Alek dismissed, bending over the notebook again, an unexpected flush on his cheeks. Ren knew he didn't mind it nearly as much as he pretended.

"Careful out there," Ren warned on his way out, serious again. "Let's not get into fistfights over the last quart of milk, right?" Because Alek was not the only one making a list right now, Ren was certain. It would soon be in the news, if it wasn't already, that citizens should be getting prepared to be snowed in for the weekend. Which meant they would all be out at the stores, buying extra toilet paper, stripping the shelves of medication, bread, and bottled water.

Ren started making a mental check list as he walked of what he should do when he got back from class. Make sure the flashlights have batteries, refill their emergency water supply. Figure out a spot on their balcony to put the stuff from the fridge in case the power went out.

Denny thought he was crazy the first time he'd gone into disaster stashing mode, called him dramatic, told him it was never as bad as the weathermen claimed it would be, but she was the first to show up when the storm started, and finally admitted that Ren was smart as they cuddled together in the dark, electricity-less apartment, eating egg rolls warmed with a camp stove. Hopefully, it wouldn't be that bad again. Ren glanced above him at the heavy clouds, wondering when it would start.

Until the first snowflakes did make their appearance, however, there was no reason not to go about business as usual. Which for a Friday meant English 101, which Ren didn't enjoy. Not just because of Justin, either. First, it seemed irrelevant to his future goals. Second, he'd already learned to speak English, so the challenge of it was already over for him. Third, the professor was one of those embittered, failed creative writers who didn't seem to particularly like teaching. Once he'd come to class with a guitar and a harmonica in a holder around his neck. He sat on his desk, played both instruments at once, sang "Like a Rolling Stone" not so much out of key but in a painfully put on gravel-ish tone, told them all to "think about that" and marched angrily out of the room. The only thing Ren thought about that was how he'd trudged all the way over in the snow to witness some sort of hippy mid-life crisis.

Professor Gibbon didn't have his guitar today, though. He did have a reminder about the biography due on Monday, and a discussion on the components of a decent cover letter. Ren sat up straighter. Cover letters could be important someday. He took his notes and drafted a template, satisfied with the lesson, but not forgetting he needed to do something about his assignment for Monday.

He had to hurry through the crowd of students shielding themselves into their winter gear to catch his teacher after class, gaining a surprised look when Ren appeared at the front desk, but Ren had to plead his case. He kept it short and relatively free of whining.

"So how can I write a biography on him if I can't even find him?" Ren finished his concrete argument. "The only way I feel I can complete this assignment is if I talk to my roommate instead."

"I don't have a problem with it," his teacher allowed, his words and his tone contradicting each other. "But you do realize Justin's sitting right there?"

"What?" Ren said, confused. Professor Gibbon pointed to the back of the room where Justin sat with his notebook open, resting his head on his hand. Ren felt his jaw drop. "No." Justin hadn't come to class in over a week! When did he get here? Ren was certain he hadn't been that interested in cover letters.

"It's up to you," Professor Gibbon dismissed, gathering his coat and his bag, obviously already finished with the conversation. "But I'd rather you and your partner work together." The way he talked; he sounded like he didn't believe Ren had tried to contact Justin. Ren wanted to rip his phone out of his pocket and show his teacher the long line of failed meeting attempts, how often he had shifted his schedule around. He had more than tried! But before he could get it out, Professor Gibbon nodded at him and headed out the door. "Good luck," he said over his shoulder.

The last of the students were clearing out as Ren shifted direction to the back of the classroom. Justin didn't move, and Ren confirmed his suspicions about why as he came to a stop directly in front of him. He'd propped himself up expertly, but he was undeniably asleep, his notebook blank. Ren folded his arms around his book, drumming his fingers irritably against the spine as he thought about what he wanted to say to this jerk who had just made him look like an idiot in front of the professor — the latest in a long inconsiderate list.

Their classroom was divided by three long tables, ten chairs lined up along each to accommodate the class, one of the smaller rooms. Justin sat at the end of the last one, farthest from the whiteboard at the front, closest to the door at the back. Where losers sit. People who come late only to fall asleep in class. People who ghost their partners.

Ren hovered over Justin from the other side of the table and couldn't remember a single thing Alek had said about getting his side of the story for why he'd been missing, couldn't gather a scrap of sympathy. Though it was exceedingly rare for Ren, all he felt as he stood there watching Justin sleep was a fiery hatred. How could he be so irresponsible? This wasn't a community college, so how did people like Justin even get accepted? It had taken all Ren had to get here. How fair was that?

Without thinking, Ren lifted his textbook high and then crashed it hard on the table right next to Justin's head. For one second, it felt deeply satisfying, the righteous pleasure of vengeance, but that moment disappeared as Ren was suddenly introduced to the consequences of what he'd just done.

Justin jerked awake, as expected, but instead of cowering, or perhaps tripping backward on his chair like the statistical majority, he leaped to his feet and instantaneously threw a right hook that connected solidly against Ren's left cheekbone, hard enough to knock him to the floor, white splashing over his vision in a brilliant starburst that faded out in rainbow static. Ren instinctively covered his head, turning away from the violence, tightening up as he waited for Justin to come kick him in the ribs for his little stunt. He blinked rapidly as his sight returned to normal, scrunching up that side of his face as he tried to figure out the damage by pain intensity alone. He'd never been punched in the head before.

"What the hell is your problem?" Justin growled, his voice raising all the hair at the back of Ren's neck because it was so quiet. Ren thought he'd feel better if Justin screamed at him. The low volume made Justin sound incredibly dangerous. Ren really should have thought this through better. And still, even though he was now on his side, half lying in the disgusting puddles of mush tracked in by the students all winter long, wondering if his cheekbone were cracked, Ren was still furious. He shoved himself to his feet, angry at himself for cowering and angry at Justin for just about everything. Ren had never intentionally hurt any living creature before, but today just might be the occasion to spoil his perfect record. He forced his hands into fists. He did his best to stand as tall as possible.

"You," Ren spat, cause, effect, and rage all in one.

"I don't even know you!" Justin returned defensively, breathing hard, still coming down from the fight response Ren had revved up in him. Seriously? Didn't know him? Unbelievable.

"You're kidding," he sputtered, surprisingly hurt more by these words than the punch. "Ren Cordero? We're partners? Supposed to be interviewing each other for Monday's assignment? You've been rescheduling on me for almost two weeks? *Ringing any bells for you?*"

As Ren spoke, harshly condescending, he gathered his courage to look Justin in the face, which washed him in immediate regret, all his fury evaporating. Something was wrong here. Ren may have taken the physical hit, but it was Justin who looked beat up, awful really. He stood there tensed and coiled, eyes hooded, fist drawn back, panting and surprisingly shaky. Ren relaxed, palms raising in surrender. He'd made such a mess of this with one careless moment. Why hadn't he taken a second to think? Alek had even warned him about it.

"I don't actually care," Justin hissed, voice still low, on edge, not shifting at all even though Ren was standing down. Ren felt guilt grip him by the throat as he registered Justin's posture. The shadows under his eyes. Ren knew these signs well, should have noticed them a lot sooner, and he felt compassion and shame swirl together nauseatingly in his stomach, not sure how to move forward from their standoff now that he'd ruined everything.

Ren had first tried his hand at healing when he was eight. The patient had been a sick, feral dog he'd found in an alley, too weak to move but with enough fight remaining in it to bite Ren's arm as he picked it up. He still had the scar. His parents were skeptical but believed in letting some lessons be learned the hard way, so they allowed Ren to make a bed for the animal in the goat shed. His mother joined him to dress his wound and try to coax him into the house, but Ren stubbornly wanted to sleep with the dog. By morning, Ren's arm was throbbing, and the dog was dead.

His dad and elder brother helped him bury it. However, Luis had harshly questioned Ren's judgment as he tore into the soil in the heat. Ren should have known better than to go near a feral dog, especially a sick one. It had been stupid. He had gotten exactly what he deserved. They were no good to anyone, so what if one died? Their father rebuked Luis quietly, making him leave Ren alone.

Ren heard what Luis said, but he couldn't make himself think he'd done something stupid. He sat near them as they worked, holding the dog, his arm heavily bandaged. His brother didn't understand. The dog bit him because it was scared, because no one had ever been nice to it. Ren couldn't stand that.

It had been years, but standing there looking at Justin, still tense, Ren could see the similarities. He hadn't thought about that dog in such a long time, but there was something fierce, feral, and wounded in Justin's expression that brought it back, his curled lips, his tight, trembling body. Ren should have approached this differently. He didn't know how to save the situation now — at least not without someone getting hurt.

"I'm sorry," Ren apologized, dropping his eyes and hands,

submitting to Justin's dominance to help him feel safer, needing to turn this around so he could talk to Justin, figure out what was really going on. "That was a jerk move; I shouldn't have done it." He knew better. He really wished he could take those moments back.

"You think?" Justin snapped, but there wasn't much strength in his voice. Ren thought he knew why but thanks to his own thoughtlessness, he didn't think he could get close enough to check. Justin still had his fists up and ready. Ren paused to gingerly touch the back of his hand against his cheek, shocked at the temperature difference. His hand felt so cold on his face, his cheek swollen and hot. He winced unconsciously, wondering what kind of damage Justin could inflict if he had the time to think about it, glad he hadn't decided to hit him more than once.

"Can we start over?" Ren offered, hoping the textbook and the punch could just cancel each other out. "Truce?" He extended his hand, but Justin eyed it suspiciously.

"Just stay the hell away from me," Justin told him hotly, turning away. Ren wilted, disappointed, then had to hurry and awkwardly catch his textbook when Justin flung it at him, discus-style, the corner gouging him in the chest.

"Ow, hey!" Ren grunted. Justin ignored him, bending to retrieve his backpack. He paused when he stood, his hand planted firmly on the table, his eyes closed. Ren felt his heart tighten up watching him; it looked wrong. "Justin?" he began, taking a cautious step nearer.

At the sound of his name, Justin turned his head, opening his eyes just enough to glare at Ren, who was studying him intently now, concerned, his EMT training prodding at him. The wild dog was still in Justin's expression, suffering, angry, scared to death. Ren held out his hand soothingly without thinking about it.

"Leave me alone," Justin commanded, slinging both backpack straps over one shoulder and hunching out of the room. Ren stood conflicted with his textbook in his hand, thinking maybe he should rush after him, despite what he'd just said. But then Ren blinked and even that tiny, unconscious motion hurt his wounded face, so he decided against it, letting Justin disappear down the hallway. Besides, even if he thought he could check on Justin without putting himself in physical danger, he didn't have time right now. So he packed up his stuff, threw on his coat, and hurried back to his apartment to change for his two-hour shift at work.

He paused just long enough to check himself over in the mirror, surprised at the reflection. His eye was fine, but there was already an impressive bruise splashed underneath it, running outward from the corner of his eye up toward his temple, his cheek visibly swollen. He grabbed a couple ibuprofen and swallowed them with water he drank straight from the bathroom faucet, feeling stupid. It was his own fault. He wondered how he was going to explain it to, oh, everyone who was going to see him in the next week or so. Like Celeste! He groaned, hanging his head over the sink. What a way to start a date. Of all the days to act like a moron. He never did stuff like that, what had possessed him?

But it was already done, no way to change it now. He'd have to figure it out later. Why he did it; what he was going to say when he was inevitably asked. Except instead of thinking up a story on what he'd done to himself, he found he couldn't stop worrying about Justin — the expression on his face, the broken posture, sleeping at the desk, how Ren had been so cruel to him without ever giving him a chance. He replayed their confrontation over in his mind all the way to the donation center. He'd given up on the idea that Justin might have a legitimate reason for not meeting with him. Because why not just say so if he did? Ren couldn't get over it. He was so shocked and disappointed with himself.

He ended up relying on what he did best regarding the startled questions he was peppered with all through his shift — telling a version of the truth. To his boss. His coworkers. The few, but regular, donors who had braved the weather to come in. "Oh yeah," Ren jokingly responded to all queries. "That? Got it in a fight, but wow, you should see the other guy!" That mostly brought unconvinced guffaws and the matter was dropped. To the very few who were still concerned and pressed him on what *really* happened, he poured on exaggerated sincerity. "But I did get in a fight. Dude got the first hit, but only one." The words were true. Except not completely. It worked here at the center, where people only thought they knew him. He'd have a harder time later, when he went home. When he'd have to confess to Alek not only how he got hurt but that he'd deserved it.

A group text arrived from Ren's Spanish teacher, canceling class that afternoon due to the weather forecast. It was still only threatening to snow, but the darkness had a weight to it now, the barometric pressure tangible in the air. The professor suggested the class use the time to review for the upcoming oral presentation, their choice of a poem or excerpt of Spanish literature. Ren wasn't worried about it. He'd already memorized Segismundo's monologue from the play *La Vida es Sueño*. A few recitations before class on Monday would do the trick for him.

That meant he suddenly had an open afternoon, a guilty conscience, and a growing need to check on his English partner. He called Denny before he left the donation center after his shift.

"Need some dating tips?" Denny purred into the receiver before any kind of greeting.

"What?" Ren asked, caught off guard before remembering that Denny was referencing his meeting with Celeste later that night. Why did he keep forgetting about that? Getting a date with her had been so high on his list of life goals he found it distressing how he had to be reminded so often. "No, that's not for hours. I've got that covered." That was a complete lie, but he had something else taking his attention right then. Ren had been focused on Justin for the last two hours. Standing there with his hand on the table and his eyes closed.

"Suit yourself," Denny told him, making him second guess the offer. Did he need dating tips? On the other hand, even if he did, could he trust taking them from Denny? She was brilliant and everything, but Alek had brought her to the apartment several times before Ren had even noticed she was a girl. "So what do you need?" she asked, changing the subject, obviously wanting to move forward so she could get back to whatever she'd been working on.

"I need an address," he said, favoring her wishes to get straight to the point, glad they weren't talking awkwardly about dating anymore. "Justin Kittrick — he's a student here. Can you figure out where he lives?"

"Can I?" Denny echoed, pretending to be offended.

"Will you?" Ren rephrased, but he didn't need to. He could hear her typing already. He hoped she wouldn't ask him what he wanted it for. He didn't have a good reason. Fortunately, Denny wasn't in the mood to be nosy, though she'd probably demand an explanation later. He added it to the growing list.

"You sure he's a student?" she asked after a couple seconds.

"He's in my English class, so yeah, I'd assume so. Is he not coming up?"

"Um, no, wait, got him," she said triumphantly, though Ren had no idea how she'd done it. He never asked, wanting to live in a place of plausible deniability. "He's in the system weird, but it says he's at Snell-Hitchcock, southwest building, room 110 on the first floor."

"You're amazing, Denny, thanks; see you tonight."

"Behave yourself," she teased, hanging up. He knew she was just saying that to say it, she had no real idea of who Justin was or why Ren was going to see him, but her comment still hit hard. If he'd behaved himself earlier, this whole thing might not have been necessary.

Was it necessary, though? Ren asked himself this repeatedly on the walk to the dorm. Maybe it was a bad idea. Justin had specifically told him to stay away. His face was already sporting the conse-quences of getting on Justin's bad side. He had a million other things he could be doing with his time right now and permission to do his biography on basically any other person in the world. If he kept walking, he could be snug in his apartment in no time at all, drinking hot chocolate with Alek, waiting for the snow. It was tempting.

"Do you really have to do this?" he asked himself out loud, standing outside the dorm entrance. He'd almost gathered enough internal momentum to walk away, forget all about it, but Justin's eyes wouldn't let him. The hand on the table. The vulnerable pause. Then a resident came out the door and politely held it open, leaving Ren no choice.

"Thanks," Ren said automatically, not sure if he meant it, stepping inside. He breathed deeply, down to the pit of his stomach, still uncertain what he was going to say. How would he even get Justin to trust him now? What if he wouldn't talk to him? What if he gave him a matching bruise on the other side?

He paused again in front of room 110, in the dark of the winter hallway, conflicted. His nerves told him to just leave. His heart told him to knock. *You don't owe this guy anything,* his logic said.

The memory of the dog came back to Ren. Even if he were totally wrong about Justin and what he thought he saw, he knew he wouldn't be able to get over it until he'd made sure. He put his palm against his arm, where the bite scar puckered his skin, then for the second time that day, he tightened his hand into a fist, this time to tap his knuckles against the door.

No response. Maybe Justin wasn't home? But no, Ren was all amped for this conversation now. If he had to summon his courage to come back later, he didn't think he could manage it. He knocked again, louder this time.

"Justin?" he called for good measure, not suspecting for one second that Denny could have given him incorrect information; his faith in her stronger than in himself. "Are you in there?"

His hand moved from chest height to the doorknob, his fingers wrapping around the old brass. "Justin," he said again, amazed how he could want two very different things at the same time. He wanted Justin to answer him. He really hoped he wouldn't. The knob turned as Ren twisted his wrist. That was a surprise. He wouldn't have put money on Justin being the kind of guy who left his door unlocked. Ren felt the latch give along with the resistance, the hinge ready to obey his next decision. If he wanted, he could let himself into Justin's dorm room. He took a moment to contemplate the consequences of that. It couldn't be considered breaking and entering if the door was unlocked, could it? And if Justin wasn't in there, then Ren would know in a matter of seconds and could leave immediately, with no one the wiser for the intrusion. But if Justin was there? Was there a reason he wasn't answering? Ren needed to find out.

"Justin, I'm coming in," Ren warned before he talked himself out of it, tugging the door and peeking timidly inside.

It was so tiny, so different from his own place, a cell rather than a room. There was a small window with a miniature desk beneath it straight across from the door. A dresser smashed against the wall on the left side of the room, and crowded on the right was a twin bed. With Justin just sitting up on top of it.

"Oh, hi," Ren stammered, surprised, worried about being responsible for waking Justin twice in a day. "You are here."

Justin blinked at him groggily. He was still wearing his coat and boots, as if he'd staggered through the door, tossed his backpack on the desk, and just collapsed into the bed. He looked terrible, worse than before. Ren suddenly didn't feel so dumb in making the decision to come check on him.

"What are you doing here? Go away," Justin commanded, his voice rough, a wild dog snarling out a warning. Ren softly closed the door. "I'm not doing the stupid assignment, got it?"

"That's not why I'm here," Ren told him, looking around. Not a single poster on the wall. Not a shred of personalization anywhere. The blanket could have been from a previous tenant or supplied by the residence hall. The desk was clear except for Justin's backpack. It looked like he'd just moved in but hadn't brought in all his stuff yet. Or like he was on his way out.

Ren brought his gaze back to Justin, who hadn't moved from the bed. Ren figured if Justin were going to attack him, he likely would have done it already. But he didn't look like he had the energy. He'd braced himself with one hand on the mattress, the finger and thumb of his other hand straddling his forehead, pressing against his temples. Ren helped himself to the chair at the desk, turning it so he could sit at Justin's level, the room so narrow their knees almost touched.

"How long have you been sick?" Ren asked him.

Justin lifted his hand away from his eyes just enough to glare suspiciously at Ren, obviously perturbed that he hadn't obeyed his request to get out. Ren watched as Justin scanned him critically up and down.

"What are you? A nurse?" Justin said, not answering the question but not denying it either, taking in the scrubs Ren was still wearing. Ren supposed the tone was meant to be condescending.

"Pre-med," Ren corrected quietly. "But I am a certified EMT."

Something slipped in Justin's expression, a tiny flash of innocence, not trust, but a glimmer that maybe he wanted to. It encouraged Ren into thinking they might be able to move forward, past this morning. Both Justin's hands gripped the mattress now, and he looked suddenly much younger, sitting there with hunched shoulders and bowed head. Shivering and helpless.

"I'd like to help," Ren offered. "If you'll let me. I'm sorry about earlier, that was not cool. I don't even know why I did it."

"I do," Justin whispered; Ren barely caught it. He didn't know what Justin meant, so he let it go. He wanted to move on.

"Can I touch you?" Ren asked for permission, not wanting to make the same mistake twice, though he was already reaching out as he said it, assuming cooperation. The one-way flow of the conversation was starting to become clear to him. Justin wasn't going to answer questions; he was too guarded. He didn't want anyone to see him weak, so he certainly wouldn't be admitting it. Ren had worked with people like him before. Hell, his own sister Siara was just like this. Justin wouldn't ask for help, but he wouldn't refuse either. So even though he didn't verbally respond, there was no resistance when Ren pulled his right hand away from where he clutched at the blanket.

"Checking your pulse," Ren explained as he turned Justin's wrist toward him, letting him rest his arm on Ren's knees. His skin was dry and hot. Ren settled his fingertips below Justin's thumb, counting as he looked at the clock on his phone — 105 beats per minute. Judging from Justin's physical appearance, Ren would guess his normal resting rate was closer to sixty.

"Can you turn your face up?" Ren asked, letting Justin's hand go. Justin looked doubtful, but after a moment's pause, he did as he was told, accepting Ren's authority even in his own room. Ren tried to rub his hands together for friction heat. "My hands are going to feel cold on your neck," Ren warned, but Justin still jumped at the contact. His temperature was so high that he shuddered under Ren's fingers. It only took a second to find Justin's lymph nodes, swollen and hard. Ren leaned back.

"Does your throat hurt?" Ren asked, narrowing down what he was seeing.

"It's like the only thing that doesn't," Justin confessed, shocking Ren. He hadn't been expecting Justin to answer like that. He'd been thinking he would have to drag every tiny bit of information out of him, one yes or no question at a time. Justin was either sick enough that his defenses were way down, or he was secretly relieved that Ren had forced himself into caring for him. Possibly both.

"I'm taking it you didn't get a flu shot this year?" Ren guessed. Justin shook his head. Ren swallowed the lecture he had prepared for that. He'd already given it to both Alek *and* Denny. Fortunately, Ren's own vaccination seemed to be holding up well.

Ren studied the room again, as if it were possible to miss something the first time. No bathroom in here. No sink. Snell-Hitchcock was one of those dormitories where all those things were communal. One huge bathroom per floor. One community kitchen. The worst place ever for a flu patient, both for his recovery and for likely spreading the contagion to the entire complex. Ren didn't like it.

"Do you have anybody who can come stay with you?" Ren asked. Justin stared at the floor, his shoulders twitching.

"Justin?" Ren tried again. "Is there someone you can call to come help you for a few days?"

The pause after the question went on so long that Ren grew worried. How high was this fever?

"Justin," Ren called him, going to his knees on the floor so he could look up into his face. There were tears in Justin's eyes, his mouth a tight bloodless line. No wonder he hadn't wanted to look up or speak. He had no one. He really was alone. Ren stared at the empty wall above the bed, the depressing atmosphere of the room. Ren stood up, folding his arms and shifting his weight on his heels. *You shouldn't have brought the dog home, Lorenzo.* Yeah, he knew. He shouldn't. He really shouldn't.

But he was going to do it anyway.

"All right," Ren said, frustrated, deciding against his better judgment. "Help me pack some stuff. You're coming home with me."

3
IN CASE OF EMERGENCY

"What?" Justin said, bewildered, not keeping up with Ren's suggestion. It had been sudden; Ren had surprised himself, but now he was committed. Ren gently pushed Justin sideways onto his bed so he could lie down while Ren began to assemble his stuff, taking control.

"You shouldn't stay here by yourself," Ren pointed out simply, feeling both horrified and amazed that he could stand at the center of the bedroom and almost touch the walls on each side without moving. "We'll both be more comfortable at my place." The rightness of the decision put him into motion. He started pulling open Justin's dresser drawers, searching for pajamas.

"Hey, wait," Justin protested, propped up on the bed. "I can't go with you."

"I'll give you ten seconds to give me a good reason why not," Ren contested, discovering that all of Justin's belongings could fit quite easily into the one duffel bag he'd located in the bottom drawer. Who was this guy? If only they had been able to complete the biography assignment, because in the last few hours, Justin had become an almost irresistible mystery. Where did he come from? How'd he get to the university? Where was the rest of his stuff? Was this really all his stuff? Where had Justin been for the last couple of weeks? And probably most important, what happened to him? What had left Justin alone in this room with no friends and so violently defensive? Because punching is not a natural startle reflex. Humans aren't born that way; they train it into themselves either through militant or traumatic repetition.

"I don't even know you," Justin repeated the same phrase as this morning. Ren paused in his rummaging to whip out his wallet, plucking out his ID, his CPR certification, and his volunteer EMT card, handing the pile to Justin for inspection.

"My qualifications," Ren countered. "And if that's not good enough, I can also get you a copy of my resume, and we can phone in some testimonials." Justin stared at the cards, his mouth open. Ren couldn't tell if he was impressed or if he were thinking that Ren might be too serious about life. He'd received both responses, and they looked almost the same.

"But aren't I contagious?" Justin asked, looking truly pitiful, almost desperate. "You could get sick too if I go with you."

Ren smiled, bending to retrieve his cards. "Nice try," he compli-mented. "But I'm already exposed, I did get a flu shot, and I've already taken care of at least four other people this winter. So far so good. I wouldn't say the same for all the poor souls who share the first-floor bathroom with you if you stay here, though. Coming with me will help in not spreading this around. I'd consider that a plus. What else you got?"

"You're crazy," Justin told him. Ren allowed him this opinion. He wasn't the first to have it, but it certainly didn't qualify as a good reason.

"Yeah, well, I did get punched in the face this morning. Could be blunt force head trauma," he answered flippantly, then wished he hadn't been so casual when he saw Justin's eyes flicker to the bruise on his cheek, his expression crumpling into shame. Then into some-thing like horror. It bothered Ren enough that he stopped moving around the room; he knelt beside the bed so Justin wouldn't have to look up at him.

"Look, I get it," Ren comforted, turning serious. "You're right; you don't know me. I was a jerk to you this morning. But I'm sorry for that, and I'm good at this. I understand you don't need me to, but I also know this year's virus is a bitch and it's a white-out this weekend. Just come with me."

"How long?" Justin asked instead of trying to list another reason, though he still sounded worried. Hesitant. His voice breathless from the strain of keeping himself upright on his elbow.

"Until you're better," Ren answered casually, not giving an estimate as to how long it would take. Alek was only down a couple days, Denny almost a solid week. Ren didn't know Justin, hadn't really examined him yet. "However long that takes," Ren finished, then stood to pack the rest of Justin's clothes and hygiene articles, knowing he'd won the exchange and Justin had submitted to his plan. He still wasn't sure it was a good idea, but Ren knew he'd do it. Ren turned his attention to the backpack on the desk, the dresser drawers empty. Justin wouldn't be up for doing homework this weekend, but his wallet was possibly in there, his keys, his phone. Ren had only just put his hands on it when Justin unexpectedly freaked out behind him.

"Don't!" Justin barked, jerking all the way up, trying to lurch over to grab his backpack out of Ren's hands. "Don't open that!" The strong reaction triggered immediate obedience in Ren. What on earth? This wasn't a half-hearted effort to protest going with him. This was genuine fear. Ren dropped the bag, lifting his hands to show he was no longer touching it. But he was instantly curious, a little apprehensive. What was in there that Justin didn't want him to see? Ren turned to him, monitoring his mottled complexion, his panting, the look of terror in his face. What kind of guy cared more about hiding what was in his backpack than what was in his underwear drawer? Despite the intrigue, concern won out. Ren wanted Justin to trust him, and he didn't want to cause him unnecessary discomfort, so he snagged the straps of the bag and brought it to the bed still securely closed.

"Sorry," he said calmly, wanting to ease the tension in Justin. "I was going to pack your phone and thought it would be in there." Ren twisted to grab the half-full duffel bag off the floor, setting it gently on the chair. "But I'll let you get it."

Justin nodded, his jaw tight, coming down hard from what that little episode had done to him. Ren could see his hands shaking as he pulled the backpack onto his lap, saw him struggle with his fine motor control to get a grip on the tab for the zipper. Filled with compassion and guilt, Ren sat beside him on the bed.

"We could just take everything," Ren suggested softly, since he couldn't help with the zipper, and he couldn't take watching Justin try anymore. Justin spread his hands over the still-closed backpack, and Ren saw him relax slightly.

"Ok," Justin agreed weakly, allowing Ren to take the bag again, efficiently tucking it into the duffel and zipping it out of sight.

"There, all set. Now, rest a minute," Ren commanded, shifting to make room for Justin to lie down again, slowing his voice to encourage the same reaction of Justin's circulatory and respiratory systems, both of which were still racing. "Breathe deep and get your heart rate down while I get us a ride."

Justin curled up on the bed, spent, arms and knees tight to his torso, staring at Ren who perched on the edge next to him. The hint-glimmer of trust was still there, but more than half-drowned in suspicion and pain. He looked so miserable, and Ren knew it was going to get worse.

"It's ok," Ren reassured. He watched Justin's eyes mist over to the point where he was forced to close them and bury his face into his pillow, embarrassed and uncomfortable. Knowing his entire body ached, Ren squeezed Justin's shoulder carefully before getting up, giving him some space to collect himself and pulling his phone out in order to call Alek. Even though it was a straight shot down 57th

Avenue to Ren's apartment, it was too far for Justin to walk. Especially in the snow.

"What's up, Ren?" Alek answered. Ren took a couple steps away from Justin, turning his back, looking out the solitary window. The snowfall had officially started, though it wasn't too serious yet, the flakes still big and fluffy. "I was just going to call you."

"Alek, where are you?" Ren asked. He hadn't meant to start with that, but he could tell from the weird echo on Alek's side that he wasn't at home. He was somewhere with a much higher ceiling, no carpet. The buzz of several other people in the background.

"The Geo building," Alek replied, a pleasant surprise. Ren tilted his head to shift his view out Justin's window, discovering it was indeed possible to see the Geo building from where he stood. "We're putting a kit together and then heading over to the museum. Looks like conditions could be perfect for thundersnow tonight."

"Wait a second," Ren said, bracing himself against the wall with one hand. What the hell was thundersnow? It sounded like a fantasy card game attack. "Back up. Who's we? I thought we were barricading ourselves in the apartment tonight."

"Yeah, we were, but then some of Denny's geoscience friends were telling her about the weather study going on at the museum tonight, and it sounded cool, so we're here with them packing up some measuring equipment and barometric scanners and then we're going to order pizza and watch the storm from the observation deck on the museum roof. It's going to be awesome! Did you want to come?"

"You sure you want to do that?" Ren checked, rather overwhelmed by the drastic change in plans. Plus, it sounded ominous. If there was thunder, that meant lightning first, right? In a blizzard. Somehow, it didn't seem so smart to watch that kind of thing surrounded by electronics under a glass ceiling on a roof right next to a huge body of water. "I mean, that's not really physics, is it?"

"Everything is physics, Ren," Denny told him, cluing him in that he was on speakerphone. "Earth, space, weather, electricity, your tendency to worry too much."

"Ok, Doctor Who," Ren shot back, not liking the whole idea and coming off hostile.

"Yes, and time, also physics, well done," Denny retorted, ignoring his tone. "So, are you coming? Bring your date; it'll be fun!"

"No, I can't," Ren denied, his insides tangling up as he remembered, again, that he had a date tonight. He checked the time, still plenty left to get Justin set up and comfortable at the apartment. "I was actually calling because I need a ride."

"What's going on?" Alek's voice came clearly through the line again, which meant he'd turned off the speaker, and Ren smiled because he wasn't the only one who maybe worried too much.

"Looks like I'm breaking a fever tonight," he responded.

"Whose? Yours? You ok?" Alek's questions toppled over each other. Ever since his own battle with the flu a little while ago which consequently led to Denny catching it after him, Alek was paranoid about Ren coming down with it too. Ren didn't blame him; Denny had scared the shit out of them.

"I'm fine, Alek," Ren reassured. "It's Justin — my English partner? He's not doing so well. I'm here with him at Snell, but it's one of those rooms that has nothing but a bed in it, so I talked him into coming over to our place. It's too far for him to walk, though."

"Oh, you found him," Alek expressed an odd mixture of sympathy and relief. "Poor guy — told you he probably had something. Wait, Snell-Hitchcock? Isn't that like right across the street?"

"Yeah, I'm looking at the Geo building now," Ren said, deciding not to tell Alek that Justin's illness could maybe explain where he'd been last night but not the previous weeks. "I can get him onto Ellis, I think. Is that ok?"

"Yeah, sure. Give me maybe five minutes? Can he make it to the corner of Ellis and 57th?"

Ren glanced over his shoulder at Justin, almost dropping the phone when he discovered him awake and staring at him. His expression was hard, pained, and scary. With his unkempt black hair partially in his face, he looked like a wolf more than a dog now, his eyes bright enough that Ren couldn't tell what color they were.

"I think so," Ren said, trying to keep his voice steady, to maintain eye contact with Justin. Really, how high was this fever? Ren was looking forward to getting Justin where he could find out and start doing something helpful. "I'll call you if we can't, and we'll figure something else out."

"All right, see you in a few," Alek solidified the plan. Ren tucked his phone into his pocket, mentally preparing himself for the tricky and uncomfortable business of getting Justin from here to there. Justin had walked home from English class, but that had been hours ago, probably before he'd even realized he wasn't feeling well.

"Ok," Ren began, attempting to keep his voice light, like this was no big deal and wouldn't be hard, like what he'd just seen in Justin's face hadn't scared him. "We're meeting my roommate on the corner so he can drive us." As he spoke, Ren closed the distance between them, taking Justin's wrist so he could check his pulse again. Still racing. The sooner they got him settled the better. Ren used his grip on Justin to help pull him to a sitting position, moving slowly to allow his impaired system time to recalibrate his equilibrium.

"Are you sure this is ok?" Justin muttered, the softness of his voice in no way matching the fierceness of his gaze. "Your roommate doesn't mind?"

"Alek? No, he's the best; you'll see."

"It sounded like an argument," Justin pointed out, and Ren was surprised he had paid that much attention, even though he'd misunderstood.

"Not about you," Ren answered gently. "Trust me; they're cool with it."

"They?" Justin checked, sounding confused, and Ren realized he hadn't mentioned Denny yet. She and Alek were together so much they seemed like one entity, and Ren sometimes forgot she didn't live with them.

"Alek's friend, Denny, will be there too," Ren explained. "They're fun to watch. I can only understand about thirty percent of what they say, but they're good."

Justin still looked unsure.

"They're my best friends," Ren assured without reservation. "There's nothing to worry about. So let's go before the storm gets bad. Can you stand up?"

He could, but it was an obvious effort. Ren thought he heard Justin mumble, "I can't believe I'm doing this," under his breath, but it wasn't clear, and Ren didn't ask or give him any time to change his mind. Instead, he slipped the duffel strap over his head, guided Justin into the hallway, and locked the door to the empty room behind them.

"What's the shortest route to Ellis and 57th?" Ren asked, knowing he could figure it out if he were outside, but he wanted to keep them in the warmth of the residence hall as long as possible. Justin glanced around as if he wasn't too sure about it either but oriented himself enough after a couple of seconds that he could point. Ren took Justin's elbow to aid his balance when walking, but it seemed now that they were in the open, Justin didn't want to be touched anymore.

"I can walk," Justin said gruffly, pulling away, and Ren caught himself before he rolled his eyes. Working around bravado was so inefficient, but since it had been a triumph to get Justin out of the apartment in the first place, he was going to let it go.

"Then lead the way," Ren invited indulgently, letting his hand drop to his side but keeping careful watch. Justin seemed the sort of person who would push himself too far for pride's sake, and it was easier to keep someone upright than pick them up after a fall. Though it appeared Justin wasn't lying; he could walk. Like a drunk, but at least they weren't going very far.

They moved through the dormitory slowly — Justin out of breath and Ren watching him, putting together his to-do list for how best to take care of him. He was paying so much attention to his future preparations that it startled and worried him when Justin stopped for what seemed like no reason at all.

"What's up?" Ren asked, tensing, ready to catch Justin if he needed it, growing confused when Justin gestured ahead of them.

"Is that your roommate?" he said, and Ren turned his head toward the glass exit door, smiling broadly enough it hurt his cheek as he recognized Alek on the other side, waiting in his enormous Carhartt coat and fur-lined Canadian trapper hat. He'd cupped his hands against the door, practically had his face squashed against it as he did his best to see against the glare of the weak winter sunlight, unable to let himself in without a resident's keycard.

"The absolute best," Ren confirmed, feeling a mix of pride and affection as Alek recognized them and started waving both hands, as if they couldn't see him standing there. Justin started moving again, slowly, but Ren went ahead to open the door for Alek, meeting with more resistance than he expected as he tried to shove it against the wind.

"Hey Alek," he greeted. "Thanks for coming."

"No sweat," he responded, nonplussed. But then he paused, mittened hand shooting out to catch Ren by the chin. "Dude, what happened to your face?" Ren twisted away both because Alek's hand was freezing and because now was not the time.

"Let's help Justin first," Ren delayed, shifting Alek's attention. Alek looked like he wanted to press him, but by this time Justin had joined them at the door, surprising Ren by reaching to hold Ren's coat sleeve for balance. Ren looked imploringly at Alek, hoping it was obvious that Justin was in bad shape and they shouldn't waste any time.

"Right," Alek agreed, eyeing Justin pityingly, automatically moving to Justin's other side to sandwich him in support. "Come on; I left the car running for you."

Two steps into the cold, Justin's body folded on him. Not a collapse, just an automatic tightening response to the drastic change in temperature. Ren heard him swear in a hiss of discomfort, his eyes squeezing shut, all his limbs pulling into his core. It made sense. Ren felt his own muscles doing the same thing, on a much less debilitating scale. It was freezing out here in the wind. Alek was the least affected since he'd been out more recently and for longer. He and Ren put their arms around Justin, half carrying him to the car.

"Halfway there," Ren noted, trying to be cheerful as he tucked his long legs into Alek's Civic and pulled the door shut. But he doubted that Justin could see anything positive in his situation at present. He was curled against the back of the seat, arms around himself, shivering rather violently, clenching his teeth to try and keep them from chattering.

"You guys ok back there?" Alek asked, watching them in the rearview mirror, his expression tight, like he felt he should be doing something, but he didn't know what.

"We just need to get there, Alek," Ren instructed, not looking forward to getting out of the car again. "It's close," Ren promised Justin. "And when we get there, we'll get you in some PJs and under a blanket, and you won't have to go outside again." Justin huddled into a ball, not answering.

"So, Ren, what did you do to your face?" Alek asked again as he drove, unwilling to let that go. Ren felt Justin flinch at his side.

"Something stupid," he told the truth.

"It looks like someone clocked you, man."

"Really?" Ren spoke up quickly, not liking the effect this conversation was having on Justin. He didn't think it was possible for him to tighten up anymore. It was making the shaking worse. "Like a fight? Does it look cool? Do you think I can run with that? That I got in a fight?"

"You?" Alek scoffed, exactly as Ren had intended. "Probably not. What'd you really do? Run into a door? Slip on the ice or something?"

"It wasn't my most graceful moment," Ren confessed without revealing anything.

"I keep telling you to slow down! I know you think you're late for everything, but you seriously aren't. Be more careful." Alek gave him the lecture, but Ren could tell he still wasn't sure about the lack of explanation regarding the injury. *I will tell him,* Ren promised himself. *Just not right now.*

"I will, Alek."

Justin twisted so he could look at Ren, who stared back, his mouth tightly closed, hoping Justin was lucid enough to read his expression. *Keep quiet.* Ren thought he detected slightly more trust in Justin's eyes, as well as wonder and surprise. Ren faced the front, sighing.

The trip from the car to the apartment wasn't any easier. Justin's muscles were so frozen it took both Alek and Ren to guide him, leaving the car illegally parked as close to the door as possible with the hazard lights on. By the time they got him into the elevator, up to the third floor, and into their room, he was moving better, but the trip had taken a lot out of him. They eased him onto the couch, letting him recover for a minute.

"I gotta jet," Alek excused himself. "Can't leave the car there." Ren turned toward him, keeping one hand on Justin's shoulder.

"Thanks, Alek," he said again.

"No problem. Listen to Ren and feel better, buddy," Alek said to Justin. "See you tonight," Alek continued to Ren. "Not sure when, though."

"I still think you should skip that," Ren tried one last time. "Have you seen the sky? The lake? The twin vortexes of doom?" Alek rested his hand on Ren's head, patting him as if he were a child.

"That's exactly the point," Alek affirmed, sounding excited. "Relax. It's not like we'll be far away. Besides, you're going to be so busy you won't even miss us. Dinner's over there for you." He pointed to the counter where his trusty crockpot was quietly simmering away. "Don't touch it until six." Alek started backing up. "Good luck on your date."

Alek's steps faded down the hallway toward the elevator, and Ren took a deep breath, placing his coat on the camp chair, ready to focus all his attention. Justin was staring again, tired and questioning.

"How are you feeling?" Ren asked. He knelt to undo the laces of Justin's boots. Justin's hands joined his, pushing him away, unwilling to let Ren take his shoes off for him.

"Like I just got kidnapped by the Hallmark Channel," Justin answered, voice still weak and breathless, but snark was usually a good sign that things weren't too bad. Patients who kept their sense of humor normally recovered faster. On the other hand, patients who didn't answer questions were harder to treat.

"Get out of your coat and get comfy," Ren said instead of acknowledging the joke, setting the boots to the side of the couch so they wouldn't be tripped over. "I'll be right back with my stuff." He left Justin on the couch to retrieve his med bag, pausing briefly to look out his bedroom window at the museum, at the gathering intensity of the storm. Rainstorms bothered him. Back home they usually meant trouble. Mudslides, hurricanes. Snowstorms were even worse. They seemed more menacing somehow.

Ren hadn't been gone long, but when he returned to the living room, Justin had wriggled out of his coat, draping it over the arm of the couch, and was now resting his head on it, slumped over awkwardly. Ren pulled out his notebook to document some stats. He started with Justin's name and the date at the top of the first blank page.

"All right, let's get some readings."

He checked Justin's pulse again, as well as his blood pressure and oxygen level, noting everything in his notebook while Justin watched him quietly, his face somewhere between overwhelmed and impressed.

"102.3," Ren repeated aloud as he wrote the temperature down, doing his best not to sound too worried. At her worst, Denny hit 102.6, but Justin was a long way from that point still. "Is that typical for you? Do you always run high fevers like this?"

"Am I supposed to know that?"

"Maybe not, but let's get serious for a minute," Ren said, sitting beside Justin on the couch, facing him directly. "I don't want to scare you, but I know for a fact that when the sun goes down, fevers go up. You're already high, so I need some information just in case. Do you have any allergies?"

"No," Justin answered, looking concerned.

"When was the last time you took any medicine, or had anything to eat or drink?" Ren hated asking these questions; he tried to skip them when he could. But it was easiest to get answers right now, before there was an emergency. Not that there would be an emergency.

"I don't know. I didn't take anything. I had coffee this morning?"

Ren felt like he needed to tone it down. He wasn't even asking anything hard yet, but it looked like Justin was scared to death.

"Relax," Ren comforted. "You're not on trial or anything." Justin winced, his hand clenching, almost a spasm; Ren frowned at him. What made him do that? "I'm just getting a picture here. Is there anything else I should know? Underlying conditions?"

"Like what?"

"Like asthma or epilepsy. Seizures, things like that."

"We read I had a seizure once," Justin said, sounding young again, this memory obviously old for him. What did that mean? He read?

"Ok," Ren encouraged, wondering if he might have gotten into something above his skill level. He'd never seen a seizure before, but if Justin's temperature went any higher and he had a history, then tonight might be the night. "How long ago? What happened?"

"I was two," Justin said, shrugging slightly. "I don't remember. It came up when we were registering for school."

"Was it a febrile seizure?" Ren asked, trying to help him. Not too uncommon for very young children, usually harmless, but a condition that could follow him into adulthood.

"That sounds right? I spent a couple days in the hospital, but they said it was fine. Is that what you're asking for?"

"That's exactly what I'm asking for. You only seized once? Is there anything else?"

"Once," Justin confirmed. "I can't think of anything else." He was scared. The exact thing Ren hadn't wanted. But he didn't know that Justin's answers to his mundane questions would be so scary. Ren considered Justin carefully, sitting there all wretched and frightened. He felt conflicted. When Ren thought up the idea to bring Justin here, he didn't think he'd be monitoring him for anything intense. He'd even planned on leaving Justin alone to sleep for a few hours while Ren went to his dance class and his date.

Now it was clear he wasn't going to either.

"Why do you look like that?" Justin asked him, and Ren smiled despite his thoughts. Stress wasn't helping.

"Just thinking," Ren explained. "It's overkill, but where is your ID, and who do I call if there is an emergency?"

"My ID is in my wallet," Justin half-answered, gesturing that his wallet was in one of his back pockets.

"And how do I get in touch with your parents?" Ren repeated.

"You can't," Justin answered, and Ren could tell he really didn't like saying this out loud. Ren felt sorry that he needed him to. "My mom left when I was little, and my dad died when I was four."

Ren swallowed any verbal expression of sympathy. He didn't think Justin wanted it.

"All right," Ren soothed, staying practical, though his mind flooded with questions. How had Justin's father died? Where was his mom? Who looked after Justin from the time he was four until now? "Then who should I call? Justin?"

"North, I guess," Justin said, looking down. Ren reminded himself to be patient; Justin wasn't being difficult and secretive on purpose. This was likely why he kept avoiding the biography assignment. He probably didn't want anyone to know any of this.

"Who is that? Are they listed in your phone?" Ren pressed. "Should we call now to say where you are?"

"Don't call him!" Justin snarled, the same as when he freaked out about the backpack. "He'll think … Don't call anyone; just forget it."

"Calm down," Ren said steadily, regretting riling Justin up again by something so seemingly innocent. Justin flushed alarmingly, panting. Ren now had way too many questions. Who was North? Why so frantic about not calling him? Justin looked like he was going into shock. "Put your head down before you hyperventilate. I won't call him."

Ren tugged Justin down onto the couch with absolutely zero resistance then went quickly into his bedroom to snag his pillow and quilt, returning to find Justin still breathing hard, lying on his side, one hand clenched in the fabric of his coat. Yeah, there was no way Ren could leave him. He covered him tenderly, helping him lift his head to slide the pillow underneath, keeping his mouth shut, listening to the wind picking up outside, putting pressure into the apartment. Ren settled cross-legged on the floor, wondering what the hell he was doing.

"I'm sorry," Justin murmured, emotionally and physically exhausted.

"Me too," Ren answered quietly, feeling the beginnings of doubt peeling back the edges of his training. It seemed the more questions he asked, the deeper the mystery of Justin became. But Justin wasn't there so Ren could solve that mystery. They weren't friends, and Justin didn't owe him any explanations.

"I'm going to make you some soup," Ren said, pushing his emotions down. "Since you can't remember the last time you ate. Just keep still."

"Ok," Justin whispered.

"I need to make a phone call first, though. I'll be in the other room for a minute."

Justin didn't answer, and Ren moved away, feeling the long night he had ahead of him stretching his soul, making him uncomfortable. He'd done this many times already, for people much closer to him. This felt different. He stared down at Justin, imprinting the sharp lines of his face, the twitch of his shoulders. What was it about Justin? What was it that made Ren act so differently? Slamming down his textbook this morning, breaking into a room, bringing a stranger home with him. Canceling his date with Celeste.

That brought him up short. He'd just said he was going to call her, but was he really going to dial her number and tell her he wasn't coming?

Justin's hand gradually relaxed as Ren stood watching him — his body forcing him to let go. Ren folded his arms, knowing his choice had been made a long time ago. Justin needed him; Celeste, humiliating as it was, honestly didn't. Ren moved unconsciously to his room, staring out the window at the snow, falling faster now. Tiny, blurred flakes pelted the museum and lake. Ren retrieved Celeste's number in his contacts, holding the phone in both hands.

"Damn it, Justin," he muttered out loud, pressing the call button without looking at it.

4
ARRHYTHMIA

"Yes?"

Ren felt as though all the fluid in his brain suddenly whipped itself into a whirlpool then drained in a rush deep into his stomach. Celeste's voice had a specific timbre, like wind chimes. It also had the unnerving ability to liquify all his muscles. He gripped the back of his desk chair to anchor himself. His mouth opened, but he was so busy giving himself mental reminders on how to be suave that he forgot whatever he'd meant to say.

"Hello?" Celeste spoke a second greeting. Ren could hear the frown in it, knowing he had to speak up soon or she was going to hang up. *Don't crack*, he commanded his voice, taking a deep breath. Of all the things he'd already done today rescheduling a date should be cake.

"C-Celeste, hi," he managed, lowering his head at the stutter. He couldn't even say her name? Seriously? Whatever, keep going, it's too late now. "It's Ren — you know, from the donation center?"

"Yes, of course," her tone changed immediately, brightening. "I'm glad you called; I forgot to ask for your number. We're on for seven, aren't we?"

Ren glanced outside, the sun already far gone from his eastern-facing window, the snow blowing in menacing tendrils across the street three stories down. He knew he was an island boy, but sometimes native midwesterners made no sense to him. He was truly afraid to see what they considered bad weather.

"About that," he said, feeling her stiffen, an almost audible static on the line. "I'm thinking we should reschedule. It's snowing hard out there, and I don't want anything to happen to you."

"That's so thoughtful," she told him sweetly, and his heart beat harder a couple times. "But you don't have to worry; I'm already here. I had a class this morning and just stayed." Ren bowed his head lower. He'd hoped he wouldn't have to explain about Justin, that the storm would have been reason enough to pick a different day. It somehow seemed less awkward to blame the snow, or at least if they agreed on the weather, it would be as if they were both making the same decision.

"I still need to reschedule," he confessed, having a difficult time choosing the right words. "My ... um." What was he supposed to call Justin? "My friend," he decided on the fastest option. "He's really sick. I thought I could let him rest here by himself, but ... he's ... I don't think I can leave him. I'm sorry."

"Ren," Celeste responded, voice suddenly icy. Ren held his breath; he'd never heard her say his name before and wished it hadn't sounded like that. "If you don't want to meet me, you can just say so."

"But I do!" Ren protested, standing straight. He would have liked nothing better than to be with her tonight, helping her, watching her move without being restrained by the donation equipment. Speaking full, complete sentences without being interrupted by the beeping of a machine. He'd wanted all of that, so much. He wanted it more than what waited for him tonight. But there were things he wanted to do and things he needed to do. Staying with Justin felt like something he needed to do. He wished he could make her understand.

"I was really looking forward to it," he told her emphatically. "Trust me, I know this is the worst possible timing, but there's no one else who can stay with him, and I'm an EMT, and I think he might—"

"Just stop, please," Celeste cut him off sharply. "If you were going to stand me up, I wish you'd done it sooner, like maybe before the storm started so I could have gone home."

"Stand you—" Ren's brain took a long time to process what she was saying. "Wait. You don't … you think I'm lying to you? Celeste, I would never do that."

"First it's the weather, then it's your 'friend'." Ren wasn't sure how he could hear the verbal quotation marks she put around the word, but they were definitely there. "Here's a little tip; make up your mind which excuse you're going with before you make the call. Or better yet, just tell the truth. I'll have you know I went to a lot of trouble to meet with you tonight."

Ren's mind was racing now, trying to find a solution, a way he could still spend time with her. First, he thought of having her come to his apartment, but he dismissed it almost as soon as it came to him. He didn't want to risk exposing Celeste to Justin's illness. And Alek and Denny weren't home; not that he'd feel comfortable asking them to take care of Justin, that was a responsibility he'd signed up for all by himself. Maybe he could take a picture of Justin to prove he wasn't lying?

What are you doing, Ren? He stopped himself as the ideas became desperate. It was a simple choice. Celeste or Justin. A choice he'd already made before he picked up the phone. If she couldn't believe him, that was on her, wasn't it? There was nothing more he could do.

"I'm sorry," Ren apologized, a new strength in his voice he hadn't expected. Now he was going to be able to talk like a real person? "This came up suddenly; the flu is like that. If you text me your email address, I'll write my experience with Dr. Farley and send it to you for your report, but I can't leave him tonight, not even for a few hours."

"Ren," Celeste repeated, but he couldn't decipher the tone now. He felt hollow and sad. He expected her to be disappointed perhaps, but not angry. At best, he thought she'd completely understand and at worst, he'd lose some points for being a flake, but he never anticipated she'd think he would lie. That stung his spirit, and now all he wanted was to get off the phone.

"I hope I'll see you Wednesday," he said in parting, hanging up without letting her respond. He lowered the phone, realizing that the ibuprofen he'd taken earlier for his cheek was wearing off. Carefully, he covered the bruise with his palm, taking a moment of self-pity, feeling beat up inside and out.

"Who was that?"

Ren jumped, the harsh question stabbing the base of his spine and jerking his heart in a painful rush. He spun around to see Justin standing near his bedroom door, leaning against the frame, his face a ghastly combination of pale, confused apprehension and hot rage. Both Justin's hands were solid fists, wild, wounded, and dangerously defensive. Ren felt his eyes widen, not sure what to do here. He thought he'd left Justin falling asleep on the couch. How long had he been standing there? How had he snuck up on Ren without making a sound? What had Ren done this time to make him look so angry?

"Who were you talking to?" Justin rephrased his question since Ren hadn't answered yet, too surprised and intimidated to speak. "You said you wouldn't call." Oh, that's what he meant. He thought Ren had slipped away to call ... whatever that guy's name was. Ren breathed out the injustice of being accused of lying twice in just as many minutes. For Celeste, it didn't matter so much, only his pride and prospects wounded, but he needed to settle Justin down quickly for several reasons. First, Justin's system wasn't handling the stress of this exertion very well; he was losing color in his face at an alarming rate. Second, Ren had no desire to get hit again, and even though Justin was not at his best right now, Ren didn't doubt he could still do some damage if he wanted to.

"What did you tell him?" Justin demanded, threatening and

ruined, raising terror and tenderness in Ren. Celeste suddenly seemed petty and childish by comparison. *This, Celeste*, Ren thought as he pondered the conflict that was Justin standing in front of him. *This is what broken trust really looks like. This is what years of being lied to looks like.* In fact, the way Justin spoke, the tone of his words and the hurt in his eyes made Ren wonder if he'd even recognize the truth if Ren told it to him. It was like he expected to be betrayed — like his life wouldn't make sense any other way.

"I didn't call him," Ren assured, wondering if it would make any difference to say it, holding up both hands in supplication. "I said I wouldn't, and I didn't. I had a date later I needed to cancel. That's who I was talking to."

"A date?" Justin repeated, still skeptical, his whole body wound tight, the same as this morning. What made him like this? Why did he think he had to fight the entire world?

"Yeah, a study date," Ren tried to soothe him. "I do go on dates. Quite often." He kept his tone light, using humor to diffuse this situation. Justin shouldn't be standing; Ren could see he was starting to tremble with the effort. "But I'm taking care of you tonight, like I promised, so I had to let her know I wasn't coming."

"You," Justin began, but then seemed to lose his train of thought, blinking fast, putting Ren on higher alert. He'd seen this before at the donation center. This was the kind of behavior donors exhibited right before they passed out.

Ren began moving toward Justin, intent on guiding him to the bed before he fainted. But he'd only taken one step before Justin cringed back, shifting his body for what looked like the preparation of a strike. Fear and pity spread in Ren's chest. Justin was such a contradiction. Such a strange combination of vulnerability and violence. It was unsettling. Ren wondered exactly what Justin could be capable of if he were functioning at one hundred percent.

"Justin," Ren called gently. "Hey, it's ok. I just want to help you. Remember? You shouldn't be moving around so much, so is it safe if I come over there to you?"

"What?" Justin seemed confused. "Safe?"

"You look like you're going to attack me," Ren explained patiently, even though he was watching Justin with a growing sense of urgency. His face was almost gray. "I'd rather not do that again, so could you not hit me if I come over there, please?"

"I'm not going to hit you," Justin responded, sounding even more bewildered. "Why would you think ..."

"Look at yourself," Ren told him softly, slowly taking another step, hands lifted as if Justin had a gun on him. "Look at your fists. You're shaking. Let's get out of this stand off before you fall, all right?"

Justin obediently looked at his hands as if they belonged to someone else, seeming surprised that they were balled up so tightly. His fingers uncurled stiffly, his mouth open, looking stricken. Ren didn't really know what to make of it. Was this what the fever was doing to him? Something else? Either way, Ren didn't like it. He'd never seen anyone so extreme. Justin covered his face with his hands, messing up his equilibrium so he fell back hard against the doorframe in such a way that Ren could tell he would lose his balance any second.

"Justin," Ren spoke as he sped to his side. He still wasn't convinced it was safe, especially now that Justin had his eyes covered, but Ren didn't want him to fall. "I'm not going to hurt you, ok? You're not going to hurt me. Because we trust each other, right?" At least, maybe a little.

Justin flinched as Ren reached to support him. He jerked his hands away from his face, looking up slightly so he could meet Ren's eyes. Ren still couldn't tell what color Justin's were, but there was still plenty to see in them. He was hurting, unsteady, uncertain — everything Ren wanted to fix. Gaining courage from his success in getting close without physical violence, Ren wrapped his hand around Justin's waist, tucking a thumb into his belt loop and pulling Justin's arm over his shoulder. It was the first time he was close enough without their coats to really feel the fever heat on him, the intensity of it. He was getting worse.

"That's it," Ren complimented, though he was growing more worried by the second. What had he gotten himself into here? It didn't help when Justin gasped painfully out of nowhere, clutching at his chest and sagging into Ren.

"What's going on, Justin?" Ren grunted as he did his best to accommodate Justin's sudden weight, the question shooting out fast, not as calm as he wanted to be. He'd expected Justin to faint, not ... whatever this was. Ren needed more information. "What hurts? Can you tell me?"

"I don't know," Justin managed, his eyes closing, but the location of his hand was a hint.

"Is it your heart?" Ren guessed. "Justin? Your heart hurts?"

"Maybe?" Justin choked out the answer, and Ren's brain opened a textbook in his memory, sorting through the myriad of diagnoses for this symptom, combating with his concern to focus only on facts instead of letting his imagination fly into panic.

"Let's check it out," Ren offered, calmer than he felt, a promise to both of them. Just because he'd never seen this before didn't mean he couldn't help. He just needed more data, then a strategy. He eased them forward toward the couch and his medical bag, murmuring encouragement the whole way. Justin seemed to recover somewhat before they got there, standing straighter, removing his hand, not putting so much of his weight onto Ren.

"Sit down," Ren instructed, breathless himself from half-carrying Justin down the hall. He lowered Justin into his original position on the cushions. "And put your feet up; come on." As he told Justin what to do, Ren grabbed his coat, balling it up into a little roll and tucking it under his ankles, checking Justin's feet for swelling. They looked ok, normal, which was encouraging. He could cross off a few more heart-related issues on his mental list.

Justin didn't look ok when Ren straightened to check him, but that was expected. He leaned sideways, propped up by Ren's pillow against the arm of the couch, letting his head swivel toward the backrest, twisted, shivering, and panting. As Ren studied, he tightened up, pushing against his chest, his face scrunching at the discomfort, shrinking into the back of the couch. Ok. So this came in waves. Ren dug into the bag for his stethoscope. Meanwhile, Justin wilted again, drained after the episode, letting Ren know they were dealing with short, intense bursts. Ren nodded, narrowing it down, nestling the buds into his ears and perching near Justin's hip.

"Can you move your hands, Justin? I'm going to listen to your heart," Ren warned him. Justin didn't have the energy to respond, and he only recoiled slightly as Ren placed the stethoscope against his chest. Ren listened as Justin's heartbeat filled his head, bowing his chin in concentration. At first, everything seemed as expected. The heart was beating fast, as if Justin were jogging instead of lying reclined on a couch, a symptom called tachycardia, but Ren already knew about that. There was nothing abnormal here. Nothing to cause that kind of reaction. He'd missed it.

"Take a deep breath," Ren told Justin, testing something, hearing the rushing whoosh of it into Justin's lungs as he complied. But he cut off, holding his breath, curling up on the couch. Ren pushed against him to keep him from folding up, needing to keep everything in place to hear what was going on, starting to understand. Justin's heart revved up hard, making him release that deep breath in an involuntary whimper. Arrhythmia.

"Ok," Ren assured, partly to himself, as if he were completely in control, listening as things slowed down inside Justin. Ren removed the stethoscope, letting it dangle from his neck. He went ahead and rested his hand on Justin's chest, over his heart, as if he could slow it that way. They needed to have a chat, but Ren wasn't sure Justin would be able to focus or remember anything he said. Still, he was going to try.

"Hey Justin, can you look at me?" With difficulty, Justin turned his head from the back of the couch, raising tired eyes. So far so good. "I think I know what's going on."

Justin winced again, more gasping, clapping both hands over Ren's on his chest.

"Easy," Ren implored, knowing sometimes even benign symptoms still felt like they could kill you. "You need to calm down. You're stressing out your heart, and it's already working overtime. What's happening to you is called arrhythmia, and it's when your pulse speeds up or beats erratically. It's like, um," he faltered for an analogy that would make sense, but he didn't know Justin well enough to know what he would understand as a comparison. "It's like a car engine," he decided. "Have you ever revved the engine in a car?" He wasn't sure, but he thought Justin might have nodded. "That's what your heart is doing, and it's a problem that perpetuates itself, does that make sense? You get stressed out, your heart overreacts to that stress, creates the palpitations that are making it so you can't breathe very well, which naturally creates more stress, and the cycle continues. Are you with me?"

"How do I make it stop?" Justin gasped, innocent and suffering. He'd clamped one hand tightly around Ren's wrist.

"You relax," Ren explained simply, hoping to convey that this should be easy.

"Ok," Justin agreed, though he didn't look like it would be simple for him, which Ren expected. Justin seemed high-strung; this might be against all his programming.

"And we need to get as much stress off your heart as possible," Ren continued, thinking of ways to help instead of all that could go wrong. "We'll start by getting your fever under control." Ren brought his other hand into the tangle against Justin's chest, pulling Justin off his wrist and folding Justin's hands gently over his heart.

"Close your eyes," Ren lulled — quiet, soft. "You're going to be fine. Stay here and just breathe."

"Where are you going?" Justin's voice sounded scared now. For all his intensity this morning, every "get away from me" and "leave me the hell alone" he'd thrown at Ren earlier, he didn't want that now. Ren patted Justin's hands in reassurance.

"I'm not going anywhere," Ren promised. "I know my apartment is huge compared to your room, but honestly, I can't go far away. I'm going to the kitchen to make you that soup. It doesn't take long; I'll talk to you the whole time. Then I'm going to get you some medicine. And then, hopefully, you are going to sleep."

Justin stared at Ren, who had never seen anyone stare like Justin did. He could see more trust there now, a touch of what could be gratitude. More than a touch of fear. The tiniest bit of protest.

"Don't move," Ren commanded firmly. "Your heart has enough to do already."

He stood up. Justin didn't look ready for him to go, but Ren wanted to get some food and medication into him as soon as possible. It hadn't been all that bright of a day to start with, but there were shadows in the apartment now. Outside, the wind began to shriek, and Ren imagined Denny explaining to him why, the pitch of her voice, the sure rapid string of her words, most of them ones he didn't know, telling him about the direction and the temperature. Probably something about Lake Effect. There was almost always something about Lake Effect. He quickly shrugged aside how much he missed her and Alek. He wanted them here, safe, warm, and present.

"Alek makes this better than I do," Ren said out loud, talking to Justin. The living room and kitchen were only separated by a partial wall, a little taller than Ren's hip. Ren had a decent view of Justin if he looked that way, but Justin could only see Ren from the waist up and only if he stayed the way he was, reclined instead of lying down.

"We made the recipe up together," Ren went on, good on his word to keep talking, for whatever comfort that could give, a distraction if nothing else. "We were trying to make it into a joke, you know — a physician, a physicist, and an engineer walk into a kitchen with a chemistry book — but that's as far as we made it. If you think of a good punch line for that, let me know."

He paused, not sure what to say next, opening the cupboard doors in search of the ingredients he needed. He scanned the lower cabinets for the pan Alek always used, the clunk and rattle of the shuffling reminding him of his mother's kitchen in Cabarete, a bittersweet reminiscence that stung harder as he remembered what Justin had said about his own mother. Ren glanced over his shoulder as he straightened with the pan, checking on Justin.

"A physicist?" Justin repeated, warming Ren's spirit since it sounded like Justin was trying to make conversation.

"Astrophysicist, I should say," Ren corrected himself. "That's Denny, but Alek's into that stuff too. They make a great team. Denny comes up with an idea, and Alek figures out how to make it happen. All this stuff is theirs." Ren paused in the soup prep to lean over the wall, sweeping his arm across the cardboard boxes where their magpie collection of tech scraps lived when not in use. "I don't really know what any of it is, but they'd be happy to tell you more than you ever want to know if you ask them." If they ever came home.

Ren broke eggs into a measuring cup, whipping them with a fork.

"They're waiting to hear from the Jet Propulsion Lab in California about some internship they applied for," Ren continued talking about his friends, waiting for the broth to boil before he poured the eggs into it. "They'll have to move to Pasadena if they get in." He stopped talking as that hit him. They would have to move. If they got in, they'd be gone in less than a month. Gone where he couldn't follow, and suddenly he no longer wanted them to succeed, didn't want to be left behind. He distracted himself with the soup.

"Here we go," Ren remarked, ladling portions into two mugs. He'd skipped lunch to find Justin and there was no way he was going to wait for the curry in the crockpot to be finished. Justin hadn't moved from where Ren left him, sitting completely still with his hands resting over his heart, head leaning against the back of the couch.

"Let it cool," Ren warned him as he set both mugs down on the coffee table. "I'll be right back." He had some meds in his bag, but he had a pharmacy in the hall closet. He tipped two pills into his hand and then went back to the kitchen for water.

"It's just Tylenol," he told Justin as he held both the water and the medicine out to him. "Should bring that fever down and take the ache away for you. Help you sleep." Justin took everything slowly but without hesitation. "Drink all the water if you can," Ren encouraged.

"How come you're so good at this?" Justin asked out of nowhere, studying the pills.

"Practice," Ren dismissed. "I told you I've already nursed four people through the flu this winter." *Though they weren't as bad*, he silently added.

"This is," Justin paused, gathering his thoughts, looking Ren up and down again. "This is really who you are, isn't it?" Ren didn't understand the question.

"Um, yeah?" he returned, uncertain. "Take the medicine."

Justin looked like he wanted to say something else but didn't. He swallowed the pills but didn't finish the water. Ren didn't comment as he exchanged the glass for the soup mug, which Justin stared into, holding it carefully in both hands. Ren wondered why he did that. He stared at everything like it was all brand new to him.

"Breathe deep," Ren told him, knowing how comforting the rich, salty scent of the soup could be if Justin's chest were still tight from the arrhythmia attack. Justin obeyed, his hands starting to shake, making Ren worried again. What now?

"You doing ok?" he asked, a stupid question. There was nothing ok about Justin, but he hadn't been shaking a second ago. He nodded a quick, voiceless response. Ren knelt at his side, reaching out to steady the mug so the soup wouldn't spill. "Can you manage a couple swallows of this for me?" He helped Justin bring the cup to his mouth, helped him tip it slightly, watched him drink as if it were difficult, as if his throat weren't working the way it should. He pulled it back for a break, monitoring Justin intently as he closed his eyes.

"That," Justin whispered. "That's so good."

Ren smiled, unbalanced, then understanding washed over him as he watched a tear escape down Justin's cheek. He was holding his breath again.

"Justin," Ren said, getting his attention though he kept his eyes closed, struggling with himself. Ren took the mug, replacing it on the coffee table, then twisted himself onto the couch facing Justin. He hesitatingly put a hand on his arm.

"Don't," Justin hissed, though not angrily. Ren paid no attention. If he wanted Justin to keep stress off his heart, then this wasn't going to work.

"No, *you* don't," Ren countered. "You're all tense again; don't do that." He left his hand on Justin's arm. His breathing had become erratic. "Your heart can't take the strain, remember? It's ok. This happens to everyone; I promise. It doesn't mean anything except you're sick. I can leave if that will make it easier but stop trying to hold it in like that." Justin's hand shot out unexpectedly, closing around the fabric of Ren's scrub top, a clear sign he didn't want Ren to go anywhere.

"It's ok," Ren invited, shifting closer. Justin's hand stayed curled in Ren's shirt while Ren put his arms around him, hoping he wasn't making a huge mistake.

"Why are you so damn nice?" Justin asked, his voice tight, covering his face with his free hand.

"The better question is why are you so surprised by it? Don't you think you deserve someone to be nice to you?" That did it. Justin broke. He lowered his face, pressing his forehead into the small hollow under Ren's collarbone, and let himself cry. Ren closed his eyes too as he registered the hurt in the sound. He didn't understand it. Why for some people it was kindness that brought all this out more than anything negative they'd already gone through. You could beat them down for days, for years, and they'd take it with a solid resolution and never make a single sound. But the second you started to be gentle with them, they would dissolve. He didn't under-stand it — even though he was the same.

"Ok," Ren encouraged, and Justin sobbed into his shirt. Ren winced. It was like he was holding a flame in his arms, a fallen star burning on the verge of extinguishing itself. He hadn't lied to Justin;

every single one of the people he'd helped through this illness had been overly emotional. They had all cried at least once. That was how Ren discovered Alek was sick in the first place; he'd found him weeping over a burned batch of cookies.

But again, as with everything else, Justin was different. Intense. Hard. Ren wasn't even surprised. He kept quiet for what seemed like a long time, thinking about it, knowing there was more going on here than illness.

"Justin," Ren eventually said once he felt Justin might be winding down. "Look, I know it's none of my business, but if you're going through something, you can talk to me. You don't have to be alone."

Justin pulled back, breaking his hold, hiding his face in both hands. Ren allowed him the distance.

"How can you be like that?" Justin said, rearranging Ren's thoughts. He said the strangest things at the weirdest times. "If you knew —"

"I'd still want to help you," Ren assured, not being able to think of a single thing Justin could have done that would change that. Slowly, Justin uncovered his face, allowing Ren to make eye contact. Tears and fever gleam still obscured the color. Ren wondered if he'd ever be able to make it out. What he could see was exhaustion and want. There was something Justin was hiding, that he couldn't trust Ren with yet, but it seemed like he might want to.

"The offer stands," Ren told him, twisting to pick up the mug again. "When you're ready, or never if you don't want to. For right now, do you think you can drink some more of this?"

Justin took the mug, his hands steady again, though he seemed unable to look at Ren anymore. Ren reminded himself that he shouldn't ask him anything; it really was none of his business. But what was Justin beating himself up over? What made him think Ren would reject him? Did it have anything to do with North? With whatever Justin kept hidden in his backpack? Would he ever trust Ren enough to tell him?

But it shouldn't matter. He didn't need to know what happened.

His job was the same, though not as simple as he thought it would be. He drank his own soup as Justin finished what he could. Then he helped him walk to his bedroom, where they had another awkward exchange about changing into pajama pants. Justin didn't have any, so Ren loaned him his favorite pair, adamant that Justin could not be comfortable sleeping in his jeans. Justin didn't have much strength, so Ren had to help him. By the time he was changed and under the covers, he could barely keep his eyes open.

"Where are you going to sleep?" was the last thing Justin asked. Ren didn't answer him. The truth was he probably wouldn't, at least not well, until the fever broke.

Ren sat next to Justin on the bed on top of the blankets, setting his hand on his shoulder again. Justin seemed to like that. He lay peacefully, breathing steady and deep. They still had a long night ahead of them, but for right now, Justin was going to get some rest.

"I'll be right here," Ren promised. He didn't move until long after he knew Justin had fallen asleep, just to make sure.

5

THUNDERSNOW

While sleep was the best thing for Justin, it was Ren's least favorite part of taking care of someone. He liked to be useful. Waiting around, quietly monitoring someone as they slept, didn't require enough effort, didn't feel like assistance. It made him feel edgy and restless. The storm and his missing friends made it worse.

He stayed with Justin for a while. The medication seemed to be helping him sleep at least, though it was not touching his temperature. Some people were like that. Their body chemistry put together in such a way that certain medications just didn't work how they were supposed to. Ren would have to experiment, but he was hesitant. Hopefully, the fever would break in a few more hours, and it wouldn't be necessary.

Once Ren was sure Justin was asleep, he opened his notebook to write some stats before he forgot them. How much Justin ate, the time he'd taken the Tylenol and the dosage. When he'd fallen asleep. The crying. His last temperature reading before Ren tucked him into bed. It had risen sharply to 103.1, which meant Ren had a new mental timer to track. If it continued to rise, or stayed over 103 for forty-eight hours, he'd have to take him to the hospital, which was less than two miles away, but somehow, with the storm and knowing how hard it would be for Justin to move, it seemed across the country rather than just across campus. It also felt like failure. He'd told Justin that *he* would take care of him, not strangers working the nightshift at the ER.

The storm intensified, and Ren grew more agitated as the apartment seemed to shrink. He ate and put away the curry, then cleaned the kitchen and made up the couch with the extra sheets and blankets they kept specifically for Denny when she slept over. Finished with domestics, he typed up his meeting with Paul Farley, just so he'd have it at a moment's notice if Celeste texted him her email address. He checked his phone obsessively. No messages from her or anyone else. He started sending texts to Alek and Denny, at first casually, then becoming increasingly worried when they didn't respond. A steady, uneasy rotation began as the sun set and hours went by. Ren would stand at the window, watching the snow, listening to the wind. Then he'd send another text. Then he'd check Justin, who shifted often, sometimes muttering in his sleep though Ren couldn't understand him. Then Ren would try to find something to do to keep himself from thinking of his friends or the storm.

Where were they? Why wouldn't they answer him? Ren flipped on the small lamp on top of his dresser, casting more shadows than light into the room, but he could clearly see Justin's face, so that's all he really needed.

Ren started the calming ritual of repacking his med bag on his bedroom floor, but the rumble of thunder broke into his concentration and brought him back to the window. It looked like the end of the world. As he stood there watching, lightning struck the lake, seeming to come from above and below the water, meeting in the middle, the shock of the broken sound barrier rippling away and shuddering into Ren's heart.

It's just thunder, he reminded himself. But even as he thought it, he knew it didn't matter. He wasn't worried so much about the thunder. He was worried for the space separating him from the museum, for how close his friends were to the lake, for how deep the snow was already and how much of it was still falling fast. He didn't know exactly what he thought could happen to them, but there was something about the early darkness, the lonely sound of the wind, the sudden peals of thunder. He couldn't help but worry.

The next strike of lightning had a strobe-like effect on the falling snow. Everything seemed to freeze in the light, snowflakes suspended as if time had stopped. An illusion, but a powerful one. And when the thunder followed, Ren jumped at its intensity. He texted Alek again and started to pace to keep himself away from the window. What were they doing that they couldn't respond? Didn't they know how much it was bugging him?

"Are you ok?"

Ren startled. Justin had this weird ability to sneak up on him, even if he hadn't moved. Ren didn't even know when he'd woken up or how long he'd been watching him. He smoothed his hands down his hips, as if wiping off anxiety, taking a deep breath as he went to the bedside.

"Just fine," Ren answered the question, forcing a smile. The last thing Justin needed was to start worrying about him. Justin had pushed himself semi-upright, turned toward Ren, his body twitching randomly with the rigors of the high fever. "How are you?"

Justin's expression darkened, and Ren could see he didn't want to answer. Ren didn't understand what was so hard about it, but he shrugged it off. He could guess how Justin was feeling just from looking at him anyway. He knew he felt cold, a very specific breed of chill that seems to come from inside and feels like you'll never be warm again, that his joints and muscles were shooting with sharp pain without warning. He likely had an intense headache, though it would be nothing compared to the backache he'd have later as the illness progressed.

"Never mind," Ren absolved him from having to say anything, standing quickly. "But since you're awake, let's get you a drink."

"That's ok," Justin began, not wanting it. But this wasn't something Ren was willing to compromise. He was already on his way to the kitchen for fresh water and an ice pack, glad to have something to do even though Justin wasn't doing any better.

"You need to keep hydrated," Ren called from the sink, amazed how relieved he was to not be alone in the space anymore, though he could hear the edge in his own voice, how harsh he sounded.

He paused to consider his stock of medicine, then grabbed the Tylenol again. It may not be doing exactly what it was supposed to, but since Justin wasn't eating or drinking much and his heart was struggling, it would be easier on him than the NSAIDs Ren had at his disposal.

"Here," Ren said as he entered the bedroom, hands full of water, ice, and medicine, but he paused, flinching as lightning cut into the room. Ren tried to ignore the look Justin gave him as he handed him the glass. "Drink up."

Thunder hit the apartment so hard it shook, and Ren dropped the bottle of Tylenol. *Pull yourself together*, he lectured himself, bending to retrieve it, thankful he hadn't opened it yet so at least he hadn't scattered two hundred little white pills everywhere.

"Uh ... Ren?"

He stood straight, the Tylenol bottle secure in both hands. Justin had never used his name before. The water glass shook slightly in Justin's grip as he sat there without drinking anything, propped up awkwardly on one arm, watching Ren with concern. It looked strange mixed with the discomfort already present on his face. Ren knelt at the bedside, fiddling with the childproof cap.

"They said there would be thundersnow tonight," Ren prattled as he struggled, trying to pretend he hadn't just jumped out of his skin over thunder. "That's what they're doing, you know? They're over there at the museum taking readings of the storm; I guess figuring out what atmospheric conditions should be to get this kind of thing." He flapped one hand behind him at the window, indicating what was happening outside. "Crazy, isn't it?"

Justin shifted, grimacing, pushing himself to a sitting position to free the hand he'd been braced on, which he then carefully and slowly rested against Ren's on top of the bottle. "Hold still," he entreated. Ren froze, more from Justin's hand than what he said, registering the heat and the shudder in the touch. "Is the storm bothering you or something?"

"Of course not," Ren dismissed, lying. "It's just thunder." In a blizzard. In the dark and cold. Completely burying the streets outside. "Take a drink," he reminded Justin, pulling out from under his hand to renew his efforts with the cap, unable to hold still. Justin obediently lifted the glass to his mouth but continued to stare disquietingly at Ren.

Another flash of light, bright enough Ren was surprised it hadn't cracked the window, followed by more thunder. The short duration between the two indicated the storm was right on top of them now. Ren's shoulders tightened automatically before he could stop them. Justin tilted his head at him, his eyes seeming entirely too large on his face. Ren needed to turn away, starting to pace again, fighting with the stubborn cap.

"Can you ... can you stop?" Justin asked him. "Why are you so afraid?" The words were sharp, but the tone suggested that Justin was trying to be gentle. Ren heard his breathing change as he spoke. It was speeding up.

"Is that what you think? I'm afraid? That's funny," Ren said quickly, succeeding at last in getting the Tylenol open so he could give Justin another dose.

Ren tried to convince himself that he wasn't afraid of thunder, or lightning. He wasn't afraid of storms. It was the cold that was doing this to him. The cold and the threat of the electricity turning off. Having no electricity was common in the Dominican Republic, it happened all the time, but no one was going to freeze to death there if it happened. It also bothered him that if Alek and Denny were in trouble, there would be no way he could get to them. That's what he hated most, though his concern was manifesting strangely, so what was Justin supposed to think?

Ren took Justin's empty water glass, setting it safely to the side, pausing to look out at the snow swirling violently through the streets, across the lake. The thunder curled him over the desk, drumming his fingers against it. How long was this supposed to last?

"Ren?" Justin called him, voice weak, and he forcefully turned away from the window to see Justin reaching out to him. He looked frightened. He was panting. Ren had to get it together; Justin needed him. "Could ... could you come here?"

"Sure," Ren agreed, still distracted but doing his best to hide it, returning to where Justin hunched miserably on the bed. He had one hand against his chest now, like before, which pinned Ren's attention immediately when he noticed. In fact, he probably should have been paying more attention this entire time. He forcefully slowed himself down. "Is your heart racing again?"

"It's starting to," Justin admitted, gasping and scared, his flushed face beginning to pale as his heart demanded more blood supply to rush inward. The start of shock, an arrhythmia byproduct.

"That's ok, you know what to do, right? Lie down," Ren instructed, not liking what he was seeing, feeling guilty. Justin shouldn't have had to call him over for help. "Just relax."

"I can't; you're freaking me out." Oh. Ren hadn't thought of that, but he should have known.

"I'm sorry," Ren apologized, kneeling again, compelling himself to chill out for Justin's sake. "Come on, put your head on the pillow. We'll calm down together, all right?" Justin shivered as Ren pulled his quilt over him, adjusting it over his shoulders as Justin lowered himself painfully on the mattress, his color returning almost instantly as he put his circulatory system into a gravitationally neutral line. "Is that better?"

"A little," Justin said, curling up into what seemed to be his natural recovery position, pulling his limbs to his core, some of the tightness leaving his jaw. "You?"

Ren was about to answer when thunder rattled every single one of his vertebrae, making him flinch, his hands convulsing around the fabric of the quilt. "God," he breathed automatically. He wished he could stop doing that, but it seemed out of his conscious control.

"Shh," Justin soothed, sounding drowsy and breathless but no longer panting now that he was on his side. He fumbled out from under the quilt until he found Ren, folding his fingers loosely over his hand. "It's ok." In that moment, Ren's heart almost broke open, full to bursting at this endearing attempt at comfort. He didn't think Justin knew how to be comforting.

"I know," he responded, smiling at Justin though he couldn't see it. "Everything's fine; we're safe. I know that."

"Then why are you all over the place?" Justin asked, holding him still at the bedside. Ren bowed his head, then decided to tell the truth. How could Justin ever open up to him if Ren didn't trust him first? Then again, the slur in Justin's question told him he probably wouldn't remember this conversation in the morning anyway. Either way, there seemed to be no harm in telling him.

"I don't like blizzards," Ren confessed. "It doesn't snow where I grew up. And I wasn't planning on Alek and Denny being gone so long. And now they aren't answering my texts, and it's just getting worse out there and ... I know there's nothing wrong, but I want the storm to stop, and I want you to feel better, and I want them to come home."

"You're something else." Justin was struggling, trying hard to stay awake. Ren had heard that expression before; Alek said it to Denny when he was exasperated with her. He wasn't sure how Justin meant it. "But that makes sense, I guess."

Ren smiled again, relieved Justin wasn't judging him for his fear. His hand still covered Ren's, but it had relaxed to the point where Ren knew it was no longer a deliberate decision of Justin's to have it there. The fever and the drugs were pulling him back under, which was what they were intended to do, and Justin needed the respite. Even though it would leave Ren alone again. "You guys are really close, huh?"

"Yeah," Ren acknowledged, selfishly talking in hopes that Justin would stay awake for a few more minutes. "They mean a lot to me." Justin's hand tightened over his as he shuddered, a concerning little spasm. "How are you doing?" Ren asked him gently, changing the subject, shifting his position so he could settle two fingers on the pulse point on Justin's wrist to analyze the speed and rhythm. Still too fast, but steady now at least.

"That's right," Justin said, his voice half-asleep already.

"Justin?" Ren checked, wondering at the random answer. "Did you hear me? You doing ok?"

"What?" Justin asked, and Ren gave up. He could see Justin was lethargic, exhausted, and he was having trouble concentrating. Trying to keep him interacting was getting cruel.

"Forget it," Ren sighed, resigning himself to how claustrophobic his bedroom was going to seem in the next couple minutes after Justin fell asleep again. "Just rest."

"It's just thunder," Justin murmured. "God, will you hold still?" Justin's hand tightened around his. Ren looked at him, bewildered. "Stop moving." Except he was holding still. He hadn't moved for several minutes now. Concern tapped him urgently at the base of his spine.

"Justin? You still with me?" Ren shook him gently, getting worried.

"It's cold," Justin said, not opening his eyes, the words hardly discernible.

"Your fever's getting worse," Ren responded, deliberately calm despite his unease, watching Justin closely, wondering if anything he was saying was getting through. Without moving his hand from under Justin's, Ren stretched backward to get the ice pack from his desk.

"You're going to hate this," he warned Justin, talking to him as if he were still a participant in this conversation. "But we need to do something about your temperature since Tylenol doesn't seem to be working for you. I'm going to hold an ice pack on the back of your neck to see if it'll help. It seems counterproductive, but trust me, the lower your temperature goes, the warmer you'll be."

When Justin didn't respond, Ren reached behind his head to press the bag against his neck. But Justin jerked as if burned with a white-hot brand the moment it touched his skin, grabbing at Ren's wrist with surprising strength and pulling him off, suddenly defensive. Ren paused, completely shocked. He knew the ice wouldn't feel good to Justin until his temperature came down, but this reaction was extreme.

"Don't," Justin pleaded, cringing away. "Don't hurt me. Please."

Ren felt pain in currents up and down his arms, not from Justin's grip but from his words, which confirmed something Ren suspected before but wasn't completely sure about. There was no questioning it now; the fever was bringing out the truth. Someone had hurt this boy. Badly. Probably many times. He ached to do what Justin wanted, forget the ice pack, bury him in blankets, assure him as many times as he needed to hear that he was safe, that Ren would never hurt him, but he knew that would be the worst thing for him. His heart needed the break. The way he was raving right now just proved even more that his temperature needed to come down. Quickly.

"Justin," Ren reasoned, probably uselessly, but he had to try again. "I'm not going to hurt you; I'd never do that. I'm trying to help. Your temperature is too high and not responding to medication. It won't be comfortable at first, but it will get better if you let me do this. You trust me, right?" Justin was shuddering in front of him, eyes open since the shock of feeling the ice on his neck but not really seeing anything, looking like he really did expect Ren to hurt him. Looking like he might not actually be looking at Ren anymore.

"Wait," Justin begged, getting panicky, keeping a tight grasp on Ren's wrist so he couldn't come any closer with the ice, as if it were a weapon. Ren relaxed the muscles of his arm, leaving it limp in Justin's hand, trying to be as non-threatening as possible. "Please."

Ren couldn't hear the storm outside anymore. There was suddenly nothing but the tone of Justin's voice, the wildness in his eyes. And even though Ren knew better, he knew he wasn't going to force it. Not when Justin was looking at him like that, sounding like that, terrified and desperate. Ren knew this suddenly had nothing to do with the ice pack.

"Ok," Ren settled him, backing off. "Look, here, you take it. Put it on the back of your neck or ... anywhere you think you can handle it; it doesn't matter to me. You pick."

Ren dropped the bag, giving Justin control of the situation, and Justin broke down, collapsing into a weak calm, releasing Ren's wrist. Ren could still feel his fingers clamped there, like the teeth of the dog.

"It's ok, Justin," Ren repeated soothingly, making himself small at the side of the bed, folding his arms over the mattress and laying his head down, his heart breaking. "I'm sorry."

Something cold and soothing came to rest against his bruised cheek, which shook him alert again. He fought against his instinct to jerk upright, forcing himself not to move, but he did open his eyes to see Justin's face in front of his. Justin had changed again, abruptly and without warning. Now he looked soft, almost concerned. Ren had never seen anyone so unpredictable before. He wondered what Justin was like when he wasn't so sick.

"What are you doing?" Ren asked, drained at the back and forth of Justin's emotions, not sure how much longer he could keep up.

"You said I could pick," Justin returned, quiet again, sleepy, like the last few minutes had never happened, his hand trembling on the bag, a sensation that shuddered all the way through to Ren's jaw. The ice felt good on his injured cheek, but the cold seemed to sink into Ren's heart. Justin was starting to really freak him out. "What happened to your face? Someone hit you?" *What the hell?*

Ren slipped out from under the ice pack. He sat on the side of the bed again, staring down at Justin, monitoring him from a different angle, needing to get higher. This situation was way out of his comfort zone now.

"You did, Justin," Ren answered him, hoping he'd snap out of it. *Please snap out of it; I don't have enough training for this.*

"I did?" Justin said, sounding uncertain, his body completely boneless on the bed, vulnerable and weighted. Ren put both hands on his chest, rubbing to keep Justin awake, genuinely afraid now.

"Don't you remember?" Ren pressed. "Justin, look at me. What's my name? Can you tell me that?"

When Justin didn't answer, Ren drew a long breath, running through the protocol on where to go from here and decided on a temperature reading. He pulled the ear thermometer from his bag. Justin barely flinched as Ren took the measurement — 103.5. Still going up.

Ren checked the time. Late, but maybe not too late? No, this was urgent. He needed some advice. Dr. Taneja would be ok with it, even if Ren woke him up. Hadn't he given Ren his cell number specifically for stuff like this? Ren kept one hand on Justin's chest, over his heart, pulling out his phone with the other, taking a moment to notice there were still no messages from Alek, Denny, or Celeste. He hoped the doctor would be more accessible.

"Lorenzo?" Dr. Taneja answered, not sounding as though Ren had woken him but confused nonetheless. Ren usually only called on Sunday afternoons or they communicated via text for shadow sessions at the hospital.

"Hey," Ren responded, gratitude and relief audible in his voice. "Sorry to call so late."

"There must be a reason," Dr. Taneja soothed, his Indian accent relaxing Ren. "What can I do for you?" Ren felt some of the crushing weight of responsibility for Justin lift off his shoulders.

"I'm looking after someone," Ren began, watching Justin intently, glad his voice wasn't betraying his fear. "And we're at the point where I'm not sure if it would be better to keep him here or call for an ambulance. Can I run his symptoms by you to get your opinion?"

"Certainly," Dr. Taneja invited. "Go ahead."

So Ren told him everything he knew so far. The febrile seizure, the arrhythmia, the dehydration and delirium, the non-response to fever reducers, the rising temperature, the changes that had taken place in the hours Justin had been under Ren's supervision and treatment. The way Justin was lying right this second, breathing fast, as still as death.

"Well, that is a tough call," Dr. Taneja said when Ren was finished. "He's definitely borderline. If it weren't for the storm, I'd say yes. However, I know for a fact they have their hands full at the moment."

"I don't want him waiting around in triage," Ren said, and Dr. Taneja hummed in the affirmative.

"Which is precisely what would happen if you took him now," he admitted. "If it were anyone other than you, I'd say go anyway, but since I know what you're capable of, here's what I would recommend." Ren grabbed his notebook and pen to document what Dr. Taneja was about to say.

"Keep him resting. I know delirium can be difficult to watch, but you're doing all the right things so far," Dr. Taneja encouraged. "If his fever goes over 104, call the ambulance. Keep waking him every hour to replenish fluids, something with added electrolytes if you have it. If he won't rouse enough to drink, bring him in."

"Thanks, Dr. Taneja," Ren said, feeling better.

"Stay calm," Dr. Taneja instructed. "Call again if you need to."

They hung up, and Ren sighed. He'd known all of that information before calling, but it was nice to hear confirmation from an actual MD. After writing a few final notes, Ren picked up the ice pack again as if it were a grenade. But it had already exploded. Gently, Ren lifted Justin's head, slipping the ice against his neck as he'd originally intended before Justin had spiraled into some crazy PTSD psychosis. Justin moaned in his sleep but didn't move. Ren wasn't sure if that was an improvement, but at least the ice was where he wanted it now.

"You are *not* going to the ER," Ren promised him, remembering how Justin had tried to use the ice pack to help him, attempted to ease Ren's pain even though he couldn't remember who Ren was. That counted for a whole lot, especially since Ren knew how delirium worked. It didn't make it any easier to watch, but he knew how it worked. He'd just seen Justin's bare soul, boiled to the surface by the fever. Part of it was fear and violence, but not all. Part of it was kindness and compassion.

Ren set a timer on his phone to let him know when he should wake Justin for another drink. Then he settled on the side of the bed, listening to the weather, listening to Justin breathe, just looking at him, exhausted from what they'd been through already, knowing they still had a long way to go.

Justin moaned again, distressed even in his sleep, and Ren put his hand on his head in an effort to still him, wishing there was more he could do. He wasn't comfortable yet either. The storm was fraying the edges of his nerves, and he was still wound up from talking to Justin earlier, from how he'd watched him fall apart, but he understood now that Justin was tuned into Ren's emotions, so he stayed where he was, forcing himself not to pace, not to look out the window. He couldn't stop himself from startling when the thunder hit the room, but at least that was softening, the time between strikes getting longer, the storm blowing away across the dark lake.

Before the timer rang for Justin, Ren's phone started playing an instrumental clip from "She Blinded Me With Science" — Denny's ringtone, which she wasn't sure if she loved or loathed. Depended on the day.

"About time!" Ren whisper-shouted into the receiver. "Where the hell are you and what have you been doing that you couldn't let me know?" He didn't really have to watch his mouth with Denny. She could handle every emotion he threw at her without taking it personally. Unlike Alek. Or Justin, who had started shaking his head side to side. Ren would have to alter his tone.

"Told you he'd be mad," Alek said, his voice muffled by distance.

"He's not mad; he's overprotective and panicking," Denny told Alek. Ren wasn't sure he liked her assessment, however accurate it may be. "Sorry, Ren; Alek forgot his charger, so his phone is dead, and I turned mine off so it wouldn't interfere with any of the equipment. I'm guessing you sent Alek twice as many messages as me?"

"I didn't count them," Ren defended, trying to make it seem like he hadn't overreacted. "It doesn't matter; are you guys done? You coming home now?"

"Well, the storm's moving on, but the damage is pretty heavy. We can't get the car out of the parking lot until maintenance comes in the morning to plow it, so a lot of the team is staying here for the night, looking through the data. We were going to do that too, but I guess we could walk home?" She said this last as if in question to Alek, to see what he thought of that idea.

"You don't have to do that," Ren told her, trying to pretend he wasn't disappointed. "Stay warm and safe. But keep your phone on? Keep me updated?"

"Aren't you going to sleep?" Denny asked.

"Not yet," Ren answered, noticing Justin growing increasingly restless as the conversation went on. His hands were clenching in the quilt, his whole body jerking at random.

"Hey, Ren, you doing ok?" The tenderness in Alek's voice made Ren's eyes sting with exhausted tears. Damn kindness. Got him every time. "You weren't that worried about us, were you?" *Alek, you have no idea. Worried isn't even the right word anymore.*

"It got intense for a while," Ren admitted, leaving it at that. Justin took a weird breath, a little gasp, and Ren decided it would be best to get off the phone, even though he didn't want to. "I'm glad you guys are ok."

"It was epic," Denny assured him, and Ren couldn't help but smile weakly. He put a careful hand on Justin's chest.

"We'll tell you all about it later, though," Alek jumped in before Denny got carried away. Because Alek could always tell what was going on with Ren, whether Ren wanted him to or not. "How's your patient?"

"He's ..." Ren hesitated, not knowing how to answer that question. Then he remembered who he was talking to. "He's a lot worse than this afternoon."

"Worse than Denny?" Alek asked. He gauged just about everything to that; it had really rattled him. Ren had a new appreciation for how he'd felt. Helpless, worried, and responsible.

"Yeah," he confirmed, defeated.

"Good thing you brought him home then," Alek praised. Ren had a sudden image of Justin lying in his own bed back in that tiny room. Lying there alone, like this, for all the long hours of the night. He heard himself make a little "huh" sound in acknowledgement to what Alek had just said, not trusting his voice. He couldn't think of anything worse than that.

"Oh hey, Chris, wait a second," Denny said to someone over at the museum. "Ren, we need to go. Will you be ok?"

"Sure," he said, trying to sound like he meant it. "I'll see you guys tomorrow."

"Hang in there, buddy," Alek said in parting. "Get some sleep."

"I will," Ren lied.

Then they were gone, and the room seemed darker. At least now Ren knew they were fine. He'd known that the whole time, but like talking with Dr. Taneja, it felt better to have confirmation.

Justin took more quick breaths, one after the other without a break to the point where Ren felt it best to try and wake him up. He didn't want to disturb his rest, but this didn't look like rest.

Ren successfully pulled Justin to a sitting position, making him coherent enough to swallow some water, though he didn't truly wake. His eyes stayed closed; he didn't speak — his brain on fire and stealing his cognizance. Ren had to support him upright with one arm and hold the cup to his lips with the other. Somehow, he did both without spilling anything.

"You were going to do this by yourself," he said disapprovingly. "There's independence and then there's just stupidity, you know."

He laid him gently on the mattress, removing the blanket. Since Justin wasn't aware, it would be best to keep him as cool as possible now. Ren refilled the icepack, replacing it under Justin's neck, making him whimper in his sleep. Ren made a note on his page.

"North," Justin cried, his hand stretching out. Ren took it, holding it to his own chest.

"Shh, Justin," he begged, disturbed almost beyond endurance to be here watching this, not able to do much to help. *Delirium is hard to witness*, Dr. Taneja said.

"Don't leave. Don't leave me here," Justin cried, trapped in his own mind. "Can't I come with you? I promise I won't ... North, it's so cold." He ripped his hand out of Ren's grip, twisting to the side. "I swear I didn't touch him. Tell them, North. I haven't even ... North, please."

Ren was beginning to see that North was more important to Justin than he'd hinted earlier. Who was he, though? And since he seemed to be the one Justin wanted most, why hadn't he wanted Ren to call him?

"Can they do that?" Justin went on, still seeing things, caught in the worst fever dream Ren had ever seen. "North, wait ... my heart ... hurts." Ren grabbed Justin's wrist when he heard this, feeling the hard, intense pulse under his fingers.

"Justin," he called, hoping to somehow get through, leaning into him as if that would help. "Calm down."

"I didn't mean to," Justin went on, not hearing Ren. "I was trying to ... you believe me, don't you?"

Ren looked around the room, desperate for something that might help shake Justin out of this. He caught sight of Justin's duffel bag and remembered the backpack inside it. Justin's phone. Would that help though? Justin had told him not to call, but that had been before. When Justin could sit up on his own and speak clearly. Ren's voice wasn't reaching him, but maybe North could?

"Get off," Justin was growling, thrashing against Ren now. Ren obeyed, even though the command hadn't been directed at him. He crossed the room to the duffel bag. Was he really going to do this? Should he?

"I'll kill you," Justin hissed, and for a second Ren thought he was talking to him. He almost dropped the bag, looking back where Justin writhed on the bed, panting, furious, and terrified at the same time. What on earth? Where had that come from?

English was so full of expressions. Ren heard Americans say the word "kill" way too casually all the time. Ren probably heard someone flippantly threaten death once a day, and none of it meant anything. This was the first time ever he'd heard what that particular phrase sounded like when it was used in its literal translation. Justin wasn't aware of his surroundings, and Ren had no idea what he was experiencing in his mind, but he could tell from the chill in his blood that Justin was being completely serious.

"Justin?" Ren said, unnerved, but the moment was past.

"I'm so sorry," Justin sobbed, practically crippled with remorse, the last few seconds of violence just a flash like the lightning. Ren returned his attention to the backpack, conflicted about opening it. He'd promised he wouldn't. Justin had told him to contact North for an emergency.

Ren carried the backpack with him, folding it in his arms as he sat on the edge of the bed. He put one hand on Justin's chest, shushing him repeatedly, hoping it might be easier to calm him now he was quieter and crying.

"Justin," he called again, bending over him. "Come on. Wake up."

"North," Justin repeated.

"I'll find him," Ren promised, not knowing what else to do. Yet even though he'd made the decision, his hands still hesitated on the zipper, knowing if Justin were awake, he would not want him to do this. But if Justin were awake, he wouldn't have to. He'd just about talked himself into it when he heard the front door open.

He looked at Justin, who was still crying softly, and then hurried toward the living room where Alek and Denny were just turning on the lights, covered in melting snow. He couldn't remember when he'd been happier to see them. Without a word, without letting her finish getting her arms out of her sleeves, Ren went to his knees in front of Denny and grabbed her around the waist, resting his bruised cheek against the fresh, wet cold of her coat.

"Aww, Renzo, is it that bad?" she asked him, softer than she usually spoke. He opened his mouth to answer, but he heard himself simply exhale in relief. "Yeah, ok. It is."

By this time, Alek had succeeded in getting out of his Carhartt and had come around to Ren's other side. "We're here," he assured, the words a comforting rumble. Ren couldn't seem to stand up. He couldn't seem to let go of Denny.

"Did you walk?" Ren sniffed, calming down. Denny was uncharacteristically running her fingers through his hair, though his embrace had gone long over her normal tolerance time.

"We hitched a ride with someone who had the common sense to park on the street," she answered. "The way you were talking, we thought we'd better come home."

"Thank you," Ren expressed his gratitude. "I could really use your help."

6

SECOND DEGREE

Ren woke in a crumpled heap on his bedroom floor, wearing his scrubs from yesterday and partially covered with the crocheted afghan that a previous tenant had abandoned on the back of the couch. He lifted his head, his cheek throbbing because he had stupidly slept on it, as close to a hangover as he would ever feel.

Ren gathered his stiff limbs underneath him, hunching over his knees, hips easing to the floor while his fingertips pushed forward, unkinking his spine before sitting up slowly and leaning back against his bed, going still after rearranging the afghan over his raised knees, watching the color brighten in the room as the sun began its ascent over Lake Michigan. Apparently, the world had made plans to continue turning. The way last night had gone, Ren had begun to wonder if perhaps dawn had been canceled.

He stopped himself just in time from rubbing both hands over his face, switching to gingerly trying to scrub the sleep from his eyes with his fingertips instead since his cheek was already tender. He looked at the mess on his desk. Justin's water glass; his stethoscope; the bottle of Tylenol; one of Alek's largest pots, half full of melted snow and floating plastic freezer bags; a few wadded-up towels,

84

some still soaked; and a wet patch on the carpet from where they'd been dripping off the desk. The part of Ren's brain that liked things settled properly in their places started ringing an alarm for him to fix all that as soon as possible. He ignored it.

Instead he turned over, rising to his knees so he could fold over his mattress. The position hurt, the ache of overuse. He'd been kneeling by the bedside for most of the night, and his muscles were telling him they'd had enough of it. He ignored that too. He wanted to check on Justin.

He was lying comfortably quiet on his side, his fingers open in soft curls instead of gripped tight and trembling. He breathed faster than normal, but at least it was steady. Ren felt his heart soften in relief to hear Justin breathing like that. Automatically, Ren reached for the ear thermometer he'd placed on the floor but grabbed his notebook instead. He didn't want to risk disturbing Justin right now. If he could sleep like this, he should just keep right on doing it. Ren flipped through his notes from last night, reviewing them now that things were quiet and he had time to think.

He didn't read for very long. He discovered after only a few entries that he couldn't. He didn't want to remember yet. Flipping to a clean page, he wrote the date at the top. A fresh start. He wrote the time and a description of how Justin looked, noting his reason for not getting any measurable stats. Then he picked up the wet towels from the desk and took them to the bathroom, seeing on his way that Denny was zonked out on the couch, and he could hear Alek softly snoring behind his closed bedroom door. He'd have to be careful not to wake them either. They'd been right there with him most of last night and deserved the break.

Tossing the towels with a squelchy plop in the corner, Ren started the water running in the shower, hurrying out of his clothes and into its soothing heat, taking a few luxurious minutes to just lean against the tile, hanging his head into the spray. It felt so nice. He'd have to try and get Justin in here sometime today. Probably not a shower, but a long soak might sound good to him later. If he were still here.

Ren bowed his head lower, thinking about Justin.

It wasn't arrogance when Ren told people he knew what he was doing. He'd studied and practiced, reviewed and trained. He spent his free time reading medical books, following Dr. Taneja at the hospital. Twice a month, he attended refresher courses with other first responders, and every thirty days, he was required to ride a shift with the campus hospital ambulance in order to keep his EMT status. It wasn't like he had no experience in the field. There had even been instances where he'd not only been first on scene, he'd been the Incident Commander in Charge. And he excelled at it.

But Justin.

Ren knelt in the shower, overcome, lacing his fingers together at the back of his neck, taking these private moments for a delayed, but expected, breakdown. Justin was like nothing Ren had ever encountered before, and he couldn't even really explain why. He stared at Ren and made him shake inside his soul. When Justin cried in his sleep, Ren forgot everything he had ever learned about manually reducing body temperature. When Justin held his breath, Ren's breathing stopped right along with him, paralyzed and unsure what to do — even though he knew perfectly well what to do!

He let himself watch it over again from this side of the morning, knowing Justin was resting easy now, breathing steadily and calm, no longer in danger. He let his mind debrief, sorting through the chaos. He remembered explaining to Alek and Denny about Justin's condition. He'd made it clear that he was going to do all he could to keep him out of the hospital even though Justin's illness had done all it could to thwart him, holding Justin hostage at the tipping point where Ren would have admitted they no longer had a choice. It had gotten personal, mostly because of the ice pack, Justin's fear, and the way he held on to Ren's shirt. Releasing him to the treatment of strangers, even ones more competent than himself, felt somehow like a betrayal of Justin's trust.

In the end, Alek and Denny brought Ren freezer bags full of snow from the balcony, and he'd wrapped them in towels and placed them all around Justin. By that point, Justin didn't even respond to the cold, and he was breathing in a tortured loop. He'd take a gasping breath and then hold it, longer and longer, he'd just hold it, before releasing in an agonizing rush, followed by another gasp and a longer pause. It wasn't as though he'd stopped breathing, exactly, but it was so close, and his heartbeat was everywhere, like a trapped bird flown into a building by mistake and searching desperately for an exit. And in that hour between two and three in the morning, the mysterious hour Ren had learned was the most likely to break a fever — that was when Justin's spiked to a dangerous 103.8.

Ren probably should have taken him in. He knew that now. But decisions like that were somehow so hard to make in the dark, tight, pressured space of his bedroom. He couldn't think outside of it. Couldn't think past the threshold, two feet beyond the perimeter of the bed, or past counting the seconds until Justin took his next breath. And just when Alek and Denny were suggesting it, letting Ren know as gently as possible that it might be time to get more professional help, the snow did what it was supposed to. Justin's breathing became less labored. His heart rate slowed, stopped jumping. The fever came down, and Justin started ranting again, as if his symptoms were working in reverse.

But oh, the things he'd said in that place. The sobbing. The visceral terror. The anguished begging. The violence.

Ren had perched protectively at his side doing his best to keep him still, pressing against his chest, speaking to him as if he could hear, while his friends stared at him, Alek straddled backward on his desk chair, one of his legs bouncing at the stress, and Denny clenched in a tight ball of anxiety on the floor, resting her head against Alek's non-moving knee. Ren tried to make them understand that this was an improvement. He tried to convince himself because Justin did not seem in the least bit improved — he was terrifying.

"What is he even saying?" Denny couldn't help but ask, her voice shrill with the strain of listening to Justin as he cried for someone to believe him, pleading not to be left wherever he thought he was. "North? What the hell is that supposed to mean?"

"It's a name," Ren replied, his voice a displaced sort of calm, pushing back the stress to a more convenient time when he could deal with it alone. He sounded hollow, but in control, though he wasn't sure how much longer he could keep it together either. Listening to Justin was ripping him up inside, making him forget what Dr. Taneja had told him, his own heart as exhausted as Justin's but in a different way. But Denny was looking at him and so was Alek. Justin still needed him. So he took one more breath and stayed still one more second, speaking to Denny evenly just to prove he could, knowing exactly how much she needed the comfort of his capability. "You don't have to stay, guys. I know it's hard to listen to. He's coming down now; I got him."

"What about you, though?" Alek asked, resistant to leave but obviously exhausted.

"You'll be in the next room," Ren pointed out. "If I need you, I can come get you."

"Except you won't," Denny snapped, which was fair. Ren gave her a tired smile.

"You'd be surprised how much you give me just from knowing you're sleeping nearby," he told her, shocked when these simple words made her lower lip tremble. It had been a long night for all of them. She stood up, wrapping herself around his arm and leaning her head on his shoulder.

"You sure you'll be ok?" she checked. "All alone listening to this?" Ren returned his attention to Justin, his flushed face and tight jawline, understanding what she meant. She knew Ren well, knew what it would do to him. Hell, she'd just seen him fall apart when they came home earlier tonight, but that had been different. He really had been all alone then.

"If you're here, even if you're asleep, I'm not alone," he told her.

They gave him final words of promise and encouragement, but then they did what he asked and went to find their beds.

Ren turned off the water, finished with his shower and still on his knees. He knew when his friends had left to sleep, but his memories blurred after they were gone. Justin had quieted — the restful kind not the critical kind; his fever finally tamed back to 102.9. Ren continued to rub his chest and tell him he was safe. He kind of remembered getting the afghan from the couch, careful not to disturb Denny, but the moment when he'd felt Justin was stable enough for him to stop watching him, when he curled up on the floor next to the bed for just a few minutes of recovery that dropped into sleep ... he couldn't remember that.

Justin hadn't moved when Ren returned to his room, so he eased his dresser drawers open in tiny fragments, just enough to snag his clothes. He dressed quickly and then headed toward the kitchen with Alek's pot so he could pour the snow water down the sink. While he may have been able to move around Justin without waking him, the dull clatter of kitchen noises stirred Denny as he set the pot down on the counter and began brewing coffee.

"Everything ok?" she murmured from the couch, her voice still rough from sleep.

"Yeah," Ren assured in a low tone just loud enough to reach her. "He's resting now. I think the worst is over."

"You should go back to sleep too," she chastened him, not knowing that just wasn't possible. He was up, showered, and dressed for the day. He had to clean off his desk, force himself to review the notes from last night, contact Dr. Taneja to give him an update, do some laundry to take care of all those wet towels. There was a quickly growing list of things that needed his attention.

"I will," he lied, hoping Denny was still half-asleep and wouldn't call him on it.

"How well do you know that guy?" Denny asked out of nowhere. "You've never brought anyone home before."

"I don't know him at all," Ren confessed, surprising himself with how bitter he sounded. He kept talking to try and smooth it out. "We were assigned to do a project together for our English class, but I don't know anything about him except he lives in one of those tiny rooms without a bathroom or a sink. It just made more sense to bring him here."

"And give him your bed?" Denny pressed. Ren poured himself a cup of coffee though the pot was only half done, needing the caffeine and a way out of this conversation.

"Well, the couch was already taken," he said jokingly, but Denny would hear what he was implying. Justin wasn't the first patient he'd brought to the apartment. *She* had been. This wasn't that far out of the norm for him. Not really. "Get some more sleep, Kaydee-bird," he instructed, taking his mug and heading to his room.

"Wait. Ren?" Denny stopped him as he walked past the couch. He didn't know why, but her simple questions were making him feel defensive. He knew she didn't mean them that way, so he forced himself to pause. "I was going to ask last night, but you were so focused, and Alek told me not to, but what the hell did you do to your face?" Ren covered the bruise automatically as she mentioned it, as if he could hide it now. He hadn't looked in the mirror this morning, but he imagined it was likely much darker than it had been yesterday. It hurt more too.

"Ha," he huffed, playing it cool. "You're going to have to wait. That's a story that needs a dramatic reenactment to do it justice."

"Give me the movie trailer version then," Denny demanded, not distracted in the least. She'd obviously already waited longer than she wanted to. Ren turned his face away, even though his bruised side was already toward the kitchen, not the couch.

"I did something stupid," he answered, switching his coffee mug to the other hand so he could ruffle her bedhead, as if that would scatter her thoughts and make her forget all about his face.

"Ren, why won't you just —"

"I need to get back in there, ok? I'll tell you later, promise. Go back to sleep." Of course, he knew it wasn't an answer. He also knew it was suspicious as hell he wasn't giving her one, but if he said anything else, Denny would know he was lying. Sometimes he wished Denny were more like her scientist colleagues. The ones who could recite the coordinates for every visible star in the Milky Way but couldn't read a social cue if their life depended on it. But no, not Denny. She was the kind of genius who could do both.

She scowled in exasperation as he passed her, and Ren knew the only thing saving him from having to explain was probably because Denny was still sleepy and likely frightened to follow him into his bedroom. Last night had been hard on her; it was a solid testament to their friendship that she'd stayed as long as she had. Ren had only bought himself a temporary reprieve, though. *You're going to have to tell them*, he reminded himself as he tiptoed through his doorway. *Eventually*.

Justin slept on while Ren did what he could about straightening his desk. He texted Dr. Taneja. He realized Celeste had never sent him her email address. Who knew a simple canceled date could make someone so angry? On the other hand, girls like Celeste probably didn't have their dates cancel very often. Or at all. Maybe he'd have a chance to talk to her on Wednesday, after he'd connected her to the centrifuge, and she had no choice but to sit there and listen. If she only knew what happened here last night, she would forgive him. Ren hunched his shoulders forward, stretching his back, not fully capable of conjuring much emotion for Celeste. He had bigger things going on.

For a little while, he stood at his window cuddling his coffee, watching the snow falling, astonished at how different it looked in the daylight. The sky and the lake had all but disappeared in the general whiteness of the low, foggy clouds, and it seemed peaceful and lazy this morning. Ren sipped his coffee, enjoying its warmth in his hand and down his throat. He deliberately did not look at his notebook, even though he knew he should organize some of the scattered thoughts and scribblings of the night before. Three stories down, a snowplow cleared a path along South Stony Island Avenue, ruining the crisp, white perfection of the drifts. Ren breathed in the scent from his mug, sighing, then reached out a hand to pick up the notebook.

He'd barely touched it when he heard Justin sneeze behind him, causing him to abandon the notebook completely. Setting his mug on the desk, Ren turned to see Justin beginning to push himself up from the bed. Saw him shudder, look around in confusion at the unfamiliar location, then sink down, groaning.

"Hey, Justin," Ren made Justin aware he was not alone in the room, keeping his voice chipper even though he was still concerned. He wasn't sure what sort of mental state Justin would wake to, or how much he'd remember from last night. Ren wondered how much he would have to tell him and how he was going to do that without falling apart. But one thing at a time; follow protocol. Justin twisted so he could look at Ren, disoriented, but not delirious. At least, Ren didn't think so. Ren chanced it coming closer, kneeling at the bedside. "You know who I am today?"

Justin's eyes softened, some of the confusion clearing, though he now wore an expression that suggested he thought Ren was asking a strange question. "Yeah," he said, voice slow and deep, in a tone that told Ren he was being humored. He wasn't sure if that made him more or less worried. He reached out to put his hand on Justin's face but hesitated, paused by memory.

"Can I touch you?" Ren asked for permission. After hearing some of the things Justin whimpered in the dark, he thought he should. Every time. Justin nodded, a simple movement that meant more to Ren this morning than it had yesterday. He rested his palm against Justin's forehead, frowning at the heat, leaning close when he heard Justin sigh, wishing he were better at this. He'd never wanted to heal someone more in his life. "Let's get some stats, huh?" Ren picked up the ear thermometer to get started on some data, though he wasn't pleased to see the reading. 103.1. For some reason, the numbers screwed in Ren's stomach like a low grade on a test. This wasn't working. He didn't think it was a good idea to treat Justin at home anymore.

"Still really high," he told Justin seriously, grabbing the notebook so he could write it down, deliberately flipping past the previous night without looking at it, like fast forwarding through the scariest part in a movie. But he couldn't keep doing that. Justin's face was full of question, and Ren knew he was still tuned to his every movement, every expression on his face. "Justin, I don't know. You probably don't remember much from last night, do you?"

"What did I do?" Justin asked, suddenly fearful, his eyes conspicuously glued to Ren's bruised cheek, making Ren's heart twist.

"You did great," Ren assured him quickly, wanting to make it clear that he'd done nothing wrong, sad that was his first assumption. Surprisingly, this statement did not have a positive effect on Justin. He turned away, tightening. Ren wasn't sure what he'd said, and he wasn't sure of the things he knew he needed to say.

He bought himself some time by helping Justin sit up so he could listen to his breathing and heartbeat. Both were moderately reassuring. Justin's lungs were clear, his heart rate fast but steady. Ren deliberated, remembering what Dr. Taneja had said. *He's definitely borderline.* Ren just wasn't sure.

"What is it?" Justin asked, monitoring him closely. "You look mad."

"No," Ren denied, sitting facing Justin on the bed, removing his stethoscope. "I'm just thinking what we should do for you." Ren watched what his words did to Justin, consumed with sympathy. His statement was supposed to be concerned, thoughtful, but Justin's eyes were full of fear and, oddly, rejection, as if Ren had just vocalized a threat. Justin raised his hand to his head, breathing hard, and Ren could see the struggle it was for him to stay sitting up. Ren took a moment to make a backrest out of the afghan and his pillow, arranging them against the wall, helping Justin shift backward and lean into it so he could rest his head but still be semi-upright.

"Justin, we need to talk, ok?"

"I ... ok?"

"You," Ren paused. He knew Justin had a hard time talking about what he was feeling, but Ren hadn't anticipated that he wouldn't be able to say it either. He reached over to put a hand on the bed between them, as if that could help them communicate. "You had a bad night." He hesitated, knowing Justin needed more information. Where should he start? How much should he say?

"Ren." Justin still seemed scared, looking at Ren's hand. "What did I do?"

"You didn't do anything wrong, Justin," Ren repeated, needing him to understand. Justin raised his head enough to look Ren in the eye, though it was impossible for Ren to maintain visual contact. The resignation was back; Justin thought Ren was lying. And he'd been expecting it. Ren couldn't stand it. Justin should never expect Ren to lie to him. He was going to have to tell him. "But I did."

"What?" Justin was still obviously confused and no wonder. Ren knew he wasn't making a lot of sense.

"Your fever spiked," Ren explained. "You ... honestly, you scared me. I should have taken you to the hospital. You didn't know where you were or who I was. I don't know why I thought ... I guess I was just being arrogant? I don't know. It was the wrong choice. You were crying in your sleep for a while, saying all kinds of things, and then you were barely breathing anymore, and I just couldn't think. It's like I forgot we could leave the room. My friends and I ... God, Justin, this sounds awful, I can't believe we did this. We packed you in snow to bring your temperature down. I really should have called an ambulance. I'm so sorry."

Ren kept his head down after his confession, not wanting to see Justin's face. He half expected Justin to turn away, demand to leave, and who could blame him. Ren had basically kidnapped him so Ren could ... what? Redeem himself from what he'd done at the end of their English class? Feel better about all the horrible things he'd thought about Justin before? It wasn't fair, and Justin was more than Ren could handle. He was too delicate, both physically and emotionally, for Ren to pretend like he still knew what he was doing. Ren took a deep breath, needing to fill the silence. Why wasn't Justin saying anything?

"I can still take you," Ren offered. "We can go; get you better help."

"You want me to leave?" Justin asked, so softly, but the question echoed within Ren in various repetitions of what Justin had been saying all night. *Don't leave me here. Can't I stay with you? Please.* The words stinging with abandonment. How many times had someone left Justin? How many times had someone given up on him? This wasn't the same, though. Ren just didn't have the resources available.

"I thought you'd want to leave," Ren responded. "I really messed up. You could have died last night, Justin."

"But I didn't," Justin pointed out. "Because of you." Ren felt brave enough to look at Justin again, wondering how it had happened. How could anyone leave this boy behind or give up on him? Had North done that? But why? Justin's eyes were full of gratitude and pleading. Ren couldn't believe it, but it was plainly there. He wanted to stay. "Thank you."

Ren held his breath. *Justin, for heaven's sake.* But he hadn't thought of it that way before. What would have happened to Justin if Ren hadn't dragged him home? What if he'd stayed alone in his room last night? Ren bowed his head.

"Don't thank me yet," Ren heard himself say. "You're still very sick, and we might not have a choice about the hospital. I think we both want you to stay here, but we're going to have to get your temperature down."

"Ok," Justin agreed. Ren shook his head. Easier said than done.

"How is your heart?" Ren asked. "You pushed it hard last night. Is it hurting today?"

"Not right now," Justin answered, encouraging Ren. "It's just tight." Ren started taking notes, going back and forth with Justin, asking easy yes or no questions. Yes, his head hurt, and it made him dizzy to hold it up for even a few seconds. He wasn't congested despite how he'd woken up sneezing. He still felt cold. No, he was not hungry.

"I know, but you're going to need to eat something," Ren lectured gently. "Especially since I have to try some heavier medication today to see about getting that fever down. You'll need something in your stomach." Justin looked really uncomfortable about the idea of eating, enough that Ren thought he should ask about it. "Does your stomach hurt?"

"No." Ok. Then what? Ren couldn't think of a yes or no question for this, but then Justin added in a rush, "my mouth does."

"Since when?" Ren asked. "Yesterday?"

"Since I woke up." Justin sounded so pitiful, like his spirit was all twisted up inside having to answer all these questions.

"Let's check what's going on," Ren said, retrieving a flashlight from his medical bag and aiming the beam into Justin's open mouth. It took half a second to see the cause of Justin's pain, but it took Ren another minute to figure out what happened.

Justin's temperature had been so high for so long it had literally boiled the inside of his mouth and all down his throat. The soft tissues there were covered in second degree burns — fever blisters.

"Oh, Justin," Ren said again, knowing that was not the best way to let him know what was going on. But he had never seen this before. He didn't even know it was possible.

"What is it?" Justin sounded worried, which was all Ren's fault. He put the flashlight back before answering.

"Burns," Ren explained. "Your fever was so high it blistered your mouth and throat. It's going to be really painful for you to ... are you sure I can't take you to the hospital?"

Justin had unconsciously raised his hand to cover his mouth. He hadn't answered yet when someone knocked on Ren's bedroom door, opening it slightly at the same time. A typical Alek gesture.

"Hey, sorry," Alek greeted and apologized, his voice low in case someone might be sleeping. "Ren, everything ok in here? What's the status?" When he saw both Justin and Ren awake, he allowed himself all the way in. "Hey, you're alive," he said to Justin. Ren didn't think Alek understood exactly how touch and go it had been. But since Ren and Justin were in a verbal stalemate about hospital negotiations, Ren just let Alek continue.

"How are you doing, buddy?" Alek asked Justin, genuinely concerned, talking to him as if they were best friends. Probably because Alek had yet to meet someone who wasn't instantaneously his friend.

"Not so great," Justin answered, immediately and honestly, and Ren had to stare at him. What the hell? But then he remembered about Alek. You'd almost have to make a delusional and dedicated choice about not trusting Alek. "But thanks, you know, for helping me."

Alek not only looked ready to continue helping, but he looked ready to adopt Justin on the spot. Ren stood by, watching with interest, his arms folded. Maybe Alek should talk Justin into the hospital.

"I did nothing," Alek said modestly. "Ren is your man. He'll have you back to normal in no time." Ren looked at the floor, weirdly out of his element listening to this, not so certain he deserved the vote of confidence. "But I came to see if I could get you guys some breakfast, or maybe we should call it brunch, we all sort of slept in today." Justin covered his mouth again, involuntarily wincing.

"We were just talking about that," Ren brought himself back into the conversation.

"Great!" Alek went on enthusiastically. "I was thinking oatmeal. Sound good?"

Justin looked pleadingly at Ren, begging him silently.

"Actually, Alek," Ren said, noticing how Justin slumped in relief as he took over. "Justin's not going to be able to handle that." The smooth, no-need-to-chew texture of the oatmeal would be fine, but the temperature would not, and Ren wasn't about to suggest Justin eat it cold. Yet.

"Ok," Alek said, already brainstorming but having a hard time coming up with better invalid food than oatmeal. Ren was mentally searching their fridge and cabinets too.

"Got it." Ren snapped his fingers as he remembered something. "Alek, were you able to get ingredients for smoothies when you were grocery shopping?"

"Sure," Alek answered, nodding slowly as he caught on to what Ren was thinking. "I had to get frozen mangoes, though."

"That's fine," Ren said, looking at Justin. "We'll try it," he told him. "If you can at least drink some calories, and we can find a medication that will work, you can stay here."

"Breakfast smoothie — coming right up," Alek acknowledged, turning to go.

"Don't put any citrus in it," Ren instructed before he left. "Use coconut milk. Oh, and spinach, please."

"Sure thing," Alek said, giving a thumbs up as he closed the door. Justin did not look enthusiastic, but it was this or nothing.

"Alek makes the best smoothies," Ren assured him. "Actually, Alek makes the best everything."

Justin leaned back into the little nest Ren had made against the wall, looking calm, but uncomfortable, tired even though he'd only just woken up. Ren returned to his position on the bed, wanting to stay close.

There was so much more he wanted to talk about, more from last night. He wanted to ask about North, learn who he was, why he was so important. Why Justin felt so strongly about not contacting him. Ren wanted to ask who had hurt Justin and how. This wasn't just a biography assignment to him anymore.

And then there was the last thing Justin ranted about last night. Words Justin had growled after Alek and Denny left. Words that almost made Ren call them back, frightened him enough he didn't know if he could even ask about them. He wasn't sure he'd written those things in his notebook. It was part of the reason he hadn't wanted to look. He wanted to have Justin confirm he'd been completely out of his mind and those things had no true basis in reality.

That had to be it. Ren looked at Justin, sitting there so still, so sick, and he knew it couldn't be real. But then he remembered the bruise on his cheek and felt the chill of uncertainty in his heart. He didn't really know anything.

He jumped when something touched his arm, so deep in thought he didn't notice that Justin had reached over to mildly cling to his sleeve cuff. Ren was beginning to like that, how Justin would hold on to his clothes, a timid, endearing request for reassurance.

"How are you feeling?" he asked, just to hear Justin's voice when it was normal.

"Like I really don't want to move," Justin answered.

"You don't have to," Ren encouraged. "In fact, it's a good idea if you don't."

"Yeah," Justin sighed. "Except I need to use your bathroom."

"Oh," Ren said. "Yeah, come on. I'll help you."

7
BLOODWORK

With the wall on one side and Ren on the other, Justin was able to make it shakily down the hall to the apartment bathroom.

"No," he said to Ren before he'd even suggested that Justin not go in by himself.

"Are you serious?" Ren returned, nodding to their current position, the only gesture available to him since he needed both hands to keep Justin upright. "You realize you didn't take a single step on your own to get here, right?"

"Then I'll crawl," Justin shot back, unwilling to yield, his voice many times stronger than his posture, completely serious. Ren didn't see what the big deal was, but he understood it was important to Justin.

"Let me at least prop you up at the sink to get you close," Ren said, watching with worry as Justin clung to the doorframe, tightening his grip on him to make sure he didn't topple over. "Take your time," he instructed firmly. "Don't lock the door. I'll be right outside if you need help."

Justin turned his head slightly as Ren practically draped him over the sink basin like a towel, giving Ren the tiniest half-smile and a raised eyebrow, looking strangely amused while Ren talked to him. "Ok," he agreed. "And did you want any in a cup or something, Doc?" he asked, sarcasm tinging his voice, and Ren felt instantly conflicted about being teased like this, an uncomfortable mix of relief, appreciation, and exasperation.

"Ha," Ren breathed uneasily, not sure what to do with a patient who was joking with him when he couldn't get over how bad he looked, then paused to think about the offer more seriously. What sort of test would he do if he had a urine sample? Not much. What he actually needed was a swab test and maybe a blood draw. When he couldn't think of anything right away, he reluctantly let go of Justin, stepping backward into the hall. "Maybe next time," he said, closing the door against his better judgment.

He leaned anxiously against the wall, waiting, listening intently for sounds of disaster, like a body falling over and cracking its skull open on the side of the bathtub. He could hear Denny and Alek talking in the kitchen, the whir of the blender, another plow outside. A phone ringing. Not a whole lot coming from the bathroom, though. Nothing outside of the usual. Maybe Justin was right to tease him. Maybe he was being a little over the top about it; he'd been accused of that before. Ren was just thinking about calling to Justin, offering to bring him his toothbrush since everything seemed to be going so well, when he heard a noise inside that did sound frighteningly close to something heavy hitting the floor.

"Justin!" Ren called, restraining himself from dashing in. Better wait a second and get some facts from out here first, just to make sure. It could have been something else, like ... no, there was nothing that sounded like that. *Damn it, Justin.* "You good in there?"

"No," came a grunted response, which oddly soothed Ren's soul. At least he was conscious.

Alek appeared in the hall, smoothies in hand, looking bemused to find Ren standing by the bathroom door. "I might need your help," Ren told him, admiring how Alek just rolled with that, processing the scene instantly. He slipped inside Ren's bedroom to set down their breakfasts so his hands would be free for whatever Ren might need him to do.

"Justin, I'm opening the door," Ren warned, pushing it carefully in case Justin had somehow landed in front of it. Alek waited patiently behind him as he assessed the scene. The faucet was still running, but Justin was crumpled on his side on the floor, eyes closed and hands against his chest, his heart obviously reacting to the physical strain of being up and moving. Ren went to his knees beside him. "Did you black out or just drop because you thought you were going to?"

"The second thing," Justin answered, breathless, taking one hand off his chest and reaching out toward the sound of Ren's voice, keeping his eyes closed.

"Smart choice," Ren congratulated him, stretching up so he could shut the water off before taking Justin's hand securely in his. "Did you hurt yourself? Hit your head or anything like that?"

"No."

"Good, let's just pay attention to your heart then. Breathe as deeply as you can."

"Ren?" Alek asked, peering in worriedly from the doorway.

"It's ok," Ren assured, even though ok in this instance just meant not as bad as it could have been. The fact that Justin couldn't stand by himself long enough to wash his hands was not good at all. "But he shouldn't move until his heart rate slows down. It's pretty stressed."

"What happened?" The commotion had drawn Denny from the living room. Justin tried to sit up at the unfamiliar voice, but Ren eased him with a hand on his shoulder.

"Don't move," Ren told him before answering Denny, Incident Commander in Charge voice securely in place. "Just taking a break, Denny," he said, trying to de-escalate the situation and calm everyone down. "In fact ... Alek?"

"Yeah," Alek acknowledged without Ren having to explain. It was getting cramped and tight in the bathroom with so many bodies staring at Justin from the hallway. It wasn't helping. "Denny, will you help me with the sheets?"

"Um, ok," Denny agreed, walking backward to start pulling apart her bed on the couch.

"Pass me those towels," Alek nodded his chin to the wet pile in the corner, forcing Ren to let go of Justin to shift them into Alek's hands.

"Thanks, Alek," he said gratefully.

"I'll be back in like five minutes," Alek promised, knowing Ren would still need his help to get Justin off the floor.

Ren returned his focus to Justin, who had curled himself around Ren's hip. The hand Ren had let go of was now twisted in the hem of Ren's long-sleeved T-shirt, wrist resting against the pocket of his jeans. "Well," Ren sighed in the aftermath, letting his palm come to rest against Justin's forehead again. "You have officially lost your standing privileges." This statement brought a low growl of frustration out of Justin. "Yeah, I know, but it's better than cracking your head open if you fall down. Here, let's get more comfortable."

Since Justin seemed to want some physical contact, Ren shifted them around, leaning against the bathtub, crossing his legs, and persuading Justin to lay his head down on top of his bent knee to help alleviate some strain on his neck muscles. "I hate this," Justin muttered as they moved.

"It doesn't last forever," Ren soothed, wishing he could say something more encouraging. "You're doing great, really."

Ren put a hand on Justin's head, almost pulling back when Justin twitched under his fingers, but then relaxing again as Justin sighed. Justin's hair was the deep kind of black that was sort of iridescent. Like a raven's feathers.

"Ren?" Denny was back, his phone in one hand, but she stopped dead when she saw them not where she'd left them. Her eyebrows disappeared into her bangs for a second, but she shrugged it off, stepping lightly into the room. "Your phone was ringing. I didn't want you to miss a call from your mom or something." Ren left his hand on Justin's hair, accepting the phone with the other one. Ren's mom called him on Sunday mornings, before Mass, and even though Denny had mistaken the day, she remembered how important taking the call would be to him.

"Thanks, Denny," he told her, trying to puzzle her out. She looked nervously out of place all of a sudden in a space she'd assimilated into so naturally that they all sometimes forgot she didn't live here. It was a little edgy and weird. If he didn't already have his hands full, he'd probably be pushing both palms against her cheeks, pursing her lips out to try and make her laugh and call him an idiot. She looked so tense, eyeing Justin, still obviously disturbed from how he'd been last night.

"Alek went downstairs with the laundry," she reported, shifting backward in slow increments. "Did you need me for anything?"

"No, we'll just wait for Alek and then probably move to the couch," Ren said, but was surprised by Justin trying to sit up again. "Take it easy," he warned him, but didn't prevent him this time. Justin kept himself braced on the floor with both hands, lifting his head to consider Denny, who stared at him as if he were a wolf.

"Sorry," Justin apologized, talking to Denny, and it hit Ren suddenly that this was the first time he'd ever seen her. He was sitting up to be polite.

"Don't worry about it," Denny saved Justin from having to say anything else. "We're all used to Ren taking care of strays by now." Justin flinched, and so did Ren, glaring at her. *Come on, Denny, be nice. You were there last night; you know how broken he is.* Denny softened, picking up on Ren's silent admonishment. She dropped to the floor so Justin wouldn't have to keep looking up at her.

"I'm a stray too," she told Justin, her voice free of the chill it had carried a second ago. Ren had never known she thought of herself that way. Alek had been the one to bring her home first. "Anyway," Denny stood up again, the sentiment of the situation starting to suffocate her. She hated getting emotional. "Hang in there. Ren will take care of you."

If Ren thought she could have handled it, he would have said something as she turned to go, but he knew better. She could take all his emotions when he threw them at her, but her own? Not so much. Once she was past the doorframe, Justin let himself back down to Ren's leg, spent. "So you do this a lot, huh?" he asked.

"Not a lot," Ren answered, feeling awkward about it. "Mostly people come to me for first aid stuff because they all know I'll have a bandage or something for a headache and I'm good at popping shoulders back into joint or whatever, but I took care of Alek and Denny when they were sick because what kind of roommate wouldn't? And then there was one of their science friends, and Genevieve, down the hall. Her roommate came to get me at midnight all frantic, but she wasn't in that bad of shape. But I usually go to them. I don't bring patients here except Denny, but she practically lives here anyway." He was rambling, and he knew it, but he felt like he needed Justin to know he was doing this for him, specifically, that Ren was making a special exception for him.

"But why you?" Justin continued with the questions. "Why do you do it?"

Ren had been asked this question before. *Why are you so passionate about this? Do you ever do anything else?* This was an answer he knew well. "Because I know how," he said without hesitation. "I hate seeing people in pain, so I'm learning how to fix it."

"But then who takes care of you?" Justin asked softly.

"Me?" Ren paused, wrapping his head around that, wondering why Justin sounded so solemn. He'd never thought about it. "No one's really needed to. I don't get sick. There's this amazing little scientific miracle called a vaccine. Surprised you haven't heard of it."

He felt Justin wilt against him and thought maybe that had been too far trying to make a joke, or maybe he'd misunderstood the question. "I have help," Ren went on. "I do have people take care of me. I mean, so far so good on staying healthy, but you know, I couldn't do half the things I do if it weren't for Alek and Denny. Alek cooks, and Denny built me a computer so I wouldn't have to go to the library all the time. She's the one who tracked down your address so I could find you."

"You asked her to find me?" Justin sounded so lost, like he couldn't understand why anyone would bother.

"You didn't look good, and I was such a jerk to you, and I'm not that way with anyone, ever. I wanted to apologize, and I wanted to make sure you were ok. I thought you might need some help."

"That's why you ..." *Yes, Justin. That's why I came. Not because of the assignment. I came to find you because I couldn't stop thinking about you. And now it seems you're all I can think about.*

"That's why," he confirmed.

Justin sniffed, tightening up, exhausted, and Ren dropped the conversation to let him process what he'd said, sad that something so simple could make him cry. He decided not to call attention to it so Justin would be less likely to try and stop; he simply sat still and quiet, looking at his phone to see who had called him. Dr. Taneja.

"Keep resting while I return this call, ok? It's my doctor friend."

Receiving no response from Justin, and, to be honest, not expecting one, Ren dialed Dr. Taneja's number, wondering what he wanted to talk about. He'd already sent him an update that Justin's fever was down a little this morning and he was lucid again. On the other hand, any advice would be welcome. Ren still wasn't sure how he was going to keep Justin coherent today, or rather, tonight. He hadn't even managed to get him breakfast yet.

"There you are," Dr. Taneja picked up with a tone that suggested some urgency. "I thought I'd stop by your apartment before I went to work to see how you're all doing over there. Do you, by chance, have a diagnostics kit?"

"Um," Ren thought as he sorted through Dr. Taneja's words. Had he ever had a diagnostics kit? They were a controlled commodity. He'd like to have one. Maybe two. Even though he had no way to do anything with them once he'd used them. At least, not legally. "Not here, no."

"No problem. I'll bring one. Remind me of your address. You're by the museum, yes?"

"Right across the street. Stony Island apartment building — that big brick box. I'll come down to meet you."

"No need; you stay with your patient. I'll see you in, oh, say fifteen minutes or so."

He hung up before Ren could explain about needing a resident keycard to get into the building. Dr. Taneja's mind was a brilliant, sparkling place. He could pull out protocol and string it up like Christmas lights, but like many highly specialized geniuses, the consequences for that kind of mind trick meant he sometimes forgot important details like keycards or wearing matching shoes.

"Good news, Justin," Ren said, setting the phone down on the tile next to his hip. "My mentor is stopping by to take a look at you."

Justin made a noncommittal grunt in reply, and Ren wondered if he wasn't dozing off again. He hoped not because there was no way he was going to stay cramped and cross-legged on the bathroom floor. His back was already talking to him about the position. Fortunately, Alek had returned from the laundry room downstairs and was ready to help Justin transition to the couch.

"Are we good to go?" Alek asked, somehow being serious and lighthearted at the same time, reaching up to rest both fists at the top of the doorway, filling it completely with his broad-shouldered gentleness. Ren tested Justin's pulse, content it was slow enough for more exertion.

"Come on, Justin," he said, shifting carefully out from under his head, supporting him to a sitting position. "Easy does it, but we're going to the couch. It'll be more comfortable."

He could tell it was hard for Justin to stand; he was weak and shifting the elevation of his head made him pale alarmingly. He leaned against Ren, panting, as they made their way toward Alek waiting in the hallway.

"Wow," Alek breathed sympathetically as he watched them move, then reached for Justin. Ren had intended to support Justin between the two of them, but Alek changed that plan. He slipped one arm around Justin's back and then simply swept him off the floor and into his arms, bridal style. Justin gasped, not used to being carried, especially like this.

"Now wait a second, Alek," Ren protested, watching Justin as he tightened up, but Alek stopped him with a look.

"It's too tight," he explained, indicating the narrowness of the hallway. Alek was already side stepping toward the living room. "This is easier." Ren wasn't completely convinced about that but couldn't come up with a good argument in the few seconds where Alek carried Justin to the living room.

Denny was already there and had thoughtfully brought Ren's pillow. As Alek gently set Justin down lengthwise and facing the kitchen, she tucked it behind his shoulders, propping him up against the armrest. Ren watched Justin's muscles release as soon as he was no longer being carried. He'd probably hated every second of that.

"What the hell?" Justin panted, looking hard at Alek, who just shrugged.

"No big deal," Alek dismissed, not understanding that while they were all definitely impressed by his ability, Justin's lack of control and warning about the situation had freaked him out. "It's not like you weigh anything."

"Alek's on the rugby team," Ren explained. "I think they have him bench press small cars. However," he looked at Alek. "Let's not do that again if we don't have to."

"Sure," Alek agreed, looking slightly confused now, like a mastiff who knows he's in trouble, he just can't figure out why. "Are you guys ok for a while? Pat from the museum called. He didn't let security tow my car, but he'd really like me to come pick it up as soon as I can get over there."

"I think we'll be ok," Ren said, still eyeing Justin as he adjusted his position on the couch, a startled raven smoothing his feathers. "Dr. Taneja is coming over."

"Oh, that's good," Alek acknowledged as Denny reappeared in the living room with Alek's smoothies.

"I'm walking over with Alek," Denny let them all know, but Ren wasn't surprised. They spent every waking moment together, and he knew it would drive Denny nuts to be stuck in the apartment with Ren and Justin. "We'll wait downstairs to let the doctor in before we go."

"Thanks so much, guys," Ren told them as they began tucking themselves into coats and hats. "Really."

"Text me if you need us to pick up something while we're out," Alek said.

"I will; be careful."

Ren's friends nodded goodbye from behind scarves and coats and headed out, giving Ren a moment to at last take a drink from the glass Denny had handed him, appreciating the chemist masterpiece of flavors Alek had decided on.

When he brought his head down after a second swallow, he noticed Justin staring at him. That unique way of staring Justin had, sorting out the logistics of the environment he'd been dropped into, wrapping his head around how the world worked within this apartment. It was kind of adorable.

"Try some," Ren nodded at the glass in Justin's hand, hoping to distract himself from what he'd just thought.

Justin considered the glass as if wishing it would disappear. Ren thought he'd have to physically help him drink like with the soup yesterday, but after a long contemplation, Justin brought it to his damaged mouth on his own. He winced as the cold liquid came into initial contact with the fever blisters, but he got a good three swallows in before taking a break. Bowing his head over the glass, he brought the back of his hand up against his mouth, recovering. Ren took a seat on the armrest at Justin's feet, watching him.

"I'm so sorry," Ren heard himself say out loud when he hadn't really intended to.

"You didn't do anything," Justin returned fiercely. Then, looking ashamed, he tried taking another drink. "This is good," he admitted.

"So, um," Ren switched topics to let Justin know he hadn't been offended, and because he hadn't asked Justin's permission about Dr. Taneja and thought he'd better give him some advanced notice. "My mentor, Dr. Taneja, will be here in a few minutes."

"Why?" Justin asked, confused and already apprehensive.

"I called him last night to get some advice," Ren confessed. "You were over my skill set. I didn't ask him to come, but I did tell him about your symptoms, and he wants to check you out himself since you don't want me to admit you."

"But I'm —" Justin started but couldn't finish. *You're what?* Ren thought. *Fine? Not even close.*

"We're mostly worried about the arrhythmia," Ren told him. "Your flu symptoms are extreme too, but we really need to keep your heart in check." Ren decided not to tell him why, not yet, not if he didn't have to. He also didn't tell him he was starting to doubt his flu diagnosis too. Alek and Denny had been sniffling, coughing, feverish disasters, but Justin didn't have anything like that. Which was actually a small favor wrapped around a big concern. There are so many scary things that start out as flu symptoms.

"This was supposed to help you relax," Ren said, forcing a laugh. "It's not working, is it?" Justin gave him a look of long suffering. He didn't want this, but he also knew he wasn't getting out of it. "I know it makes you uncomfortable to be vulnerable like this in front of strangers." This statement gained him a look of intimidated surprise. Ren went on as if he hadn't noticed. "But Dr. Taneja is great. He'll likely only be here a few minutes, so please just keep breathing and it'll be over soon. Hopefully, he'll have a better plan to help you."

Justin shook his head, but Ren didn't know what it meant. And he didn't have time to talk anymore since Dr. Taneja started knocking on the front door.

"It'll be fine," Ren promised, setting his glass on the coffee table so he could let Dr. Taneja in, all productive energy and overpowering mustache. Dr. Taneja always looked as though he'd stepped out of a spaghetti western movie.

"Lorenzo!" Dr. Taneja greeted enthusiastically, making Ren melt inside. It felt so good sometimes not to be the highest medical authority in the room. "Goodness, what have you done to your face?"

Ren couldn't believe he'd forgotten to warn Dr. Taneja about the bruise on his face, specifically the part where he didn't want him to mention it. Ren could *feel* Justin flinch even though he was across the room and behind him.

"I thought I'd take up boxing," he tossed out, hoping to redirect Dr. Taneja's attention. "But I'm pretty awful at it, so I don't think I'll keep it up."

"That is wise," Taneja told him, still considering the bruise. "Your schedule is full enough, though if you wanted, I could help you spar a little. Used to do some fighting myself when I was younger."

"Crocodiles or tigers?" Ren joked, successfully shutting down all talk of boxing and bruises for the time being. Dr. Taneja gave him a side eye, rotating his shoulders as if physically changing the subject.

"Who do we have here, then?" Dr. Taneja asked, noticing Justin now. Ren noticed Justin too. He was putting on a brave face, but Ren could tell he was internally terrified. Taking pity, Ren went to his side, kneeling in front of the couch.

"Justin," Ren said, introducing them properly. "This is my mentor, Dr. Taneja. Dr. Taneja, this is," he took the tiniest of pauses, "my friend, Justin."

"Sorry to meet you under the present circumstances," Dr. Taneja said, setting down his bag. "And for the last-minute notice, but Lorenzo is worried about you and that means so am I. All right if I have a look at you?"

Justin looked at Ren, who nodded. Ren rested a hand over

Justin's, who immediately flipped his palm over to grip Ren tight. Ren blinked but didn't move.

"Ok," Justin agreed quietly.

"Wonderful. Take off your shirt," Dr. Taneja instructed, opening the bag to remove his own stethoscope. Justin's hand jerked in Ren's, a very clear "is he crazy?" on his face.

"It's fine," Ren whispered encouragingly, used to this. Justin grudgingly began pulling it off. Ren started to help him, but Dr. Taneja had instructions for him too.

"Can I see his chart, Lorenzo?" he asked, assuming correctly that Ren would have written down stats.

"Sure," Ren said, jumping up to do as he was told. "It's in my room. Be right back."

But as soon as he'd lifted it from his desk, he hesitated, taking some extra seconds to finally flip through to the data from last night. He wanted to see what he'd written there. There'd been several hours where he had taken a temperature reading every twenty minutes. Liquid intake measurements. Blood pressure. Oxygen level. Notes on Justin's appearance, the sound of his held breath. The quotes of what he'd said. Ren felt cold remembering this, hearing Justin as if he were still in the bed next to him in the dark. On impulse, he tore a page out, crumpling it in his hand and throwing it into the waste basket next to the desk. No one needed to see it.

Ren grabbed his quilt, bundling it under his arm and striding with more confidence than he felt to the couch. Justin needed him.

"Ah, yes, perfect," Dr. Taneja welcomed him back. "Go ahead and drape that over his shoulders."

Ren obediently handed over the notebook and went to wrap Justin in the blanket. Dr. Taneja had shifted him to a seated position, leaning slightly forward so he could listen to his heart and lungs from behind, and Justin was visibly shaking from the chill and the exertion. But even so, Ren couldn't help but pause.

It was astonishing how much information a person's frame will give up about them to someone who knows how to look.

With a few moments of consideration, and a little help from what Justin had said in his fever dream last night, Ren saw that someone had put out cigarettes on Justin's upper shoulders and the back of his neck, many times. No wonder he'd startled so badly when Ren put the icepack there. The nerves in skin couldn't always tell the difference between extreme cold and heat. There was a weird puckering along his left bicep, a remnant of trauma but Ren couldn't tell what kind. His vertebrae were visible in a line down his back. Alek was right; he probably didn't weigh much of anything.

Ren swallowed the sudden lump in his throat and shielded Justin in his quilt, covering his back, wishing the blanket could protect him from more than just cold. Dr. Taneja paused in his reading, giving Ren a knowing look and a nod. He'd seen it too.

"Lorenzo, you'll find the kit in my bag," Dr. Taneja told him, thankfully giving him something to do. "Could you please do the blood draw for me?"

"Oh," Ren said, shaking his head to clear it of the images of Justin's back. "Sure."

"What?" Justin asked, lifting his head from where he'd been studying the coffee table.

"I'd like to test you for anemia," Dr. Taneja explained. "It could be the cause of your heart irregularities, and if that's the case, I'd like to get you on a nutritional supplement as soon as possible. But the only way I can confirm is with a blood sample. And you'll want Lorenzo to take it, trust me. He's better at it than I am. Young eyes, steady hands, all that."

"He's joking?" Justin asked hopefully, holding the blanket tightly closed around him. Ren wasn't sure which part he meant — the part where they needed the blood sample or the part where he wanted Ren to get it.

"It's ok; I work at the plasma center," Ren told him, keeping his voice easy, opening the diagnostics box and laying the contents on the table. "I do this all the time; don't worry." He patted Justin gently on the shoulder as he went to get some BSI gloves, his eye protection, and wash his hands.

"But ... seriously?" Justin sputtered.

"Lorenzo is perfectly capable," Dr. Taneja vouched for him. "I've been trying to get him clearance as the backup flight nurse, but the administrators insist he has to be licensed first even though he could outdo our current staff with one hand tied behind his back."

"Flight nurse?" Justin asked, voice raising in pitch.

"The one who goes with the helicopters," Ren answered, coming to his side again, gloves in place.

"Anyone can get an IV started in a still, quiet, well-lit room," Dr. Taneja said. "It takes talent to do it in a moving helicopter."

"Have you ever?" Justin asked, staring hard at Ren as he perched on the coffee table.

"In a helicopter? No. But I've placed thousands of needles, and I have yet to collapse a vein. It'll be ok; I promise. I'll be gentle."

"That's not it," Justin muttered.

"I just want to help, Justin," Ren told him, throwing all his concern into his voice. "We can do the swab test first if you want?" He looked behind him at Dr. Taneja, who was standing slightly to the side, arms folded, monitoring the procedure. "You did want the swab test too, right?"

"Yes. I'm not entirely certain we're looking at an influenza virus here. I'd like to check that too." Ren nodded.

"Just get it over with," Justin begged, slipping one arm out from behind the cover of the blanket. Ren scooted closer, grabbing his pillow and resting it on his knees, placing Justin's arm on top to keep it steady, and then taking a breath as he saw what he was up against.

For all he'd just bragged and had Dr. Taneja back him up, he knew this wasn't going to be easy. Justin didn't have great veins, and they were shriveled from dehydration. It was going to be hard to get a good stick, and he only had the one needle. He twisted the piece of elastic around Justin's bicep to keep more blood in the arm and hopefully fill out the vein. Then he pulled the cover off the iodine swab to clean the area with one hand while slipping two fingers of his other into Justin's limp grip.

"Squeeze and release for me," he instructed, eyes glued to Justin's arm where his antecubital vein was just barely visible to Ren's trained gaze.

"Ren?" Justin said but seemed to not know what he wanted to say after that. Ren settled the tubes into his lap and prepped the needle apparatus.

"Don't move," he cautioned him, meeting his eyes, seeing the need for reassurance there. "I'm not going to hurt you, Justin." There was trust and pain in Justin's expression, his lips tight. "Are you all right?"

"No," Justin whispered. "But go ahead." Ren felt as though their whole relationship thus far could be summed up in that tiny eight-word exchange.

"Make a fist and hold it. You're going to relax your fingers on the count of three." He expected Justin to turn his head at this point. Almost everyone did, even Celeste didn't like watching the moment where the steel pierced through the skin, and she was practically a professional donator. But Justin kept his eyes just as fixed to the spot as Ren did.

"One," Ren lined up the needle. "Two." He pressed his thumb against Justin's arm in an automatic, practiced gesture. "And three. Relax." Justin slowly released his fist while Ren pushed the needle in. His hands and voice had been steady, but inwardly he breathed a deep sigh of relief when there was immediate backsplash against the cupping area for the tubes. Flight nurse, indeed. "Got it," he said, as if it had been easy. As if he hadn't been scared that he'd screw it up.

"Holy shit," Justin exhaled as Ren fitted the first tube, watching carefully as it filled.

"Yes, well done," complimented Dr. Taneja, though Ren wasn't sure that's what Justin meant. Ren pulled back the first tube to exchange it for the second, feeling the heat of Justin's blood as he held the vial in his palm. In a few more seconds, both tubes were full, and Ren reversed the entire process, settling a white gauze square over the needle, pressing it down as he pulled out.

"Keep pressure on this," he said, cleaning up the biohazards. The needle went into a plastic container, which went into a red, clearly marked sharps bag. The blood tubes were neatly labeled and packed safely into the diagnostics box. The piece of elastic twisted off Justin's arm, and Ren lowered it to apply some tape to the gauze piece. Not a single drop of blood stained the white pillowcase. "Doing ok?" Ren checked Justin.

"I didn't feel a thing," Justin said, sounding sort of spooked about it, though Ren took it as a compliment.

"That's always the goal," he replied, allowing himself to feel cocky now he'd succeeded, though inside his soul was shaking. It was harder to do things like that with Dr. Taneja watching. With Justin not turning away. With only one needle and all that build up about how good he was supposed to be.

After all the drama getting blood, swabbing the back of Justin's blistered throat was nothing. In another few minutes, Ren had his gloves off, the box was packed securely into Dr. Taneja's bag, and Justin was being encouraged to lean back and sip his smoothie as Dr. Taneja did his finishing touches.

He asked questions. How long had it been since the last arrhythmia occurrence? What had Justin been doing at the time? Was there anything else Justin could tell him? When had his symptoms started? Lorenzo, what happened after three in the morning when the notes skipped to seven?

"I fell asleep," Ren said, guilty because he had fallen asleep and because he'd hidden part of the notes from his mentor. But there was nothing important on that page. Justin deserved at least that privacy. Dr. Taneja hesitated in his interrogation, as if realizing he was semi-chastising Ren for getting less than four hours' worth of sleep, and only after Justin had been stabilized.

"All right, you two," Dr. Taneja said briskly. "I'm going to run some tests and get back with you later. In the meantime, you keep resting as much as you can." He stared hard at Justin, but only for a moment before turning to Ren. "I'd recommend benzocaine for his mouth; it'll help with the pain. Keep doing what you're doing, but if something changes, call me."

He then put an arm around Ren's shoulders, pulling him several steps away and speaking directly into his ear. "Watch his heart; I'm not happy about it. I'd like to get a chest X-ray and an ECG, but I don't want to move him unless we absolutely have to or his test results indicate we should. It could still resolve on its own, so we're going to just watch for now. Do you know what happened to him?" Ren could only shake his head. "Well, keep him safe here with you. It looks like all the injuries are old, but make sure when he recovers that he's not returning to a dangerous situation. Right?"

"Right," Ren promised, hurting inside, not knowing what he could really do.

"You're doing very well, Lorenzo, so don't sound so unsure."

Dr. Taneja let him go, retrieving his coat and bag and moving toward the door.

"Lorenzo will take excellent care of you," Dr. Taneja assured Justin, who sat still on the couch, looking dazed. "But don't forget to take care of yourself, Lorenzo," Dr. Taneja said in parting.

"Thank you," Ren told him, hating how inadequate those words always seemed for how much gratitude he felt.

"Anytime," Dr. Taneja responded, and disappeared behind the door, leaving Ren and Justin alone. At the sound of the door closing, Justin looked up to meet Ren's eyes.

"Can I put my shirt on now?" he asked, making Ren smile tiredly.

"Yeah, you can."

"And what were you whispering about?" Oh, so he had been paying more attention than Ren thought, but he wasn't sure Justin wanted to talk about any of that. On the other hand, there were some things Ren wanted to know, and if Justin brought it up first, why not take the opportunity?

"He asked me if I knew what happened to you," Ren spoke before he'd decided if it were a good idea.

"What?" Justin asked, sounding like he regretted bringing it up.

"You have burn scars on your shoulders, Justin. I'm not sure if you knew that? And you stopped whatever workout routine you had going and you aren't eating right or enough." As he spoke, Ren drew closer, watching as his words shut Justin down. He pulled his shirt over his head and pulled his arms to his chest, staring at the coffee table.

"How do you know that?" he asked.

"Because I've been trained to look," Ren said. "All EMTs are legally obligated to report signs of abuse and neglect." By the time he got to the part about being required to report, Justin was staring at him in panic. "But I'm not an EMT right now; I'm just your friend with EMT training, so you don't have to worry. I know you don't want to tell me anything, and I don't have any right to ask, but can you at least tell me if you're safe? Is there something going on?"

"You have no idea," Justin muttered, but Ren thought he might.

"Was it North?" Ren asked suddenly, amazed at his directness. "Did he hurt you, Justin? Is that why you don't want me to contact him?"

"No," Justin answered quickly and sharply. "No. He never," but his throat tightened around whatever he was going to say. He covered his mouth, in every kind of possible pain.

"Are you sure I can't call him?" Ren asked gently, kneeling at Justin's side, putting a hand on the couch. "You were asking for him last night. The whole night, Justin, you were begging for him. He's important to you. Don't you think he'd want to know where you are?"

"He doesn't care," Justin whispered, with the same conviction Ren saw in his eyes when he expected to be left behind or lied to. He truly believed it.

"Justin, how do you —"

"He doesn't care," he repeated, trying to sound forceful but just coming off wounded. "No one does."

"No, that's not true," Ren challenged. "Justin, look at me." He did, reluctantly. "I care," Ren said with conviction. "Dr. Taneja, my roommates, we all care what happens to you." And even though he could see that Justin didn't doubt him this time, he could also see it didn't really help. Because this pain was tied to no one but North, so only North could fix it. "So please, tell me, are you safe?"

"I don't know."

Ren took a deep breath, worried about this answer. What kind of trouble was Justin in? How could he protect him?

"Is there anything I can do to help you?"

"No."

But Ren wasn't sure if that was the truth or just what Justin suspected was the truth. He was sitting hunched over, arms folded protectively around him. Very slowly, Ren shifted from the floor to the couch next to Justin, surprised how much he wanted to hold him. Wanted to promise him everything would be ok. He wished they knew each other well enough that he could.

"Is this ok?" he asked, gauging how Justin reacted to him sitting so close.

"It's fine," Justin answered, then looked over at Ren as if something had struck him suddenly. "Is your name really Lorenzo?"

"Yeah," Ren admitted. "Hardly anyone calls me that, though."

"That's cool," Justin muttered, his hand on his chest.

"How's your heart?" Ren asked him, ready to switch topics again. "Does it hurt?"

"Kind of."

"Did you want to go back to bed? Would that be more comfortable?"

"Could I just lie down here for a while?"

"Sure," Ren acquiesced, preparing to stand up until Justin put his hand out.

"You don't have to get up," Justin said, and Ren didn't know what to do about that. It sounded like Justin wanted to rest on his leg again, or at the very least he didn't want to be left alone. Ren could get behind that. He understood that feeling.

"Put your head down, then." He maneuvered them around on the couch, leaning back and helping Justin lie down across his lap on the pillow, more than slightly uncomfortable and unnerved. This was the boy who'd punched him in the face yesterday? The one who growled and glared and ditched out of his homework assignments? Was he really so lonely that one day had tamed him literally into Ren's lap? Ren threw the quilt over him, conflicted, covering his shoulder with his hand, remembering the scars he'd seen there, wondering what had happened, what Justin wasn't telling him. He felt Justin sigh, felt his heat under his hand. Ren leaned his head back, feeling the tightness in Justin relax in intervals, feeling him twitch as he drifted off, secure enough, at least in this moment, to fall asleep.

"What am I going to do with you?" Ren whispered.

8

COGNITIVE DISSONANCE

Ren woke to whispers, stirrings in the room, the not-quite-silent hush of his considerate roommates doing their best to be quiet. He could feel more than hear the rumble of Alek, the fluted higher pitch that was Denny, and closest of all, the slightly too-fast breathing of Justin underneath him. Shifting incrementally, Ren sat up, trying to guess how long he'd been out. It seemed he'd fallen asleep and then slumped over until his head was pillowed on Justin's not-so-soft hip. Meanwhile, Justin had curled up and flipped around so he lay on his side, face toward Ren's stomach, elbows bent and holding Ren's shirt. Ren didn't know how to feel about that. On the one hand, it was too damn sweet, but on the other, it made him sad. Especially since Justin's face was not peaceful. His brow furrowed in discomfort. It looked as though his jaw was locked. His hands clung to Ren's shirt a little too hard. Carefully, Ren rested his palm on Justin's forehead, disappointed but not surprised to discover he was still burning. Ren moved again, awkwardly, until he had one of Justin's wrists, taking count of his pulse. Still too fast and not quite as strong. Was his blood pressure lowering?

Ren debated on what he should do. Should he wake Justin to take a blood pressure reading? Or should he remain where he was to make sure Justin rested undisturbed? Ren was biased toward moving. Now that he was awake, he was getting claustrophobic and desperate to shift away from Justin, who was too hot and close on his lap.

As a distraction, Ren tipped his head to see where his roommates were and what they were doing. He could smell Alek's curry, which they were both eating at the table surrounded by all their electrical debris. They made tiny adjustments between bites, whispering together in that distinctly comforting way Ren loved best. As if nothing in the world were going on outside of their project. As if Ren weren't sleeping on top of a stranger a few feet away.

"I'm telling you," Alek whispered forcefully without raising his voice. "It's the channel. We're not tuning in to the right frequency."

"It's two hundred and twenty miles above the earth, Alek," Denny hiss-whispered back. "What we need is a repeater. There's no way you're going to reach them without one."

"But we *are* bouncing off the — oh hey, Ren," Alek stopped mid-sentence as he noticed Ren awake and watching them. "Did we wake you?"

"I don't think so," Ren replied mildly, shrugging his shoulders to relieve some of the tension he was feeling. "This isn't the most comfortable napping position."

"Oh, I don't know," Denny said teasingly, turning so he wouldn't miss the sly smile on her face. "You look pretty cozy to me." Ren didn't respond out loud, but he screamed at her with an exaggerated head tilt. *Really?*

"So, how long have you guys been home?" Ren asked, fidgeting under Justin, changing the subject.

"An hour?" Alek answered, looking to Denny for confirmation, too innocent to pick up on what Ren and Denny hadn't said. "Yeah, about an hour. We were in my room, but we got hungry. It's almost two," Alek answered the next question before Ren asked it. Ren inwardly groaned. He was getting tired of falling asleep in weird places and positions without meaning to. But then he thought of Justin and reminded himself that cramped and stiff as he was, he was still better off.

"Do you want some help getting out of there? You're all twitchy," Alek offered, though how he was going to assist getting Ren out from under Justin was a mystery. Maybe he thought he could just lift him in one quick swoop to let Ren out, though judging from the last time Alek had picked Justin up without warning, Ren didn't want him to try it.

"No, it's fine. I'll figure it out," Ren declined, looking down at Justin's hands still fisted up in his shirt. He'd have to start there, somehow untangle all Justin's fingers. Maybe he should just take the shirt off? Ren shimmied his shirt up his back, pulling it over his head so Justin could keep hold of it, feeling Denny and Alek staring at him curiously as he contorted out of the sleeves. He wouldn't be surprised to see Denny with her phone aimed at him if he looked up.

"You want some curry?" Alek asked, still casual about what was going on. Ren was now sitting shirtless under Justin, considering the best way to hold the pillow up, trying to mentally liquify all of his limbs so he could just pour himself off the couch.

"Um, no, thanks, Alek," he whispered, only half-listening. There was too much heat in curry; it would be too painful. Ren had both hands under Justin's head now, elevating his pillow a few degrees at a time, tensing the muscles in his legs and back, beginning to twist toward the armrest, shoving himself against it. Justin tightened, freezing Ren to the spot, but after pulling Ren's shirt closer against his chest and practically burying his face into the fabric, Justin went still again. And then Ren let out the breath he'd been holding, relying on gravity more than anything to start pulling him toward the floor.

Using every technique he knew about moving individual muscles, Ren rotated behind Justin's head, down on his knees beside the couch, and lowered the pillow with Justin on it into the place he'd been sitting. A few more steady, slow seconds as he brought his hands out from between the pillow and the couch cushion and he was ready to stand up and walk away freely. He breathed a little "whew" of relief as he turned toward the table, where Denny applauded him, tiny soundless claps.

"That was almost a Cirque du Soleil act," she said appreciatively, with only a trace of sarcasm.

"I'll add it to my resume," Ren told her, bowing without any real emotion, still groggy and frustrated, hunching toward the hallway. "Be right back; I need to get another shirt."

He took his time, checking the snow out his window, then using the bathroom, wetting a washcloth with hot water, and holding it against his face, pressed against his eyes. His bruise had darkened to the deep purple black of its highest trauma, all the blood clots raised to the surface. He languidly breathed the warm, humid scent from the cloth, thinking. Alek and Denny would probably have questions when he returned to the living room, so he stood in front of the mirror for a few more minutes, mentally preparing himself for whatever they might want to know. He also wanted to think a second about Denny's teasing grin and what she'd said about Ren sleeping with Justin on his lap. It bothered him more than he wanted it to.

He wasn't sure how to get her to understand that there had been nothing cozy about that position. Denny had probably forgotten how much time she'd spent in Alek's lap when she was sick. Justin needed reassurance; he'd been upset by Dr. Taneja's visit. He needed to keep his head down. Ren needed to stay near him to make sure his heart rhythm stayed regular. There was nothing more to it.

Ren gave himself a questioning look in the mirror, surprised how defensive he felt. There really wasn't anything more to it, was there? No. He didn't know anything about Justin; it was impossible. Concern was a neighbor to affection, but they weren't the same thing. Ren was worried about Justin, that's all. He was curious about Justin because honestly, how could a sane person spend any amount of time with Justin and *not* be curious about him? He looked at the bruise again, touched it carefully with the back of his hand, remembering how it got there. Remembered the scars on Justin's back, what he'd said, remembered that Justin probably wouldn't even allow them to be close after this was all over. The best thing to do would be to get him well and get on with their lives like with Genevieve down the hall. Getting any more involved might not be the healthiest choice. But Justin asked not to be left alone. He kept holding Ren's clothes.

His reflection shook his head at him as he bowed over the sink, disturbed and conflicted, hands on either side of the basin. He decided to reschedule this inner dialogue for a better time. When Justin was well and out of trouble. When Ren had more data. Then he'd reassess his feelings and what Denny believed they might be. In the meantime, he had plenty of other things to do.

Justin slept on, still not as peaceful as Ren hoped, but at least quietly. Ren resisted the urge to touch him, feeling Denny's eyes on his back and forcefully turning toward the table, taking the chair between his friends where he could still keep an eye on Justin. They pulled their attention from the NASA website on Denny's tiny, home-built laptop to welcome him back. And as Ren expected, to ask him questions. He pulled his legs underneath him, sitting cross-legged on the chair, and got ready to answer everything they threw at him. After all they'd done for him yesterday and today, they deserved any information they wanted. Almost.

"So what'd Dr. Taneja say?" Alek asked first. An easy question, really, a relief, but since Justin's full diagnosis was still unknown, it rattled Ren anyway.

"He took some samples to test for a couple things," Ren answered, folding his arms on the table top, looking at the electronic mess in front of him, wondering how quickly he could turn the topic to what they'd been up to while he'd been sleeping. "He's going to call us later when he knows more."

"Testing for what?" Denny wanted to know, perceptive. "I thought he had the flu?"

"He does," Ren answered, reaching forward to poke at some of the wires. "I mean, we're almost sure he does, but there's something going on with his heart that is more typical for anemia. So we're testing the iron level in his blood." He paused to check his friends, remembering that sometimes he got off on medical tangents they couldn't keep up with.

"And last night? What'd he say about last night?" Denny continued the interrogation, making Ren jump before he remembered that Denny hadn't been there for all of last night. She'd missed the really messy stuff. "Was any of that even true?"

I really hope not, Ren thought, but couldn't say that out loud.

"Maybe," he said instead. "It's impossible to tell without going over it with Justin, but I'm not doing that. He had no idea what he was saying, so I don't think it matters much. I think we should just forget about it." Oh how he'd like to.

"What if it happens again?" Denny continued with the questions Ren was deliberately not asking himself.

"It won't," Ren almost snapped, turning his face and his bruise away from her, noticing Justin shifting out of the corner of his eye. "Not if I can keep his fever down."

"Wouldn't he be better off at the hospital? Did that not even come up?" Denny was staring hard at Ren now. He could tell though he wasn't looking at her. He was watching Alek nervously twisting wires together, a physical manifestation of how it probably felt for Alek to sit and listen to Denny and Ren talk like this. Alek always liked everyone on the same page; this was disturbing him. "It's just ... I don't think I can scoop more snow into bags tonight."

"You won't have to," Ren replied, his voice quiet but his tone too harsh, immediately hurt and almost angry at Denny. She thought she'd had it bad last night? What about Justin? He'd been the one really suffering. "You won't have to do anything. Either of you. I brought him here; he's my responsibility. I'm sorry it's ruining your weekend, but he had no one else, and that doesn't work for me. Thanks for your help. I won't ask for it again."

"Ren, chill," Denny soothed. "Don't get so defensive. It's not ruining my weekend; it's ruining *you*." Now Ren did pause to look at her, feeling challenged. "I'll be the first one to say you do great things, and you know a hell of a lot, but you're not a doctor yet, remember? He's not actually your responsibility. You're really sweet to help him, but you said you don't even know him. And I'm just saying a repeat of last night is going to be too hard for *all of us*, including Justin. I thought for sure the doctor would have taken him to the hospital. It seems the best option to me."

Well of course it seemed the best option to her. If Ren were to read about Justin in a case file, he'd say the same thing. He'd thought it was the right choice this morning too. The hospital could provide tests and medications Ren simply didn't have. But they couldn't provide the warm quiet of his apartment. The smell of the curry. The special weight of Ren's quilt. The soft sounds of people just going about their business, a calming background reassurance.

"On paper, it looks that way," Ren allowed, his tone softened, speaking delicately. "But I think it would be a step backward if we were to send him away. It would be like we gave up on him, and you heard him last night."

"You're saying we should keep him here, without proper medical care, because he has abandonment issues?" Denny checked, her restatement making it sound so ridiculous that Ren paused to rethink it before he remembered even Dr. Taneja had agreed it was best. At least until the test results came back.

"Exactly," Ren said, obviously not the answer Denny was expecting judging from her expression. "But I'm not ruling it out," he added. "I'm going to do all I can for him, but you're right; we can't do another round like last night."

Denny shrugged, a quasi-agreement, though she still looked skeptical.

"So now *that's* settled," Alek broke in hurriedly, springing on the first chance he saw to switch topics, eager to create harmony between them again. "Ren, how'd your date go yesterday?"

At first, Ren didn't understand what Alek was asking. What date? But then he remembered Celeste.

"Oh, right," Ren heard himself whisper, feeling his shoulders droop.

"Right, so are you seeing her again?" Alek wanted all the details. Except they were so disappointing.

"Was it bad?" Denny asked gently, reading Ren's body language outside of Alek's enthusiasm. "Did she ghost you?"

"No, she was ready, but I didn't go," Ren confessed. "I couldn't leave Justin."

"But you called her, right?" Denny said, nodding at him, sounding like his mother. "You let her know what was going on?"

"I did," Ren defended himself, sinking lower into his chair. This day was proving to be almost miserable. He felt trapped in a never-ending string of disappointment and waiting and scenarios he couldn't fix. "She thought I was lying to her. She was pretty mad, so no, I don't think I'll be seeing her. Ever."

"Lying?" Alek repeated, as if the word were new to him, sounding hurt. "You?" Denny moved around the table to place her hands against Alek's back, as if he were more disheartened about this than Ren.

"Sounds like you dodged a bullet, then," Denny told him. "If she can't handle a cancelation due to medical emergency then you guys were sure to fail." Ren lifted his head slightly. He'd never thought of it like that, but Denny had a point. Anyone Ren dated would have to understand he could be called away at a moment's notice for something. There were probably hundreds of cancelations in his future thanks to the career he'd chosen. Come to think of it, all the doctors he truly admired lived alone.

He looked at Denny and Alek, his brilliant friends who always seemed to be with him no matter what, realizing that any day now they were probably going to receive an acceptance letter, and he felt a little nauseated, empty, and cold.

"Hey, Ren, don't worry about her," Denny said, calling him back from visualizing his future. But he wasn't worried about Celeste anymore; he had so many bigger problems looming over him. "She doesn't deserve you anyway."

Ren allowed himself a tiny smile, more to show Denny he appreciated what she was trying to do than that it was working.

"I'll get you some curry," Alek offered, getting up, knowing in his soul that whenever someone was upset all they really needed was a hot meal.

"No, thanks, Alek," Ren began to protest again, but he shut up when he saw the look Alek was giving him. Alek stood with his arms crossed, knowing almost all there was to know about Ren, understanding him better than Ren's own brothers.

"Nope, we've talked about this," Alek reprimanded. "Just because Justin can't eat doesn't mean you starve. I'm getting you some lunch."

Denny patted Ren's shoulder as Alek left for the kitchen, and Ren felt a little better. He was hungry; he'd forgotten he did that, though now that Alek had brought it to his attention, he did remember the other conversations they'd had about this very thing. It wouldn't do Justin any good for Ren not to eat.

"Why don't you get your book?" Denny suggested. "We can go over that Spanish oral thing you wanted me to quiz you on. The test is what? Monday?"

Ren nodded, the empty feeling in his stomach subsiding. *See, Justin?* He thought. *Friends take care of each other.* He went to do as Denny said, ready to push his dark thoughts out of his mind and soul. So he pulled *La Vida es Sueño* from his backpack and decided to be in the moment. Enjoy this quiet time with his friends on a snowy afternoon while Justin rested. Enjoy Alek's curry. Soak up as many moments as he could with these wonderful scientists instead of worrying about what it would be like after they were gone.

He returned to his seat, plopping instead of sinking into it this time, thumbing through the book to find the pages with the soliloquy on them.

They waited for him to eat before starting, since he couldn't chew and recite at the same time. As he ate, Alek and Denny returned to their mechanism, disconnecting a wire here, tightening one there, moving around each other with professional familiarity. Outside, he could hear the wind, and he knew the sun was past its tipping point for going down, but for right now, everything was soft light and coziness. The almost exact opposite of a hospital.

"Show me where you're starting," Denny said when he was ready, and he obligingly handed over the tiny gold book, pointing out the beginning of the thirty-line soliloquy. Denny spoke maybe a dozen words of Spanish, all of them taught to her by American cartoons and commercials, but her analytical mind could match the words on the page to what she heard Ren say easier than Alek could.

"Ready?" Ren asked nervously, just because he felt so dumb in the seconds before he got into it. Denny gave him a thumbs up while Alek nodded, so Ren brushed himself off and started reciting, *"Sueña el rey que es rey."* And he began to pace the short distance between the table and couch, closing his eyes as if that would help him read the words off the page he kept in his brain. He knew he was gesturing, like a chorister conducts a choir, because this particular monologue had a specific cadence to it, and it somehow felt right to emphasize the downbeat with a cut of his hand. Denny had to stop and slow him once as he unconsciously sped into that rhythm. He tried harder to enunciate carefully.

"Y los sueños, sueños son," he finished, standing still and opening his eyes to see how he'd done. Denny had a hand over her mouth, eyes intent on the book, nodding thoughtfully. "Did I miss anything?" he asked but had to shift his focus to Alek who was spinning his finger in the air in a "turn around" gesture.

"The words are all fine," Denny assessed. "But you move too — ow, Alek, what?" Alek had elbowed her in the side, jerking his head toward the couch. Puzzled, Ren looked over his shoulder, locking eyes immediately with Justin, taking him by surprise. How did he even do that? Move so quietly? Stare like that.

"Hi," Ren greeted him in a frightened burst, feeling stupid. He hadn't meant to wake him with his pacing. Justin's eyes and mouth were both open. He'd curled against the armrest of the couch, Ren's shirt still in his hand. Ren felt worry bloom in his chest and the back of his throat. Justin looked disoriented. Had his fever gone up again?

"Justin," Ren called as he dropped to one knee in front of the couch. "You with me?" Because he really didn't look like it. He was looking at Ren like he didn't know him again. "What's my name? Can you tell me?"

"Ren," Justin answered, still staring, looking confused. "No ... wait. It's ... um." Ren didn't like it one bit.

"Never mind. What class do we have together?" Ren asked, testing him.

"English," Justin replied, much faster, relieving Ren. "But that's not what you were speaking." Oh, that was it. Ren nodded, understanding. Justin had woken up to Ren wandering around the room reciting Spanish poetry. He probably thought he'd gone crazy.

"Right ... sorry," Ren apologized, hearing Alek chuckle softly behind him, hearing the relief in it. Seemed he wasn't the only one to think there was something wrong. "I was practicing for my Spanish oral. I didn't mean to wake you up. Denny was testing me. How are you feeling? Doing ok?"

"You speak Spanish?" Justin asked instead of answering Ren's questions, sounding like Ren had been keeping secrets on purpose. Alek was full on laughing at the table now, and Ren waved a hand at him to knock it off.

"Wow, you guys really don't know each other at all, do you?" Denny accused, her elbows high in the air as she rested her hands behind her head. Justin went back and forth between them, unsure where to focus. In the end, he settled on Ren, his expression wounded, like he thought he'd done something wrong.

"So what?" Ren defended, making sure Justin understood it wasn't a big deal. There was no reason why he should know anything about Ren. "I'm getting you something to drink," he told him gently, standing up. "And we need to check some stats now that you're awake."

"But ... wait," Justin said, though Ren was only going to the kitchen, pulling out a new container of Gatorade. "What's so funny? What'd I say?"

"Ren's *native* language is Spanish," Denny offered, though she somehow made it sound condescending. Or challenging? Ren couldn't quite pin the nuance, but it wasn't friendly. Like she wanted to make a point that she knew Ren better than Justin and always would.

"Really?" Justin again searched out Ren for confirmation. Ren allowed himself a small smile of pride, carrying a glass of Gatorade back to the couch. Justin eyed it suspiciously, checking Ren's face for any sign he might be able to get out of drinking it.

"It's true," Ren revealed. "I grew up in the Dominican Republic. Here, take a drink."

"That stuff is disgusting," Justin said, leaning away from the cup, and Ren knew exactly what he meant. Gatorade was unique in that it only tasted good when your body really needed what was in it. For normal people, it did taste gross. For dehydrated people, it was heavenly.

"I guarantee you, today it will taste fine," Ren promised, extending the glass again. Justin continued giving him that look, the one that said Ren was keeping something from him, but he hesitantly took the glass and sipped. Ren watched his eyes go wide, smiled as Justin held the glass out in front of him to check the contents again. Then he shook his head and took another swallow.

"It's good, isn't it?" Ren prompted, and Justin glared at him from over the rim of the glass with his mysteriously colored, fever-bright eyes.

"How the hell do you do that?" he asked after draining half the contents, making Ren suddenly feel warm all over. He moved away to gather his things from his bag, the blood pressure cuff, thermometer, and notebook, suspecting his face had blushed and wanting to hide it. "Or does everything just taste better here?"

"If Alek makes it, yes, everything does just taste better, but in this case, it's a mind trick; your body is craving the electrolytes. Here, let me see your arm." Ren wrapped Justin's bicep in the cuff, anxious to get a reading to alleviate the concern he'd felt earlier about Justin's blood pressure. He wanted to make sure he'd been imagining it when he thought it might be weaker. It turned out to be ninety-five over sixty. Borderline. Again. Technically, it was still normal, but it was lower than the previous readings. At least Justin's temperature had also gone down, not much, but it was under 103 now, and Ren considered that a major accomplishment. Even the pulse rate had improved. Maybe another good nap could finally break this.

"Well?" Alek asked from the table where he and Denny were watching Ren do his doctor routine, genuinely concerned to learn Justin's status.

"Actually, it's looking ok," Ren said, nodding encouragingly at Justin. "Heart rate's down, temperature's down a little. But your blood pressure went down too, and that's not so good? But it's not bad either. You need to keep drinking, though. How are you feeling? Any better?"

"Not really," Justin said hesitantly, as if worried he was going to give the wrong answer.

"That's not surprising," Ren assured him. "How about your heart? Does it still hurt?"

"No," again with the hesitant answers, but Ren thought he should feel lucky Justin was answering at all. "But it feels weird. Tired? I don't know. Hot maybe?"

Ren didn't know what to say. It wasn't a symptom he recognized, and he couldn't really translate it to something he did. And until Dr. Taneja called back with the test results, he was stuck with the same things he'd been doing. He wrote a few more notes into his book so he could research it in more detail.

"When did you learn English?" Justin blurted abruptly before

Ren was finished. He tilted his head at the strange return to their previous topic, and he could feel Denny and Alek tuning in intently from the table. "How old were you?"

"Um, I don't remember," Ren began, ending his last sentence. "I guess I was fluent by the time I was ... uh ... ten, I think. Why?"

"Because you speak it perfectly." Justin sounded hostile, or maybe that wasn't the right word. Intense, perhaps. Whatever the tone, Ren felt his face flush again. "You don't have an accent or anything."

"Everyone has an accent," Ren said quietly. "I've just made it a point to make mine sound like yours."

"Ren," Alek called him, sounding giddy. "Ren, do the thing!"

"I don't think so," Ren shot back without looking at his friend. Sometimes when the physicists were over, Alek and Denny liked to show off Ren's ability to do accents. They usually brought it out as a parlor trick shortly after Denny won the inevitable contest on who could recite pi the farthest. Then Ren would entertain with the accents as a smooth follow up, something to ease any tension about Denny being the smartest in the room. It never failed. They all ended up laughing. But he didn't really feel like doing it now. It seemed too much like showing off, even though that's not why he'd practiced so hard.

"Aw, come on, Renzo; why not?" Denny persuaded. Ren bit his tongue before suggesting she start reciting decimal places instead. He started slowly putting his gear away in the med bag, ignoring them. At least, he tried to. But then Justin softly touched his shoulder, and his attention snapped to him like a magnet.

"What are they talking about?" Justin asked, partly curious and partly anxious.

"Nothing," Ren said, glaring at the table where Alek sat with big puppy dog eyes and Denny was grinning in triumph even though he hadn't agreed to do anything. "They're being weird."

"No, it's awesome," Alek argued, then spoke to Justin. "Ren can speak English in any accent you can think of."

Ren rolled his eyes, zipping up the bag. That wasn't even true.

"Yeah?" Justin said, sounding interested.

"Show him, Ren," Alek pleaded.

"Justin's head hurts," Ren pointed out, standing to put away the bag, ready to walk out of the conversation.

"Justin?" Alek said, beseechingly, trying to shift the vote and knowing Justin was the only one who could tip it the way he wanted. Ren paused at the side of the couch on his way to his room, holding the strap of the heavy bag to keep it on his shoulder, knowing Justin did not care about stupid stuff like this. It was too inconsequential, too random and strange. But he wanted to hear Justin's answer before walking off.

"Actually, I would like to hear it," Justin said quietly, reaching over to take Ren's shirt cuff between two of his fingers. "If that's ok with you." Something very like pleasure radiated from Ren's wrist where Justin's hand was hesitantly holding him.

"I need a book," Ren acquiesced, sighing, not near as put out as he was making himself sound. "Not that one," he said preemptively to Denny, knowing she was still holding *La Vida es Sueño*. "An English one. Be right back."

He heard some excited chatter from Alek as he left the room, and he wondered what was being said while he wasn't there. Nothing bad, he knew, but he was still curious. He looked at what he had book-wise that might be interesting to read and came up short. Mostly all he had were textbooks, an outdoor emergency care behemoth that weighed more than three gallons of milk, and that dumb copy of *Pride and Prejudice* he'd purchased when he'd been way too excited to impress Celeste. But it was either that or *Early Childhood Development*, so he picked up the emergency care guide.

"A little light reading, eh?" Denny joked when he returned bearing the beast in both arms.

"You want me to do this or what?" Ren challenged, coming to stand near the center of the room, making a triangle of the couch and the dining table. He opened the book near the center so it would be easy to balance in his hands. "What first?" he invited, standing like a machine that needed a quarter inserted for it to work, a circus side-show act.

"Jamaican," Alek said, making Ren purse his lips as he centered around that. He deliberately did not look at Justin, knowing he'd screw up if he did. The intensity of Justin's stare would render him completely speechless. He concentrated on the book, the placement of his tongue against the back of his teeth, and began to read.

As Ren read through the treatment for different kinds of puncture wounds, his friends tossed out accents at random intervals. Whenever he played this game, Ren's mind would wind back to Cabarete, the heavy, hot wetness of the air, the scent of the ocean, the sticky-sweet taste of mango. The warmth of his goat's fur under his hand. And he would see them in his head — the tourists. The Germans in packs consisting of their entire family, all wearing matching shirts. Dutch girls on spring break who kissed him and British men who clapped him on the back. Canadians whose smiles opened on their faces as they recognized their speech patterns in his words. Americans who laughed and wanted to pat his goats, take their picture together. He could hear the creak of his wooden cart, the sound of hooves clicking along the path home after sunset, feel the heaviness of coins in his bag. He read in a Boston accent, feeling the familiar ache of homesickness settle into his heart. Something that always happened, but he didn't talk about. Every person in this room was far away from home, after all, and he always felt dumb how it seemed to bother him more than anyone else.

He wasn't sure how long he'd been going, or how many accents he'd run through. In all honesty, he'd done this so often he wasn't paying that much attention. He heard the new requests from outside his consciousness, the only thing he could physically feel was the heaviness of the book in his hands.

But then he heard Justin say, "Dominican," and his tongue stuck tight in his mouth, his voice catching in his throat, the whole experience slamming to a stop. The book slipped from his hands, crashing loudly onto the floor. Ren jumped back from it, surprised. No one ever asked for that one. Not once had anyone asked for what would have been his own true accent. And worse, he discovered he couldn't even do it. He bent to the floor, carefully gathering his book with shaky hands, straightening the pages so he could close it correctly, horrified at himself. He couldn't do it. He'd worked so hard to shed it, the accent that would have marked him the same as every other fruit vendor on the *playa*. And he'd done so well ridding himself of his native identity that now he couldn't bring it up if he wanted to. He felt ashamed, traitorous.

"Yeah, I, um, I think that's enough for now," Ren said, his voice small and tight.

"Ren, it's ok," Alek began, but he knew if Alek said anything to him right now, he'd do something embarrassingly weak. He hurried toward his room, clutching the book like a shield against his chest, dodging Justin as he reached for him on his way by.

"Ren ... what?" he heard Justin ask, and he wanted to tell him it wasn't his fault, but he couldn't yet. He just had to get out of the room. Alek was talking; Ren could hear it behind him as he replaced the book, breathing in jerky little gasps, hardly able to see past the blur that had misted his eyes. Denny was talking too.

"No," Denny said, surprised and soothing at the same time. "You didn't do anything; just give him a minute."

"Hold up, Justin," Alek instructed, a clue to Ren that Justin was trying to get up to follow him. The last thing he wanted was for Justin to see him like this.

"You stay on that couch, Justin!" Ren tried to yell past the lump in his throat before he sat on the edge of his bed and dropped his face into his hands. But when he closed his eyes, all he could see was his mother, the sad but proud expression she wore as she hugged him one last time before sending him in the cab to the airport in Santo Domingo. And then all he could hear were the affectionate but accusatory words of his brothers. They had wrapped their emotions carefully, but Ren heard it anyway. They said they would miss him, but they meant he shouldn't go. Why would he want to leave? Didn't he care what that would do to Mom? Sometimes it made Ren feel so selfish that he hadn't stayed, doing the same thing his family had done for generations. Ren felt like he'd rejected all of that by choosing something else, stripping himself of his own accent. What kind of son betrayed his family like that? How could he be so ungrateful?

He was so caught up on how he'd lost part of himself that he didn't hear Justin until he was at the doorway.

"Ren?" Justin asked, and Ren squeezed his eyes more firmly closed, wiping his hands across them. *Damn it, Justin.* "Hey ... I'm sorry. I didn't mean to ..." He sounded like he wasn't sure what he should be saying — that he was afraid of making it worse.

"I thought I told you to stay on the couch," Ren said, and his voice sounded cold.

"Can ... Can I come sit with you?" Justin asked, unsure, and Ren could suddenly hear how breathless he was. He forced himself to turn his head toward him, finally seeing him as he stood huddled against the doorframe, neither Alek nor Denny supporting him, his face almost white. He'd come on his own, barely able to walk, but he'd come anyway. Ren felt both touched by the gesture and annoyed that Justin had ignored his instructions.

"For heaven's sake, Justin," he said, immediately getting up to come to Justin's side, folding around him. "God, you're shaking like crazy. Come on. What'd you get up for? I told you to stay still." Ren pushed aside his feelings, more than ready to be rid of them, making space to focus entirely on Justin. His patient let go of the door, submitting to Ren's support readily, a hand closing around Ren's shirt at his shoulder while Ren put an arm around Justin's waist.

He let Justin lean on him, heavy and trembling, leading him the few steps to the bed and easing him down. He pulled a blanket over him, kneeling on the floor at his side. But Justin didn't seem to like their positioning. "Not down there," he muttered. He tugged weakly at Ren until he'd returned to his original place, perched on the bedside. Justin was still breathing hard, his hand pushed against his chest.

"Take it easy," Ren told him, rubbing his arm, hating that he'd caused this. "You shouldn't move so much."

"Yeah … but," Justin protested, hardly able to talk. "You looked so upset … and I," he broke off into a groan of frustration.

"Hey," Ren comforted. "Careful. Don't get so worked up. I'm fine."

"You're such a liar." Oh wow. That was a shock. Ren had never considered himself a liar before. Sure, he told lies, but it was usually so he wouldn't bother anyone or hurt anyone's feelings. No one had ever said it so bluntly before. But then again, Justin didn't have a lot of energy to mince words. Ren bowed his head, ashamed.

"Denny says you're homesick," Justin went on, the word coming out of him like he'd never said it before. Which wasn't surprising. How could Justin ever be homesick if he'd never had a real home? The thought made Ren feel even worse, spoiled. He had so much Justin didn't; he had no right to feel like this.

"It's stupid, but she's right," Ren allowed, not able to look at Justin anymore.

"It's not stupid," Justin returned. "Tell me about the Dominican Republic. How'd you even get here?"

Despite his better judgment, Ren found himself telling Justin all about his brothers and sister. He talked about the goat cart and hauling the mangoes from his orchard to the beaches, selling them to tourists to help feed his family. He described his little nephews, showing Justin the bracelet that Mateo, the eldest son of his eldest brother, had gifted to him before he'd left, which he hadn't removed since Mateo tied the knots on it more than a year ago. But once he got to his mother, he suddenly couldn't talk anymore. He sighed, feeling drained.

"I hate it sometimes; how much I miss them. Alek's family lives in Hawaii, but he's coping with the distance just fine."

"Alek says you're going to talk to them tomorrow," Justin volunteered, his voice stronger now that he'd been lying down. "He says you'll have your accent back after that whether you like it or not."

Ren huffed, but he was sorry he'd done it when his throat closed on him again. He put his hand on his mouth, trying to hold it together. He felt Justin shift closer to the wall, felt him tugging on him, pulling him down, and he allowed it. He let Justin drag him until he was lying on his side, their knees touching, Justin under the blanket, and Ren on top of it. Ren turned his face toward the mattress as tears broke free, feeling the wetness spread on the sheet beneath his uninjured cheek.

"I don't really understand," Justin confessed. *Of course, you don't*, Ren thought. *We're so different.* "But it sounds like they depended on you for a lot, so that would probably make it harder to leave them."

"Yeah, maybe," Ren said, trying to be casual, though he was inwardly astonished that Justin was being so perceptive.

"Is that why you take care of everyone?" Justin asked. "Because you feel guilty about leaving your family?"

"I don't know," Ren muttered. *Shut up, Justin.*

"I'm sorry," Justin apologized again. "I didn't know I'd mess everything up."

"You didn't," Ren said in forgiveness.

"I just wanted to hear, I don't know, how you really sound, I guess. It seems like you're so many things for so many different people. I wanted to hear your voice when you aren't any of that."

"This is my voice, Justin," Ren reminded him, sitting up, resting his head on his hand, watching Justin.

"I know … but," Justin said, sounding sleepy again, and confused, as if he were struggling to get his point across. "When you were doing that test thing, whatever that was you were saying, it sounded so nice." Ren leaned back slightly, gauging whether Justin was making fun of him. But it didn't look like it. He had his eyes closed, taking quick breaths with gaps between.

"Well, it's a poem," Ren explained. "So it's kind of supposed to."

"That's not what I mean," Justin argued. Ren was glad Justin had his eyes closed so he wouldn't see what his words were doing to him.

"Shh," Ren told him, not knowing if he could handle much more. "You need to rest."

"I just woke up."

"Yeah, well, your sleep isn't really rest right now," Ren explained. "You have every reason to be exhausted." *And say weird, disconcerting things about my voice.*

"Will you say that poem again?" The request was so innocent it almost broke Ren's heart.

"If you want me to."

Before he began the recitation, he caught movement at the edge of his vision. Curious, he turned to see Denny standing in his doorway, arms crossed. Her face was twisted into an expression he'd never seen on her before. She looked worried and angry, afraid. Ren didn't understand what her issue was. When she noticed he'd caught her staring, she gestured for him to come with her. He shook his head, holding up a hand with his fingers spread, indicating he'd be done in five minutes. Then he could come see what she needed. She put her hands on her hips, not used to him ignoring her.

"Come with me," she mouthed the words, putting more emphasis into her face so he'd have an easier time reading her lips.

"Not yet," he mouthed back.

"What the hell?" She bit into each silent word.

"Ren?" Justin asked, opening his eyes and shifting as if he'd sit up, pushing himself to see why Ren had just gone silent. He looked over to the doorway where Ren had been looking at Denny, but she'd disappeared. Ren wondered why she wanted him — why she looked so mad.

"I'm here," he assured Justin, putting his hand on his arm, one thing at a time. He shifted into Spanish, like Justin wanted, using its tone to lull him to rest. "*Descansa tu corazón. No te dejare.*" He slowly moved his palm from Justin's arm to his chest, feeling his heart jump under his hand, throbbing like a wounded bird. He sighed.

9
VOLUNTARY MANSLAUGHTER

Denny was waiting for him. And he knew every minute he remained at Justin's side was just making her increasingly impatient. She was likely sitting with Alek, bristled and pissed that he was ignoring her. Which wasn't what he was doing, not really. He was anxious to see what was up with her, why she looked so worried, why she was so insistent to talk to him. But he just couldn't bring himself to go yet. He wanted to be sure Justin was truly asleep, and he wanted to settle his own spirit too.

Ren had successfully slipped off the bed without disturbing his patient and was again kneeling at the side, focused entirely on minutiae and writing down everything he saw. He didn't like what Justin had said earlier about his heart or the lowered blood pressure. And he especially hated that he didn't know what any of it meant. He checked his previous stats for any kind of sign or pattern he might be missing, looking at the details from a distance.

He saw immediately that Justin wasn't getting enough fluids. And it wasn't good for his heart rate to be this elevated for this long. But Ren just couldn't think of any way to slow it down other than breaking the fever. Which should be happening soon now if past patients were any indication of the typical timeline for this thing.

Except Justin wasn't typical. As unpleasant as it sounded, he should be writhing in pain by now as his immune system gathered the waste of the destroyed and weakened virus into his kidneys, producing an agonizing backache that signaled the end of the illness, the last thing to happen before each patient had complained about being hot and thirsty, the transition to the recovery period.

But it was like Justin was stuck somehow. Even now, Ren could see Justin was breathing irregularly, pausing like he'd done last night for longer than he should. He couldn't stand or sit up for very long without messing up his heart rate. It could be simple dehydration doing it, or the anemia Dr. Taneja suspected, or it could be something life threatening like a blood infection. There was even the chance for sudden cardiac arrest during arrhythmic episodes.

Those were the absolute worst-case scenarios, though. Ren didn't think they were at that point yet, and he reminded himself, again, that he was probably over thinking it. Justin just needed more time, more rest. As much comfort as Ren could give. Which meant he should probably get him the pillow and quilt from the couch.

Denny was halfway out of her chair the second she saw Ren coming into the room, but he put both hands out to stop her.

"I'm not ready yet," he said quickly, snatching up the pillow, blanket, and his shirt from the couch. "Give me a couple more minutes. He's almost asleep."

"Ren," Denny said darkly, warningly, and started a nonverbal argument. Denny and Ren specialized in silent fights; they'd learned quickly that if they had a disagreement, they had to keep it away from Alek. He loved them both so hard that for them to have discord with each other was almost physically painful for him. Even now, though they weren't saying anything out loud, Ren could see Alek tightening up, hunching over a schematic on the table, actively trying to ignore them.

Ren stared openly at Denny, letting her read him fully. *What?* His posture told her. *What's so urgent you have to tell me right this second? I'm not avoiding you. I want to know; I really do. Whatever is important to you is important to me too, but unless it's a real emergency, which is doubtful as you're sitting there breathing correctly, sound and well, I think you can wait.*

Denny was one of the few people he knew who could translate all these thoughts from his stance, and he knew he'd gotten through to her as she sank all the way back into her chair, pouting, breathing out a puff of frustration like a furious little dragon. He nodded a thank you to her.

"I'll hurry," he promised, and she shrugged as if it didn't matter to her anymore how long he took because she was done with him. It was only a defense mechanism, though. He really did have to hurry if he didn't want to truly hurt her feelings.

His room was covered in shadows when he returned, the result of more clouds rolling in from the lake. Without the thunder, however, it seemed gentle today, a protective cover, turning the space into a little healing cocoon.

Ren deftly slipped his hand under Justin's head to help him lift it enough so he could rest on the pillow again, allowing his spine to align and his breathing to ease. Without really noticing, Ren set down his shirt on the bed too, for no reason except he wasn't sure what to do with it.

"I'm sorry," Justin murmured. "Did you say something? I keep falling asleep."

"That's exactly what I want you to do," Ren told him. "I will have to wake you up more often to drink something, though."

"Sure," Justin muttered noncommittally, drawing in another breath that he held.

"Justin, why are you breathing like that?" Ren asked, hoping to bring his attention to it enough for him to stop. "You keep taking a breath and holding it. Why?"

"I didn't notice." That was fair enough, though frustrating. Ren spent some extra time fishing his pulse oximeter from the med bag.

"I'm checking your oxygen saturation level one more time," Ren warned him before clipping the meter to Justin's finger. Justin didn't even move, and Ren wondered if it was because he was simply ok with Ren touching him now or if it was because he was just too sick to recoil anymore. The reading came back at ninety-five percent, the lower end of normal. Still, Ren would feel more comfortable with a bigger cushion. Say, ninety-eight.

"Breathe deeper, Justin," he instructed.

"Ok," Justin agreed, mostly asleep. Ren shook his head, knowing that hadn't communicated well, but he could also feel Denny's impatience.

"I'll be in the other room," he told Justin. "Denny needs me for something, but I'll be back to check on you, and we need to figure out how to get some more calories into you soon. Is that all right?"

This seemed to rouse Justin more than anything else Ren said. He shifted, opening his eyes. "You're leaving?" he asked, suddenly anxious.

"No," Ren assured, putting a soothing hand over Justin's after removing the oximeter. "I'll be just outside the door. You're not alone, Justin. We're all here. Ok?"

"You're coming back?"

Ren sighed, hurting for Justin, feeling guilty for something he hadn't even done. "Well, you know," he tried to joke. "This is kind of my room, so yeah, I'll be back. Here, I'll put some music on." He was already moving to the computer, adjusting the sound on the speakers and bringing up his favorite piano album.

"This is what I use to relax," Ren said. He then physically pushed Justin back to the bed, resting his hand on his head for a little longer than necessary. "*Respira*," he told Justin. "Keep breathing deep now. I'll be back soon."

"Thanks," Justin said, closing his eyes again, his body folding as Ren took small steps backward toward the hallway. The last thing Ren saw was Justin's hand curling around the shirt he'd left on the bed, bunching it up against his chest as he tucked his arms close to his body. Ren gently closed the door, hoping whatever Denny had to say wouldn't take too long. He was still worried.

The few steps down the hall were a 180-degree flip from still and dark to bright and frazzled. Again, Denny bolted from her chair when she saw him, and this time he let himself feel curious.

"Get your coat," she commanded through clenched teeth. "We're taking a walk."

Feeling intimidated despite their height difference, Ren began putting on his shoes, hoping for a compromise. He'd just told Justin he would be in the next room; he didn't want that to be a lie. Maybe she'd settle for the hallway? Alek watched them quietly, his innate empathy absorbing all the weird energy between them. Ren saw the same question on Alek's face that was running through his mind. What the hell was going on?

"Can we stay inside?" Ren pleaded, gesturing toward the balcony door at the snow. She stared at him, unimpressed, and he felt his resolve start to crumble. In fact, he was seconds away from picking up his coat when she threw up her hands.

"Fine, we'll go to the lounge. Come on."

"Denny?" Alek asked, standing now too, wondering why he was being left behind. Ren watched Denny soften immediately. She turned to Alek, nuzzling into him since he was too tall and broad for her to hug around the neck or waist if they were both standing. Instead, she tucked her fingers into his pockets, pressing her forehead against his solar plexus, a posture Ren had seen many times before but always felt out of place watching.

"Ren should get out of here for a little while," Denny explained to Alek. "But someone needs to stay in case Justin needs something, right? And since you're the only one strong enough to lift him, I'm going to take our boy on a walk so he can clear his head and be his brilliant medical self again tonight. Make sense?"

Now Ren felt incredibly out of place, listening to her talking like that. Is this how they always discussed him? He didn't need a break; he needed a solution. He needed to do some research on heart symptoms. Needed to be next to Justin to soothe him in his sleep.

"Yeah," Alek agreed, pacified. "That makes sense." He carefully bent to hold Denny, and Ren could see he did this as often as she let him, but always waited for her to initiate the contact. It looked special and precious, and Ren admired their relationship at the same time he felt jealous he didn't have one like it. That he was "their boy," as if they were a couple who had adopted a puppy. On the other hand, why wouldn't they think that? They had other social circles. The geoscience group, the physicists, the robotics club, several employees at the museum, even those pale, wide-eyed outcasts that came over for anime marathons sometimes. Ren had ... well. He talked to a lot of people at the training meetings he attended. He worked well with his fellow EMTs when he did the ambulance runs, tried to make conversation with his coworkers at the plasma center and the regulars who came in to donate. Oh, and there was Dr. Taneja too. But the point was Alek and Denny brought people to the apartment all the time, for dinners, for video game parties, for geeky, engineering projects and stargazing on the balcony. Ren simply came home to them. Maybe he really was just their boy.

"We'll be back soon," Denny said, pulling away from Alek.

"Justin's asleep," Ren put in, wanting to contribute to the conversation, feel like he had some control over something. "I didn't tell him I was leaving, so hopefully he'll stay that way until I get back. But I'll have my phone in case you need me to come right away."

That last comment made Alek look anxious, like he wanted to ask what sort of conditions would be required to call Ren back before Denny was ready.

"You'll do fine," Ren reassured, really hoping they would just take a walk to the lounge and be right back. He suspected Denny had more on her mind than simply giving him a break, though. She looked way too worried, and he suspected Alek knew that too, but they were both going to humor her.

"Let's go," Denny said again, grabbing Ren's sleeve and tugging him toward the door. He shared a last look with Alek as he allowed himself to be dragged into the hallway, one of long-standing endurance. They knew Denny was like this, and they loved her for it.

Ren obediently followed Denny down the stairs to the lounge, which was even darker than his room. Someone had turned on the electric fireplace and left it running, so there was a cheerful glow to the area, and it was refreshingly empty. Denny led him to the couch in front of the fireplace, sitting him down so she could hold the taller position. She folded her arms, leaving the lights off so she was standing in silhouette in front of the fire. Ren didn't feel comfortable about the position. He felt like he was in trouble, but he couldn't imagine why.

"What's going on, Denny?" He hated being the one to break the silence, but he couldn't take it anymore. Why did she feel she had to bring him all the way down here? Why keep secrets from Alek?

And even though Denny had practically dragged him in her hurry to tell him whatever she had to tell him, now she hesitated. She didn't seem to know where to start. He watched her face contort between her need to share whatever information she had and her desire not to hurt his feelings. It made Ren want to help her, some-how, but he was at a loss as to what he should do. He had no idea why they were even here.

"Kayden?" he said gently, making her cringe. "You ok?"

"You big-hearted idiot," she snarled, which only made his sympathy melt more toward her. She only insulted people in that tone of voice when she really cared.

"What did I do?" he invited. "Sit down?" He reached for her, but she dodged him, moving instead to perch on the armrest of the couch, maintaining her height over him, splitting her face between the fire's glow and the shadows. This was obviously really bothering her. He turned toward her, pulling one leg underneath him and holding onto his ankle, waiting and ready.

"Do you know anything about Justin?" she finally asked accusingly, confusing him.

"No," he said simply, shrugging it off. That's what was bugging her? "I mean, I know what I need to know about his medical history. I didn't know your geo friend either; what was his name again?"

"Evan, but this is not the same."

"Why not?" Ren asked innocently.

"Because *I* know Evan, and I know he's a good person. None of us know Justin."

"I'm still not seeing much difference," Ren said, though there were so many differences between Justin and Evan he didn't think he could list them all. However, from a medical perspective, those differences didn't matter. "I'm going to be looking after thousands of people I don't know. Justin's no different than Evan."

"Except you weren't falling in love with Evan."

Ren pushed himself against the armrest, as far away from Denny as possible, his turn to fold his arms. "I'm not falling in love with Justin either," he defended himself, wishing she would just let that go. This crazy theory she kept throwing out there, first teasingly and now with actual concern. And even if it were true, which it wasn't, what difference did it make to her?

He watched her shoulders lift as she took a deep, calming breath, as if seeking patience, pinching the bridge of her nose like she did when confronted with a monumental problem.

"How about we skip the part where I talk you out of your own denial?" she requested.

"Or how about we agree to disagree on that particular point and move on to why you would care so much and why you seem to think it's a problem?" Ren returned, shutting her down again.

"Ren, I'm worried about you," she said quietly, in a vulnerable tone she never used. It made the hair at the back of Ren's neck stand up, the shadows of the room taking on a sinister darkness. It made no sense when he compared it to what Denny was saying. "You're like my brother, ok? I don't want you to get hurt."

"Then get straight and tell me what you really want to tell me," Ren pushed, off balance, unused to Denny speaking this way, hating the mystery and the edginess of Denny's demeanor.

"Fine," Denny almost snapped, the verbal equivalent of ripping off a bandage, which initiated about the same amount of painful relief for Ren. Finally. "Since you weren't interested in Justin's background, I decided to look it up for you."

This comment brought Ren straight up off the couch. He didn't want to hear any more, didn't want anything Justin had said last night confirmed in any way. But Denny anticipated what he'd do and shot for the doorway like a thrown dart, moving faster than he'd ever seen her, slamming both hands on either side of the frame and spreading her feet to each side too, blocking the exit. He'd have to physically lift or push her out of the way if he wanted to leave.

"No, you don't," she challenged him as if she took up the same amount of space in the doorway as Alek did. Ren hated that she might be harder to get past than the Japanese-Hawaiian rugby player. Denny lifted her face to glare at him. "And it looks like you do know some stuff after all."

"That's not right, Kayden," he told her, angry at being caught like this. Angry at her for invading Justin's privacy, knowing how much it meant to him. "That's not fair."

"Maybe not," she allowed. "But I did it, and I'm not sorry because you need to know some things."

"No. If Justin wants to tell me, he can when he's ready. Now please move."

"Justin is never going to tell you," she responded, hard and adamant. "So I am."

"Don't make me pick you up," Ren begged, but they both knew it was an empty threat. Denny was small, but she was vicious.

"You go ahead and try."

They glared at each other, a silent, intense contest of wills where Ren suddenly realized how tired he was. He felt himself shrinking in submission, hating the part of himself that did want to know what

Denny had found out. But he'd made promises. He wouldn't look in the backpack. He wouldn't call North. Technically, he was still keeping them even if he let Denny tell him everything, but it still felt like a betrayal.

"Does it really matter?" he heard himself asking, but his tone was so quiet he didn't know if Denny could hear him. "I told him I'd take care of him, and I'm going to do that no matter what. And then he'll be back to his own life and out of ours, and we probably won't ever see him again."

"I thought about that," Denny informed him. "And if I thought it was true, I'd let you go upstairs. But the way you look at each other, the way he follows you, holds on to you."

Ren broke eye contact, drained, knowing she was right, at least partially. Justin did something to him, and there had been something different in how Ren was treating him. Closer. More intimate. And he liked it. He didn't want Denny to damage what was happening. He didn't want it to be ruined.

"Did he ever give you a reason why he canceled all your appointments to meet up for that assignment?" Denny asked, and Ren felt as though he were on top of something high. He felt Denny take his hands, taking charge, and he allowed her to pull him to the couch where they sat together, turned toward each other.

"Ren," she asked again. "Did he ever tell you where he was?"

"In meetings," Ren responded woodenly, staring at the paisley patterning of the couch cushions. "He said he was stuck in meetings off campus."

He heard Denny sigh, preparing to shatter this explanation. He felt his spirit tense up as if she were going to hit him. She kept hold of his hands.

"He was in court, Ren," she told him, ripping off another bandage. "For the past two weeks, he's been on trial."

"Ok," Ren accepted numbly. "For what? Drug possession? Traffic violations?" He threw the suggestions out half-heartedly. Hopefully. He heard Denny take another breath.

"He's on trial for murder."

Ren pulled his hands back from Denny, covering his ears but still hearing Justin last night. The ranting after Alek and Denny had gone to bed. *I'm sorry*, he'd sobbed. *I didn't mean to. I just wanted him to stop. He wouldn't get off. Please.* Ren had known something horrible had happened to Justin, but he hadn't known it ended that way. With someone's death. He didn't want to believe it.

"Maybe it wasn't him," Ren said, but he didn't sound convincing. "Maybe they got the wrong person."

"No, Ren," Denny went on, her tone so careful. "That's not what the charges are. He's confessed and everything. The court is trying to decide to what degree he should be held accountable, voluntary or involuntary manslaughter. The jury is out right now deciding on the verdict. Justin might be going to prison."

"Might?" Ren checked, feeling cold despite his proximity to the fireplace. He could see Justin in his memory, standing in their classroom, tight with violence, poised to attack. He saw him sobbing, curled in a ball on his bed. Heard him telling Ren that he didn't know if he was safe, that Ren had no idea what was going on and there was nothing Ren could do to help. "I mean, it can't be that bad. They let him go to class and stay in his own apartment, right?"

"Ren, you're missing the point. He beat someone to death with his bare hands, do you understand?"

Ren laced his fingers behind his neck, fighting the urge to start rocking back and forth, remembering Justin's hesitant hold on his sleeve, his constant apologies, his tears, his scars. His fear.

"He didn't mean to," Ren heard himself defending Justin. "It was probably an accident. Or self-defense."

"Are you kidding me?" Denny squeaked. "That makes it even worse! It means he can't control himself. And this wasn't an isolated incident. Justin has a long history of violence. He's been suspended for fighting, kicked out of three different schools. He's been in the foster system since he was four, but it doesn't seem like any family could handle him for long. He's changed hands a lot, then ran away and disappeared after getting a driver's license. He tried to get into the Air Force when he turned eighteen, but they wouldn't take him because he spent time in a juvenile correctional facility for assault. Do you hear what I'm telling you?"

Ren didn't respond. He didn't know how.

"You needed to know," Denny went on. "Before you get in too deep. He's just not safe, Ren. I don't want him to hurt you."

"He's not going to hurt me," Ren said automatically.

"He already did," Denny replied. Ren found himself looking at her questioningly as she cupped a careful hand over the bruise on his face. "He hit you, didn't he?"

Ren felt his breath catch, shocked she'd figured that out on her own, even though he shouldn't have been surprised. "No," he said immediately. "That really was an accident. It was all my fault. I startled him, and he was —"

"Don't. Stop it," Denny broke in, shaking her head through the whole explanation. "Do you hear yourself?" Ren watched, amazed and hurt, as tears rolled down Denny's face. "You sound like every abuse victim in the history of forever. He punched you in the face, Ren! And you're going to blame yourself for that?"

Ren cowered, not knowing how to explain. It had been his fault. Because he'd thrown that textbook down right next to Justin's head. He'd started it.

"Please," Denny begged, crawling unexpectedly into his lap, wrapping her arms around him and burying her face into his neck. He clung to her, wishing they could come to some understanding just by being physically close. "Please don't let him. If something happened to you ..."

"Nothing's going to happen to me," he whispered, not knowing how he found the words or his voice. "I'm just trying to heal him, Kaydee." *Because you're worried over nothing. There's nothing between Justin and me.*

"Please, let's take him to the hospital," Denny pleaded, still crying. "You've done enough."

Ren held still, drowning in thoughts. There had to be more to this. He didn't doubt Denny's facts, just how they'd been presented. Because there was more to Justin than violence. There was a frightened boy who had been consistently abandoned. He was begging for someone to listen to him, to believe him, to stay with him. Ren knew without a doubt that he was responsible for the bruise on his cheek. He'd provoked Justin, on purpose. Maybe it had been like that before. Maybe it had always been like that. The scars on Justin's body were real; someone had done that to him intentionally. Someone had taught him about pain. Someone had shown him violence to the point where he probably didn't know how to handle situations without it.

"I really haven't," he said, feeling the truth of it through his whole bloodstream. There was so much more he could do. That he meant to do. If it were true, and Justin was on the verge of being sentenced to prison, then there was plenty Ren was going to do.

Denny pulled back, detaching herself so she could look at his face. She was a mess. Ren tugged his sleeve over his hand so he could begin wiping her eyes.

"Ren," she began, but he continued before she could say anything else.

"No," he countered. "It doesn't matter. I'm an EMT; it's not up to me to make judgments. Justin's not on trial with me. I promised him I would take care of him until he's better, and I'm going to keep that promise."

"But he *killed* someone."

Ren cringed in spite of himself. "He was set up," he said, meaning it. From the time he was four years old, Justin had been set up for failure. There was no doubt in Ren about that.

Denny was staring at him, her mouth open, as if she couldn't understand a single word he said.

"How can you be so stupid?" she asked, and Ren was surprised how much it hurt. He turned away from her, sitting still and stubborn. "I hope Justin does go to prison," she went on fiercely. "Just so you can get away from him in one piece."

"That's awful," he said, horrified, surprised how eager she was to cast Justin aside. Just like everyone else. "Why would you even say that?"

"I just want to protect you," she protested. "Since you don't seem capable of doing it yourself." He wanted to argue that point. He wanted to tell her he knew what he was doing, knew what he was getting into. But the truth was he had no idea. The truth was that Justin could be every bit as bad as Denny suspected. He didn't have enough information. He didn't have Justin's side to this story. And he really couldn't fight Denny's logic. Or that she was doing this because she cared about him.

"I appreciate that. I appreciate *you*," Ren emphasized.

"Then listen to what I'm saying to you," she tried one last time.

"I am listening," Ren affirmed. "I heard what you said, and I'm thanking you for telling me, but I'm not abandoning him. If he's going to prison, then I want to give him some kindness before he goes. He's so sick, Denny. Worse than I've ever seen anyone, and I think part of that is because he is so alone. Didn't you hear him last night? How many times did he say he was sorry, huh? How many times?"

"Someone is still dead, Ren, and your face is still bruised. Sorry doesn't fix it."

It does for my part, Ren wanted to say, but he knew better.

"You're right," he said instead. Denny's favorite words. His best bet if he wanted to get anywhere in this conversation. "I'll be careful, ok? He's in no condition to hurt anyone; he can't even stand up on his own. He'll be out of the apartment soon enough, right? You won't have to worry about it."

"Too late."

"I'm going upstairs," Ren said, signaling the end to their stalemate. "We're not saying anything to Alek, right?"

"Of course not," Denny snapped. "But what are you going to tell him?"

"Do we have to tell him anything? I brought Justin home to get well, and once he's better, he'll be gone. End of story."

"The only person who believes that is you."

"Are you coming?" Ren invited, standing and holding out a hand to help her up. But she was closed off to him, cross-legged and cold on the couch. She wouldn't turn her head to look at him. He let his hand drop, sad and disappointed. "Suit yourself."

"You're an idiot."

He nodded, doing his best to keep his face expressionless. He'd been told that before too. Though he didn't want to, he left Denny alone in the dark lounge, heading slowly back to his apartment, but he couldn't really see where he was going. His mind was reeling, and despite how sure he'd made his voice sound to Denny, he was almost completely undone.

Damn it, Justin! Just when he'd started to think there was something happening between them. Justin had asked him to recite the poem. He'd followed Ren to his room to make sure he was ok; he listened as Ren poured his homesick heart out to him. He'd put an ice pack over the bruise on Ren's face. He kept reaching out to hold onto his clothes. He'd cuddled up to Ren's shirt on the bed. How? How had he beaten someone to death? What pushed him that far?

Ren felt a burst of pain in his throat and chest at the same time he heard himself sob in the stairwell. He'd given up his chances with Celeste for this? He'd stayed up all night and got into a fight with Denny for *this*? Denny was right; he was an idiot. He plopped down on the stairs, emotionally paralyzed, hiding his face in his hands, hating that he cared too much. Every time, he cared too damn much.

"Ren?" Denny's voice at the bottom of the stairs. "Oh, no, hey, come on. I'm sorry." Her voice broke as it came closer. He didn't pull his hands away from his face to look. Her scent touched him first, followed by her hands as she enveloped him, draping herself over his back. "I'm so sorry."

"Me too," he choked out.

"I didn't want this," Denny said, petting his hair. "I just thought it would hurt less if you found out sooner."

"Nothing ever hurts less," he said bitterly. Denny held him tighter.

"There is someone out there for you, Ren," she promised, an empty thing to say given their current situation. "But it's not him." Ren hadn't even realized how much he'd wanted it until Denny had taken it away. Except she hadn't. She'd just delivered the message. Ren should have known from the beginning. He'd done this to himself, just like his face. He folded his arms around his knees, tucking his head into the hole, an ostrich in the sand.

"What about Genevieve?" Denny suggested desperately. Trying to staunch the gaping, bleeding wound she'd torn open in Ren's soul. "I know she's interested."

"You said yourself she's a superficial disgrace to the university," Ren challenged, looking at Denny sideways from the curtain of his arms. But the new topic had given him a chance to breathe again.

"I ... did say that, didn't I? Well, maybe —"

"And she couldn't keep up with a conversation unless it happened on Sesame Street."

"Ok, wow, jeez, how do you remember all that?"

Because I listen to you, Denny. Because I respect your opinion. Because you really are the smartest person I know. I just wanted you to be wrong. Just this one time.

"Anyway," Denny went on, stroking his back. "You have Alek and me. We love you." Yeah, but for how long? Ren started pulling himself together; he didn't want Denny to be upset about this anymore. It wouldn't help, and she couldn't help. He wiped his face, careful of his bruise, and then leaned over to kiss her cheek.

"That's all I need," he said, wishing it were true.

"I'll help you," Denny offered. "With Justin, I mean. I know promises mean a lot to you. Just please ..." she hesitated. They were in such a fragile place, and she didn't want to ruin it.

"I'm not falling in love with him," Ren assured her.

"Keep telling yourself that."

Denny kept hold of his arm as he stood from the stairs. She kept it all the way to the apartment, and just as he touched the doorknob, she gripped him extra tight, making him turn to look at her.

"You're not mad at me, right?" she asked.

"No," he replied honestly. "We're ok, Denny."

She seemed satisfied with his answer, though neither of them was happy at the situation. But Ren was a systems man, which meant he was going to continue following protocol, his routine, something he could do without thinking too much, something he could perform without being emotionally invested. He felt his heart cool and close as he opened the apartment door, felt the skin of his face smooth into a calm mask for Alek's sake. He hadn't meant to bring them into the nightmare this was turning into. He'd just been trying to help.

Alek perked up when he heard them coming in the door, but his face fell immediately when he saw them.

"Uh, what happened?" he asked. Denny and Ren exchanged quick, alarmed glances.

"We took a walk, Alek," Denny shrugged, recovering faster than Ren did.

"To where? You guys look exhausted. This feels like one of those time travel movies where you walked out the door, got sucked into a wormhole, spent like three months in medieval Europe fighting the crusades and then came back an hour after you left because Denny did something astronomically clever. So is that it?" He stared hard at Denny. "Did you invent time travel without me? Because we had an agreement."

Ren felt himself tearing up listening to Alek's innocent little story, loving how Alek made it seem completely plausible. As crazy as it sounded, Ren really wished that it had been what they'd done when they walked out the door. He would have much rather invented time travel with Denny than find out Justin was a murderer. He had no idea how long that was going to take to really sink in. Maybe never.

"We'd never fight the crusades without you, Alek," Denny assured him, so casual about it that Ren wondered how often they talked about this. He loved them both so hard in this moment it hurt.

"Ren?" Denny called, waving a hand from across the room to focus his attention. He'd taken one step into the room and frozen. He hadn't even closed the door. "Aren't you coming?"

He nodded, pulling the door shut, joining them once again at the table.

"So can you," he paused to clear his throat and take a breath. "Can you tell me what this thing is for?" His voice almost abandoned him before he finished the question, and he kept his eyes fixed on the project on the table that had kept them both busy for the past couple weeks. He didn't want Alek to see the tears still in his eyes, which was silly because he knew Alek would pick up on his tattered emotions almost instantly.

"Ren," Alek said his name gently, and he knew what was coming. He was going to ask him what was wrong, which would make him fall apart, and he didn't know how he was going to rescue the situation after that.

"It's a radio," Denny saved him. "Based on the BaoFeng BF-F8HP dual band, but we amped it up, of course." Ren nodded like he understood.

"Um," Alek cut in softly, but Denny continued to talk right over him. She was probably staring at him too, letting him know they were going to completely ignore Ren's odd behavior.

"If it works like it's supposed to," Denny went on. "We'll be able to talk to the space station, but we need to work on bouncing the signal off a repeater so we can broadcast far enough."

"No, we need to work on the dial mechanism so we can tune in to the right frequency," Alek protested, and just like that, they went off again, ping-ponging ideas and suggestions off each other with Ren sitting silently in the middle. Before long, one of them made a heated comment that resonated somewhere in the brilliance of the other and suddenly they had a new strategy that was sure to work. Ren rested his head on his hand, calming himself watching them do their thing as the afternoon passed softly under the snowfall, doing his best to let his attention focus completely on what they were doing, deliberately ignoring his time with Denny in the lounge. He didn't want to think about it. Wished he didn't know.

But his heart kept tugging him towards his room. He had to check on Justin, had to wake him up to drink something, maybe eat something too. He had to, but he was afraid. He didn't know how to act around Justin now, how to keep him from suspecting that Ren had invaded his past so completely. *Damn it, Justin, why?*

Alek didn't look up when Ren stood to make his way to his room, but Denny did. They had a moment of mutual understanding, of secret, and she gave him a small nod, acknowledging that even though she didn't agree, she wasn't going to stop him. The increasing dark as he walked away from the setting sun felt like he was stepping into quicksand instead of into shadow. Not even the soft music of the continued piano album soothed him. What was he going to say? What was he going to do if Justin grabbed his sleeve again?

He let himself in, feeling like a stranger in his own room, uneasy and defeated. But then he saw Justin curled up tight on his bed and all of that stripped away in an instant. He suddenly didn't care what Denny had said or even what Justin had done. Ren felt he'd been punished enough already.

"Justin?" he called him gently, kneeling at the side of the bed and reaching over to shake him awake. Justin was shivering under the quilt, still burning up, his face tight with pain. He was doing the held breath thing again, a disquieting length of time between shaky inhales. "Justin, wake up."

Justin's eyes opened, then almost immediately rolled back into his head for a moment before focusing with difficulty on Ren's face.

Ren felt the muscles in his back tighten in preparation for an emergency. Justin winced, struggling to sit up, gasping.

"Wait a minute," Ren soothed, not liking what he was seeing. "Just stay down."

"I can't breathe," Justin panted, scared and desperate, which spurred Ren into motion. He took hold of Justin's arm, helping to ease him upright while he maneuvered himself behind him on the bed, leaning against the wall and pulling Justin against him in a reclined position to open his chest cavity, noticing Justin was breathing, just shallowly. Somewhere quicker than normal but not quite as fast as hyperventilation.

"Lay your head back," he commanded. "But not too far, just enough to keep your airway straight. You can breathe; you're just doing it too fast. Slow it down. Deep breaths like we talked about before."

Justin struggled with his breathing, trying to do what Ren said. Ren reached around to test his pulse, which he couldn't feel in his wrist so he switched to his neck. It was thrumming, speedy as a hummingbird. Was this because he'd woken him up? Ren had never seen anything like this before ... outside of a heart attack.

Just as Ren was opening his mouth to call for some help, he heard Justin take a double inhale, a second pull that seemed to inflate Justin's lungs properly and completely. It made Justin give an involuntary exclamation of relief. His next breath seemed more normal. Ren felt Justin's heart rate begin to slow under his fingers. He rested his head against Justin's neck.

"What the hell was that?" Ren whispered.

"Don't you know?" Justin panted. Ren unconsciously pulled Justin closer to him, hardly noticing when Justin reached a hand up to cling to Ren's wrist as he moved it from Justin's neck to his chest.

"No," Ren murmured. He hated admitting it, but it was true. They stayed still together for a while longer, both breathing hard in the aftermath. Ren's brain was sparking, flipping through pages, switching through lectures at the speed of light. He knew what he needed. He needed another oxygen reading, another blood pressure test. He needed to compare the numbers to what they'd been an hour ago. He needed Dr. Taneja to call him with the test results. And he needed to listen to Denny and take Justin to the hospital. It no longer had anything to do with what Justin had done and everything to do with his condition. But first, Ren waited. Waited until Justin's breathing matched his own, waited until he could feel Justin's pulse in his wrist again. Waited until he was calm and relatively still under his hands.

"How are you feeling, Justin?" he asked quietly, noticing a quick spike in heart rate when he spoke. Justin groaned.

"Like shit," he answered, the first time he'd ever not held back about it. Ren would have been proud of him if he hadn't been so worried.

"I'm sorry," Ren apologized. For failing him. For everything that had happened to Justin before Ren met him and everything that could happen to him after he left this apartment. "Listen. I know it's not how you wanted it, but I think it's time we —"

He never got to finish. Alek rushed into the room without knocking, surrounded by a sense of urgency. He didn't even pause to see Ren supporting Justin on the bed. It made Ren tense. What now?

"Ren?" Alek called, as if he expected him not to be there. "You need to come. The resident dean is here looking for you."

The what? The resident dean? The guy whose e-signature came on every official notice for the building regarding rent rates and policy changes? Craig something or other? Ren couldn't even remember if that was his first or last name. What could he possibly want with Ren? They'd never met each other.

"Can he come back later?" Ren requested. "We need to get Justin —"

"Sorry, Ren," Alek interrupted. "You really need to come. Like right now."

Justin fidgeted, trying to get off Ren so he could get up. Something Ren didn't want.

"Take it easy. You don't have to move," Ren told him. If the dean wanted to talk to him, he could come in here. Ren was busy. This was important. Vital maybe. But it seemed he was the only one who thought that. Justin continued to shift away, and now Alek was helping him.

"Go on, Ren," Alek demanded. Something he rarely did. He was sitting on the bed, easing Justin into his side, wrapping an arm around his shoulders. "There's a police officer with him."

Ren stood up, drenched in sudden apprehension. He locked eyes with Justin, staring at him hard. Could this have anything to do with … no, how could it? Still. Justin shied into Alek, terrified. This was too much. Everything was moving way too fast. Ren's talk with Denny, Justin's scary breathing episode, the dean. The police? When had this become his life?

"Justin, you ok?" Ren checked, unwilling to leave him for any reason.

"I've got him, Ren," Alek assured, and while Ren didn't doubt his sincerity, he did doubt his ability. If Justin began hyperventilating again, or something worse, Alek would panic. He would have no idea what to do. Ren didn't even know if he knew what to do anymore.

"Go," Justin seemed to be begging him to see what was going on rather than giving him permission. "It's ok." But it really wasn't. None of this was ok.

"I'll be right back," Ren promised. "You keep calm. Keep breathing."

Justin nodded weakly as Alek shielded him in his arms. Ren backed out of the room, keeping his eyes on Justin until he had no choice but to turn. He wiped his hands down his hips. *You're the Incident Commander in Charge*, he reminded himself. *Start acting like it!* He straightened his spine, lengthened his stride, and marched purposefully to the door.

10

HYPOTENSION

Several details came to Ren's notice almost simultaneously as he stepped into the living room. The first was Denny, standing awkwardly at the table, steadying herself with one hand, for once appearing her actual height. It hit him hard how tiny she really was, and he felt a pang of brotherly devotion. *I'm here*, he nodded at her. *I'll take care of it.*

Relief smoothed Denny's face as Ren joined them. She also looked pointedly innocent. Ren could see she wanted him to understand that she had nothing to do with this. Ren held out a calming hand, a soothing gesture from a few steps away. He knew that. He didn't blame her.

The last big thing Ren noticed after his rapid exchange with Denny was that in addition to Dean Craig and the officer, there was a third person standing just outside the open doorway. He could see how Alek missed him, positioned behind the other two and wearing black, giving no visual clues as to who he might be or why he might be here. Ren met all their eyes one after the other, and he wondered why he felt so guilty. He didn't even know for sure why all these people were suddenly looking for him.

Because they had asked for him, specifically. Alek said they'd asked for him. Not Justin. This might be completely unrelated. Except Ren knew it wasn't. Somehow, this had everything to do with Justin. The atmosphere in the apartment seemed suddenly charged, full of static electricity, as Ren came to a stop just past the coffee table, putting himself in the middle of the room, hopefully a position of authority. *You have nothing to hide*, he reminded himself. *Just get this over so you can get Justin some help.* Who knew what was going on back in his bedroom, how Justin was doing? He'd looked so scared.

The dean came forward first to meet Ren, acting as the mediator in the exchange, arm extended as if he wanted to shake hands. Ren wanted to fold his arms and tuck into himself for protection, but that would clearly send a wrong message, so he forced himself to close the distance, take one unhurried step forward, and shake the dean's hand as if they were old friends instead of meeting in person for the first time. He noticed how the dean's eyes shifted to his cheek and then quickly away again, very pointedly trying to pretend like he hadn't noticed anything unusual about Ren's face. Ren was grateful that at least they weren't going to have to talk about *that.*

"Sorry to disturb you," the dean apologized, his voice indicating he'd grown up much farther south than Chicago. Ren decided from the grip of his handshake and his tone that he genuinely meant it. He was not comfortable about escorting policemen into his resident apartments. He pulled Ren closer to rest his other hand on his shoulder, touching heads with Ren and whispering in his ear. "I don't know what's going on here, but I suggest you cooperate; they have a warrant."

It was all Ren could do not to react to this helpful, though almost threatening, little tip. Was it supposed to be friendly? Ren felt a nervous smile creep onto his face, his defense mechanism switching on, his fingertips tingling with adrenaline.

"Lorenzo Cordero?" the police officer asked, executing a perfect dominance posture, filling the doorway, obscuring the mysterious third man still standing in the hall.

"That's me," Ren answered, trying to be casual.

"Mind if we come in and ask you a few questions?" the officer continued, sounding like every cop television show Ren had ever seen. He looked the part too. He was tall and lean like Dean Craig, though younger, maybe mid-forties, sandy hair buzzed close to his head. In a different uniform, he would have been a perfect Nazi. He offered his badge for Ren to read — Officer Frederick Geisler, CPD. Ren wanted to tell him to leave, that he was too busy just now to answer anything.

"Uh, sure," he heard himself agree, voice still shaky, confused, remembering the warrant. "Are you guys from ICE? Is this about my visa? Because I just renewed it last September. I can get you the paperwork if you need to —" Because he didn't want this to be about Justin.

Officer Geisler ignored his nervous chatter, began talking over him as if he also just wanted to get this over with. "We're looking for a missing person — Justin Kittrick. His phone records indicate you were the last to correspond with him. We understand you were to meet him last Thursday evening at eight-thirty pm. Did you see Mr. Kittrick at that time, and do you have any information as to where he might be?"

Dean Craig moved out of the line of fire now the interrogation had officially started, standing closer to Denny, who looked apprehensive, despite how she'd expressed her desire for Justin to be taken away to prison such a short time ago. Ren knew she hadn't really meant it. Not when the reality of that was standing here in the apartment — badge, belt, gun, and all.

"He didn't meet me at the library. He never showed," Ren answered, telling the truth the wrong way again. He saw Denny's eyes widen across the room.

"And do you have any information as to where he might be now?" the officer repeated, not accepting Ren answering only half the questions.

"What do you want with him?" Ren checked, wanting to find out their true intentions here. Because Justin could not be arrested right now. Ren had to protect him from that. Surely, they would have some compassion if Ren told them what sort of shape he was in? The officer stared at him, hard and uncompromising, making it clear that he absolutely would not understand.

"Go ahead and tell him, Fritz," the man in black said quietly, a deep, surprisingly reassuring sound. The good cop? But he wasn't in uniform. Or maybe he was; Ren couldn't really see him yet as he was still keeping back in the hall. Officer Geisler shrugged, like this was the least important thing he had been assigned to do today.

"Mr. Kittrick is required to present himself at the Circuit Court of Cook County on Monday, January twenty-first, at ten am," Officer Geisler rattled off, as if he were reading something. "I am legally obligated to deliver to Mr. Kittrick the official summons for a verdict hearing at that time but was unable to locate him at his last known address and have been unsuccessful in reaching him by phone. Can you give me any information as to where he can be located?"

A summons. For the verdict. That meant the jury had decided about the murder. Ren felt a flash of heat bolt down his back, and the room got slightly hazy for a second.

"You're not going to arrest him?" Ren asked, knowing his questions were weird, that this would give him away that he did know where to find Justin. But if all they needed was to give him a court summons … no, Ren still didn't want them to see him. The shock wouldn't be good for him.

"Not at this time; however, if Mr. Kittrick fails to appear, a warrant for his arrest will be issued, and he will be cited for contempt of court."

"But if he doesn't know about the hearing, how is he supposed to show up?" Ren asked, surprising himself with his own audacity, making Officer Geisler tilt his head to the side, his nostrils flaring in impatience. Ren couldn't blame him; he knew he was being difficult.

He also knew Officer Geisler was his least favorite person in the room, even though he was just trying to do his job. He didn't know Justin hadn't abandoned his apartment on purpose. He didn't know that he was so scared or sick. The problem was he also didn't care. And he likely wouldn't change his opinion even if Ren told him the truth. He might even feel as though Justin deserved it. That's what made Ren hate him.

"It is Mr. Kittrick's responsibility to notify the court of any contact information changes including new phone numbers and addresses, whether temporary or permanent," Officer Geisler explained coldly. "As he is well aware. If you cannot give us any information of his whereabouts, and I am unable to speak with him, then the documentation I left at his last known address will serve as sufficient notice, and he will be held accountable for appearing at the appointed time."

That actually sounded good to Ren. He had the details now; he could pass the message to Justin later, when he was settled and safe in the hospital with proper meds and monitoring equipment. Ren wondered if Justin would be required to "present himself" in court if he were still in the hospital on Monday morning at ten am. He wondered if a doctor's note was good enough to postpone a sentence hearing, and for how long. He was certain Dr. Taneja would write him one. He wanted more time before Justin was sentenced for him to heal, for Ren to understand what had happened. He hadn't even had a chance to talk to Justin about it yet.

"I guess we're done then," Ren heard himself say, steady and clear. Because he sure as hell was not allowing this officer and his shady bodyguard anywhere near Justin, despite his assurance that he wasn't there to arrest him. He was too gruff, too mercilessly intimidating, and Justin's heart couldn't take it. "If I see Justin, I'll tell him to check his messages."

"Young man," Officer Geisler began, getting terse, and Ren felt his chin lift automatically in response. Every time he'd been "young manned" all his stubbornness came to the surface like oil rising on water. "Do you understand that —"

"Fritz? May I?" the shadow man cut in gently, a hand appearing on the officer's shoulder from behind.

The officer stepped aside to allow his partner entry with a sort of "be my guest" kind of flourish, looking at Ren roughly, as if to say Ren was in for it now. Though the voice from the hall had been soothing, Ren felt as though he'd made a big mistake as the unidentified man came into full view. He was almost as big as Alek, but cut, broad-shouldered and narrow-waisted, and he had military written all over him from his hairstyle to the way he moved, though he was wearing civilian clothes — a simple black sweater and jeans. His features were similar to Officer Geisler, though he was dark where Geisler was fair, and disfigured slightly by two scars — one that dipped into his right eyebrow and one that slashed along his chin. Ren suddenly felt as tall as Denny, more intimidated by this man than the police officer. What was he going to do now?

The man in black also reached out a hand to Ren, making his insides squirm as he noticed the man's right hand was a prosthetic. Ren forced himself to extend his hand even though it felt like he was purposefully exposing himself to something dangerous, like a lion or a loaded bear trap, watching as his skin was enveloped in smooth carbon fiber. Extremely smooth, and not the least bit clumsy. Wow. Ren found himself suddenly marveling as they shook hands. This was not an ordinary prosthetic; it was too elegant, sophisticated, and sleek. The dexterity in the fingers as they closed around Ren's was fluid enough to write a dissertation on. He could probably thread a freaking needle if he wanted to. If they weren't in a standoff about Justin, Ren thought he would very much like to sit down with this man and learn all about his robotic arm. There was a part of him that wanted to drag him over to Denny right now so they could both pull back the sweater sleeve and start poking at it.

"Wow," Ren breathed before he could stop himself, completely awe-struck. "That's beautiful." He bit his tongue before he said anything else embarrassing. Normal people didn't geek out about things like that; it was inappropriate and ill-timed.

To his credit, the man held still, leaving their hands clasped, letting Ren admire his mechanically replaced limb, and he didn't say any of the things Ren would have said if their positions had been reversed. Stupid, immature, tension-easing things like "take a picture" or "my eyes are up here." The thought made Ren lift his gaze, finally making eye contact, noticing immediately that the gentleness of this man's voice extended also to his black eyes. The man smiled softly as he realized he finally had Ren's full attention.

"Elias Kaplan," he introduced himself with an efficient sort of clip, and Ren wondered how much of a struggle it had been not to say his rank along with his name. Because he was military, or had been. No doubt. So what was he doing here now, looking for Justin? He released Ren's hand, hiding the distracting prosthetic behind his back, falling automatically into parade rest. "You're Justin's friend?" He sounded hopeful.

"I don't really know him," Ren denied. "We have a class together. English. We're partners for an assignment." He paused to look at Officer Geisler, who was fiddling with his radio near the door. "But you probably already know all about that."

"From the texts, yes," Elias nodded, but grew serious quickly, leaning closer and lowering his voice, as if sharing a secret. "Can you tell me if he's all right? I'm really worried about him."

Ren studied Elias some more, hearing the nuance in what he said. He was nothing like the officer. He was telling the truth; he was invested. Ren found himself wanting to tell him everything. He felt they would understand each other perfectly. But he just couldn't do that. There was too much risk to Justin.

"I don't know," Ren stuttered, unsure what to do. He couldn't look at Elias anymore; he'd run out of half-truths and the heart to tell them. He just wanted everyone to leave.

"Please," Elias went on earnestly, lifting his hand as if he meant to grab Ren's shoulder, but lowering it again awkwardly as he changed his mind about touching him. "I need to find him; it's important. Won't you help me?" Me. Not will you help *us* find him; he'd excluded his companion. This was personal to him. Ren wished he'd come alone. The apartment was too crowded to communicate properly. There was too much threat, and Justin was so fragile.

"That's complicated," Ren whispered, for only Elias to hear. "It's not a good time."

"What do you mean?" Officer Geisler asked, making Ren realize that even though he didn't look like he was paying attention, he was still entirely focused on what was going on. Ren shot a look over to Denny, who hadn't moved, hoping she could give him some guidance.

"It's *him*," she mouthed soundlessly as they made eye contact, but he didn't understand what she meant.

"Do you know where Justin is?" Elias questioned, sharper, pulling Ren's attention away from trying to figure out what Denny was trying to tell him. It wasn't an unfriendly edge, more like he really wanted to see Justin and couldn't wait any more to find out.

"I just," Ren hesitated, feeling detached and antsy, like he wasn't ready for this. Why couldn't they just leave them alone? "I can't let you see him now." There, Ren might as well have confessed Justin was here, or at least that he knew where they could find him.

"Why?" Elias asked, looking at Ren in concern. Disappointed and uneasy.

"Is he here?" Officer Geisler said, almost at the same time, sounding angry. Ren held up his hands defensively, wondering how much trouble he was going to be in for deliberately withholding information from law enforcement.

"He is, but —" Ren faltered, feeling like there wasn't enough air in the room. Alek and Denny had once packed over thirty scientists in this space, triumphantly declaring that the collected IQ of the apartment was higher than a full session of Congress. You couldn't move without squishing against someone, and still it felt more open and breathable than it did right now.

Probably because Officer Geisler was suddenly looming over Ren, as near as he could get without touching him, eyes flashing, looking like he wanted to take Ren and shake the information out of him. Surprisingly, Elias's simple look of pleading was worse.

"Where?" Geisler asked, so close Ren could smell his cinnamon gum. Ren told himself not to cower. He needed to explain himself quickly, needed to make them understand that they could cause serious complications if they went storming around the apartment. "Take me to him."

"No," Ren denied, still protective even though he was frightened and intimidated. It was a bad move, and he knew it. They still had a warrant and could search the entire apartment if they wanted to. "He just can't ... Let me explain," he begged.

Except he didn't have to. Ren heard Denny call his name, and when he straightened from under Officer Geisler's fury to see why, he saw Elias staring open-mouthed toward the hallway. Ren checked over his shoulder, half turning, and groaned to see Justin, white-faced and shaking, leaning on the corner where the hall to Ren's bedroom gave way to the open living room space. Alek was standing behind him.

"Oh, Justin," Elias moaned in shock and sympathy, just loud enough for Ren to hear. Justin was staring at Elias, in terrible obvious pain, and Ren saw his lips move. He couldn't hear, but Ren knew what he'd said, had listened to him say it for hours. North.

North? Elias was North? Of course. That's what Denny meant; she'd figured it out before Ren. It was North, here, searching for Justin even though Justin didn't think he would care, didn't want to call him. But North had tracked him down anyway, wanting to see if Justin was all right.

Justin was definitely not all right. Ren saw Justin sway, too weak and dizzy to be standing up in the first place, and the shock of seeing North suddenly in the apartment was making everything worse. Ren could tell that Justin was seconds away from blacking out.

"Justin, sit down," Ren commanded, sharp and immediate,

taking charge, not knowing if he'd have enough time to get to his side. "On the floor. You sit down right now."

It didn't look like Justin heard him. He continued to stare, hard, at North, his speeding breaths visible in his diaphragm. Then Ren watched his vision go unfocused, watched him start blinking rapidly, shaking his head as if to clear away the hot buzzing of his crashing consciousness. Ren darted for him, hoping to make it in time to catch him, but Officer Geisler grabbed his arm. He let Ren go almost immediately as he realized what Ren was trying to do, but just that tiny delay was too much. Justin was already falling.

"Alek!" Ren yelled, but Alek had not been blessed with a quick reaction time, and Justin was falling forward, away from him. He made a clumsy, too-slow attempt and missed.

Ren made a desperate jump, like a baseball player diving to catch a ball, colliding with Justin on his way down, Justin's head hitting Ren squarely in the chest and knocking them both to the floor. They crashed against the coffee table, shoving it across the carpet. A corner caught Ren in the back as he fell, scraping a long, painful gash through his shirt. He grunted but kept his focus on cushioning Justin's head and neck. They landed awkwardly against the shifted table, Justin unmoving, hot and heavy across Ren's torso. Ren floundered, pinned painfully on the corner of the table, trying to get out from under Justin so he could see what he needed to do to get him conscious again.

North turned out to be the fastest responder in the room, rushing to help lift the unconscious Justin off Ren, who scrambled to his knees, ignoring whatever the coffee table had done to his back to see what Justin's status was, realizing that whatever had started earlier in the bedroom had progressed to something critical.

Ren allowed North to keep hold of Justin and began calling out instructions. "Sit him up, no, *up*; keep pressure off his chest." He started pulling on them, rearranging them to his specifications, grabbing North's artificial arm without thinking and dragging it across Justin's collarbone, above his heart, leaning Justin forward over it in a tripod stance to ease his breathing. North instinctively brought his other hand around Justin's forehead to keep his face from dropping too far forward. Ren nodded appreciatively. "Hold him steady like that; make sure his airway stays clear. Alek, my bag, please. Denny, bring me a cold, wet dishtowel. You!" He barked the last at Officer Geisler, who was standing off to the side, coming to terms with what the hell was going on. "Call an ambulance."

"Justin," North was calling tenderly to the boy in his arms while Ren gave orders to almost every person in the room. "Oh God, you're burning up." Ren felt a hand on his arm and knew it was Denny, so he reached up without looking to accept the wet towel, wrapping it around Justin's throat. He was about to ask for another when Justin opened his eyes, coming back from his faint and beginning to struggle against the hands that held him, disoriented and terrified.

"Don't move," Ren told him firmly, placing a restraining hand on his back at the same time North tightened his hold. Ren settled his fingers against Justin's carotid artery, noticing the irregular pound of Justin's heart, full throttle arrhythmia. "You passed out and fell." And it was the worst thing that could have happened. It was like the only thing keeping him this side of critical had been his own stubborn resolve. Now that he'd fainted, he was crashing. Ren was surprised he'd been able to regain consciousness at all. "We've got you. It's going to be ok."

"Ren," Justin said, breathless and frantic. "Something's wrong."

Ren registered a thump at his side as Alek put the med bag within reach. He hurriedly pulled the blood pressure cuff and pulse oximeter out, strapping them to Justin as quickly as he was able.

"I know," he assured, trying to sound steady and calm, looking at the oxygen reading, waiting for the cuff to finish deflating. He'd only seen this kind of thing happen once before, to an elderly woman he'd picked up in the ambulance from a dialysis center. It had something to do with dehydration. She'd completely bottomed out; they hadn't been able to save her. Ren checked the oximeter. Justin's level had dropped to eighty-five percent. *Shit.* "I'm going to fix it. It's your heart; remember we talked about your heart and relaxing? You need to do that now. Breathe as deep as you can for me, yeah? And stay calm." Next the blood pressure reading — 80 / 50. *Damn it.*

"Ren," Justin begged, trusting him. Ren tried to think. Justin's pulse was close to 140 beats a minute but speeding up with every passing second; he was deteriorating way too fast. His numbers didn't match the dialysis patient yet, but they weren't far off. Ren reminded himself to stay calm too. "Ren, I can't breathe."

"You can," Ren told him, filling his voice with certainty. "There's nothing wrong with your lungs; you understand me? They're clear. They're working fine. So you keep focusing on taking deep breaths and stay awake. Ok? Stay with me." *Please, stay with me.* Ren knew Justin felt as though he were drowning right now. The ineffectual beats of his heart were weakly pumping blood throughout his body, resulting in lowered blood pressure and decreased oxygen to his organs. Justin's brain was receiving screaming signals from everything that used blood that there was no air. Ren couldn't imagine how terrifying that would be, or how he would possibly stay calm in such a situation. But Justin was doing his best, both his hands clenched in fabric, North's shirt on one side, and Ren's on the other.

"Fritz," North called sharply to the officer. "Where's that ambulance?"

"Three minutes out," Geisler responded.

"Will someone go down and let them in?" Ren asked. Dean Craig looked more than willing to leave, his face almost as pale as Justin's.

"On it," he said, dashing for the hallway.

"Alek," Ren called without taking his eyes off Justin, knowing his roommate was standing somewhere close, watching, freaked out. "I need some pickle juice in a cup." Then he remembered about Justin's mouth, all the fever blisters. It would be agonizing for him to drink it, but it was the only thing Ren could think of that might keep Justin's blood pressure up and stop him from going into complete cardiac arrest. "And a straw if you have one."

Ren could feel North's gaze, hard and wondering. He knew it

sounded crazy, but the pickling brine was as close as they were going to get to a chemical defibrillator. What Ren really needed was supplemental oxygen and Bretylium.

"Ren," Justin panted, his voice raising in pitch, twitching in panicked distress. Ren recognized the movements. Justin's muscles were cramping up.

"Listen to me, Justin," Ren ordered, putting his head close to Justin's so he'd be sure to hear him. "I promise, you're going to be fine. I've got oxygen coming for you; it'll be here any second. Hang on."

"Here," Alek said from behind Ren's vision, handing a cup over his shoulder. Ren snatched it, the tang sharp in his nose.

"Justin, I'm going to have you drink this. It's going to hurt like hell, but we need to keep your blood pressure from dropping anymore." He held the straw to Justin's mouth, poking him in the lip because his eyes were closed tight against the pain. Justin opened his mouth and obediently used his next panting breath to suck up some of the brine.

And immediately gagged on it, his entire system shocked by the extreme taste and the burn of the salt. Most of the mouthful ended up on the carpet and Ren's thigh. Justin coughed thickly, and Ren worried he might have just made everything worse.

"No, you don't; don't you dare throw up. Justin, I need you to breathe. Take a second." Ren paused, but not for long, watching Justin attempt to swallow the taste of the juice out of his mouth, doing his best not to vomit. "Ok, now you've got that out of the way," Ren went on after it looked like Justin was as recovered as he was going to get, as if it had been no big deal and he'd expected it. "Let's try again."

"I can't," Justin whimpered, drawn up tight in North's arms, releasing Ren so he could cling to North's sleeve across his chest. "Ren, I can't." *I know, Justin. I know this is hard and you're scared to death. I'm asking you to do something that makes no sense to you, but you keep calling my name because you trust me, because you are expecting me to make this better, and this is all I've got.*

"You have to," Ren encouraged, but not gently. "Now try again."

Justin's head drooped, exhausted by the frantic beating of his heart, by his own panting and pain. But his blood pressure was still dropping. Just when Ren thought he'd have to tip Justin's head back and spoon feed him strawfuls of pickle juice, he weakly drew up another mouthful. And this time he was prepared for how awful it would be and kept it down, swallowing with difficulty.

"Again," Ren ordered, after allowing him to take a couple rest breaths.

Justin managed to keep down another half dozen swallows of pickle juice before the paramedics arrived, wincing each time, crying without tears. Ren continued to ignore everyone in the room, especially North, even though Ren knew he was staring at him and wanted Ren to make eye contact with him. But he just didn't have time; he needed to keep Justin from crashing. The pickle juice seemed to ease the cramps, and Justin's numbers weren't going down anymore. But they weren't coming up either, and Justin's heart was still racing dangerously.

When the paramedics showed up, Ren didn't waste time on them either. He knew them. Grayson Tanner and Stefany Lopez, both also med students, but much farther along in their courses. Ren should have let them take over, yet he found himself unwilling to step out of the scenario and yield to their direction. He didn't want to back out of the way for Grayson, didn't want to wait for Stefany to figure out what to do. So he decided to stay in it, take charge himself, even though they were in uniform and he wasn't, and they technically outranked him. He was the student and they were his trainers, and he had been fine with that on every op except this one. He knew Justin's history. He'd been first on scene. Justin kept calling his name.

"Oxygen," Ren requested before they were truly in the door, still on his knees next to Justin, who was taking those awful gasping breaths and holding them again.

"Cordero?" Grayson wasted time expressing his surprise to find him here.

"Oxygen," Ren demanded again, snapping his fingers, and this time Grayson moved to do as he was told.

"Tell me what's going on here, Ren," Stefany invited.

"Male patient, eighteen," Ren told her quickly, and she started scribbling down the history. He kept talking as he accepted the oxygen mask from Grayson, attached it securely over Justin's mouth, and cranked the flow all the way up to fifteen liters a minute. Somehow North took the pickle juice and handed it off to someone. Ren continued talking. "Temperature 103.3, blood pressure 75 over 50, heart rate," he faltered, saying this out loud made it terrifyingly real. But Stefany needed the numbers. "Heart rate 170 beats a minute and irregular. Oxygen saturation level eighty-five ... no ...eighty-eight."

Somewhere outside of what he was doing, he heard North vocalize distress about the statistics. Ren continued without looking at him.

"Suspected influenza, anemia, and dehydration. No allergies."

Now let's get on with it, he thought, watching Justin. His eyes were closed, concentrating, sucking in greedy breaths of oxygen, still conscious, though trembling hard, lying limp against North. Grayson had replaced Ren's personal blood pressure cuff with the one from the ambulance.

"Justin," Ren called, taking his hand and squeezing it gently. "You're doing great. We're going to have to move you now; we're taking you to the hospital. I'm going with you, though. I'm riding with you."

"I'll take him," North offered, just as Alek appeared at Ren's side, bending over to hand Ren his quilt from the bed. Ren accepted it and, together with North, wrapped Justin up, warm and secure. He was slipping into shock, even with the oxygen supplement.

"You can't," Ren said, knowing it was a terrible idea to let a man with a missing arm carry Justin.

"No time," North refuted, and Ren knew he was right. "I'm here, Justin," North told him, his voice low, intimate. "I'm going to pick you up; hold on."

Justin wrapped his arms around North's neck, weak, frightened, and shivering, resting his head against North's chest as if he were a child. Grayson helpfully kept the oxygen tank level with Justin as North stood up, though he looked doubtful, switching his gaze back and forth between Ren and Stefany.

"No, sir, you can't carry him. Ren, you know we can't allow…" Stefany began, but stopped as Ren glared at her. Of course he knew. North was not medically trained, at least to their knowledge. He could drop Justin, injure him further, and they would be liable because they had allowed it to happen. But right this second, Ren trusted North more with Justin than he did anyone else in the room, and he didn't want to waste time with the gurney on the stairs.

"Go on," Ren told North, pushing Grayson so he'd be sure to follow despite what Stefany was saying. "He's right; there's no time." North nodded, striding forward in a secure march. Grayson looked pained but followed with his gear.

"Ren, what do you think you're doing?" Stefany growled, but he didn't care. Officer Geisler was on his way out too, following North, speaking into his radio. Stefany watched him walk past with her mouth open, as if she were ready to make an official report about Ren right this second. In the end, she turned back to him. "You better get in line, or you're not getting in my ambulance."

"I'm going with him," Ren countered fiercely, not making any promises about any future broken protocol. He was going to do what was best for his patient. "And it's not your ambulance. Now let's go; we're wasting time."

Stefany's lips slammed together as if holding back all the sharp words she suddenly wanted to say but couldn't because she was a paramedic on duty. She spun on her heel and started jogging after the others. Ren was right behind her until he heard his name called sharply from behind.

His living room looked small in the aftermath, darker and empty. Denny and Alek came up to him, looking stricken, not used to emergencies and especially not used to watching Ren handle them, but despite being afraid, their hands were full of offerings. Denny held out his coat while Alek had his backpack. Ren smiled at them gratefully.

"You guys are the best," he acknowledged. "I'll call with an update as soon as I can."

"Be careful," Denny told him, knowing there would be no talking him out of going wherever Justin went. Alek looked like he wanted to say something, but he was too shocked to make a sound. He squeezed Ren's arm on his way out, putting everything he wanted to say into the pressure.

"Thanks, guys," Ren said, closing the door and dashing down the hall to catch up with everyone. The elevator was already on the first floor; they hadn't waited for him, but he hadn't expected them to. He flew down the stairs, almost tripping as he skipped as many as safely possible, meeting up with them out front of the building as they were strapping Justin securely onto a stretcher. He still had his eyes closed, his chest rising and falling in a slow and heavy way, as if each breath were a difficult, dedicated effort.

When the time came to transfer the stretcher into the back of the vehicle, Ren was right there on one side with Grayson on the other. Stefany shot him a look as he took what should have been her place, and they had a quick stare down.

"I'm going with him," Ren reminded her, knowing she didn't like it and knowing there would be a disciplinary meeting with someone about what he was doing. But that was so far away. Ren wasn't thinking about that. Mostly he was focused on Justin's next breath and heartbeat. He felt Justin's trembling hand on his sleeve, gripping him weakly. "I'm here," he told him. "I'm not leaving."

"Just follow protocol," Stefany ordered, headed for the driver's side door. Ren didn't take the time to feel triumphant about this, just nodded to Grayson so they could finish getting the stretcher secured inside.

"North, come on," Ren called out the back of the ambulance. North was standing close to Officer Geisler, conversing rapidly, but jerked his head up when Ren called him by the name Justin used.

"I'll meet you there," Officer Geisler said, turning towards his patrol car. North grabbed Ren's offered wrist and hauled himself into the back of the ambulance. Grayson pulled the doors closed, and Ren tapped the back window to signal Stefany that they were clear to move. Then he shifted his focus to Justin.

"I'm starting an IV line," Ren told Grayson. He wanted to get Justin medication as quickly as possible. While the anti-arrhythmic drug could be administered via a muscular injection, the delay in effect was almost two hours longer than if it was administered via IV. Ren didn't want Justin to have to wait that long, didn't think he could. He also knew Grayson wasn't the best at IVs, they were in a moving vehicle, and Justin's veins were not great.

"I don't think so," Grayson started, but Ren didn't care. Justin needed every minute he could give him.

"Can you just stick to what you're good at and shut up?" Ren returned, already pulling an IV kit from a cabinet behind his head. "I'm taking full responsibility. North? Come up here by his head. Come talk to him."

North looked as though he wasn't sure what he should do, sensing the discord, but in the end began to obey Ren.

"You can't take the responsibility," Grayson countered but couldn't reach Ren to stop him. North made it even more difficult by squeezing between Grayson and the stretcher to get to Justin's head. "I'm the one who'll get in trouble."

"Justin?" Ren spoke to his patient, covered in Ren's quilt and silently panting. "Drop your hand to the side, ok? Just let it hang while I get this ready for you." Justin let go of Ren's shirt, letting his hand fall limp as Ren tightened a tourniquet above his elbow. And even though Ren had told him to do it, he jumped in alarm to see the hand fall like that, to feel it slip from his clothes, as though Justin had lost consciousness again. He sped up his prep work, ignoring Grayson, though he could hear him prattling on.

"Cordero, don't," Grayson kept entreating. "Wait, you're gonna do the hand?"

Yes, he was starting the IV in the hand. Normal ambulance procedure would put it in the crook of the elbow because the veins were larger there and it would be easier to do while moving. But it wasn't as safe as the hand. Justin could start seizing, which would jerk his arm tight to his body, could break the needle somewhere inside him. It would be more difficult, but the hand was the best location choice, and if Ren were successful, it could be used throughout Justin's entire hospital stay. Ren hoped the combined effort of Justin's struggling heart, the tourniquet, and gravity would be sufficient to pool enough blood in the veins so he could feel them.

Grayson used his long arm to its full advantage and reached over Justin to push Ren away. "Come on, Cordero, stop it, I'm not playing with you." Ren glared at him.

"No one's playing," Ren clipped. "Are you telling me this isn't the best choice?"

"If we were still, it would be," Grayson allowed. "But we're moving, and you aren't cleared to do it anyway."

"I'll clear him," North spoke up from his position of protection at Justin's head. Justin also had lifted the hand closest to Grayson, blindly fumbling for his arm to pull it away. "Do what you need to do," North said to Ren. They shared a look of trust, gratitude, and expectation, and Ren nodded, hoping North's faith in him was not misplaced. Grayson reluctantly backed off, muttering something about Ren getting him fired. While Ren knew that was a possibility, he also knew it would be less likely if Justin didn't die. And that would be less likely if he could get this IV going as soon as possible.

Ren gently took Justin's hand, keeping it low against his thigh, trying to get his head in the moment, ignoring anything outside of Justin's hand. The angle was weird; he'd never done it this way before, and not in a jostling vehicle. But Justin could hardly breathe, his body was not getting the oxygen it needed, so Ren proceeded, dismissing immediately the dorsal venous arch on top of the hand. No need to take unnecessary risks. He'd use the cephalic vein located at the wrist below the thumb, large, straight, and easy to cannulate. In theory.

"Justin," Ren let him know what he was doing. "I'm starting an IV in your wrist." Justin was in so much pain already, Ren wondered if the prick of the needle would even be noticed, but he also knew he wouldn't be as graceful as he had been in the quiet of his apartment. Ren held his breath, didn't blink, tightened all his muscles to brace what they were doing, somehow hold it apart from any movement the ambulance might unexpectedly make at a crucial moment. Steady hand. Sure stick. Justin flinched slightly as Ren eased the needle in, but kept still enough, everything still enough, that the placement was a success. Ren taped it securely in place, knowing this needle would be Justin's best friend for at least the next few hours and possibly the next few days.

Grayson looked stunned when Ren finished — stunned and impressed. He took Justin's hand, checking Ren's work and at the same time injecting a solution into it. Bretylium. Finally.

"Almost there, Justin," Ren reassured him. "We've just given you some medicine that will slow your heart down. It'll start working soon." Ren leaned over him as he spoke, and Justin opened his eyes to look at him. To stare at him. Justin had his mouth open inside the oxygen mask, breathing hard. His eyes were so full of fear and pain it made Ren hurt too. Made him feel guilty. It shouldn't have come to this; Ren should never have allowed Justin to decline to this point.

And they were at the worst part now. The part where there was nothing left for Ren to do except wait. It would take several more minutes, maybe as many as twenty, for the medication to fully enter Justin's bloodstream and do what it was supposed to. Twenty grueling minutes for Justin to continue struggling for air, for his heart to throb and jerk and race. And Ren could do nothing for him anymore.

"Stay with me, Justin," Ren pleaded, wishing his voice sounded better, less afraid. He didn't want Justin to hear it. Fear was such a contagious thing. "Stay awake."

11

SCOPE OF PRACTICE

Once an ambulance arrives at the emergency department, there is a transfer. Everything switches. The paramedics let down the stretcher, wheel it inside, and shift the patient to a waiting bed and team. Paperwork is torn from a clipboard and tucked into a folder. Information goes back and forth between the ambulance and the ER staff.

Ren always remained on the ambulance side. Bring the patient in, pull the paperwork, return the blood pressure cuff to its waiting hook, and answer questions. Once the ER people had everything they needed, he'd go back to the ambulance to wait for the next call. Staying afterward was new, unusual, and to be honest, demoralizing.

Justin's condition required a team on high alert, and Stefany had done a good job on the radio before they'd arrived assembling the proper people. There was someone from cardiology, phlebotomy, two techs, and a nurse who crowded Ren and North away from Justin. Ren wanted to fight them, cling to Justin's hand and refuse to move, but North pulled him back like an irresistible force of nature.

"Let them do their job," North told him, and while he hated it, Ren had to admit he would be out of his league among them. He submitted and stood quietly anxious at North's side, arms folded tightly across his ribs, his backpack on the floor against his leg, watching the ER team with grudging admiration.

The nurse stepped in immediately with the techs on her sides. Between the three of them, they had Justin stripped and into a gown in seconds. Then they began efficiently hooking him to everything they had, another blood pressure cuff, a pulse oximeter. The portable D-size oxygen tank from the ambulance was replaced with the permanent flow attached to the wall. Stats appeared on the black and green screen to Justin's side, a continuous line of data show-casing Justin's rapid heartbeat, a frightened spike popping up hard every time someone unfamiliar touched him. His oxygen level had increased to ninety, but that was the only improvement Ren could see.

After a few minutes, the energy in the room died down slightly, the phlebotomist leaving, taking one of the techs with him. The cardiologist left shortly after with the remaining tech, and Ren watched the nurse bow out of the room as the ER doctor arrived. Ren felt his muscles constrict, unconsciously standing straighter as he recognized the woman coming purposefully to Justin's side. Dr. Angelique Delacroix.

She was covered in royal purple scrubs, with almost none of her dark skin visible, but he knew it was her. Knew from the deep brown hair, streaked with gold and plaited in hundreds of tiny braids that normally fell to her waist, but were now pulled into a large knot at the base of her neck. He knew from the confidence in her stride and the sharpness of her eyes, also dark and streaked with gold, as she took in everything around her in an instant. Ren had only seen her twice before, but he knew her well.

She'd turned up unexpectedly during one of Ren's EMT classes, asking permission to sit in and listen. No one knew why she was there or why she had taken a sudden interest in this particular instructor or lesson. Ren didn't even know who she was then, though she'd been introduced before she'd taken a random seat. She sat there silently, until Ren answered a question that seemed to surprise her, and suddenly Ren found himself the object of her tiger-eyed stare as she continued to drill him about who he was and how he would handle case after case until she'd completely exhausted his soul and knowledge, turning him into a stammering mess in a matter of minutes to the tune of the other students nervously giggling all around him; all of them secretly relieved they weren't in his shoes. When class dismissed and she left the room, Ren stayed in his seat for a long time feeling slightly violated.

He'd almost refused to go when he received an email from her the following morning asking him to come have coffee with her at the hospital, but in the end, he'd been too intrigued not to accept. He even bought and brought the damn coffee, though he hadn't been able to drink it during what seemed like an impromptu hiring interview with dashes of autobiography and a quasi-history lesson thrown in at seemingly random intervals that kept Ren perpetually knocked off balance. He sat there, stunned by her voice, which was deep, intense, and full, rooted into the very core of the earth. She asked him about sucking chest wounds and then turned around and asked what he knew about herbalism and spiritual healing methods. He'd done his best to keep up, but in the end, he accidentally spilled coffee all over himself, his hands shaking hard at the twists and turns and just the strange *intensity* of the conversation that he lost his grip on the cup, staining his clothes and damaging some of her notes.

That had caused her to sigh and pull back, slowing down, thanking him for coming and suddenly he was out in the hallway with several napkins and a sense that he had just failed an exam. It felt like being dismissed by an undercover deity. In revenge, he'd asked Denny to pull up everything she could find on Dr. Delacroix.

"I'm surprised she didn't eat you," Denny told him as they sifted through the information. Angelique was forty-five, had spent her childhood in the French Quarter of New Orleans before attending college at Harvard and later made Chicago her permanent home after her residency there. She had never married and had a reputation for bringing most of her students to tears on the rare occasion she taught a class. "Did you notice if she stole any of your hair?" And Ren had shoved Denny's shoulder, rolling his eyes, but then that night he sat up in bed worried about that very thing. That had been last semester, and since he didn't appear to be cursed by anything other than being an awkward nineteen-year-old, he'd forgotten all about her until now.

As Dr. Delacroix approached Justin's bedside, Ren couldn't take it anymore. He broke away from North's hand on his shoulder, meeting her on Justin's other side as if he'd protect him from her somehow, though he couldn't bring himself to look her in the eye, and Justin needed her badly at the moment. Angelique didn't acknowledge him; she was devoting her full attention to Justin, slipping one hand into his and placing the other gently on his forehead.

"Hello, baby," she crooned at Justin with so much actual affection in her voice Ren was startled. He'd never heard her talk like that. "My name is Dr. Delacroix." Justin shifted, breathing like fish do when they're out of water, staring at this tiger woman at his side. "We're giving you fluids and pain medication in your IV there, and it seems you've already received a dose of anti-arrhythmic in the ambulance. We'll give you a little more time to see how it's working before we try anything else. I hope to have you feeling more comfortable very soon." She paused, conspicuously turning her gaze to Ren, who had to remind himself a little too late to close his stupid mouth. He couldn't tell if she recognized him, and he wasn't sure if he'd be insulted or relieved if she had forgotten him completely.

"Is this your friend, darling?" She continued to talk to Justin. Instead of answering, Justin did his normal trick of reaching over to Ren, intending to attach himself to his clothes, but Ren cut him off before he could, gently encasing Justin's hand with both of his, careful of the IV. "I see." She moved her exquisite head to where North still stood in the corner. "And you?" she asked.

"Elias," North said, and Ren admired the strength of his voice. "I'm ... was ... Justin's social worker."

"Ah," Angelique breathed in response, seeming disappointed with the selection of outcasts who had followed Justin into her triage room. "Who has legal custody of Justin currently? Does he have a living will or advance directive?"

"No, nothing like that," North responded, and Ren could tell he was ashamed for some reason. "And he's eighteen. He has legal custody of himself, no known relatives." Ren knew why she was asking these questions. If Justin blacked out or flatlined, Dr. Delacroix wanted to know who was allowed to make medical decisions on his behalf. Since neither Ren nor North could legally do so, she would assume that right if the situation came to it. Ren didn't know if he liked that, but it was out of his hands now. This wasn't like the ambulance; he had no authority in this room at all.

Angelique nodded, accepting the answers and assimilating them into her master plan. She moved the hand on Justin's forehead to his chest, as if holding his heart.

"All right, love," she spoke again to Justin. "I'm going to give you five minutes for the medicine to bring your heart rate down before we try something else. You just lie here quiet, just like this. Your friends are here to help you relax, but I am going to borrow Lorenzo for a moment to ask him some questions. We'll be right outside the door." So she did remember him after all.

Her eyes were on fire when Ren finally met her gaze, and he wondered how she could keep her expression so fierce when her voice was so soft. He looked away quickly, turning behind him to gesture for North to come take his place at Justin's side. North seemed more than happy to do that, stepping up immediately and leaning with concern over Justin.

"I'll be right back," Ren promised, though he did not want to follow Dr. Delacroix into the hall. But it was like he was already gone, no one acknowledged his departing comment. Angelique held the door open for him to go out first, and he walked past her as if to an execution.

It turned out not to be that bad, but it was close.

"Well, Lorenzo," Angelique began, tucking Justin's chart into the slot by the door. "Still in the med program then?" The way she said it made Ren wonder if she thought he would have been kicked out by now. Though he supposed he hadn't made that great of an impression on her the last time they'd been together.

"That's right," Ren responded, though he felt she hadn't expected an answer. "Nice to see you again, Dr. Delacroix."

"Hmmm," she replied ambiguously, no trace of the gentleness he'd just seen in her remaining outside of Justin's room. "Do you want to explain yourself?"

Now he was confused and not sure where to start. Did she mean the stuff he'd pulled on the ambulance? Letting North carry Justin? He stood there deliberating, leaning against the wall, listening to the bustle all around them. Carts being pushed, typing, footsteps, monitors going off, murmurings of conversations happening outside of triage rooms just like the one he was having right now. And out of the corner of his eye, Ren saw Officer Geisler just arriving through the main entrance. Great.

"Maybe you tell me what I did and then I can explain why I did it," he suggested, not wanting to give her more than she had on him already. Mostly he wanted to get the lecture finished so he could go back inside with Justin.

"I heard from the ambulance team that you placed an IV on the drive over here," she said, her tone so dangerously neutral that Ren wanted to sit on the floor. "Is that true?"

"Yes, ma'am," he confessed, not seeing any point in denying it, wondering how much more the ambulance team had told her. "I thought it would save time."

"You know that's out of your scope of practice, don't you? I could have your status revoked?"

"I ... do know that, yes." Ren could practically feel the discomfort of the coffee spilling on his lap; he was right back in her office again, stuttering under her scrutiny. Jeez, this woman.

"And you did it anyway. Why?" Ah, what the hell? He was already in trouble.

"Because I'm better at IVs than Grayson," he said simply, no trace of arrogance. "The cephalic vein was the best location, and I wanted to get the medication into his system via IV as soon as possible because an injection would take two hours to work and an IV would take twenty minutes. And I didn't want to wait until we got here because that seemed too long when it didn't have to be." He hung his head, wanting to disappear.

"Well, forgive me, but I'm surprised," Angelique finally said, truly sounding that way. Ren risked looking at her, seeing her standing with her hands on her hips, head tilted to one side, looking at him as if he had suddenly revealed a secret identity she'd never known about. "I didn't think you had it in you."

That stung, but Ren wasn't in a position to protest.

"And in a moving vehicle on icy roads, no less," she finished, very quietly.

Ren wasn't sure where to go with that. Did she sound impressed? At least she didn't sound mad. He thought it might be safe to change the subject.

"What's going to happen to Justin?" Ren asked, not really caring about anything else. He knew he'd done the right thing, maybe not the legal thing, but the right thing, and he could live with that.

"If he's lucky, his heart will start slowing to a normal pace in the next few minutes. If it doesn't, we'll have to use the manual defibrillator." Angelique answered his question as though speaking to a comrade, to an equal. Ren didn't know how, but it seemed she'd gained a new respect for him during their conversation. That didn't mean he liked her answer, though. The defibrillator was a last resort, the ultimate in turning it off and turning it back on again for human hearts. If Justin's heart couldn't return to a normal rhythm on its own, Angelique was planning on using an electric shock to stop it in its tracks with the idea that it would then correct.

"But he's awake," Ren whispered. *It'll hurt. It'll hurt so much.* Officer Geisler had made his way over to them, standing a respectful, but expectant distance away, as if waiting in line for his turn.

"He's awake now, but if we let him keep going like this for much longer, his heart is going to fail. You know that," Angelique went on. "I don't like it either, but if I have to choose, that's what we're going to do. So I suggest you get in there and calm him down."

Ren nodded, feeling the weight of responsibility for Justin being returned to him, wondering if that would have been the case if he'd somehow displeased Angelique with his explanation of the IV. He gripped the handle of the triage room door, intending on going in, but Officer Geisler spoke up behind him.

"Actually, I'd like a word with you first," he said, breaking into the conversation. Angelique lowered her mask specifically to scowl at him.

"Oh no," she snipped at Geisler. "You're going to have to wait, officer. You can have your say when our patient is out of danger and resting."

Geisler didn't look very happy about that, but there wasn't a whole lot he could do. He didn't have a warrant for the triage room. "Can I ask you some questions then?" he compromised.

"That's fine," Angelique agreed. "You go on now, Lorenzo. Go talk him down. I'll be there in a few minutes to check on your progress."

Never in his life did Ren believe he would be pulled out of a room for violating medical rules only to be later defended from the police and sent back in to continue. He would have never thought Angelique Delacroix would turn over a patient into his care. But he certainly wasn't going to question anything Dr. Delacroix said to him. And if she thought, even a little, that he might have a chance to help Justin escape defibrillation, then he was all for it. But what the hell was he supposed to do?

North looked serious when Ren returned to them. Both he and

Justin had their eyes closed, and North held onto Justin's hand, bowing over him in defeated pain, self-admonishment almost radiating from him. Ren checked the screen with Justin's numbers displayed on it. Oxygen up to ninety-four, which was considered just shy of normal. Heart rate still fluctuating between 160 and 170. Ren had no idea what he was going to do to help that, but he'd be damned if he allowed Justin to be put through any more trauma without thinking of something.

"Hey there, guys," he greeted softly. Justin opened his eyes at the sound of Ren's voice, and Ren put a hand on his head. "Miss me?"

"Where did you go?" Justin wheezed, just that tiny sentence dropping his oxygen to ninety again.

"Shh," Ren shook his head at him. "I was just outside with the doctor. You're in luck, Justin, she is *legendary*."

"She is?" North asked, as if he'd nominated himself to speak for Justin.

"Oh yeah," Ren assured, hoping to ease Justin's fear about being here, trying to lighten the weight on Justin's heart. "Highest survival percentage of any doctor in the state."

"You ... you're my doctor," Justin protested. Ren smiled bitterly.

"No, I'm not," he admitted, ashamed. "If I hadn't been pretending to be, you wouldn't be here right now, Justin. It wouldn't have come to this." Justin's heart performed a frightening little shudder; the reading on the screen looked like a dog shaking itself dry. Justin whimpered, eyes closing again. Ren needed to try harder. Five minutes was not long, and Justin was still terrified. Ren put a hand on Justin's chest. *Slow down.*

"What did she say?" North asked, gaze heavy on Ren. "The doctor. What's the plan?" *Oh no, don't ask me that,* Ren inwardly groaned. *I don't want to tell you; it won't help.* He pressed harder on Justin, searching for the feel of the heart under his hand. If only he could calm it, physically hold it still. If only he could match it to — wait a second.

"Synchronization," Ren heard himself say, remembering walking through his door to find Denny, Alek, and about five metronomes, all pulsing out of rhythm. Alek was so close Ren wondered how he wasn't getting knocked in the face by one of the pendulums, a stopwatch in his hand. "We're going to try synchronization." *You're going to what, Ren? You're saying this out loud, you idiot.*

"What's that?" North sounded unsure, and Ren didn't blame him. He was certainly winging it with this, but mostly he needed to give Justin something to do, something more physical and focused than lying there struggling to breathe, waiting on the invisible assistance of drugs. "A procedure?"

"Physics," Ren answered, looking only at Justin, noting that the glimmer of trust in his eyes had turned into something resembling blind faith. Though Ren wasn't sure how that could have happened when he'd done nothing to improve Justin's condition since the beginning. This would be his last chance. He did not want to watch him be shocked.

"Justin, we're going to make a closed circuit, your heart and mine. Where's your hand?" He took Justin's right hand and guided it upwards towards his chest, then rethought it at the last second and, extremely careful of the IV, helped Justin reach under his shirt for skin-to-skin contact. If there was even the slightest chance this would work, it would be better with as few barriers as possible. There was a tiny shriek from the monitor as Justin's heart spiked with the movement.

"Ren?" Justin asked as Ren pressed Justin's hand against his own heartbeat. North looked extremely skeptical but kept quiet.

"It's a calibration," Ren tried to explain, holding Justin's wrist to keep his hand fixed in place, easing himself delicately on the bed close to Justin, hip-to-hip. "Though I've never done it this way before." Ren slipped his right hand through Justin's gown sleeve, reaching through to where his heart would be. He couldn't believe he was going to try this.

"What are you trying to do?" North encouraged more explanation. Ren tried to think of how best to explain and have anyone take him seriously. First, he wondered what Denny would say, then dismissed that quickly as he realized he'd never get anyone to understand that way. He decided to be as forthright as possible. It wasn't like he had a lot to lose.

"If you place five metronomes next to each other on a table and set them off one after the other, all different speeds, they will continue to keep pace without ever changing. Shh, Justin, you just breathe now; trust me." Justin's fingers were curling against Ren's skin, as if he were trying to pull away. Ren held him securely.

"Ok," North accepted, sounding confused, but that's because Ren had only given him half the information.

"But if you take those same five metronomes, out of sync, and instead of setting them on a fixed table, you put them on, say, a skateboard, or something that will allow them to oscillate, within seconds every one of those metronomes will tick identically."

"And that applies to this situation how? I'm not following," North asked, not condescendingly. His voice had hope in it, as though he couldn't understand but he really wanted it to work. Ren was also hoping. It was such a long shot. Mostly he wanted to provide Justin with a distraction that sounded completely plausible. This could all be an elaborate mind game that worked a treat, or it could be a waste of time that broke all of Ren's credibility. Hard to tell at this point, but Ren just didn't have anything else.

"Let's say Justin's heart is one metronome, ticking fast, not keeping time the way it should," Ren laid his experiment out, grateful Denny wasn't here to tell him in excruciating detail how many ways he was messing this up. "And now I've put my steady, slower metronome heartbeat next to his. The position I've just set is what's known as a Josephson junction, which is two superconductors, our hearts, being joined by a weak coupling system, which would be the connection of our hands here, but will result in a joint supercurrent at the same pace due to the Kuramoto model of synchronization." Ren paused in his wild and possibly inaccurate description to glance at Justin's monitor. No change. And the only thing he could feel under his hand was Justin's labored breathing and fever heat. But they weren't moving yet. There needed to be some small movement, a rocking of some sort.

"Justin, if you have any energy left, try to move with me, ok?" Ren invited as North stood to the side, utterly transfixed. Ren began an awkward shifting, just barely, keeping Justin's hand in place, lowering his head to his chest to concentrate. "Pay attention to everything slowing down. It'll only work if we can move together."

But Justin absolutely could not move. Even with Ren's help, his hand was trembling against Ren's chest with the effort of partially holding his arm up. He'd started blinking fast again, his body worn out and on the verge of giving up. Ren felt defeated, sad, and completely out of ideas. What was he even doing? He wasn't even remotely sure he'd gotten the science right. Just because he'd seen it done in metronomes didn't mean anything in this situation. Ren slumped over Justin, feeling ridiculous for even suggesting this.

He was about to remove his hands and sit up, tell them to never mind, he had no idea what he was even talking about, when North scooted in close on Justin's other side, slipping his real arm around Justin's shoulders. He moved behind Justin, propping him up and letting him rest against his chest while he wrapped both arms around him, reaching forward. His prosthetic arm gripped Justin just above his elbow while Ren felt his organic hand close on his forearm above his wrist. Ren met his eyes. He still looked doubtful but determined too.

"Thanks," Ren told him, several layers of gratitude in one word. "Let's try rocking and see what happens. Justin, you just relax and breathe, ok? We've got you."

Ren had never felt so much like a quack. This was not medicine; this was supernatural nonsense. *No*, he tried to correct himself. It was science; he had seen this work himself. Just not with hearts. Still, there were worse things he could be doing with his five minutes. Justin was supported here in the hospital, with Ren in front of him, whispering assurances, and North behind him, holding him securely, all of them rocking together in a slow and steady rhythm, quiet, soft. If everything went horribly wrong, if the medicine failed and the defibrillator didn't work, at least in these few minutes, Justin would know North was here, holding him.

Ren felt his own chest tighten as he thought about that, feeling the coming helpless shaking that always happened to him after handling intense situations as he'd just done with Justin. If he wanted to keep it at bay, he'd have to keep moving. If he were to hold still, if things got too quiet while they waited, he was going to break down. And there was nowhere to hide right now if he did. He took another breath, trying to just focus on what he was doing, stay here in this moment with Justin and North. He needed to be Incident Commander in Charge for just a while longer.

"It's working," North whispered, and once he said it out loud, Ren could feel it. Justin's breaths had deepened, getting slower and more effective. His heart slowed and strengthened, to the point Ren could feel it throbbing under his palm. Inwardly, Ren shook his head. No way. There was no way this was working, but he knew better than to say anything dumb like that. It had been his idea, so he certainly wasn't going to admit he hadn't had any real faith in it. *It's not working, North*, he thought. *The medicine is working*. This was all a smoke and mirrors trick.

But there were lecturers who were keen on the placebo effect, on how powerful a tool the mind could be in things like this. Shifting Justin from a place of unfamiliar terror to being rocked in North's arms might have had something to do with the dropping heart rate, though Ren wouldn't be publishing a paper on the radical effects of the Josephson junction when used to synchronize heartbeats anytime soon.

"There you go," Ren congratulated softly, as if he'd planned the whole thing and been certain of its success. Justin's face smoothed into quiet exhausted relief. He leaned against North in perfect trust, as calm as Ren had ever seen him. It stirred up a warning flicker of something uncomfortable in Ren, so he turned his face away to look at Justin's numbers. So much better than when he'd come in. Justin's heart rate had slowed to a respectable ninety beats a minute, and his oxygen had come up to ninety-eight percent. Blood pressure an almost textbook 105 / 70.

"Much better." Ren heard Angelique behind him. He heard the relief in her cheery tone and realized how much she'd wanted the medication to work too. "Well done. I see you're all very cozy here, but can I get you two to back up?" Ren extracted his hand from Justin's sleeve and then helped him detach from under his shirt. Likewise, North eased Justin onto the pillows, reluctantly standing up.

"I won't be long," she apologized, setting her stethoscope into her ears. "Just need to listen to your heart, darling." Ren tried to stand and let her get close, but Justin had a tight grip on his sleeve. He had to use his other hand to gently pull him off so he could get out of Dr. Delacroix's way.

"I'm getting your blanket," he offered, relinquishing his place to Angelique. "I'm not going anywhere." *Believe me, I know how hard it is to be alone with this woman.* Meanwhile, North had seen Officer Geisler still standing in the hallway.

"Justin, I'll be right back," North promised, disappearing out the door to see what Geisler was still doing here. Ren hoped he'd tell the officer to get lost; there was no reason for him to still be hanging around. It should be pretty obvious at this point that Justin couldn't keep a court date in this condition. Ren picked up his quilt, the scent of the apartment rushing up to him as he moved it, a little piece of softness in this not soft space, and he draped it over Justin, pulling it to his waist protectively and waiting for Dr. Delacroix.

"Has anything like this ever happened to you before, sweetheart?" Angelique was asking Justin as Ren finished fussing with the blanket. Justin shook his head, unable to look at her despite her gentleness. Ren would have to tell him later how special it was that she was speaking to him so warmly. Maybe he'd even tell him about the coffee episode. Justin might think it was funny.

"Well, now we've gotten things under control, we can figure out what happened and why so it doesn't happen again," Angelique went on, her voice coaxing and careful. "I'd like to do some tests while you're here. I'm going to have someone come down with an EKG machine in a few minutes to measure your blood flow and heart patterns, and I'd like to leave you hooked up to it for a few hours to monitor how things are going. I'm going to take a blood sample from you, and we're going to keep administering fluids; you definitely need them."

"Dr. Delacroix?" Ren spoke before he had thought much about whether he should. "I already took a blood sample this morning. We, um, were thinking Justin's arrhythmia could be caused by anemia. It's already in the lab." Angelique looked at him over her shoulder, face mask covering her mouth, her eyes hard.

"Oh?" was the only thing she said, all the honey gone from her tone. Yeah, Ren might not have wanted to volunteer that information. But he didn't want Justin to have to do things twice either. The test results could already be available, which meant he could start getting an iron supplement sooner. "You're taking it upon yourself to do blood samples now? But how did you ... No, wait, it was Dr. Taneja, wasn't it?"

Ren hesitated. It was one thing to confess his own sins. He didn't want Dr. Taneja to get into trouble for helping him smuggle anonymous BSL II samples through diagnostics. His hesitancy quickly turned to confusion. How did she know it was Dr. Taneja?

"Oh, never mind," Angelique said, turning away. Ren wondered if she was only giving him three words now because she was saving them all for the disciplinary report that she was going to type up later. It wasn't necessarily illegal, what he and Dr. Taneja had done this morning. But Justin hadn't signed permission for anything, and he technically was no one's patient, so if something had happened and he'd wanted to, he could sue them for malpractice. "I'll see what I can find out from the lab then."

She stood up, pocketing her stethoscope. "I'll order the EKG machine." Then she looked at Ren again, and he couldn't read her expression. Exasperation? Amusement? "You and I need to have a talk later," she said threateningly. He nodded, submissive. "Stay with him, but for God's sake, don't touch anything. You understand me?"

Oh, yes, Ren understood. It wasn't for God's sake; it was for Ren's. He was on incredibly thin ice, and the only reason he was even allowed to stay in this room was because Justin obviously wanted him.

"Yes, ma'am," Ren acknowledged, frustrated, depleted, and slightly disoriented. Angelique sighed, as if she weren't sure she could leave him alone with Justin, but she was a busy woman, and now that Justin was out of immediate danger, she did have other things she needed to do. She shook her head, waving a hand at him dismissively, and went off to take care of other patients. Ren unconsciously slumped as she left, resting both hands on Justin's bed.

"Did I get you in trouble?" Justin asked hesitantly, and Ren could feel his gaze on him. He lifted his head to comfort him, seeing the worry in his eyes, emphasized by exhaustion.

"I got myself in trouble," Ren replied, smiling. "It's nothing you have to worry about."

"But ... why? What did you do wrong?" Justin wondered out loud, his voice so endearing that Ren paused before answering, pulling the blanket higher over Justin's chest. It was good he had enough breath again to talk, even if this was what he wanted to talk about.

"I didn't do anything wrong," Ren said, and he heard Alek snort in his memory because of the slipperiness of his answer. "Everything I've done was technically the correct thing to do; I'm just the wrong person to do it."

"But ... if you did the right thing?" Justin sounded confused, upset. There was a catch to his voice that Ren didn't like. "Why is it like that?"

"Calm down," Ren eased him, putting a hand on his arm, needing him to stay quiet and restful. Justin reacted by curling towards him and clinging again to his sleeve. "It's because I'm an

EMT. Just an EMT, I should say. And when this all started, I wasn't even on call. Technically, Dr. Taneja and I should have had you sign some paperwork before we took a blood sample, and Dr. Taneja should have taken it, not me. I wasn't supposed to let North carry you, and I really wasn't supposed to start your IV."

"But North cleared you. He said it was ok," Justin protested.

"That worked for Grayson," Ren explained. "But North isn't your legal guardian or medical power of attorney. Him saying it was ok didn't mean a thing."

"So what's going to happen?" Justin sounded anxious. Ren shifted so he could put one hand on his chest.

"I'm not sure," he answered honestly, keeping his tone light despite the severity of the words he was using. "Maybe nothing? I think the worst that could happen is getting sued for malpractice, stripped of my EMT credentials, kicked out of the med program, and sent back home." Justin clung to him tighter, alarmed.

"Sued? They can sue you?" he asked.

"No," Ren smiled again, leaning closer. "But you can. If that's something you wanted to do?"

"God, no."

"Looks like I'm safe," Ren responded, though he didn't feel it. Dr. Delacroix could still do plenty to hurt his career. He very well could leave this hospital without his volunteer EMT card if she wanted that to happen.

"How about you?" Ren changed the subject, smoothing invisible wrinkles in the quilt to soothe the tremor he felt starting in his hands. Not yet. Dr. Delacroix would be back soon; North and Officer Geisler were still talking out in the hall. Justin was awake and needed him. He couldn't fall to pieces yet. "How are you doing? Is it easier to breathe?"

"Yeah." In fact, if Dr. Delacroix hadn't specifically told him not to touch anything, Ren likely would have fiddled with the oxygen flow. Justin probably didn't need it up so high anymore. Instead, Ren shifted the blanket, his fingers lingering over some of the fabric patches. His mother had made it using scraps of clothes, old favorites from Ren's childhood. There was a piece of soft cotton from a pair of pajamas he'd loved, the last remaining corner of his baby blanket, the logo of a T-shirt, several sections from his father's old work shirts. A piece of faded flowery print that had been his mother's best Sunday dress. Each snippet a memory, each stitch a tie to his family. *Keep it together.*

"Ren?" Justin called him, very softly.

"What is it, Justin? You all right?"

"I'm so tired."

"Well, your heart just ran its own private marathon, you know."

"I don't think I can stay awake." He did sound tired, but comfortable — the pain medication easing him down. "Is it ok if I ..."

"You can sleep now," Ren gave him permission, knowing Justin probably would have drifted off a long time ago if it hadn't been for Ren specifically asking him not to in the ambulance. "It's all right."

"If I do," Justin hesitated, and Ren watched his brow crease. "Will I wake up again?" *No, really?* Now Ren put both hands on either side of Justin's face, forcing them not to tremble.

"Of course," he assured quickly, shocked and sad that Justin had even worried about that. Ren wished he could tell him it hadn't been that bad, but it absolutely had been. "Your numbers are good; you're safe now. Jeez, you poor thing. I'm sorry." Ren knew Justin had been scared, terrified even, but for some reason he hadn't thought about that. He touched his forehead against Justin's, wanting to be closer but not sure how to manage it.

"Rest," Ren encouraged. "I'll be here."

"Did North leave?" Justin asked sleepily.

"No, he's outside talking to someone. He'll be back soon." *And there is no way I'm letting him go anywhere while you're sleeping,* Ren promised silently.

"Talking to who?" Justin murmured, but Ren didn't want to remind him about the policeman. Didn't know if he'd even seen him there in the apartment, his entire focus had been on North. Ren didn't want to tell him about Monday, or the court summons. He didn't want to think about that now, and he didn't want Justin to think about it either.

"I can't see from here," Ren half-lied. It was true he couldn't see Officer Geisler from this angle, but he knew he was out there, waiting. Outside this room, the world was still moving. The snow was still falling. The sun was going down. "Quiet, now. Rest your heart. It's going to be ok."

Justin's eyes were already closed, his chest rising and falling slower and slower. Ren straightened, watching him sleep, feeling uneasy. His hand shook when he reached out to smooth the blanket one more time; something else that was coming for him whether he wanted it to or not.

"It's going to be ok," he repeated to himself as the shivery feeling traveled up his arms and into his chest, all the panic from the afternoon that had gathered quietly in the back of his mind, waiting almost politely for him to finish his duties as an efficient responder, catching up to him now in the stillness. Ren grabbed on to the blanket with both hands, feeling lightheaded all of a sudden, too warm. *Damn it.* His knees were shaking now along with his hands and shoulders, so he went ahead and knelt on the floor, his fists above him, clinging to the blanket, to his family, to Justin.

"It's ok," he told himself firmly. *Everything's fine. Justin's sleeping peacefully.* Ren let go with one hand so he could cover his mouth. He didn't want to make any noise here, but he was quickly losing control over things like that. The sob came out in a weird sort of wheeze, followed immediately by another, desperate little wails of anguish from a tragedy that hadn't even happened. He heard himself gasp, choking on his own attempts to be quiet, knowing he was lying to himself.

Nothing was ok.

12

AFTERSHOCK

Ren felt battered, helpless in an emotional hurricane, where his only safety was the hand he kept gripped to the quilt. He knelt on the triage room floor reliving in graphic detail how Justin had collapsed in his apartment and every hideous moment after. He watched the scenarios play out, each a clear traumatizing version of all that could have gone wrong at every critical point. Ren tightened and chastised himself for every poor decision he'd made regarding Justin, every risk he'd taken, every moment he could have done better. How basically everything he'd done since he'd slammed his textbook next to Justin's head yesterday morning had been a mistake.

And now he couldn't stop shaking in the aftermath, powerless and paralyzed by images that hadn't happened. Oh, but they could have. The difference between the reality and the what if was as thin and fragile as a butterfly wing, the quickness of a single heartbeat, and the realization made Ren tremble through all his limbs. He couldn't even lift his head. It went on much longer than before. Ren was usually shaky for a while after certain emergency calls as his body managed the remnants of extra adrenaline, but not like this.

Because damn it, Justin. Ren cared about him, despite everything, more than he should, and it was creating additional stress in an already stressful situation. It wasn't just the adrenaline making him shake this time; Ren had been *terrified*. He was still terrified. It might be the first time it struck him so hard that he literally held someone's life in his hands. And not just anyone's life — Justin's. Ren didn't hear the door to the triage room open over his own shuddering, horrified breathing.

"Lorenzo? Fritz would like to — *what happened?*" North's question startled him, crashed him back into reality. He cowered, embarrassed and frightened by the alarm in North's tone. "What's wrong? Justin!" North's footsteps rushed to the bedside. Ren was too far down to see anything, but he could feel North's shadow.

Ren did his best to pull himself together. Understanding that his position was giving North the wrong impression about Justin's condition, he forced his trembling body up, hunching over the bed, his head still hanging down to hide his face. He hadn't meant for anyone to find him on the floor.

"Quiet," Ren cautioned, more clearing his throat than requesting silence. He put his hand on Justin's chest. North's sudden attention and raised voice was causing him to stir in his sleep. "It's all right," Ren assured all of them at once. Then he tried to make eye contact with North, not quite managing it. "He's sleeping," Ren explained, his tone pitched low, even his words trembling. "He's going to be fine." He spoke quietly, his voice ruined, eyeing the patch on his quilt made from his mother's dress.

"Then what were ... oh, I see," North stood straight, realization and tender relief in his voice. Ren hunched lower, ashamed. He normally did this in private, hiding until his hands steadied, until he could wash his face and present himself to the world as though nothing had phased him. He felt weak and exposed standing here with North staring at him. Pathetic. "I was wondering when it was going to catch up to you."

"What?" Ren asked, hating how his voice sounded.

"You look like you're having a panic attack. Come on, come over here and sit down." North spoke carefully, gently, walking around the bed surprisingly lightly for such a large man, placing a hand on Ren's shoulder to guide him to the chair near the door. His soft touch did not help; it almost buckled Ren's knees. "It's all right," North assured, but it just made Ren feel worse. They should be focused on Justin right now, not him. There was nothing wrong with *him*; he was just being dramatic and weird. This wasn't panic; it wasn't even close. Wasn't that bad.

"I'm fine," Ren protested, pressing his shaking hands tight under his arms. He clamped his teeth shut before he said anything else. If only North had waited one more minute to come in.

"You're not fine; you're amazing," North said emphatically. "But trauma needs to be processed at some point. Sit down now. Can I get you some water?"

Ren shook his head as North physically turned him around and pressed him gently into the chair. He didn't want anything except for his body to obey him again. He scrubbed his sleeve across his face in an attempt to wipe it dry, aggravating his bruise, deliberately not looking at North. When *was* this going to stop?

"Hey, Elias," Geisler's voice from the partially open doorway. Ren didn't look at him either. "Everything all right in here? I thought you were sending Lorenzo out? I need to get going."

"A couple more minutes, Fritz," North answered, standing directly in front of Ren, staring down at him. "He's —"

"No, it's ok," Ren said, jumping up, more than willing to focus on literally anything else. "Stay here with Justin. I'll go."

Before anyone could say anything to him, Ren ripped the door all the way open and slipped past the police officer, forcing him to back up awkwardly fast. Ren kept his arms crossed, hoping to hide the ridiculous shivering if he kept all his muscles clenched tight. Hopefully, this wouldn't take very long. He leaned against the door as he closed it, keeping his eyes carefully on the tile, noticing how the overhead lights reflected off it, each scuff from shoes and wheels.

And he waited for Geisler to yell at him. It couldn't be any worse than what he was already telling himself.

"You all right, boy?" Geisler asked him, and he nodded in painful exaggeration. *Yes, now please get on with it. Don't look at me anymore.* Geisler sighed, and Ren watched him shift his weight, staring at his boots.

"How much trouble am I in?" Ren blurted, not able to wait any longer.

"Trouble?" Geisler repeated, surprised but Ren didn't know if that was from what he'd said or how he'd said it. "Probably a lot, but nothing on my end."

"Huh?" Ren asked, the second time he'd been confused in less than five minutes.

"I understand why you did what you did," Geisler said, words Ren never thought he'd hear from him. "You knew he was sick and wanted to protect him, but it would have been better to just say so when I asked you the first time. I'm not that much of a jerk. I would have listened to what you had to say, and we would have taken care of him."

"I'm sorry," Ren apologized quietly, sheepish. That seemed so obvious to him now. "What's going to happen to him?"

Geisler sighed again. "That's up to the jury," he dismissed. "They may have to postpone for a while due to all this, but he will still have to appear in court for the verdict and possible sentencing."

"But —" Ren began, but Officer Geisler held out a hand to stop him.

"Listen," Geisler quipped. "You're an incredible young man. I've never seen anyone out of uniform do what you just did. You're going somewhere. And that's why if you're as smart as I think you are, you'll go home now and let Elias deal with this. Justin will have to answer for the crimes he's committed. That's nothing you can protect him from, and you'll only hurt yourself if you keep trying. Take my advice and stay away from him. He's trouble."

Ren leaned hard on the door, tired and weak, even his soul felt shaken. Denny had said basically the same thing. And the words sounded true if he were looking at the case file. His growing loyalty to Justin made him do things like break medical protocol and lie to police officers. But there was what looked right on paper and what *felt* right inside him. Abandoning Justin now, even leaving him with North, was wrong, and he didn't think he could live with himself if he did that. No matter what it cost him.

He covered his mouth with his hand again, thinking about the consequences waiting for Justin. The hospital might delay his sentence, but it wasn't going to go away. Justin had still killed someone, beaten someone to death according to Denny. Maybe it really would be better to go home. Maybe Ren wasn't thinking about this clearly. Maybe he'd confused his feelings. But how could Justin be a murderer? He just didn't seem ... but then again, Ren didn't know him, did he? He had no idea what Justin was like when he was well and functioning. He could be every bit as dangerous as Denny tried to tell him.

His chest hurt, filling with repressed anguish, and the shaking intensified again. Without meaning to, Ren tilted against the wall, hunched over, overwhelmed, and so tired. Why was this taking so much out of him? *Just get up, Ren. Go home. Do the smart thing for once.*

"Hey," Officer Geisler exclaimed, surprised to watch Ren crumple in front of him. "What's the matter with you? It's not the end of the world. Come on." He hovered over Ren, putting a hand on his back, putting pressure on the almost forgotten scrape from the coffee table. Ren cringed away from him, hearing himself make a wounded yelp of pain, wondering if this could possibly get any worse.

"Kid," Geisler started impatiently, and Ren couldn't blame him, but then something changed in him suddenly. Ren had his eyes closed, but he felt Geisler pause next to him, then felt him back up. "I'm going to find that doctor," Geisler offered, and Ren heard his boots marching away. It took several more seconds for his words to connect into meaning in Ren's head. He was bringing Angelique over here.

That actually would be worse.

Shaky, miserable, and weighted, Ren forced himself upright using the doorknob and the wall. No matter what, he could not let her find him out here in the hall like this. His hands were shaking so hard now he could barely let himself in Justin's room. *Stop*, he commanded them. *Stop doing that; it's getting weird.* But it was like Geisler had touched every exposed nerve in his body, and now they were all tingling and firing at once.

"Lorenzo!" North whisper-shouted as he staggered through the doorway and dropped onto the chair. "Jeez, look at you. It's ... you're getting worse. What happened? Fritz promised he'd go easy on you."

"He ... I'm sorry," Ren managed. "I can't stop."

"Take your time," North invited, but Ren didn't want to. He wanted to stand up, go to Justin, wanted to ask him so many questions. "Is there anything I can do?" North also put a hand on Ren's back, beginning to rub it in comfort. Except it hurt, so Ren cringed away.

"Please don't," he begged, shuddering. *Don't touch me. Don't look at me. I don't want to be here; I don't want to think.*

"You're just like Justin," North muttered, frustrated, but then he too paused. He shifted the hand from Ren's back to his shoulder, taking another step closer to him. What was he doing? Ren felt his shirt lift away from his back, felt it unstick in tiny painful tears from his skin as North plucked at it. He twitched in irritation under North's hands. "Oh, that's right," North continued talking to himself. "You crashed into that table, didn't you?" Since he didn't really seem to be talking to him, Ren felt it safe not to try and answer. He wished everyone would just leave him alone, yet his wish remained unfulfilled as Angelique arrived followed by Officer Geisler. Perfect.

"Lorenzo, what's going on?" Dr. Delacroix demanded, sounding annoyed that she'd been pulled away from whatever she'd been doing. Ren wanted to tell her it wasn't his idea for her to come. She didn't have to stay on his account. "Oh," he heard her exhale, stopping short as soon as she saw him.

"He hurt himself on a table corner," North offered when Ren couldn't speak. "Looks pretty scraped up, but I'm not sure about the shaking. Panic attack, do you think?"

"No," Angelique said, a sting of disappointment in her tone. "That's not what this is." She sounded disgusted, and Ren knew exactly why. He was disgusted with himself too. "Lorenzo, get up. Come with me."

The firm command soothed Ren slightly. At least someone was in control here, solid on what should be done. She also sounded like she knew what was happening to Ren. She might know how he could make it stop. He obediently got to his feet, ready to follow her without question.

"Where are you taking him?" North asked, sounding unsure as to what his role should be regarding Ren.

"My office," Angelique quipped, her strong fingers circling Ren's arm to direct him in front of her, stilling Ren's spirit despite her ferocity. "We have a lot to talk about." Oh, they were going to do that now. Ren had no idea why, but he was secretly relieved. She was taking him to her office where she would sit him down and hopefully rip him to pieces. He knew he deserved it. Having it over would be such a release. When she started walking, he docilely allowed her to lead him.

"Now wait a minute." Officer Geisler blocked the doorway, starting a power struggle. Ren admired his courage, but his bets were on Angelique. "Son, you want me to go with you?" Angelique arched an eyebrow, somehow making such a tiny gesture the elegant equivalent of spitting in his face. Her fingers dug deeper into Ren's arm. Ren didn't dare say a word.

"I don't think a police escort will be necessary, officer," she told him impatiently.

"I disagree. You've been nothing but vicious to him since he got here," Geisler challenged, and Ren suddenly took back most of what he'd thought about him. "If I were in his place, I wouldn't go anywhere with you without a witness. Why can't you take a look at him right here?"

"Lorenzo, you want all these people staring at you with your shirt off or do you want to come with me?" Angelique smoothly asked, never taking her eyes from Geisler in an extreme alpha contest. Ren didn't want either option.

"You," he almost whispered to the floor, deciding to just get it over with.

"Excuse us," Angelique followed, triumphant, and Geisler reluctantly stepped aside to let them pass. Ren lifted his eyes only enough to keep a final image of the room in his mind. Geisler and North, standing near the door looking out of place. North especially looked torn between guarding Justin and Ren, and Ren felt grateful knowing North had decided, consciously or not, to include Ren as someone worthy of guarding. Meanwhile, Officer Geisler glared at Angelique, his expression shifting subtly between admiration and anger. Ren felt oddly grateful to him too.

Ren then looked beyond them, to where Justin slept unaware. Ren found that moderately satisfying. If something happened in the next few minutes that shut him outside the hospital, unwelcome to return, he thought he could accept that he'd done all he could. North was there now. Justin wouldn't need him anymore. The door closed behind them.

Angelique kept her hand on Ren's arm, pushing or pulling him appropriately as she guided him through the emergency department corridors and onward to her own office. Her fingers lightened in pressure as they went, and by the time they reached her door, she was hardly touching him at all.

"Sit down," she ordered almost before Ren was past the threshold. "Let me see your hands." She kept an efficient clip in her voice, not exactly sharp, but definitely not tender. Ren was glad about that. If she'd been too nice to him, called him any of the pet names she'd used with Justin, he'd probably lose the tenuous control he was currently clinging to. It was easier to just do what she said, not think too hard or too long about any one thing. He sat in the same place as when he'd visited her months ago, holding his trembling hands out for her inspection as he looked around her office. It hadn't changed.

There were several cardboard boxes stacked randomly about the space, haphazardly full of manila files. She had pictures on her desk, her doctorate degree hanging as expected behind her chair. It looked comfortingly like almost every doctor's office Ren had ever been in, though he was surprised to see the coffee cup he'd brought her still on the desk, his name written on the side of it bearing testament that it was indeed the same one. Why was she keeping that?

She focused his attention by taking hold of his outstretched hands, squeezing them in her own as if trying to still them. She'd removed her mask and gloves while he'd been staring around and now stood in front of him, the definition of authority and powerful grace. Ren didn't know how it was possible to be so full of fear and reverence, but that's exactly what he felt.

"How often does this happen?" she asked him, jerking her chin toward their hands. He wasn't sure how to answer her. There wasn't an exact system to it. He hadn't taken notes on himself, and he couldn't always predict when it would strike. "Is it every time?"

"Every time what?" he asked, unclear what she wanted. Every time he set an IV? No, he did that fifty times a shift at the donation center, to the point where he sometimes caught himself not paying as much attention as he should. After every ambulance run? Again no. There just wasn't a clear pattern. She rolled her eyes to her ceiling, dropping his hands.

"What do you think?" she snapped, and he flinched. She tilted her head at his reaction, backing off and visibly gentling herself before going on, her patience spread thin in her voice. "But it's happened before?" He nodded. "Often?" That made him shrug. He didn't know what either of them considered often, and he was growing afraid of giving any answer as her frustration with him increased.

"Ugh, you're such a *mess*, Lorenzo, honestly. Here, make yourself useful." She unceremoniously picked up a coffee mug full of pencils and thumped it on the desk in front of him. He almost asked her what he was supposed to do when he spotted the electronic sharpener near his elbow. She wanted him to sharpen pencils? Ok. Whatever. He selected a plain yellow one first, struggling with the trembling in order to connect the tip with the tiny hole in the sharpener, leaving gray smudges around the edge.

"Does it always last this long?" Angelique tried a different question, thankfully one he did know the answer to.

"No," he replied, listening to her carefully over the grinding of the sharpener but keeping his gaze fixed on the pencils, weary through to his soul. "It's never gone on this long."

"And what do you normally do to handle it? Does Dr. Taneja know?"

"I don't," Ren stammered, never believing he'd ever have to talk about this and not sure how to start now. "No, he doesn't. I don't let anyone ... Dr. Delacroix, do you know why I'm like this? What's wrong with me?"

"Who said that? What makes you think anything's wrong with you?" Angelique's questions came out like gunfire, sharp and hard. Ren felt tears sting his eyes. There had to be something wrong.

Dr. Delacroix sighed dramatically, snatching a box of tissues from under what looked like an oatmeal-colored cardigan and handing them to Ren. "Here," she said, gentler. "Lorenzo, you're going to have to figure this out."

He nodded. He knew that. He'd been trying. Nothing he did seemed to make any difference.

"It'll be a goddamn shame to lose you," she finished, almost too quiet for him to hear, making him pause.

"What?" he checked. Lose him how?

"Keep working," she changed direction again. "You think those pencils are going to sharpen themselves?" Ren jerked at the abrupt switch in her tone and topic. He did not know how to have a functional conversation with this woman.

"It's not common," Angelique continued to talk, though they weren't looking at each other. She was leaning against her filing cabinet, arms crossed. "People like you." Like him? There were other people who went through this? Doctors? How did they control it? "Have you gone over the methods of processing trauma in your classes yet?"

"No," he told her, watching her intently now, as if she held the key to his future. She pointed to the pencil mug again, reminding him he hadn't finished his assignment. He absently picked another from the group, hardly looking at the sharpener anymore.

"When you experience an incident," she began once he'd started working again. "Something that requires you to think on your feet with intense physical and mental focus, most people's minds force them to process everything at once, which overwhelms them to the point where they mess up, slow down, or freeze completely. In some ways, that's protective, and it's healthiest as you can deal with each situation as a whole. I admit, I thought you were like this when I had you in here before; you were so nervous you couldn't keep your hands still enough to hold a cup of coffee." She paused, studying him.

"Seems I was wrong," she admitted. "There's no way a person with that processing style could have threaded that IV like you did, especially in the back of an ambulance. But the extreme reaction you're having to that means you're processing outside of the incident. You can separate experiences as they come at you, dealing with them compartmentally and at different times. It lets you perform astonishingly well in the moment, but then afterward you have to handle the stress repercussions. I imagine it's like having dissociative identity disorder."

Ren jerked his head up from the pencil he'd just replaced into the mug. Yes, that was it! That was exactly it. There was the Incident Commander in Charge, and then there was just Ren.

"You know what this type of processing is good for?" Angelique asked. Ren didn't even try to come up with an answer. He chose another pencil.

"People who process this way make excellent surgeons," she continued. "Also they do well in the chaos of emergency rooms. You'll see a lot of them in the military because they work so well under incredible pressure, but Lorenzo, listen carefully now. It's important. You have to come up with some method of handling the aftershock. Since you're processing it outside of the experience, your mind can't figure a clear stopping point. Without one, you'll keep going over it, your system will continue producing cortisol and adrenaline in excess. That's what makes you so shaky, but it does other damage over prolonged periods. This is a cycle that will start building one experience over the other until it crushes you."

"Like burnout?" Ren asked innocently, tuned in to every word Dr. Delacroix said. He'd never heard his own feelings explained to him so clearly before. Never had it make so much sense.

"Like suicide," she corrected, her voice cold, and he recoiled from her. She'd had it correct until this point. That was something he was certain he'd never do.

"Well," Ren stuttered. "That's not ... I'm not going to ... I would never." She pushed away from the cabinet, disturbingly quickly, suddenly inches away from him, slamming her hands on her desk, leaning down to stare fiercely into his face.

"Shut your mouth. That's the easiest thing to say right now; you're just starting out. I'm not talking about a gun-in-your-mouth kind of suicide. I'm talking about drinking too much after work, taking prescribed medications for too long without cause. The slowest most painful kind. You'll be able to chip away at yourself for years because when you're in the moment no one will even be able to tell. You can't sit there and tell me you know it won't happen to you. Not a single person who has done it, or come close to it, thinks that's how it will go for them. But it is a *pattern*, and you are falling right into it. Dr. Taneja isn't doing you any favors either, pushing you faster than your classes can keep up, trying to get you cleared for life flight service. It's nonsense. What are you? Second year of pre-med?"

"Yes," Ren replied, completely rattled, surprised she even knew that.

"You shouldn't be doing what you're doing. You shouldn't even know how. I don't care how good you are at it; you're going too fast and too far without building the proper coping mechanisms for dealing with it, and it's going to break you."

Ren swallowed hard, intimidated by how passionate she had become, how forcefully she was trying to make him understand. Why did she care so much? But even if she were right, about some of it, definitely not all of it, how could he stop now? The people he'd helped. What would they have done if he hadn't rushed his learning?

"But what about Justin," he protested, not knowing how he found the strength to contradict her except he felt he had to make this one point for himself. "He could have died if I hadn't gone ahead in my training."

"No, you would have brought him to the hospital sooner like a *sensible pre-med student*, and he could have received treatment before he got critical. I'm disappointed in Dr. Taneja; if he examined him this morning, he should have known to bring him in. The responsibility for that should have never been yours."

Ren curled up at her words, how she'd so quickly and firmly put him in his place. She was right, and he'd known that before she'd told him. He'd had red flags almost from the start.

"So what do I do?" he asked, hoping she wouldn't tell him to quit medicine.

"How are those pencils coming?" she returned, frustrating and confusing him simultaneously. What the hell was with the pencils? He needed some guidance here. He picked up the mug, tilting it toward her so she could see that every single one now had a sharp point, unlike her lecture. "And your hands?" Again, he humored her, hoping if he did they could get back to answering his question.

Setting the mug carefully on top of a pile of notes, he spread his hands so she could see them, though he ended up studying them more than she did, amazed at the change. She smiled in self-satisfaction, watching him as he turned them over incredulously. The tremor had stopped. He was back to normal; at least where the steadiness of his hands was concerned.

"I suggest you learn to knit," she told him. He shifted his gaze from his hands to her face. Learn to what? "Or some other small, repetitive, portable task. I like knitting since it produces theta brain-waves, has distinct start and stop points to anchor your mind to, and if you get good at it, you'll have a coping mechanism and clothes all in one." Ren let out a breath, feeling as though he'd just staggered off a wildly spinning carnival ride. Knitting? Really? Though she seemed to be correct about that too. Sharpening pencils was also a mindless, repetitive task, and that had obviously worked.

"I also strongly suggest you slow down," she went on, taking his hands in hers to return his attention to what she was saying. "You're so young. You have a very promising career ahead of you. There's no need to rush it. There's also no need to ruin it." Her voice gained volume and speed, shifting topics again before he'd had a chance to wrap his mind around the last one, before he'd finished being aston-ished how she'd worked such an effortless miracle with his hands. Something he'd been struggling with for years.

"Obviously, you can't unlearn what you already know," she admitted. "But I am going to insist that you stick only to procedures you are cleared for. You're allowed to cannulate donors at the plasma center during your regular shifts and *nowhere else.*"

"So, you're not going to revoke my EMT credentials?" Ren hesi-tated to ask, but he wanted to be clear.

"I should, but no, I'm not," she replied reluctantly. "You should be focusing solely on your classes right now, but you are very talented, Lorenzo, and the program is better because you're in it. Your skills have been crucial in saving lives, including your friend's today, but unless you get yourself balanced, you won't be an asset to anyone for very long. Do you understand me?"

"Yes," Ren agreed, though he was internally resisting it. Despite her heavy warning, he was still certain he'd never take anything that far.

"All right, now let's take a look at your back."

"It's superficial," Ren dismissed, feeling lighter after their strange, scary, and yet somehow productive conversation. Despite the confusion, he felt better. More resolved and focused. "I'm fine. We can go back so you can do your real job."

"My shift ended half an hour ago," Angelique informed him, surprising him yet again. Ren felt humbled; he hadn't known she thought him worth so much effort. "Now take off your shirt, please."

Ren didn't want to; he'd already taken enough of her time, but there was never a point in trying to do anything but what Dr. Delacroix told him, so he pulled his shirt over his head, exposing his damaged back.

"Oh, honey," Angelique breathed at once, and Ren realized he was now, without a doubt, no longer a student to her. He'd become in that one instant a patient, and he thought he was ok with it now. "That's more than superficial. How did it happen? Something about a table?"

While Angelique gathered supplies from the bottom drawer of a cabinet, Ren told her about Justin collapsing. How Ren tried to catch him but fell onto the coffee table. He winced as she started cleaning, blinking curiously at the small pile of antiseptic wipes she dropped into the waste basket at the side of her desk.

"There's some deep bruising here," Dr. Delacroix told him as she worked. "It's going to be tender for a few days, but the bleeding's all done if you're careful. The abrasion goes almost the entire length of your back. Have someone help you put antibiotic ointment on it twice a day to keep it from getting infected. What about this one? What'd you do here?" Angelique sat him up straight and lightly touched an unnoticed bruise on his chest, the place where Justin had flung his textbook at him. "And here?" She brushed the back of her hand against his cheek. Ren looked down at the desk and the pencil mug, replacing his shirt, wishing he could hide all his wounds inside the fabric. He already knew how those injuries would be taken out of context, and he wasn't sure how to explain them. Unfortunately, Angelique had the same training he did and picked up on his hesitation.

"Who hit you, Lorenzo?" she demanded.

"Justin," Ren heard himself confess. Somehow, this tiger of a woman was going to demand all his secrets before letting him go. And somehow, he was ok with that. "And I know what it looks like, but it really was my fault."

He watched her struggle to keep her face neutral, trying not to judge without his explanation. "I'm listening."

She meant it, and because she was so still, focused on his every word, he found himself telling her more than he'd intended. He spoke of the English assignment, the textbook, the punch to his face, and then following Justin home to his apartment. He told her how empty it was, how broken Justin was, went into perhaps too much detail about how hard Justin could stare at a mug of soup. And he acknowledged how it all looked wrong, and that he'd been warned to stay away from Justin by several people, but he just … couldn't.

He hadn't noticed he was crying again until he felt Angelique dab his face with a tissue. He hadn't noticed she was holding his hand again. He hadn't known his emotions were so twisted up around Justin, this boy he had only just met, until he began verbally untwisting them out loud to Dr. Delacroix of all people.

"I should go home, shouldn't I?" Ren sniffled as he finished, hoping she had a clear answer to this problem the way she had for everything else. She smiled, shaking her head.

"Now what's the point of asking me a question like that when you've already made a decision? You don't want me to tell you what you should do. You want me to confirm that the choice you want to make is the right one."

Ren tilted his head toward her, annoyed by her perception. She was right. Again. But so what?

"But I can't do that; I don't know what the right choice is," Angelique confessed, though by this point Ren expected no less. It hadn't been fair to ask her. This was his problem.

"I need to head home," Angelique said, standing and gathering her coat from the back of her desk chair. *Wait,* Ren wanted to say. *You can't leave yet. I still don't know what to do.* "My next shift starts tomorrow morning at eight, and I'll see how Justin's night went."

"You're admitting him?" Ren asked.

"Not yet. I need to see the data from the EKG before deciding how long he needs to stay."

"So he's going to be stuck in triage all night?" Ren checked. The emergency room turned into a surreal place after nightfall. It was never perfectly quiet, but the stillness it did have possessed a physical weight. Haunted and strange. Ren didn't like the idea of Justin being trapped there overnight. It was creepy.

"I don't have much choice. It's hospital policy, but I think it'd be good to have a friend stay with him," Angelique gently suggested, pulling a purse from her desk drawer, fishing in it for keys. "Maybe you two can talk tonight. I think there are some answers you're looking for that only he could give you. Maybe you should think about asking him instead of asking me."

"Dr. Delacroix?"

"See you tomorrow, Lorenzo," she said, shifting into the hallway and heading toward the parking structure. He would go the opposite direction, back to the emergency room. She was gone before he could thank her.

Ren didn't have a good grasp on how long he'd been gone; it felt like a very long time, but the only change in the room since he'd left it was Officer Geisler was nowhere to be seen. North had stayed. He stood guard over Justin's bed, his back perfectly straight, head reverently lowered, eyes fixed on Justin's sleeping face. His hand held tightly to Justin's; his fingers closed as if he were afraid Justin could disappear at any moment. He looked as though he could maintain that position for eternity, his face a mask of duty and devotion.

The scene felt so special and closed that Ren hesitated at the door. They were finally together; he shouldn't intrude. Angelique said Justin should have a friend with him, but Ren didn't think it mattered too much which one. In fact, Justin would probably prefer North. They had a longer history and more to discuss. Maybe he should give them some more time. Ren turned to go, but his movement across the glass windows must have caught North's attention because he hadn't made it very far before North called him back.

"Lorenzo, there you are."

Ren paused, turning awkwardly to see North beckoning him from the doorway.

"I was getting worried," North told him, opening the door wider to let him in. Ren paused. Why would North be worried about him? "Are you feeling better?"

"I'm fine," Ren murmured dismissively. "How's Justin?"

"I think you'd know better than I would. He's been asleep since you left, but he's been talking. He's asked for you a few times."

"He did?" Ren couldn't believe it. "That's strange."

"Oh, he's always been like that. Ever since I've known him," North responded, misunderstanding what Ren meant.

"No, I know," Ren clarified. "It's just, last night he was asking for you."

North stared at him, looking touched, remorseful, and hurt. Ren wondered if telling him had been a good idea. They stood looking at each other, North just inside the room and Ren just outside of it, held together by Justin.

"Did you need to leave?" North asked, noticing how Ren wasn't coming inside. *Yes*, Ren thought. *While I still can.* Except he already knew he wouldn't. "Can you stay for a while?"

"Sure," Ren heard himself agree, no longer able to fight the invitation, the insistent pull he felt coming from where Justin was sleeping. It may be another poor decision, but what was one more added to his already impressive list? Justin had asked for him.

"Where's the doctor?" North kept on with the questions as Ren woodenly submitted to a long night in triage.

"She went home; her shift's over," Ren answered, glad these were still easy questions. He couldn't imagine what else North might want to know. The things Ren wanted to ask himself. "She'll be back tomorrow to read Justin's data and see what to do." As he spoke, he noticed the bulk of the EKG machine resting on a cart pushed close to Justin and the growing printout detailing how effectively Justin's heart was delivering oxygen-rich blood to his body. Ren had no idea how to read it.

"Justin has to stay here until then?" North asked, surprised. Ren doubted he'd ever hung out in triage like this before if that shocked him. Once a patient was stable, it could often take hours to decide what to do with them. Sometimes, they could almost be forgotten in the wake of incoming emergencies.

"That's what Dr. Delacroix said," Ren replied, shrugging. "He might need to stay longer depending on his condition." Most patients who had heart episodes like Justin's were kept for at least three days, with regular doses of medication to keep their hearts beating regularly and a steady monitoring of how it was performing. Ren was more surprised that Justin hadn't been admitted already than that he would be staying at all.

"Ren?" Justin twisted on the bed, as if trying to turn toward the sound of Ren's voice. His hand lifted weakly, searching for him, and Ren was powerless not to go to him. When he got close, he saw that he wasn't awake. He'd been talking in his sleep just as North said. Ren took his hand anyway, watching as North returned to his position on Justin's other side.

"I'm right here," Ren assured in a voice little more than a whisper. "*Duerma.*"

He felt North studying him curiously, felt the pressure of question as heavy as the snow-laden clouds outside. With Justin between them, Ren raised his eyes to meet North's.

"Can I ask you something?" North began at the same time Ren said, "I have so many questions."

13
QUID PRO QUO

"I don't know if I can answer everything," North gave the caveat before Ren figured out what he even wanted to ask.

"It's none of my business, really," Ren acknowledged, still pinned awkwardly to Justin's side. He held Justin's hand, noticing that Justin had curled toward Ren on the hospital bed, as close as he could without falling off.

"I think all the things I want to know fall into that category too," North admitted. "How about this? No restrictions on questions asked, but we both reserve the right not to answer. Deal?"

"Deal," Ren accepted readily, liking North more by the minute, though Ren was still confused why Justin hadn't wanted to contact him. North seemed so friendly, and Justin obviously loved and trusted him. "You can start."

North let out a breath, unprepared for this invitation. Ren understood completely, which was why he wanted North to begin. Ren had so many questions; he hoped whatever North asked would help him choose one.

"All right," North stalled, unsure. He tilted his head, looking with painful affection at Justin. Ren had a hard time reading his face; it was conflicted. There was so much love there, but also so much hurt. Even though North said it was ok, Ren wondered if asking about what happened between them might be too personal.

"Who *are* you?" North began bluntly, making Ren smile tiredly. This was going to be a lengthy discussion.

"I'm Lorenzo Cordero," Ren answered. North stared at him, his mouth a neutral line, forcing him to add something. "You can call me Ren, though; everyone does. I'm just a student."

"You're not *just* anything," North contradicted. "I've never seen anyone like you before. What kind of student knows about pickle juice and starting IVs? That was incredible."

Ren was at a loss; it hadn't been that incredible. And according to Dr. Delacroix, none of it would have been necessary if he'd just brought Justin in sooner. He still felt ashamed.

"I do IVs all the time." Ren shrugged. "I work as a tech in the plasma donation center at the other end of the hospital. And I'm a volunteer EMT."

North paused, deep in thought, lightly brushing his fingers against Justin's forehead. Justin murmured something, turning his head toward North without releasing Ren's hand.

"I'm grateful you were there," North whispered. "Can you tell me what's wrong with him? What happened?"

"No one's told you anything?" Ren answered with another question, surprised North had been here so long without anyone giving him information. North looked frustrated, but not with Ren.

"The nurse who hooked up that thing said a little," North said, gesturing toward the EKG machine. "Something about his heart beating irregularly, but I think I'd understand more if I heard it from you." There was a hint of distrust in North's words, and Ren knew he was thinking back to how Ren had denied knowing Justin. How that most certainly looked like a huge lie after Justin had been discovered in Ren's bedroom. Ren found it interesting how many facts about Justin seemed like lies but were actually the truth. Somehow Justin seemed to twist perception so everyone who interacted with him came away with a completely inaccurate picture. Ren found that difficult and frustrating.

"We think he has the flu," Ren started, then hurried to explain better as he saw North's eyebrows crunch together in almost offended disbelief. They both knew the flu didn't look like this. "Or at least it started that way. I'm pretty sure he's anemic too, but the lab work hasn't come back to confirm anything. All I do know is he has a very high fever, he's dehydrated, he hasn't been taking care of himself for a while, and some combination of those things messed up his heart rate, lowering his blood pressure and oxygen intake level."

"How close were we to losing him?" North went on, making Ren slightly nauseated. He didn't want to think about that again, didn't want to talk about it. Wasn't it enough that they hadn't lost him? Did North really need to know how bad it had been? Especially since Ren didn't think he was the only one blaming himself for how sick Justin was. He felt North was thinking it was his fault too, even though that was impossible. He hadn't even known.

Unconsciously, Ren slipped two of his fingers out of Justin's hand so they could cover his pulse on his wrist. He could clearly see the heart rate on the monitor just behind North's shoulder, but somehow it was a comfort to feel it. Still beating. Steady at last.

"The only other patient I saw who was like that didn't make it to the hospital," Ren told North, surprisingly keeping his voice steady. North covered Justin's shoulder, as if frightened Justin might disappear if he didn't hold Justin's spirit in his body with his hand.

"Could it happen again?" North wondered.

"Maybe, but I think he's going to be ok now," Ren reassured. "He probably won't crash again. Not with the drugs he's getting, and the lab will figure out what caused it soon."

"I just don't understand," North said, not talking to Ren anymore, looking forlornly at Justin. "You should have called me."

"I don't think he knew he could," Ren answered for Justin, making a guess. He watched shame and sadness drip down North's face in place of tears. "When was the last time you saw Justin, North?"

Because it seemed as though it had been a while. It seemed like they had so much history, but then something had broken between them. Ren wasn't sure which of them had done the breaking, but he thought maybe it could be mended now they were back together.

"It's been more than a year," North revealed. "It was right after ... he was sixteen then."

"Why so long? What happened?" The words were out of Ren's mouth even though he knew it probably wasn't a question that could be answered. Nor could any of the others that had popped into his head after North's verbal backtracking. Right after what? North looked confused and hurt.

"When I asked Justin who to contact in case of an emergency, he gave me your name," Ren began, wanting North to know that. "But then he got upset when I suggested we call you, and he made me promise not to."

"I bet," North muttered, looking at Justin with exasperation.

"I thought it was because ... I'm sorry, but I thought he was hiding from you. I thought maybe you'd hurt him." North stiffened, causing Ren to lift a peaceable hand toward him. "Justin didn't say that, though; he wouldn't talk about you at all. At least not when he was conscious." Ren paused, wondering if he could repeat these things out loud. He wondered if Justin would be ok if Ren did.

"Conscious?" North prompted when Ren's silence continued too long. "You said he asked for me in his sleep before. Is that what you mean?"

"Not exactly. He wasn't really sleeping during this. His fever spiked last night," Ren explained. "He said all kinds of things. I don't even know if all of them are true, but mostly he begged for you." Ren hesitated momentarily, seeing what he was doing to North. He felt as though he were beating him with his words, like this was a mental torture session instead of an explanation. He went on anyway; he felt like he should. "He asked to stay with you. He cried about it. He said he was sorry so many times."

"What's your question?" North asked, voice hard. Ren could tell he'd steeled it on purpose to keep himself from sounding too emotional, and he was pleading for another question so they could switch topics.

"I asked Justin if we could call you this morning since it seemed he wanted you last night, and he told me you didn't care about him. But I can see that's not true. So I guess I'm asking what happened between you?"

"Justin doesn't think anyone cares about him," North muttered, still sounding bitter, though there was more sadness to his tone than before. "And he does his best to stop anyone from trying. But in our case, I made a mistake."

"You don't have to answer," Ren reminded him about their agreement, seeing how much this was hurting North. He still wanted to know, but it looked as though he was going to have to drop it.

"What else did he say?" North asked instead. "Last night?"

Ren took a moment to wrap his emotions tight, preparing to give that information up, knowing it would be hard but also knowing it would be a relief not to bear it alone anymore.

"He was delirious for hours," Ren cautioned. "It was bad. Are you sure you want —"

"Yes," North said, the closest to a demand Ren had yet heard from him.

"There were a lot of fragments," Ren tried to organize this better, give some sort of summary of the disjointed, distressing wounds in Justin's spirit that he had given voice to in the dark. "He seemed afraid of being left behind or alone. He asked why he couldn't stay with you." North winced as if Ren had hit him but motioned for Ren to continue. "He also kept asking for someone to believe him. Mostly, it seemed he was speaking to you, but he mentioned someone else too. He was so scared. He said —" Nope. Ren couldn't do it. Not yet. The words were sticking in his throat. He had to change the subject, sensing this conversation would keep circling around the biggest issue, the deep sucking abyss of the murder trial and the events that caused it, in an awkward, uncontrolled whirlpool.

"North, who hurt him?" Ren shifted instead of finishing. "I've seen the scars. Someone burned him. How come no one did anything to stop it?"

"I stopped it," North declared, and Ren suddenly saw what North had been once, not all that long ago. A soldier, a leader, and a defender, powerful and protective. If he wanted to, North could easily be the most frightening person Ren had ever met. All the cautions Ren had received so far about Justin being dangerous seemed suddenly weak. Justin wasn't dangerous. But North could be.

"You said you're his social worker?" Ren asked, feeling unsteady at North's intense change in tone, feeling his understanding of the situation shift once again. "You don't look it," Ren murmured, mostly to himself as he tried to figure out how North had gone from what had most certainly been a military background to working as a liaison for minors in a district office.

"I suppose not," North acknowledged, the edge gone from his voice. "But you don't look like an EMT either."

"I'm sorry," Ren apologized. "I'm just trying to figure this out."

"I used to be in the Air Force," North disclosed. "I piloted an F-35, but then this happened," he lifted his prosthetic, letting Ren fill in the gaps however he wanted regarding the injury, "and I was put on medical leave.

"After that, the social worker position sort of fell into my lap, and Justin's file was literally dropped into it. He was fourteen; no one knew what to do with him. He kept running away, getting into fights. I think giving him to me was supposed to be some kind of hazing thing, or maybe they thought I could use some military tactic to get him in line."

Ren felt his heart harden at this. He didn't know any of the people North was talking about, but he hated their casual laziness. They were supposed to protect Justin.

"I was new," North continued. "Justin was my first case. I went to visit him to get acquainted, but as soon as I saw him, I knew something wasn't right. I didn't really know what I was doing, what the procedure was for removing a child from an unsafe place, but I knew I had to get him out of there. I gave him ten minutes to pack a bag while I argued with his foster mother. Then all of a sudden, he was in the car with me, and I just … brought him home. He slept on my couch. He didn't act anything like the kid in his file; I thought maybe I'd somehow picked up the wrong one."

Ren felt the corners of his mouth trying to lift upwards. Basically, he and North had done the exact same thing. Walk in unexpectedly on Justin, find him in trouble, then take him home without thinking too much about what sort of consequences there would be.

"By Monday, we were both in trouble," North went on, and the tiny smile that had started in Ren disappeared again. "My supervisor was furious. Justin's foster mom was in the office, insisting she was trying to act in Justin's best interests, but it still felt wrong. I thought Justin should choose. From the looks on their faces, obviously no one ever thought to get his opinion. Including Justin. He said he wanted to go home with me again, but we weren't allowed to do that."

"Why not?" Ren asked, not understanding. If that's what Justin wanted, and if North was ok with it too, then what would stop them?

"It's against the law," North revealed, his tone indicating that he didn't think it was the best law. "I'd never been cleared to have foster children in my apartment. I didn't have permission to keep or care for him. It didn't matter he was being hurt, or that I wanted him with me."

"So, it was all for nothing?" Ren wondered. "He had to go back?"

"No. That was the one good thing that came out of it. I had a doctor look at Justin, and there was more than enough evidence to keep him separated from his host family."

Ren was getting the picture now. How awful for Justin. Trapped and alone. Hurt by people who were supposed to be taking care of him, forced to accept consequences for choices he hadn't made.

Both Ren and North had their hands on Justin, covering him protectively, keeping him safe from people who were not there, from situations already over. If only Ren had known him then. If only they'd been friends. He hadn't been living in the same country, but he still felt somehow that he could have helped him if only he had known.

"So then where did Justin go?" Ren asked. "If he couldn't stay with you and he didn't go back to them?"

"There weren't many options for Justin. He had a history, and surprisingly the very people who are supposed to be advocates for children like Justin are sometimes prejudiced against them. It didn't help that he was a teenager by this point. No one wanted to bother with figuring out why he got into so many fights or ran away so often, why he was being difficult with his host parents. It's hard to find the time or the energy, I guess. Or after a while it seems people become desensitized to that kind of thing. There aren't enough resources, you know, so it's hard to keep struggling to fix a terribly broken system when it feels as though you're not making any progress or have any help."

"But he must have lived somewhere," Ren pushed.

"The best we could do was a group home. Not far from here, actually."

Ren sorted through this new information. It was starting to make sense why Justin in his delirium had pleaded so hard to stay with North. It may have been the first warm and comforting place he'd slept since he was four years old. And it also sounded as though it had done something good for North too. Ren couldn't be sure; he'd only just met him a few hours ago in an atmosphere that was anything but calm, but there had been something in North's voice when he spoke about Justin being there with him. How different could their lives have been if an uncompromising law hadn't kept them from each other?

"Ok, so that was years ago," Ren heard himself saying, putting together the jagged remnants of North's memories that he'd been given. "Did Justin ever see them again? The people you saved him from?"

"Never," North responded quickly. "The court ordered separation for life. They can't foster again, and they had to pay a fine."

"A *fine*?!" Ren said, louder than he should have, but he couldn't believe it. Justin had suffered abuse for months, maybe years, everyone knew about it, and the consequence was a fine? Where was the justice in that?

"I couldn't believe it either," North agreed.

"But then what happened?" Ren pressed, becoming bolder in asking his questions. The further they went into Justin's past the more Ren wanted to know. What happened to Justin after he was transferred to the group home?

"Actually, I was hoping I could take a turn asking questions," North brought him up short, and Ren realized their conversation had been extremely one-sided in his favor. He lowered his head, nodding, though he couldn't guess what North would want to know that could be more interesting or important than what they were currently talking about.

"Go ahead," Ren invited, hoping to get North's questions out of the way so he could return to the mysterious years in Justin's life they hadn't spoken of yet.

"How long have you and Justin been friends?" North asked. Ren looked down at Justin, at the hand he was still holding. He couldn't help but smile at him.

"I don't know that we are friends," he answered. "I know it looks like I was lying, but I really did just meet him yesterday. Before that, it was just the texts you already saw. We've been in the same class since the beginning of the month, but we never talked to each other. I can't even remember seeing him in there, but I wasn't paying attention."

North looked sadly bemused at Ren's confession. "Yesterday?" Like that couldn't possibly be the truth, though Ren had no reason to lie.

"Yeah," Ren insisted, getting defensive about saying this all the time. "We don't know each other. The whole point of the assignment we were partnered on was to do an interview and write a biography, but you saw how well that was going."

The light went out of North's eyes. "Justin doesn't open up easily or trust anyone. It's nothing against you."

"I know that," Ren allowed, running a gentle hand through Justin's hair.

"Which means you should also be able to see why I'm having a hard time believing you. I know you're not lying, but I've never seen Justin like this."

"Like what?" Ren asked, thinking he might know what North was talking about, but he wanted it confirmed out loud. Especially since it seemed as though everyone was getting confused as to what sort of relationship Ren and Justin had. Ren included.

"Just look," North gestured toward Justin, how his body gravitated toward Ren even in sleep, how he held on to him tightly. "There's a lot of trust here for knowing each other for only a day. You must be very special."

"He's just very sick," Ren protested, unable to speculate in this direction. Justin was sick and no one had noticed or cared except Ren. No one had been there for him but Ren. That didn't make Ren special; it made all the people who should have been there for Justin horrible failures. "I did what anyone would have done."

"But what did you do exactly?" North asked suddenly, as if he'd been looking for the right opening for it this whole time. "How did Justin go from frustrated texts on your phone to your apartment in less than a day?"

"It surprised me too," Ren admitted for the first time. "I wasn't even going to work with him anymore; I'd asked my teacher for another partner and everything. But then Justin showed up to class on Friday."

North was staring intently at Ren, engrossed in the details, hungry to hear what had happened to Justin outside of his protection. The loyalty in his face made Ren embarrassed all over again about how he'd behaved. How he'd treated Justin like everyone else in his life, acting on assumptions rather than finding out the truth. It was disappointing to Ren that he'd done this so easily, that he'd let his anger take control of him.

"I was already mad at him for missing our Thursday meet up," Ren told North, finding it harder to admit this to him than to anyone else. "And then when I went back to his desk to talk to him and saw he was sleeping, it just made it worse." Ren paused, not wanting to continue, but North was still staring at him, compelling him to keep talking.

"I slammed my textbook on the desk by his head to shake him up," Ren pushed himself to admit, feeling a tightness release in his chest as he said the words. He'd said it before, to Angelique, but it felt different telling North. "It was awful; I hadn't even spoken to him yet, never gave him a chance to explain. I just assumed the worst about him. That's why I deserved it when he woke up and gave me this." Ren slid his fingers over his bruised cheek.

"I wondered about that," North admitted softly. "I wouldn't say you deserved it, but I'm surprised you were in a fight."

"We didn't fight," Ren denied. "I was ready to; I almost hit him back, but something seemed wrong. He left, and I let him go, but later I wanted to apologize and make sure he was ok. I found him sick in bed with his clothes on. He said he didn't have anyone he could call to come help him and, I just ... have you been to his apartment?"

"It's not his, but yes," North answered. Ren stored that information for a future question.

"Then you see why I couldn't let him stay there alone. I want to help him, North. I think you and I are the only ones who want to." His throat closed again, making it impossible to continue talking. He wanted to lower his head and nuzzle into Justin. He wanted North to turn away and not look at him while he did it.

North's elegant robotic hand curled around Ren's wrist,

squeezing with soft, reassuring pressure. Ren marveled all over again at the precise control North had over it. If he could do this with a prosthetic hand, what sort of amazing pilot had he been?

"You are helping him," North said, genuine and quiet. "And it seems he's going to let you. I can't tell you how special that is or what it means to me that you took the initiative to find him, especially since I know how hard he works at being invisible most of the time. You saved his life." A pang of guilt hit Ren at the heartfelt compliment, knowing he hadn't always made the best choices when it came to Justin. The room darkened, more than one kind of shadow filling it.

"You saved it first," Ren responded, trying to give something back to North, who looked so broken across the bed, failure weighing him down in a visible way. He tried to smile at Ren's statement, but they had entered that place in the conversation again. The uncertainty. The painful thoughts of how their current circumstances could have been prevented if only they had, in their respective ways, done a little more a little sooner. For Ren these thoughts were present but useless; he hadn't even known Justin two days ago. For North, this regret cut deeply.

"I wish I could," North murmured, and Ren found it strange how he knew exactly what he meant even at the same time he had no idea at all.

"I don't understand," Ren wondered out loud, overwhelmed with helplessness, an ache in his spirit that he wished would break open.

North wilted, looking at Justin, and Ren knew they were both thinking about the sentence waiting for him. How it didn't matter what either of them felt. Justin's future depended on whatever the jury had decided was the truth. And from what Ren had noticed about Justin and how others perceived him, he couldn't help but succumb to dread.

"North, what's going to happen to him?" Ren asked, wanting North to reassure him, wishing he would tell him the whole story, explain how it had been just another misunderstanding and Justin hadn't killed anyone. Ren watched North's soft black eyes shift to mirror Ren's own worries and doubts and knew they were both powerless to stop what was coming for Justin. It was too late.

Ren couldn't tell if North had been about to answer him, but their discussion paused naturally as Justin stirred. His hand clenched in Ren's, then pulled away as he shifted on the bed, coming back to consciousness. When his eyes opened, both Ren and North stood quiet and ready. Because it wasn't Monday yet, so Ren was going to do anything Justin needed to feel safe and comfortable.

"Welcome back," Ren greeted, unable to tolerate the silence. He forced a smile.

Justin's eyes dragged up to Ren's, and Ren was relieved to see recognition. Always a good start. Justin made a weak attempt to sit up, but Ren knew the cocktail he was getting through the IV would make it difficult for him to move without help. He probably felt as though he had no muscle tone at all.

"Hold still," Ren advised, reaching for the automated controls on the hospital bed. He remembered Angelique telling him not to touch anything but felt he'd be safe raising the bed so Justin could recline. "I've been wanting to play with these buttons for hours now, and I'm not missing my chance. Just sit tight."

"You're still here?" Justin questioned.

"I'm not going to leave you," Ren scolded gently. "I promised, didn't I?" Some fear relaxed from Justin's face, replaced by something powerful Ren couldn't make out. It made him want to put his hand against Justin's cheek. He might have if they had been alone.

"How are you feeling, Justin?" North asked, which made Justin turn his head toward him, reminding Ren that not only were they not alone, Ren might be in the way now that North was here. He should probably offer to let them have some privacy, even though he didn't want to.

"North," Justin said the name in surprise and reverence. His large eyes teared up, and he redoubled his efforts to sit straight, a cadet suddenly finding himself in the presence of a much-respected commanding officer. Ren took pity and bent down, sliding his arm behind Justin's back and taking the elbow closest to him, sensing that any caution against unnecessary movement would go unheeded. While Ren helped Justin, North carefully perched on the edge of the bed, opening his arms. Ren pushed Justin right into them, letting go so North could encase Justin in an embrace he'd obviously been saving for their entire separation.

"I'm sorry, Justin," North apologized, the weight of lost time heavy in the words, clinging to Justin as though afraid he could somehow run away from him before he could finish. "I should have told you. I should have told you first."

"North?" Justin repeated his name, puzzled. North reluctantly released Justin so they could speak face to face, easing him back against the raised bed, but he kept their hands clasped, resting in Justin's lap.

"I've been looking everywhere for you," North said, shaking Justin's hand slightly, partially reproachful. Ren stood up straight, shifting into invisibility in the background to just watch. So Justin had been hiding from North after all.

"Why?" Justin asked, so innocent and yet with so much apathy that Ren had a hard time not touching his shoulder. How could he ask that? How could he look at North's devoted, affectionate face and not know North loved him? Then again, the way his life had been, why would Justin recognize something like that?

"Why?" North repeated, incredulous and exasperated. "Because you vanished without a trace, Justin! You wouldn't take my calls. No one would give me any information. You just —" he cut himself off, collecting his emotions and wrapping them under tight control. He softened his voice. "I was so worried about you."

Justin's heart skipped, the tiniest little hop on the monitor. It wasn't enough to trigger any system alarm, but Ren saw it out of the corner of his eye. It suddenly turned the conversation into a different kind of delicate. The heart rate steadied immediately, but Ren was now on high alert, watching and listening.

"I'm sorry," Justin murmured, eyes lowered to Ren's quilt, his free hand beginning to pluck at it in discomfort. His apology sounded cold to Ren, robotic, the apology of a boy who had been forced to say he was sorry for everything.

"No, Justin, don't," North protested. "There's nothing you need to be sorry for. If you thought you couldn't come to me for help then that's *my* fault, not yours."

"What?" Justin said, confused and lost, finding it difficult to put his thoughts into words. "I thought you didn't want me to ... you asked to be ..."

Ren watched Justin's heart rate start to climb, not drastically, but it was definitely speeding up. Justin started to tremble. Ren seemed to be the only one noticing.

"I know I did," North confirmed. "I asked to be transferred. And I should have told you why, but I didn't think you'd run away before I could talk to you."

Justin's breath caught, and his shoulders tightened. Ren's eyes went to the monitor as the numbers on it changed color, and he sighed. It was time to intervene.

"Hey, sorry," Ren interjected, taking a step closer to the bed, melting inside when both heads turned to look at him, surprised he was still here. "I really hate to interrupt, but I think we should take a break here."

North's head tilted, not understanding and not appreciating being stopped now that he was finally able to talk to Justin, so Ren jerked his chin toward the monitor. "Unless you want a whole team of nurses coming in?" North also checked the monitor, beginning to nod slowly.

"You're right," North acknowledged, though Justin didn't seem ready to change the subject.

"But," Justin stuttered, breathing fast. "North."

"Justin, please," Ren entreated, finally giving in and putting a hand on his shoulder. "You're asking a lot from your body right now.

I think we should talk about something that isn't so emotional so you can calm down."

"I am calm," Justin insisted, holding tight to North as if he'd been the one who had run away, his shoulder stiff under Ren's fingers. "I just need to know why."

Ren drew closer, leaving his hand on Justin's shoulder and placing his other one over Justin's chest, not sure if he were trying to support him or restrain him. Justin didn't shrug him off, but Ren could feel how he wanted to.

"This isn't how I wanted to tell you," North said, backing down. "Not here. Not like this. Let's wait like Ren says. We're together now; we have time to do it right."

"But," Justin said, becoming more frantic despite their entreaties for him to relax. "No, we don't. They're going to ... he's dead, North."

Justin's statistics had risen enough that Ren heard the alarm go off outside the door.

"I know," North placated, also putting a hand on Justin's chest right next to Ren's. "Officer Geisler came to my place looking for you, and he told me some of what was going on. We're going to figure it out, though, Justin. I'll start the arrangements tonight. You don't have to worry."

"Breathe, Justin," Ren reminded him, feeling helpless and morbidly curious. The way Justin said it. *He's dead.* It made it sound like he was surprised. Like he wasn't there when it happened. But if that were true, how come he'd confessed to the murder? Or maybe Denny was wrong? But Denny was never wrong.

The nurse arrived then, bustling into the room with purposeful calm, and Ren watched her with approval. Not a shabby response time. She wore periwinkle scrubs; her brownish-blonde hair held in a sloppy twist by an enormous hair clip. Her name tag read Abbie M., RN, and Ren guessed her to be in her late twenties.

"Hello," she greeted them all, but zeroed in quickly on Justin. Ren let go of him to move out of the way, but North stayed where he was. Abbie silenced the alarm. "Everything all right?"

"Yes," Justin muttered, the least qualified to give the answer but apparently the only one capable of speech. Abbie studied him, reading the room carefully now that she'd seen her patient conscious and responding. She checked the output from the EKG, folding up the long line of paper slowly gathering in a pile on the floor and tucking it onto a hidden shelf on the cart under the machine. Then she went through Justin's stats, took his temperature, and checked the volume and drip rate of the IV bag. Meanwhile, as they were all forced to be silent by her presence, Justin's heart rate leveled out again, though his face was hard and impatient. She softened the lighting in the room, dimming it down significantly. Ren checked his phone, surprised at the time and the number of politely inquisitive texts from Alek and Denny. He should probably call them soon to give them an update.

"Warm enough?" Abbie asked Justin, finally running out of things to look at or change. "That's a lovely blanket; did your mom make it?"

Justin shook his head, shy. "I think his mom did," he answered her, gesturing toward Ren. Abbie glanced at Ren quickly, the tiniest furrow of confusion creasing between her eyes. She moved on quickly.

"Well, it's beautiful, but I can get you another one if you're cold. Or anything else you need?"

"I'm all right," Justin responded, unable to look at her or anyone.

"Just press the call light if that changes," Abbie invited, showing him where it was on the bed. "I'm right outside."

"Can you give us an update?" North asked, coming to life suddenly as he realized she was on her way out. She looked at him, then at Ren, considering.

"We're running a test," she told him, as if they didn't already know that. "And we're waiting for the doctor to determine the outcome of the lab work."

"The labs came back?" Ren asked, pouncing on that detail.

"What's the diagnosis? Anemia?" Now Abbie was really studying him as he stood there in his jeans, covered in awkward.

"The doctor will go over it with you," she promised, moving toward the door.

"Which one?" Ren pressed, hoping they weren't going to wait until Dr. Delacroix returned twelve hours from now. "Dr. Delacroix?"

"No, I think the one who ordered the bloodwork," Abbie answered. "He's on another floor right now, but he's been paged and will probably be down soon. Try to lie still," she said in parting to Justin.

Abbie slipped quickly from the room as Ren processed. The labs were finished, and they were waiting for Dr. Taneja to come talk about them. But Dr. Taneja's real job was on the third floor; he specialized in internal medicine. Justin wasn't officially his patient, which meant that no matter who had ordered the bloodwork, they were going to have to get permission from Angelique for any kind of treatment. Which could take a while.

Ren looked back from the door toward North and Justin, who were staring wordlessly at each other. He sensed that if they started talking again, it would escalate as before.

"Are you ok?" North uttered the first question hesitantly. Justin shrugged. North's expression tightened, used to these non-answers but not liking it. "Are you in pain?" He tried again, getting more specific.

"Not anymore," Justin responded quietly, speaking only of the physical kind. He turned to Ren. "What are they giving me?"

"Fluids, pain medication, and an anti-arrhythmic drug to keep your heart rate steady," Ren answered readily, glad to still be part of the conversation, however awkward it may be.

"Ren is really good at this," Justin told North, who smiled.

"I'm glad you found a good friend, Justin," North responded.

"Hey," Ren broke in as another uneasy silence fell. "Is it ok if we take a minute and call your other friends?" Justin looked confused. "Alek and Denny," Ren reminded him. "They're worried."

Justin checked silently with North, studying him, watching for any sign that he could get away with asking more questions. Ren would have loved nothing more than to bring it all out in the open, but he thought it would be better to wait until after Dr. Taneja came and they'd learned more about what was going on.

"Let's call them," Ren urged. "Then you and North can try to talk more about that other stuff. I can leave; you can have some privacy. Just promise me you'll take it easy, ok?"

"You don't have to leave," Justin said quickly, his face flushing. "Unless you need to," he amended carefully. "Just because I'm stuck here doesn't mean you have to be."

"I'll stay as long as you want me," Ren promised. "I'd like to hear what Dr. Taneja found out, and, well, anything else you'd like to tell me." He knew that was not a subtle hint, but it was out in the open now.

"I guess," Justin said, his eyes slipping down. "You have a right to know."

"No," Ren said. "I'd be lying if I said I wasn't curious, but you don't owe me anything. It's completely up to you."

Many emotions crossed Justin's face. Without seeming to realize it, he reached over to Ren, tentatively taking hold of the hem of his shirt. Ren felt warmth radiate from Justin's fingers.

"Ok," Justin acquiesced. "Call them."

14
INFUSION

"Ren! Oh man, it's good to hear your voice. Dude," Alek rambled, exhaling his relief in near non-sensical phrases. Ren smiled automatically, familiar with how Alek sounded when he was worried. He looked at North and Justin the same way he would have looked at Denny if she'd been present, forgetting that they didn't know Alek the way he did. They both wore neutral expressions, unsure if this was supposed to be funny or concerning.

"Everyone's fine, Alek," Ren told him first thing, knowing that would be the most important piece of information exchanged in this entire call. The last time Alek and Denny had seen Justin, he'd been strapped to an oxygen tank and carried out of the room with Ren sprinting after him. "I've got you on speaker with Justin and North. We wanted to check in."

"Good thing you called," Denny sighed coolly. "Alek's out of counter space."

Now Justin definitely looked confused. North more so. Ren decided to ask a question he already knew the answer to for their benefit. "Stress baking, huh, Alek?"

"What? Me? No. Just trying some new recipes," Alek denied, almost drowned out by a squawk from Denny.

"Alek, there's like fourteen loaves of bread here. That's what? Seven times your weekly average?"

"It means he was worried about you," Ren whispered to Justin, translating Alek's behavior into the emotion that had driven it, wanting him to understand. "You're making bread?" He returned to Alek on the phone. "Not cookies?" It felt peaceful and normal talking to his friends, especially since he didn't have to give them horrible news. Well, not yet. A shiver of dread rippled through him, tarnishing the moment, as he remembered the court date for Justin. He repressed it with a vengeance.

"Oh, we got cookies," Denny drawled. "You don't have a table, but we've got cookies. We've got an entire chocolate chip mountain; it's impressive. I've given away dozens, Ren, but I'm not making a dent here."

"Amateur," Ren teased her, though he knew perfectly well the sort of production Alek was capable of in a stress-induced baking frenzy, and Ren could only eat two of Alek's massive, gooey cookies in one sitting.

"Anyway," Denny huffed. "How are you guys? What's going on over there?"

"Yeah, Justin, buddy, you ok?" Alek echoed, growing serious again. "Is he ok, Ren?"

Ren looked at Justin, giving him first chance to answer before he did any talking for him. But Justin looked too overwhelmed to speak, clinging to Ren's hem, mouth tight, touched in a way he probably couldn't explain that people he barely knew were so invested in his wellbeing.

"He's doing better," Ren eventually answered, feeling Justin's hand clench on his shirt. He sat down on the edge of the bed, keeping the phone positioned between them. "I think he's pretty comfortable at the moment?" he said the last as a question, wanting Justin to confirm. Justin nodded while North rested a companionable hand on his head. "He's definitely getting better pain medication than I've got at the apartment."

"So are they going to let you come home soon? You need a ride?" Alek offered hopefully.

"Not yet, Alek, thanks though. They're doing some tests, so Justin's going to stay at least until tomorrow sometime."

"And you're staying with him?" Denny asked, and Ren hoped he was the only one to hear the slight edge in her tone.

"I'm staying," Ren confirmed, a matching edge meant only for her. She made a frustrated little huffing noise, moving away from the phone. Yeah, but what else could he do? Triage was no place to spend the night alone. And he'd made a decision.

"Tough break," Alek empathized. "But if that's the case, you need me to bring you anything?"

Ren almost said no without thinking; he didn't want to put Alek out any more than he already had. He'd pushed the limits of all politeness by bringing Justin home with him without even checking with Alek first. It would take Ren forever to return the favors he'd already received, and it somehow made it worse that Alek wouldn't require him to even try.

But then Ren noticed his phone battery. It wouldn't last the entire night. He wouldn't worry about it, but tomorrow was Sunday. He couldn't be without a phone on Sunday morning, no matter where he was.

"My phone charger?" Ren timidly requested. "But I can come get it."

"That's already in your bag, man," Alek returned. "Guess you haven't had a chance to look in there yet."

"You packed my phone charger?" Ren asked, surprised and moved at Alek's never-ending thoughtfulness.

"Yeah, I just started grabbing stuff. You can go through it when you get bored tonight. It was the only useful thing I could think of while you were being a superhero."

"Come on, Alek," Ren dismissed, feeling awkward. He was a far cry from being a hero.

"Come on, nothing! I've never seen you be all medical drama serious like that. It was pretty cool."

"You were crying, Alek," Ren pointed out flatly, wanting to remind him that it had also been extremely scary. Medical dramas were one thing. What happened earlier with Justin had been all too real and terrifying.

"Well, sure, but things can be cool and awful at the same time, you know. Oh, hey, is your back all right? Ten points for the catch, but the fall looked like it hurt."

"You fell?" Justin murmured, looking at Ren questioningly. "What does he mean? Your back?" He started tugging at Ren's shirt, trying to twist him to see what Alek was talking about.

"It's bruised a little, no big deal," Ren allowed, resting his free hand over Justin's to hold him still. He didn't want Justin to see his back, didn't want him to blame himself for anything. "You'll never guess who treated us, though."

"Dr. Angelique Delacroix," Denny responded without a moment's hesitation, her need to be right trumping whatever frustration she might be trying to cling to about Ren and his choices. Ren slumped. While he was glad she was talking again, she had stolen his thunder. "Did she remember you?"

"She did, actually," Ren admitted. "Not sure that's a good thing, but she did a great job getting Justin stable again." *And me*, he added in his head.

"She didn't do anything; you did," Justin interrupted, voice shockingly clear and almost hostile.

"Easy, Justin," Ren calmed, wondering where the energy had come from. "Believe me; she did a lot for both of us."

"No, seriously," Justin continued, unexpectedly passionate. "What'd she do? You're the one who did the IV and figured out that whole Kuramo-whatever synching thing. She just stood around and asked a bunch of questions." Ren couldn't disagree. Looking at it from Justin's perspective, it probably did look like she hadn't been very involved.

"What'd he just say?" Denny broke in, intrigued and vaguely impressed. "Are you talking about the Kuramoto model?" Great. Now Ren was going to have to explain what he'd tried to do and have Denny laugh at him for the next six months. "Why did that come up? How do you even know about it?"

"I don't; Ren used it," Justin deflected.

"Ren?" Denny said his name as a demand; she wanted information.

"We just did an experiment while we waited for the medication to work," Ren sighed, wondering how to say it that would sound the least stupid. "We tried to synch our heart rates with a Josephson junction and some oscillation."

"Did it work?" Denny sounded so interested, the opposite of how he'd expected her to react.

"Yeah, it did," Justin answered for him, apparently unable to talk about himself but more than ready to answer for Ren. Ren wasn't sure how he felt about that.

"Almost instantly," North added.

"The medication worked," Ren protested, but it seemed no one was listening to him. Apparently, everyone except Ren had forgotten there had even been medication or that he'd risked his EMT status on making sure Justin got it quickly.

"That was really clever, Ren," Denny complimented, tossing Ren into the Twilight Zone with one casual sentence. "Don't forget what you did; I'm going to want to see if we can duplicate the experiment when you get home."

"No," Ren protested, off balance, never anticipating this sort of response to what he'd tried to do. "We can't duplicate that." *Please, never again.*

"I have some ideas," Denny rebutted nonchalantly. "I'll see if there's any literature first, though."

"Knock yourself out," Ren relented. There was no stopping her anyway.

"Hey Ren," Alek broke in. "You said North was there?"

"You're letting everyone call you North now?" Justin whispered under his breath. Ren hadn't thought about that. North had used his full name when he'd introduced himself earlier, both to Ren and to Dr. Delacroix, and Officer Geisler called him Elias. Justin might have been the only one to use the nickname until now. But honestly, for Ren, Alek, and Denny, they couldn't help it. They'd listened to Justin call that name for hours.

"I'm here," North raised his voice so Alek could hear it over the phone but then toned it down again just for Justin. "They're your friends; I don't mind."

"Oh, cool, hi there," Alek began rambling again, an indication of his discomfort. "Glad you and Justin found each other, but, um, I was wondering." *No, please don't ask Alek*, Ren mentally pleaded, considering hanging up before Alek could say anything about the strange manner in which North arrived at the apartment. "What was up with the police officer?"

Leave it to Alek. Damn it. Justin and North traded heavy glances. Ren wasn't sure which side to defend — Justin's right to privacy or Alek's innocent curiosity.

It turned out, he didn't have to choose.

"We'll have to talk about it later," Ren delayed as he heard Dr. Taneja's heavy accent outside Justin's door, never more grateful to be interrupted than right this second. Dr. Taneja sounded as though he was also talking to someone on the phone, his voice growing louder as he came closer. "Dr. Taneja is here to go over the lab work with us."

"Keep us updated?" Alek requested, disappointed. Ren felt bad but not enough. He didn't want to have that discussion over the phone. He wanted to sit together and explain things gently. If anything needed to be explained. Maybe Denny would do it for him. No, unlikely. Alek had probably speculated about it already, and if she hadn't broken out the truth by now then she never would. She was going to make Ren do it. Because that's what he deserved for bringing home felons, wasn't it?

"I will. Thanks for all your help. We'll talk soon," Ren promised, knowing he'd never be able to thank them enough.

Dr. Taneja walked into the room as if it were empty. He had his eyes on the floor; his mustache twitching as he pursed his lips around what Ren could only assume were twenty arguments that he couldn't find a place to slip in through the tirade coming from the phone. Ren couldn't hear any words yet, but he recognized Angelique's voice. He wondered who had called whom. What sort of argument they were having. It didn't make sense for them to have anything to argue about.

"I'm not encouraging anything," Dr. Taneja darted in when Angelique paused to take a breath, tucking papers under his arm so he could hold the phone and close the door behind him. "He came to me. I don't see the problem."

"Well, you didn't see him today," Angelique snapped, her words clear now that Dr. Taneja had come inside, her tone exasperated from the receiver, and Ren abruptly realized they were arguing about him. "He was a wreck." Perfect. Ren fidgeted on the bed, turning his face away from Justin.

"I'm looking at him right now," Dr. Taneja retorted, obviously annoyed, standing there staring unambiguously at Ren, clutching his paperwork and tucking his fist against his hip. Ren felt Justin's and North's eyes on him suddenly, adding to the count of people staring, making it almost unbearable. Of all the things they could be talking about, they'd decided on him? Ren wasn't sure if he felt angry, frightened, or embarrassed.

"You're going to ruin him," Angelique accused mercilessly, her voice sharp and loud in the room. Ren dug his fingers into the fabric of his jeans. How long were they going to keep talking about him? Couldn't Dr. Taneja see that this was a conversation he should have kept in the hallway?

"So you've said," Dr. Taneja replied coldly, unaware of the

awkward atmosphere. Ren felt North's robotic hand on his shoulder and unconsciously leaned into it. "Multiple times. If you feel that way, you should take it up with him yourself. This has nothing to do with my reason for calling. If you want to continue yelling at me, you'll have to schedule a time with my receptionist."

It was Ren's turn to grip Justin for reassurance as Angelique sputtered, too angry for words, astonished by Dr. Taneja's audacity. North bent low to monitor him, but Ren just shook his head. He felt like the only child of divorced parents. Had Dr. Taneja ever met Angelique in person? Did he know what he could be starting by talking to her like that? Justin patted him clumsily, whispering a question Ren couldn't decipher.

"Look; you're in charge here, all right?" Dr. Taneja said to Dr. Delacroix, slightly deflated. "I've told you the results, and I'm certain you're not going to withhold treatment because of who took the samples. Now will you call in the order?"

"Of course I will," Angelique huffed, her pride as a doctor being called into question.

"Thank you," Dr. Taneja said bitingly, and thankfully turned off the speaker to finish the conversation semi-privately. "Yes, right now. I know. Of course I do! Probably more than ... if you say so. I'm still going to let him decide and so should ... because ... fine. I will talk to him, ok? Ok!" Dr. Taneja rammed the phone into his scrubs pocket so hard Ren thought he might tear through it.

"Infuriating woman," the doctor muttered, shaking his head.

"Is there a problem?" North asked.

"Nope, not a word," Dr. Taneja denied, plucking a pen from his breast pocket and shoving it at Justin. "Not until I get these forms signed. Sorry, young man," Dr. Taneja softened, speaking just to Justin now. "I wasn't going to make you when I thought you'd be recovering at Lorenzo's apartment, but now that you're here and I've got test results that require immediate treatment and future prescriptions, there's just nothing for it. Understand?"

"What's he signing?" North interjected, protective. He may not be Justin's official social worker anymore, but he was obviously still very much in business of acting on Justin's behalf.

"And who are you?" Dr. Taneja demanded, still ruffled from talking with Angelique.

"Elias Kaplan," North answered readily, standing by Justin's side, straight and honestly intimidating. Though Dr. Taneja didn't seem to be intimidated in the least. "I'm Justin's guardian."

"Lorenzo?" Dr. Taneja asked for confirmation, staring North in the eye as if he could best him in any fight he may want to start. Maybe he really did used to wrestle tigers. Or maybe he lacked the social graces to notice that he kept verbally putting himself in danger. Ren couldn't tell; he'd never seen Dr. Taneja so agitated before.

"It's ok, Dr. Taneja," Ren said peacefully, emphasizing his mentor's title to make sure everyone in the room would give him the respect he deserved. "Justin wants him here."

"I see. Well in that case, what I need signed is a document giving me and Dr. Delacroix clearance to diagnose and treat illness, a standard hospital waiver, a statement indicating I have given you a copy of HIPAA law and hospital policy, which is right here by the way, and a privacy agreement where I am given permission to share information with other individuals as identified such as a primary care physician." As he spoke to North, Dr. Taneja handed Justin papers, rapidly pointing with amazing efficiency to all the specific lines requiring Justin's signature or initials. "And this one is for your insurance," he finished, though Justin didn't seem to know what to do with it.

"I don't think I have insurance," Justin confessed. This statement drew all the remaining hostility out of Dr. Taneja. Ren watched him gentle, saw compassion soften his jaw as if he'd just now remembered that Justin was barely a legal adult.

"You should," North offered helpfully. "I'll have to check with Kasey about it, but you should be covered until you're twenty-five.

He would have gone over the paperwork with you in the exit interview; do you remember?"

Justin shook his head, closing up as if ashamed.

"Justin, did you have an exit interview?" North pushed, attempting to be gentle though traces of impatience were creeping into the frown lines on his mouth. Justin shook his head again, the tiniest of movements. North closed his eyes, pushing his palm to his forehead. Ren knew Justin would take this gesture as anger directed at him, but Ren thought it looked more like North were mad at himself again.

"Well, we can go over that part later," Dr. Taneja dismissed, taking back all the signed papers.

"Can you tell us what's going on?" North requested, also quieter, not as threatening. Ren wanted to know too. Hopefully, there was nothing wrong with Justin that time and treatment couldn't resolve. "What are the results?"

"I can't tell you until Justin says it's ok," Dr. Taneja answered. Dr. Delacroix must have really yelled at him. Not that Dr. Taneja didn't adhere to policy; Ren followed him around the hospital enough to know that, but the way he said it indicated he was being more tensely by-the-book than normal. Any other day, the fact that North was in the room would be reason enough to think Justin would be all right with him hearing the diagnosis. "Justin, would you like these two to step outside while I go over your test results with you?"

"No, they can stay," Justin gave permission, and Dr. Taneja nodded. Because they had all known that in the first place.

"I thought so," Dr. Taneja said, shifting the papers around until he found the ones he needed. He cleared his throat. "And your blood-work confirms some other things we thought as well. You did test positive for influenza B virus, and the CBC test came back with extremely low hemoglobin levels, a definitive symptom for anemia. The good news is you tested negative for HIV, so the cause of your anemia is likely an abrupt change in diet and can be corrected easily. All that tells us how we got here," Dr. Taneja lifted a hand, rotating his wrist to indicate the hospital room. "Now I'm going to tell you what we can do about getting you better and back home again."

"Ok," Justin accepted, his voice quiet.

"Most of this will be taken care of by Dr. Delacroix, as she's the doctor who admitted you to the emergency room," Dr. Taneja explained, keeping his voice professional. "She's having an iron infusion brought in that we're going to administer through your IV. It'll take about four hours. That'll kickstart the recovery, but you'll need to take an oral iron supplement and change your diet to make sure you don't end up here again. As for the virus, there isn't a lot we can do but let it run its course and treat individual symptoms as they come. Do you have any questions about what I've just told you?"

"How long will I have to stay here?" Justin asked, holding the papers Dr. Taneja had passed him. The printouts of the results. A paper on anemia and what foods he should eat containing high amounts of iron.

Three days, Ren wanted to answer. That was standard for monitoring a patient like Justin to make sure his heart rate stayed within normal parameters and give him a chance to get over the virus while getting IV hydration. He was so certain he almost opened his mouth to answer for the doctor.

"That will be for Dr. Delacroix to decide," Dr. Taneja said instead. "She'll be back in the morning to talk about that with you. Until then, you keep resting. Lorenzo, do you need a ride home? I won't be finished until eleven, but it's a bad night to walk, so I can take you if you need me to."

"No, thanks, Dr. Taneja, but I'm staying," Ren said again, wondering why everyone expected him to just leave Justin here.

"I'll see if I can have a cot brought in then," Dr. Taneja accepted the answer, turning toward North. "Do you need one?"

"No," North answered. Justin jerked his head over to him, worried.

"You're leaving?" Justin asked, as though he might never see him again. North bent over Justin, covering his shoulders with his hands, squeezing him.

"I wouldn't if I thought you'd be here alone," North assured him. "But I have some calls to make; things to take care of right away. I need to talk to Kasey about insurance and probably talk to your lawyer. Do you have a lawyer?"

Justin side-eyed Ren nervously but then gave up. "Yeah," he answered. "But I don't know her number. It's in my phone. Her name is ... well, her last name is Kelly."

"Kelly," North echoed, rolling the name around as if searching for a mental match. "Tamsyn Kelly?"

"I think so."

"Makes sense. Our office has worked with her before. I can find her number," North said thoughtfully. "But is there anything else? Do you have any paperwork? A file or something so I can get caught up?"

"Yeah, it's —" Justin paused, his eyes flitting over to Ren again, looking embarrassed. "There's a file in my backpack. It has everything in it. My phone is in there too, but it's probably dead."

"That's ok. It doesn't matter, but where can I find the backpack? The apartment?" North asked efficiently, no judgment in his tone. He really was perfect for Justin.

"All Justin's stuff is at my place," Ren answered for him, understanding at last why Justin had been so possessive and weird about his backpack. He hadn't wanted Ren to see the file about the court case. Didn't want Ren to know he was on trial for murder. "The backpack is in my room. Alek can find it for you. I'll let him know you're coming to get it."

"Thanks, that's a big help," North expressed gratefully, though he sounded tired now. He pulled his wallet from his back pocket, retrieving a business card and handing it to Ren. "Will you call me if something changes?"

"Of course," Ren promised, knowing he would call North for any reason at all. Now that he had permission and a phone number, he would never again hesitate about contacting North.

"It's going to be all right, Justin," North assured. "Ren is here with you, and I'll be back before eight tomorrow; I promise." Justin looked at North, covered in the fragments of broken promises. Like they were shards of glass he was going to cut himself holding because he was going to try, one more time, to see if they would hold true and together. North must have seen this too; he returned to Justin's bedside, pressing his forehead against Justin's, closing his eyes.

"I won't if you won't," North whispered to Justin, words that must have some secret meaning. Justin relaxed as soon as he heard them. "Have Ren call me if you need something."

"I'll see you tomorrow," Justin whispered his hope out loud, looking at the blanket, resigned. North nodded comfortingly, though he didn't seem satisfied. Ren knew he wanted to stay here, but he also knew there were battles outside this room only North could tackle. They were a team now, Ren and North. He couldn't believe it was possible, but somehow that made Ren feel even more responsible for making sure Justin got the treatment he needed. He didn't want to let North down.

North shook Ren's hand, eyes filled with gratitude, then also shook Dr. Taneja's as he made his way slowly toward the door. He looked over his shoulder at Justin, as though he wanted to say one last thing, but in the end, he forced himself into the hall, and Ren watched him speed up as he walked purposefully toward the exit. Ren wasn't ready for him to leave yet either. There was more he thought they needed to talk about, even though there were more important things for North to do, and they were definitely running out of time.

"I need to head upstairs," Dr. Taneja said, bringing himself back to their attention. "Justin, I probably won't see you again. Dr. Delacroix will be taking over from here, so best of luck to you. As for you." Dr. Taneja settled rather fierce brown eyes onto Ren. "If you need anything, you'll come to me, yes?"

"I always do," Ren said dismissively, feeling uncomfortable, remembering what Angelique had said to Dr. Taneja about him.

"Evidently, you don't," Dr. Taneja countered darkly. "We don't have to get into it now, but sometime soon, I'd like to talk about what Delacroix told me today and why you've been hiding it."

Ren hunched his shoulders, wanting to say something petulant like, "Do we really have to?" He truly didn't understand why everyone wanted to make such a big fuss about him. Why couldn't they just trust that he knew what he was doing and leave it at that? However, he felt that if he wanted to continue under Dr. Taneja's mentorship, he would have to agree.

"Sure," he yielded, mostly so he could put it out of his head for a while. Maybe Dr. Taneja would forget all about it. Actually, chances were almost guaranteed that he would. But Angelique wouldn't. Pity.

"Take care then, both of you," Dr. Taneja said in parting, leaving Ren alone with Justin in the yellowish dark of the negative pressure room.

"So," Ren said, forcing some cheerfulness into his voice as he dragged the chair closer to the bed. He'd be here awhile, might as well pull up a seat. "Now we know what's going on with you. That's good."

Justin didn't seem close to convinced. He stared at Ren with his mouth open, the way he'd looked when Ren was speaking a foreign language. "*That's* all you're going to say?" He choked on the confusion in his question. Ren shrugged, as though whatever they'd just heard and learned about each other was no big deal.

There was *plenty* he wanted to say, though. What'd North mean the apartment wasn't his? What was an exit interview, and why didn't Justin have one? Who was Kasey? Was Tamsyn doing a good job as Justin's lawyer or was she being as careless as the rest of the DCFS employees responsible for Justin's wellbeing? And the huge, burning question Ren desperately wanted and also did not want answered. Had Justin really killed someone?

"What do you want me to say?" Ren questioned mildly, sitting down, putting himself at eye level with Justin.

"I don't know," Justin said, frustrated, resting his head and staring at the ceiling. The bed remained in a reclined position, but Justin had curled to the side, almost sitting up, facing Ren. He still wore the oxygen mask, but now that things had settled down in the room and the silence between them turned awkward, he started fidgeting with it. No one had turned the flow down yet; it was still maxed out at fifteen.

"You can probably take that off now," Ren invited, knowing how irritating it could be to have that much air blowing in your face when you no longer needed it. "It might freak out your nurse, but I think you can chance it."

Upon receiving permission, Justin practically tore the straps from the mask in his haste to get it off his face. He took a moment after flinging it to the side to examine himself, the hospital gown, the IV, all the electrodes connecting him to the EKG machine. The increasing panic on his face made Ren tense in preparation to hold him down. He looked like he might be at a breaking point, ready to start desperately and recklessly ripping lines off his body, which was a good and bad thing. It meant he was feeling better, but Ren knew it was a false sense of wellness.

"You still need all the other stuff," Ren said preemptively. "I know it feels like you're tied up, but if you touch anything else, it'll set off all the alarms this room has. Take a deep breath and chill out."

Ren partially stood from the chair, watching as Justin didn't respond to his words. He hovered over him, ready to grab his wrists, trying to think of something to distract Justin from thinking too hard about how he couldn't get up. "Justin, look at me. Relax."

As Justin immediately shifted to the command, Ren was amazed anew at how big Justin's eyes were and how even though they were so wide and focused on him, he still couldn't decide on the color.

They were dark, or maybe they weren't, and clouded. They *were* still full of fear and frustration.

"You're going to be all right," Ren calmed, watching as his words flipped the fear, twisting it into disbelief. Justin pulled his knees to his chest, wrapping his arms around them. "You aren't going to be stuck forever."

"Just the next four to fifteen years," Justin murmured, ducking his head behind his knees. Ren bit into his lip, realizing Justin was making a very dark joke about how long he could be sentenced to prison.

"Can I get you anything?" Ren tried to change the subject, not sure if he were ready for Justin to start lowering his guard over the details of the trial. He could no longer pretend to know nothing, but he surprisingly didn't want to talk about it yet either. Because once he knew the real truth, there would be no going back. He wanted to stall. "Maybe some ice? Are you hungry?"

Justin lifted his head, his expression quizzical, fierce, and defiant. "Why aren't you asking me what you really want to ask me?" he challenged. He sounded like he was up against a wall with nowhere to go, his voice stronger than it had been since yesterday morning. Ren thought carefully about how he wanted to answer him, deciding to risk turning off the oxygen flow at the wall before saying anything.

"I did want to ask you," Ren allowed, returning to where Justin could see him, sitting down again. "But it's none of my business."

"You saved my life," Justin returned, and Ren began to wonder if Justin maybe wanted to tell him but somehow couldn't volunteer the information unless Ren demanded it from him first.

"Justin, you don't have to tell me anything," Ren maintained.

"I killed someone," Justin finally blurted out, and Ren sighed, wishing he hadn't said that.

"No, you didn't," he countered, amazingly calm, not knowing anything about it but somehow feeling it just wasn't possible. Or maybe that he didn't want it to be possible.

"I did," Justin confirmed, sounding displeased that Ren wasn't believing or even reacting much to this revelation. "I'm not like you, ok? I'm not a good person."

"Shut up, Justin," Ren surprised himself by saying, but it felt good to rip the velvet gloves off how they talked to each other. He knew what was happening now. Justin had been too sick before to put up much protest about anything. But now, with his physical pain dulled to nothing and his heart behaving as it was supposed to, now Justin could act more like himself. The boy who kept his distance from anyone who might try to care about him just as North had said. "You're not a bad person either."

"How do you know? You don't know anything about me." Justin's tone shifted somewhere between indignant and despondent.

"So, tell me," Ren dared more than invited, even though he thought he knew more than Justin suspected.

"You should go home, Ren," Justin shifted, pulling back. "Go back to your friends; they're worried about you."

"They're worried about *you*," Ren pressed, leaning forward. "So is North. So am I. I don't want to leave you alone, Justin, and I don't think you really want me to either."

"How can you be like that?" Justin demanded, perplexed. "Didn't you hear what I said?"

"It wasn't your fault, Justin," Ren insisted. "You don't remember, but you talked about it last night. You said you didn't mean to, that you were sorry. You said you just wanted him to stop. That doesn't sound like murder to me, Justin. It sounds like defense, and I can't believe they're putting you on trial for it. The whole thing is a joke."

Now Justin looked completely stricken, tamed and quiet. "You already knew?"

"Yes," Ren confessed, feeling guilty. "Denny looked it up after hearing some of the stuff you said when you were out of it. She told me about the trial, that you'd confessed to a murder."

"And you still ..." Justin was suddenly speechless, turning away to look at the IV in his hand. "Why?"

"Because I promised I'd take care of you," Ren told him, because it really was that simple. *There are some people in this world who do keep promises, Justin, and I'm one of them.* "And I believe that *if* you really did kill someone, it was because you were forced to. Is that what happened? Was he hurting you?"

"Me? No," Justin said, so quietly, slowly pulling Ren's blanket over himself as if for protection.

"Someone else then? No, wait," Ren stood up, running a hand through his hair. "You don't have to answer that." He went to the stock cabinets, nervously turning on the faucet so he could splash water on his face.

"I was in a bookstore," Justin began almost defiantly behind Ren, which made him shut off the water and hang his head over the sink, listening intently. "I used to hang out there a lot because it didn't close until midnight." Ren took a slow inhale. There was so much Justin had given him in that sentence.

"It wasn't that late, but it was already dark outside," Justin kept talking when Ren didn't turn or respond. It seemed there would be no going back now. "I heard some arguing in a corner, a girl trying to get some creep to leave her alone."

He wouldn't stop. He wouldn't get off. Ren hid his face in his hands, kept his back toward Justin.

"I got between them, told him to get lost. He backed off and left, the girl thanked me, and I thought we were done. She stayed in the store another thirty minutes, and I watched her. She was shook up, you know? She called someone and was waiting for them to get there. I didn't offer to walk her out, but I should have. God, I should have."

Justin paused, overcome with regret. Ren carefully looked over his shoulder to see if Justin needed any help, checked his stats on the monitor to see if talking about this was damaging in any way. He opened his mouth to let Justin know he could stop if it were bothering him. At least, that's what he meant to say.

"Was he waiting for her outside?" Ren asked instead, prompting Justin to continue, anticipating the scenario of these strangers. This situation Justin stepped into without knowing how horribly it would end for him.

"He grabbed her in the parking lot," Justin confirmed. "Started dragging her. It was dark; no one noticed. Her friend didn't even see him; she was looking for a spot to park or something."

"But you saw him," Ren affirmed, hanging on Justin's every word.

"I ran out there, but he almost had her in his car already. I yelled at him, tried to get him off her. He used to be her boyfriend; that's why he was fighting so hard. I don't even remember what happened after he tried to punch me. There was screaming. I just kept hitting back until the police came and pulled me off him."

"And he was dead?" Ren asked, not sure why.

"No," Justin responded. "Not then. I put him in the hospital, but he didn't die until later."

"And the girl? Was she ok?"

"Yeah, she was fine. Scared. I remember her sitting with her friend with a blanket over her, both of them staring at me when I was being handcuffed."

"Were you hurt?" Had anyone even checked? The girls, hadn't they explained what really happened? They were witnesses; they knew Justin had only been trying to save someone. This was all wrong.

"I took a few hits, nothing serious," Justin responded, all the emotion stripped forcefully from his tone.

"And they're putting you on trial for this?" Ren asked, incredulous. This was nothing like what he'd imagined happened, not even close.

"That's what manslaughter is," Justin said, closing his eyes as Ren turned to face him. "He's dead because of what I did to him; his parents want me executed."

"God, stop. Just stop."

"You don't have to stay," Justin told him, keeping his eyes closed.

As if he thought now that Ren had the truth, he'd want to run away and Justin didn't want to watch him leave. "I get it."

"No, you really don't," Ren fumed, furious and vindicated at the same time and not able to keep it out of his voice even though he knew Justin would take it the wrong way. "This is wrong. You saved her, Justin!"

But he could easily see how it could have been thrown out of context. The couple had dated once. The girl wasn't injured. No one could prove her ex meant to harm her. Ren could hear the arguments now. Why had Justin felt the need to go so far? There are other ways to stop someone without the use of lethal force. And knowing Justin's history ... yeah, it was easy to see how it'd been twisted to be all Justin's fault.

I didn't mean to, Justin had cried. *Please, listen. You have to believe me.*

But he'd been on his own with no one to speak for him.

"Justin," Ren said again, because Justin had curled into a miserable ball under the blanket. Ren closed the distance between them, putting a gentle hand on Justin's shoulder. "Justin, thanks for telling me. It means a lot."

It meant a piece of Ren's soul could ease about Justin. He wasn't a killer, at least not intentionally, and everyone who had told Ren that he was being an idiot for sticking with Justin were wrong.

"It doesn't change anything," Justin lamented, and Ren had to admit this could also be the truth. Because there was still all that evidence that looked as though Justin were a danger to society, and Ren wasn't certain anyone would take the time, especially now when the trial was basically over, to consider looking at it another way.

"You're right; it doesn't," Ren told him, which made Justin lift his head, steeling himself to be hurt by whatever Ren said next. Ren tightened his hold on Justin's shoulder. He looked absolutely wretched, expecting Ren to desert him like everyone else. "Because I still want to be your friend," Ren confirmed, as serious as he could. "And I'm staying with you."

Justin's eyes welled up, and he darted behind the blanket again with a frustrated hiss. "You're unbelievable," Ren heard him say, muffled under fabric and tears.

"Yeah, you are," Ren returned before letting it drop. Ren wanted to call Denny and tell her off. Tell her she needed to do better research before she formed opinions about people from what she found online. He also wanted to call North and beg him to figure a way out of this. There was no way Justin should go to prison. He'd been trying to help.

But the trial was over. The jury had made a decision. Ren was still reassuringly holding to Justin, pondering how the sentence could be changed if the jury had decided Justin was guilty, when Abbie came in with an IV bag full of the rust-colored iron solution. He held a finger to his lips and shook his head at her when she began asking them if they were ok. With professional understanding, she quickly slipped the bag onto the pole and inserted another line into Justin's existing IV. Ren shuddered, watching as the iron bled into the color-less saline solution, a treatment that looked more sinister than bene-ficial. Abbie lifted her hand to her ear in a "call me" gesture before tip-toeing out the door.

Ren wished there was someone he could call. Wished he weren't walking into this so late in the game. Justin peered out of the blanket suddenly, looking up at the IV pole in surprised fear, noticing how the color had changed. He turned to Ren, who tried to smile, knowing that even though he couldn't do much, he could make sure that whatever happened to Justin, he wouldn't go through it alone.

15

CONVALESCENCE

"What the hell are they putting in me?" Justin asked, sounding disgusted and horrified.

"It's iron," Ren told him. "And yes, that's how it's supposed to look."

"Like they dumped out an old toolbox and mixed it with chocolate syrup?" Justin checked, pivoting his gaze between the bag hanging on the IV pole and the place where the needle disappeared into his vein. Ren unexpectedly burst out laughing.

"Never heard anyone say it that way, but you're right," Ren explained himself, smiling at Justin, who was watching him closely again, his face serious but not offended. "Why are you staring at me like that?" Ren couldn't help but ask.

"I didn't know you knew how to laugh," Justin said, still serious, though there was something else there too. Something unrestrained, almost teasing.

"And I didn't know you were funny," Ren returned.

"Yeah, well," Justin deflated, squinting again at the line. "And this is really supposed to help?"

"It'll definitely help with the anemia, which will strengthen your immune system so it can do what it's programmed to do and kick that flu virus for you. In a couple of days, I bet you'll feel brand new. We should have come here a long time ago." Ren finished with his voice lowering into regret. "It wouldn't have been so bad," he admitted, hanging his head.

Justin fidgeted with the tape on his hand, smoothing the edges. "Ren," he began, unsure. Ren raised his eyes to pay close attention. Because whenever Justin said his name, it was important. "What's the deal with you? I don't get it."

"What's not to get?" Ren sought out more information. "I'm a pretty simple guy."

"Then why are all the doctors fighting about you?"

"Oh, that." Ren had hoped Angelique and Dr. Taneja's spat on the phone had been long forgotten. "I don't know."

Justin's face closed immediately; all the tentative trust shut off so fast Ren almost gasped. He thought Ren was lying to him, so he was pulling back. It made sense, but Ren was going to have to act quickly to convince Justin he was telling the truth.

"I mean, I know what the fight is, but I don't know why they think they need to have one," Ren remedied what he'd just said, watching Justin relax again. "Especially Dr. Delacroix. I thought she'd written me off a long time ago."

Justin continued to look interested, and they had a lot of time to kill before morning, so Ren went ahead and told him how he'd met Angelique and how he'd just as quickly fallen from grace with her only to have perked her interest again with one carefully placed IV in an unauthorized place in the back of a moving ambulance.

"Wait," Justin said, wrapping his head around Ren's description. "You sure you're talking about the same person? Because I've never been called so many pet names in my life."

"You're a patient; that's different," Ren explained. "But she makes almost all of her students cry or quit, and you heard her talk to Dr. Taneja. She doesn't teach regular classes anymore, and she only presents one or two lectures a year. Anything she does for students is strictly one-on-one by invitation only."

"How come she's allowed to do that?"

"Because she's awesome at her job. Having her name on a federal grant application means it's practically guaranteed to be funded. And any student who can claim her for a mentor or get a letter of recommendation from her can probably just pick whatever job they want anywhere."

"And she's going to be your mentor?" Justin asked, sounding surprised, or perhaps impressed.

"No way! Dr. Taneja is my mentor. I wouldn't last five minutes with Dr. Delacroix. Like I said, she's tough on students, and she hasn't invited anyone to shadow her for a long time."

"Why?" Justin wondered out loud. "Something to prove or what?"

"I think it's just because being an ER doctor is really difficult," Ren said, almost enjoying himself. If he brought his attention in enough, focused on the sound of Justin's voice and the safe-for-the-moment topic, he could pretend they were just friends having a regular conversation. "She doesn't want to waste her time on people she knows would break under the pressure. Not everybody can handle it."

"You can," Justin encouraged, sounding completely convinced.

"No," Ren denied, almost shuddering when he remembered what it had taken for him to perform this afternoon and what it had done to him afterward. "That's not for me. That's not the kind of doctor I want to be anyway."

"Then what kind do you want to be?" Justin asked.

"I want to be a pediatrician," Ren disclosed. "Have my own practice with steady hours, you know? I want to help children."

Justin looked skeptical now, different than when he'd thought Ren was lying to him. This was more like he thought Ren didn't know what he was talking about.

"So, if you aren't her student and you don't want to work in the

ER, why does she care so much what you do?" Justin asked, as if Ren knew the answer to that.

"See, that's where we're both confused," Ren said. "I have no idea; I didn't even know she'd been paying any attention to me since she had me in her office months ago. It's weird."

"She wants you in the ER," Justin speculated. "She knows you can do it, and she doesn't want anyone to screw it up for you before she can get you in. That's why she's so pissed."

"That," Ren started to protest but then paused to consider. Could that be true? No, no way. She hadn't mentored a student in years; there were all sorts of rumors about what had happened to the last one. "You think?"

"That's why I said it," Justin said dryly. "You should think about it. You're pretty damn good at it."

Except you almost died because I'm not any good at it, Ren wanted to tell him. He decided to turn the conversation back to Justin instead.

"What about you?" Ren flipped. "What do you want to do?" But his question almost crippled Justin, making him wish he hadn't asked. Justin opened his mouth, then closed it, shaking his head, seeming to shrink.

"I don't think it'll matter what I want," he revealed, dark and sad again.

"You're not going to jail, Justin," Ren promised, though he knew there was no way he could know and definitely no way he could guarantee. He just couldn't imagine Justin being punished for trying to save someone. Justin obviously thought differently.

"I've already gone to jail for this," he shot back, bitter.

"What?" Ren sputtered, thrown off balance. "What do you mean?" Justin looked sorry he'd said anything. "Justin?"

"I mean the first time this went to trial, I was sentenced to six months in juvie," Justin tossed out quickly, sounding mad and hopeless. "So yeah, pretty sure it'll be the same."

"Wait, back up," Ren scrambled. Just when he thought he understood what was going on. It was like Justin specialized in shock value, and Ren had to think about what that word meant. "Like a juvenile detention center?" Denny said Justin had spent some time in a correctional facility. But that couldn't have been for this, could it? "And what do you mean the first time? You can't be put on trial twice for the same thing."

"It doesn't matter," Justin said, melting into the bed.

"No, Justin, it really does," Ren contradicted, forcing himself not to lean too close to Justin in his sudden intensity. How much more twisted could these facts be? "When did you beat this guy up anyway? How old were you?"

"Sixteen," Justin answered brusquely, looking at Ren the way Ren suspected he looked at the prosecuting attorney. Cooperative, but only at the most minimum level required. Now Ren was very confused. He knew sometimes the judicial system took a while, but almost two years seemed extreme for something to come to trial. But Justin had just said it had already gone to trial when he was still a minor and this was the second time. But that was impossible. What the hell was Justin talking about?

"That was over a year ago; why is this coming up now? Or again?" Ren couldn't help but ask, needing Justin to explain since every time Ren tried figuring out an explanation it was wrong.

"Because he just died eight weeks ago," Justin said, annoyed, as if it were obvious, sounding as though he'd like to change the subject, but Ren wasn't finished. In fact, he'd pounced up from the chair, beginning to pace as he always did when he needed his brain to put details in order. "Ren, what the hell?"

"Exactly," Ren muttered in agreement, thinking, moving back and forth in the tight space. "So, if he just died recently, what did they send you to jail for the first time? Assault?" Because that could be it. Justin beat up this person, who was sent to the hospital but didn't die. Justin consequently was sentenced to six months in a correctional facility as a minor on assault charges, was released and thinking everything was over, but then was arrested again because the person he beat up over a year ago suddenly what? Died eight weeks ago? But how would that involve Justin at all?

"Ren, stop that," Justin commanded instead of answering. "I hate it when you — hold still."

Ren turned his head to look at Justin, and he tried to stop pacing, he really did, but this information had lit him up like a stick of dynamite. Something didn't add up. And something needed to be done about it. Now.

"You're telling me," Ren clarified. "They're trying to convict you for this guy dying even though you beat him up over a year ago? They can't do that. Did you even see him?"

"Ren ... come on, knock it off," Justin begged gruffly, reaching for him from where he lay pinned to the hospital bed. Ren forced himself over to the bedside, standing next to the chair with both hands on his hips.

"How can they say it was you?" Ren almost barked the question, not necessarily at Justin, though he was conveniently the only one in the room. "That makes no sense. What did your lawyer say?"

"Can we quit talking about this?" Justin said, but Ren could hardly hear him.

"It couldn't have been your fault," Ren continued, overcome with how much he wanted that to be true and also how powerless he felt about convincing everyone he was right about it. "There's no way."

"But it was!" Justin shouted, and now Ren had to close up and start paying attention. Justin was panting, his outburst taking more energy than he had to spare. He'd put a hand against his chest, glaring at Ren even though his other hand was still outstretched, resting against the guardrail. He bowed his head, his back curling. Justin gasped in some more oxygen so he could keep going now that he had Ren's focus. "He died of complications from the brain injury I gave him, ok? It *is* my fault. Because every time I try to do anything right, I fuck it up. It's always like that, and it's always going to be like that, got it? Quit trying to pretend I'm —" he cut himself off, choking on the word for whatever he suspected Ren thought.

"Justin," Ren tried to pacify him, too late. The hand that had been reaching for him pulled back as Justin rested his palm against his forehead.

"Just go away," Justin demanded. "Go pace somewhere else. I'm tired."

"Justin, I'm sorry," Ren began, amazed he was being sent away over this. If Justin wanted to change the subject, they could change the subject. He wasn't convinced in the least, but they didn't have to talk about it anymore.

"Leave me alone," Justin commanded again.

"Justin, I'm on your side about this," Ren tried to explain, but Justin wouldn't look at him. He was fishing around all the various cords and tubes on the bed, searching for the remote with the nurse call button, as though he were going to flag down someone to physically remove Ren from the room. "I'm just trying to help you."

"I never asked you to!"

Ren felt his teeth click shut, shocked, remembering how he had indeed volunteered himself into Justin's life. Justin's first words to him had been a request for Ren to stay away after a punch to the face. Anyone with common sense would have run in the other direction and never looked back.

"Get out," Justin said again, voice very quiet now, face turned away.

"Fine. I'll leave if that's what you want," Ren gave in, remorseful, hurt, and angry. He grabbed his coat and backpack, ashamed and suddenly lost.

He marched past the triage rooms and out of the emergency wing entirely. *Damn it, Justin; I'm just trying to help. That's all I've been doing since I found you. Despite what everyone's been telling me about how I shouldn't. And this is how you react, huh?* How ungrateful could a person get?

"Idiot," Ren murmured to himself as he wandered the darkened hospital, through the busy emergency waiting room, into the main part of the building. First, he walked unconsciously to the closed plasma donation center, needing to put some distance between him and Justin. Why the hell was he so mad at Ren anyway? All he wanted was to clear Justin of this crime Ren still wasn't convinced he was responsible for. How was that a bad thing? He pivoted against the closed doors of the donation center and headed toward the hospital entrance, fuming.

Ren flopped onto one of the more comfortable chairs in the front reception area near the gift shop, where everything was dark and closed for the night. It was the perfect place for a pity party. What was Ren supposed to do now?

Go home, was the immediate answer from one part of his mind, and he had to admit that seemed a tempting choice. It was getting close to eleven; Dr. Taneja had already offered him a ride. All he had to do was hop in the elevator across reception and take it to the third floor. Dr. Taneja wouldn't even ask him why he'd changed his mind. It would be easy. His apartment would be warm and smell like Alek's baking. He could get some food; he hadn't eaten anything since this afternoon. If he tried hard enough, he could maybe cut this whole experience from his emotional database. *Justin Kittrick? Who's that? No one I know*. The thought was meant to be sarcastic, but Ren found it cut deep. Just when he'd thought they could start being real friends. But Justin didn't have friends, North said. Well now Ren could see why if he pushed them away every time they tried to help him.

Ren swept his legs up and over the armrest of the chair, folding his arms and, being careful of the wound on his back, scrunching down until his neck nestled against the opposite armrest.

"I left my blanket," he whispered to himself. *Ugh*. How was he supposed to get that back? Maybe Abbie could help. He could go ask her. She'd probably look at him funny, but what else was new? That's what everyone was doing to him lately. Officer Geisler, Angelique, North, Denny, they all looked at him with the same damn question on their faces.

Ren covered his face with his hands, mentally and physically exhausted. His body sank deep into the chair, pinched between the armrests, his coat and backpack on the floor beside him. All his nervous energy quieted here in the dark silence of the reception area, shorted out like a burnt fuse and leaving him boneless, draped in the chair like an afghan. He'd have to get up in a minute, though, if he wanted to catch Dr. Taneja.

He pulled out his phone to check the time, almost dropping it as it started ringing in his hands, breaking the atmosphere. The number wasn't one Ren recognized.

"Hello?" Ren greeted, dragging himself upright in the chair.

"Hi, Ren, it's Eli — it's North," came the answer. "How are things going over there? Justin ok?" Ren rolled his eyes, glad North couldn't see him.

"Don't know," he replied curtly. "He kicked me out."

"Oh good!" North exclaimed immediately, sounding oddly relieved, which made Ren's jaw drop. What? Good? He felt tears sting his eyes, and he blinked them impatiently away. He was not going to get upset about this; it shouldn't matter.

"Yeah, it was great," he said facetiously. It was one thing for Justin to have done it, but it hurt more than Ren expected to hear North happy about it. Fine thing to say to the guy who'd saved Justin's stupid life!

"Sorry, Ren," North apologized, his tone softened significantly. "That didn't come out right. He probably said some pretty cruel things to you, didn't he? But it does sound more like the Justin I know, which means he's feeling better. Are you ok?"

"It doesn't matter," Ren murmured. He rubbed his sleeve aggressively against his face, wincing.

"I know it's not the best way to show it, but I know Justin likes you," North defended, and Ren shrugged even though North couldn't see him. Not the best way to show it? Try the *worst way* to show it. He was so tired. "Where are you now? You're not with Justin?"

No! Ren wanted to yell. *Weren't you listening? He kicked me out! I'm going home, like I should have done hours ago. I don't need this mess.*

"I'm waiting for Dr. Taneja," Ren said, his voice icy, looking toward the elevator as though he expected to see his mustached mentor appearing out of it any second. "He said he'd give me a ride."

"Oh," North vocalized his disappointment, but seriously, what did he expect? "Of course, but can I ask what happened? What did Justin say?"

"He told me why he's on trial," Ren practically snarled. *Cool it*, he admonished himself. *It's not North's fault Justin is a jerk.* "But it doesn't make any sense. When I tried to ask him some more questions, he got mad and wanted me to leave."

"He told you what happened?" North repeated, incredulous. "Ren ... you don't understand what it took for him to do that."

"Is it true?" Ren heard himself ask, glossing over how hard it might have been for Justin to say anything. He didn't want to give Justin any credit right now. But if Justin wouldn't give him the details, maybe North would. "They're really blaming him for this guy dying more than a year after Justin attacked him?"

"It does look like the events are related," North answered sadly. "Though I haven't had a chance to hear back from Ms. Kelly yet about how the trial went. I wish I'd been there, but I just didn't know it was happening. I thought that was all behind us."

"It's not fair," Ren unexpectedly blurted out, sounding whiny to himself despite his conviction. "Even if they are related, Justin saved that girl. It's not a crime to prevent a crime."

"It is according to the Hunts," North corrected him, also sounding cold.

"What?" Ren asked, confused, feeling as though his brain had somehow slowed down after sunset. He wasn't sure how much more of this he could take.

"William Hunt," North went on. "He works for Citadel, financial trading. He and his wife, Lisa, live out in Oak Brook, one of the wealthiest families in Chicago."

"And they matter because?" Ren prompted, realizing just at this moment that he had a headache.

"Because they believe Justin killed their son. They're the ones pressing the charges, and they can take it as far as they need it to go."

"But North," Ren sputtered, curling over to lay his head on the armrest, closing his eyes. "That's wrong; they can't really do that, can they?"

"Unfortunately, they can, but in this case, they aren't going to have to try very hard. The report makes a convincing argument that David, that's his name, died as a result of his previous injuries."

"What exactly did Justin do to him?" Ren pondered out loud.

"Think about it," North answered. "Look what he did to you half asleep and running a fever. Now imagine him healthy, angry, and actively trying to hurt you." Ren decided not to go too deep into a vision like that. Just thinking about how Justin looked after that first punch was bad enough.

"So what do we do?" Ren asked, then wanted to smack himself. He didn't need to do anything. He wasn't obligated in any way to defend or help Justin. In fact, Justin had basically told him he didn't want Ren to help at all.

"You've done plenty, Ren; I can't thank you enough," North said, his voice warm, though still worried. "Though I wish you could ... no, never mind. Go ahead and head home. You sound tired."

"What do you need me to do, North?" Ren requested, because even though he was tired, North sounded worse. Ren felt nothing but respect for North, which meant he also wanted to help him.

"It's not fair to ask you, Ren," North told him, though Ren could hear how desperately North wanted to ask. He also thought he knew what it was.

"You want me to stay with him," Ren said it for him.

"I know he can be difficult," North admitted. "But yes, I do want someone to stay with him. I can't stand thinking of him in that room all night alone. I've never seen him sick like this before, and I know he's scared, though he'll never admit it. And I don't think there is anyone better than you to watch him while I'm trying to sort this mess. But I get that he hurt you, and he probably will again even if he's trying hard not to, so I understand if you need to leave."

"I'd stay if I thought he'd let me anywhere near him." Ren gave the excuse, but it sounded weak. Justin hadn't asked Ren to come to his apartment, but that hadn't stopped him. What sort of person was he if a little argument would make him break his promise? And Justin wasn't the only one who got annoyed when Ren fidgeted too much. Denny had almost screamed at him about it. It even bothered Alek, who was arguably the most laid-back guy in the world. Ren had pushed too far, despite Justin asking him to stop. He probably owed him an apology.

"I think you'd be surprised," North encouraged. "I'll bet he's sitting in that room mad at himself and wondering why he said what he did. He'll act rough, but if you can be strong and walk back in there, I don't think he'll say anything to stop you."

Ren felt the beginnings of loyalty swell inside his chest, and he knew there probably wasn't much he wouldn't do in order to gain North's approval. But in this case, North was asking him to do something he secretly wanted to do anyway. He just needed an external reason. Somehow it made it easier thinking of it as a request. Ren could go back and sit with Justin as a favor to North. It was like receiving permission.

"All right, fine," he gave in, putting more annoyance into his voice than he felt. He heard North sigh in relief.

"Thank you, Ren," he said. "I know it's not obvious, but Justin trusts you. I'll check in again later."

"Great," Ren answered, hoping when he did that there would be some good news. North hung up, leaving Ren alone in the dark. He rested his arms against his knees, allowing his body to droop, giving himself a minute before he gathered his energy to return to Justin. It was going to be a very long night. Although, probably not as long as last night. Nothing could be worse than last night.

"Let's hope not," Ren whispered, pushing himself upright and once again picking up his coat and backpack. Maybe it was time to see exactly what Alek had put in there; it seemed unnaturally heavy now that he thought about it. He tossed it over his shoulders, sagging under the weight and beginning to plod through the hallways towards the emergency room entrance. He felt neither brave nor strong. Mostly he felt defeated.

Justin's room looked abandoned from the outside. If Ren didn't know better, he would have wondered if Justin had been moved. The lights remained as Abbie had left them, off except for the one behind the bed on the wall. As Ren stepped closer, he could see Justin through the open blinds of the hall window. He was turned away from the entrance, possibly asleep. Ren felt guilty about how easily he'd almost left him behind.

As quietly as he could, Ren let himself into the room without knocking. Since he wasn't interested in what Justin had to say about him being here, he figured he could skip the part where he pretended to ask permission. And if Justin were sleeping, he didn't want to disturb him.

But Justin wasn't asleep. He turned to look over his shoulder. When he saw Ren, he almost pulled the quilt all the way over his head, turning his whole body away from him on the bed. Ren let that go, remembering what North had said, returning to his seat and calmly putting down his stuff.

"Hey," Ren called softly, a gentle alert that he was back even though he knew Justin had seen him.

"You done freaking out?" Justin asked, the sound muffled from his position.

"Yep," Ren answered casually, keeping his emotions carefully closed.

"I thought you went home," Justin accused, his body folded tight.

"I thought about it," Ren said, deciding to be honest.

"Is North making you stay?" Justin asked suddenly, and Ren could hear the pain again. It made him pause, sad how he'd almost hurt Justin by leaving him, especially after he'd been so mad at everyone else who had done that.

"He *asked* me to stay," Ren acknowledged. "But he can't make me do anything I didn't want to do in the first place."

Justin shifted slightly, rotating his torso backward so he could look at Ren properly. He kept his arms folded against his chest and his hips didn't move, leaving him looking uncomfortably twisted. He studied Ren carefully, gauging his mood and motives. Ren kept still and silent, feeling as though he were being assessed for danger by a wild animal. He tried to be as non-threatening as possible.

"He's pretty awesome, huh?" Ren allowed when he couldn't take the staring anymore, still speaking of North.

"He's a fighter pilot," Justin volunteered.

There was so much respect and admiration in Justin's voice, talking about North as though he still jumped in his plane every weekend to take out terrorists, and Ren remembered something Denny told him. Justin had tried to join the Air Force but had been turned down. North must have been so influential for Justin, such a positive role model.

"That's really cool," Ren complimented, feeling as though Justin would accept these words as if Ren had said them about him.

"Yeah," Justin agreed, then the conversation sputtered into awkward silence again. Ren could tell neither of them was going to bring up what happened, for their own personal reasons, but now it seemed they didn't know what to do with each other. Ren almost asked Justin how he was feeling but thought it might not be the best way to start talking again. So he leaned back as far as he could without tipping the chair over, interlocking his fingers and pressing them against the top of his head. He wondered if Dr. Taneja had remembered to ask for that cot.

"You think your table is really buried in cookies?" Justin asked, sounding innocent in his disbelief. Ren smiled.

"Denny might have given them all away by now," he said,

picturing it, almost smelling it. "But yeah, Alek can do some serious baking when he's worried."

"Wish we had some," Justin muttered, forcing Ren to sit up.

"Are you hungry?" he checked.

"I can't tell, maybe," Justin said noncommittally. "Is that ok?" Ren leaned forward carefully, stretching out a hand.

"It's more than ok," Ren assured. "It's a good sign."

He dipped down, pulling his bag up and plopping it on Justin's bed between them. "Should we see what's in here? Alek might have packed something edible," he suggested. Justin shrugged, arms still folded, though he did turn his hips, lying on his back now, head resting but turned toward Ren again.

Ren undid the zipper, pulling apart the opening to peer inside. He found his phone charger, and there was a small plastic bag with a spoon in it that Ren set on the bed.

"This is promising," he said lightly, drawing out a travel thermos and unscrewing the cap. He had to turn it toward the light, sniffing it experimentally, recognizing the scent. "Thanks Alek," he breathed.

"What is it?" Justin asked, maneuvering himself upright against the angled upper portion of the bed, interested in spite of himself.

"Proof that Alek likes you more than me," Ren answered, handing over the thermos and reaching for the spoon. "That's the last of the rice pudding. Alek threatened my life if I touched it."

"It's probably yours," Justin countered, though he took the container, looking almost wistfully inside it. "I don't think I can eat it."

"It's soft enough; it shouldn't hurt your mouth too much," Ren told him. "Trust me; he sent it for you." Ren dropped the spoon into the pudding, nodding reassuringly. "See if you can handle a bite or two."

"What are you going to do? If I'm hungry, I know you've got to be," Justin returned.

"I'm fine," Ren assured. "Go on."

Justin took a deep breath, practically inhaling the spoon, keeping it in his mouth as he tested the bite, closing his eyes. Ren decided he liked watching Justin eat. He did it with an appreciation of someone who hasn't always had ready access to food, who had to fight with himself between shoveling huge bites into his mouth as quickly as possible and savoring each bit to make it last longer. With the pudding, savoring won out, and Justin moaned appreciatively with his mouth full.

"Ok?" Ren checked. Just because he thought the pudding wouldn't bother the blisters in Justin's mouth didn't mean it was true.

"How does he do this?" Justin asked, releasing the spoon so he could plunge it back into the thermos. "I've never tasted anything like it."

"I have a couple theories," Ren responded. "I figure he's either an alchemist or he sold his soul to a crossroads demon." Justin raised an eyebrow at him, not bothering to give an answer to this because he was busy taking another bite.

"Want me to see if I can find you something else?" Ren offered after Justin quickly emptied the thermos.

"It's ok," Justin absolved him. "I'm done."

"Is there anything you need?" Ren continued, wanting to be of service.

"No," Justin sighed, leaning against the bed, his hands resting loosely in his lap. Ren moved everything to the side, giving himself the freedom to stand up to help tuck Justin in.

"How are you doing, Justin?" Ren felt it was safe to ask now. "How's your heart?"

"It hurts," Justin admitted, voice catching slightly. Ren barely heard it. He pulled the quilt up to Justin's chin, letting go to rest his palm against his chest, worried. The pulse had been steady for a long time now; the pain medication should be taking all of Justin's discomfort. He shouldn't be feeling much of anything. Justin began to curl up; Ren could almost see the weight of his life crushing him against the bed. He wondered what Justin was thinking right now, recognizing that the pain Justin felt was more an ache in his soul than anything physical.

"That's normal," Ren comforted him, grateful North had talked him into staying.

"How long?" Justin began but couldn't finish the question. Ren understood why. There was usually a tipping point in an illness, especially a long intense one like Justin's, where it became too exhausting to hope, and it just felt as though there would never be an end. For Justin, as always, it was worse because even if he felt better, he was still convinced his life would not return to normal. His future was as dark and cold as the storm on the lake had been last night.

"Not much longer," Ren said, knowing they both knew he had no idea what he was talking about. But he wanted to give Justin something. "Get some sleep, Justin; you'll feel better in the morning."

"What about you?" Justin asked. "Weren't they supposed to bring in a bed for you or something?"

Ren shrugged. That wasn't anything Justin had to worry about. "They're probably busy; I can go find out in a while. Close your eyes."

Ren eased himself into the chair, which was stiff and cold and too small for him to adjust in. He pulled one leg up to his chest so he could rest his forehead against his knee, securing himself by gripping his ankle on either side.

"Ren, you can't sleep like that," Justin pointed out.

"Wanna bet?" Ren murmured. He was tired enough that he thought he could sleep standing up in the corner. He wished he had a blanket, though. The ER was kept pretty cool most of the time, but after ten it seemed they turned the heat way down. He uncoiled himself momentarily to pick up his coat from the floor.

"You cold?" Justin asked him.

"I'm Dominican; I'm always cold," Ren returned, wishing Justin would just quit watching him and go to sleep already.

"Why don't you come here," Justin invited, no emotion in his voice. Ren paused putting his arms through his sleeves to see Justin scooting as close to the side of his bed as he could get, pressing himself against the guardrail and opening the quilt and hospital blanket up for Ren to lie down beside him.

"Because I don't know the weight limit on that bed, and there's no point both of us being uncomfortable," Ren argued, not making any attempt to get closer.

"Don't be stupid; there's room."

Ren tried to translate Justin's tone. Was he just trying to be nice, or did he actually want Ren in bed with him? They'd done it before. For a few minutes at the apartment when Justin was under a blanket and Ren was on top. That position had been at Justin's request too.

"There's a chair in the waiting room I was using before," Ren offered, almost as a test. "I can crash out there for a few hours. You don't have to make space for me."

Justin's face fell slightly, making Ren sure. This was more than a gesture of politeness. This was how Justin said he was sorry. This was how Justin could ask for something he might want without having to actually ask. "Ren," he said again, so much meaning in the name, part coaxing, part frustrated.

"You sure you're ok with this?" Ren asked one more time, slowly pulling off his coat again.

"Would you hurry up? My arm is getting tired," Justin said. Ren kicked out of his shoes, leaving them beside his backpack. Trying not to think too much about what he was doing, he slipped under the familiar weight of his mother's quilt. Justin lifted his arm more, drawing back as though he were going to toss the corner of the blanket farther over Ren, but Ren grabbed it away from him before he could.

"Watch that IV," Ren cautioned him. "I didn't risk my career for you to rip it out now."

"Shit," Justin whispered, horrified at what he'd almost done, because he apparently hadn't even thought of that. He also probably hadn't meant for Ren to hear him, but their heads were close together now. Ren tried to relax but found it difficult. He lay stiffly on his back. Now that he was under the covers, he could feel Justin's unnatural heat beside him. This probably wasn't the best idea. If they had a different relationship, Ren would have slipped his hand beneath Justin, allowing him to pillow his head in the crook of his shoulder. He wasn't even sure if he could chill out enough to fall asleep now that he had to pay attention to make sure he didn't get too close.

"Hey, Justin," he began, trying to think of another sleeping situation that would be more comfortable.

"Don't make it weird," Justin ordered. Ren shut his mouth.

Taking turns making tiny, hesitant adjustments, they began to settle in. Ren inched himself onto his side, facing the sink and the door while Justin turned the opposite way toward his IV pole until their backs braced against each other. Ren drew his arms close to his chest, feeling Justin's breathing against his spine and the edge of the bed close to his hip.

He lay there a long time, eyes open, watching as shadows went back and forth outside in the hallway. Justin's breaths lengthened and slowed as he drifted off, and he twitched a few times as his brain transitioned into sleep. It made Ren smile, comparing their current situation to last night, how drastic the differences were. How much he had learned in the past twenty-four hours, not just about Justin but also about North, Dr. Taneja, Angelique, and even Denny and Alek. And everything that had seemed to be crashing in on top of them suddenly moved too far away to even think about. Even the dawn was an eternity from now, from this moment, confined in a too-small hospital bed next to a fevered, unpredictable partner. As if there would never be a morning.

Justin began to whimper as he slept, murmuring unintelligibly though he stayed motionless. Ren flipped around clumsily, listening with a heavy heart as Justin unconsciously wept. He raised himself onto his elbow so he could lean over him, not surprised to see tears on Justin's face.

"Shh," Ren whispered, wanting to help but not wanting to wake him, putting a careful hand on his upturned shoulder. "Justin, it's ok."

You were going to leave him, Ren berated himself. *You were going to let him suffer alone.*

Ren sat up a little, curling protectively over Justin, gently pulling at him. Justin didn't resist, submitting loosely to wherever Ren moved him, twisting himself up and against Ren, the hand with the IV strapped to the wrist raising to hold onto Ren's shirt near his collarbone. Ren did his best to keep Justin's hospital gown straightened and covering him, wrapping it over him and then wrapping his arms around him too.

"*No llores*," Ren begged Justin to stop crying, to be still, to rest. He lifted a hand to gently press Justin's head against his chest, propriety be damned.

"I just want," Justin cried, but it didn't seem he would allow himself to give voice to what he wanted, even in sleep. Ren held him tighter. He knew what he wanted. He wanted his life back, his health. He wanted to go home with North. He wanted to be wanted.

"I know," Ren assured.

"Ren," Justin whispered, relaxing against him.

"I'm here," Ren promised.

16

LONG DISTANCE

Justin slept soundly and well the rest of the night, and Ren knew that because he did *not*. He sacrificed his comfort for Justin's, straining to keep Justin securely in his arms. He found that if he maintained this position, Justin would lie quietly. Ren watched Justin's racing heart slow to seventy-eight beats per minute there in the dark, a physical indication that Ren was not wasting his efforts.

Abbie came to check on them several times throughout her shift. When she first caught them together in the bed, she paused at the door, her hand reaching toward her throat in surprise.

"Oh, I was supposed to bring you a cot!" she whispered in distress, ashamed of having forgotten. "Should I bring it now?"

"I think it's too late," Ren replied, not unkindly, gesturing at Justin. "We're fine."

But she fussed enough that Ren allowed her to take down an extra pillow from the cabinet above the sink, propping it somewhere under his head and between where his shoulder was scrunched against the guardrail. Then she removed the empty iron IV bag, adjusted the gravity feed on the remaining solution, and promised to return in a while. Ren started telling time from Abbie's dedicated rounds. Each time her silhouette appeared in the doorway, Ren knew he'd given Justin another ninety minutes of peaceful rest.

Meanwhile, Ren was dying inside. Being so tall meant he struggled for comfort in a regular bed on his own. Sharing a triage room hospital bed was a unique blend of torture. Justin kept his hand secured in Ren's shirt, his head resting on Ren's diaphragm. It would have been endearing if Ren had been able to get situated before Justin decided he was never moving again, but he hadn't thought that once Justin settled it would be *forever*. Justin's body burned into Ren, miserably hot, and it felt as though each time Ren tried to shift, it irritated the bruised scrape down his back.

He couldn't say he didn't sleep at all, though. He knew he drifted off from time to time, but never for long. Somehow, the tiny cycles of rest made the night go on even longer. He was in the middle of one of these miniature naps when his phone rang, dragging him awake.

The triage room hadn't changed; it was still as dark as it had been when they'd tried to go to sleep, and for a minute, Ren wasn't sure he'd heard anything real. When his phone buzzed a second time, and then a third, he began desperately attempting to free himself from under Justin. It wasn't as difficult as when he'd slipped out from under him on the couch yesterday, but by the time he'd rolled himself off the bed and into a crouch on the floor, the phone was quiet again. Three rings. Sunday morning. Ren knew exactly who had called him.

His family didn't have a phone in the house, but the pastor of La Iglesia Santa Elvira allowed them to use the one in his office on Sundays before Mass. They dialed Ren's number, let it ring three times as a signal, and hung up. He would then return the call so the church did not incur any long-distance charges. The only reason Ren could call them back was because Denny had given him an old phone still connected to her mom's international plan at a fee far less than if he'd tried to get one on his own. She said it didn't matter, but he demanded to pay his share every month. Before he'd met Denny, his only correspondence with his family was through email and handwritten letters.

Ren quickly put on his shoes, intending on taking his phone out so his conversation wouldn't wake Justin, but he'd forgotten to plug it in last night. His battery was at seven percent. He'd have to talk while attached to an outlet, doing his best to keep the volume down.

Keeping an eye on Justin, Ren dialed the familiar number, waiting for the phone connection to bridge the 1900 miles from here to home. He closed his eyes, picturing them all in the office. His brother, Marco, would be sitting on the priest's desk, trying but not necessarily succeeding in not touching anything. Marco's wife, Isabel, would be standing, leaning between Marco's knees with baby Diego, who Ren had never seen in person, in her arms. Ren's eldest brother, Luis, would stand sheltering Ren's mom, holding her shoulders supportively in his hands, his two boys on either side of her, faces eagerly turned up as if that would help them hear better while Paloma, Luis' wife, would be seated, patient and graceful, in the priest's chair. Ren's only living sister, Siara, closest to him in age, would stand in a corner, arm across her body, one hand lifted and perpetually adjusting her glasses. And Ren's mother would stand, one hand gripped tight on the phone, the fingers of her other just barely brushing the top of the desk.

"Enzo!" The jubilant chorus of voices greeted him, and he breathed the word in as though it had been an embrace.

"Hi, guys," he returned, his lowered voice almost cut off from how much he loved them. His mother noticed immediately.

"Why are you whispering?" she asked. "We can barely hear you."

Ren debated how to answer. His entire immediate family listening to these calls had proved to be the most effective lie detector test Ren had ever taken. Tiny shifts in his voice that his brothers wouldn't notice would be picked up by Siara. He had yet to come up with a tone neutral enough that he could get something past them all, and they'd already read into the pause.

"My friend's still sleeping," Ren let them know. "And I can't take the phone out. How are you all?"

"Friend?" Siara double checked him. "In your room? What kind of a friend?"

"Did you have a girl spend the night, Enzo?" Marco teased.

"Lorenzo, you didn't?" His mother had undoubtedly removed her hand from the table to clasp it around the cross pendant hanging from her neck. Ren wished he were physically with them so he could glare at Siara and shove Marco off the desk. Were they trying to get him in trouble?

"No, Mama," Ren tried to keep his voice steady, mature, innocent. "I'm not even at the apartment. One of my friends had to be taken to the hospital yesterday, and I stayed with him." The fact that they had shared a bed was irrelevant.

"Oh, the poor thing," her whole demeanor flipped in an instant. "Is it your roommate? The one I sent the birthday package for?"

"Alek? No," Ren answered, setting himself a mental note to ask about that package. It hadn't arrived yet. "I'm here with someone else; his name's Justin. I don't think I've ever mentioned him to you before." At least, not by name; Ren might have complained about him last week when he was still trying to pin him down for their assignment. Back when that was the biggest inconvenience in his life.

"Is he all right?"

"He will be," Ren said, as if he could will it to happen with only his own conviction. "But he does need rest, so I've got to stay quiet. So tell me what's been going on?"

A deluge followed, voices leap frogging over each other, a whole week's collection of news they had saved for him. Someone would start a story, then someone else would contradict a fact, or be too excited not to interrupt and tell their favorite part. The speech patterns wove around each other, with plenty of "guess what's" from Ren's little nephews. He sat hunched in the chair near the bed, elbows on his knees, resting his forehead on the quilt, eyes still closed as he translated the changes that were happening at home from the scattered sentences that came across to him.

For the grand majority of these chats, Ren felt a closeness. Felt wrapped by their voices, warm in their love. But it seemed as though they couldn't let a week pass without some little dig, some verbal disappointment about where he was and how he could remain gone so far and so long. This week it took the form of a seemingly playful remark by Marco about how big baby Diego was getting and how it was a shame Ren had never seen him. The words were subtle enough that Ren wasn't sure if they were meant to hurt him or if it was his own guilt doing it on its own. Either way, he could hear it loud and clear. *If you were only here, the family wouldn't be struggling as hard. If you hadn't gone away. If you ...*

Whether it was there or not, Ren's mother could always hear when it was getting to Ren. When his answers grew shorter as his heart and conscience weighed him into silence. At this point, she would send everyone out of the room so she could speak to him in private. This was both Ren's favorite and least favorite part of the call. As the youngest son, he always treasured any time he could have his mother all to himself, but on the other hand, he felt as though he had to be on his guard. He couldn't tell her all he might want to tell her because he could never make it seem as though coming here had been a mistake. Whatever he said would have to be both the truth and the most positive bits of his life. Most of the time, he didn't have a hard time doing that.

"Now," Eva Cordero invited in the quiet pause after Ren's siblings left. "Tell me all your secrets." Ren smiled sadly, wishing he could. He lifted his head, checking Justin who had begun to shift, almost waking, the hand that had been clinging to Ren's shirt pawing around the pillow, as if looking for him. Ren rested his hand over Justin's to reassure him, hoping he would stay asleep.

"You go first," Ren prompted. "How are you?" His question had many levels, and he wanted his mother to answer them all. He knew it wasn't fair to expect her to disclose things when he didn't always return the favor, but then again, he knew he could handle it.

"I'm the same," she replied casually. "I live between the extremes of missing you and wanting you back and being so proud of you I can't help but talk about you to strangers at the restaurant. I served a couple from, oh, what did they say? Minnesota? Is that close to where you are?"

"It's two states over," Ren said, pulling up his mental map of the US. He knew his mother would have no idea those states were several hundred miles across. That all of the Dominican Republic could fit into Florida, the very tip of this country. "You could drive there," he tried to orient her. He didn't know how long it would take to drive to Minnesota, nor how far of a drive it would be from the southernmost border to the northern one, but his answer was enough for his mother.

"I thought so," she preened, and Ren gave a huff of amusement, watching Justin slowly but undoubtedly waking up. His mother seemed to believe that the US was the sort of place where all Americans knew each other. "They'd heard of your school. They said it was a very good one."

"It is a good one." He felt he needed to confirm that for her. An MD from this place would allow him to give her a life he hadn't been capable of imagining.

Justin was definitely awake now, groggy and puzzled, beginning to look around to orient himself. Ren kept hold of his hand, squeezing it and causing him to turn toward Ren, blinking up at him adorably.

"Hang on a second, Mom," Ren paused his conversation, switching from Spanish to English. "It's all right, Justin. We're still in the hospital. You can go back to sleep if you want."

Justin shook his head, twisting onto his back with remarkable grace for someone who'd just woken up attached to an IV and an EKG machine. As Justin resettled himself in his new position reclined on his back, Ren took his hand again without thinking. Holding it and stroking his thumb along the top. Justin watched him, but he didn't move and he didn't speak.

"Do you need to go?" Eva asked, hope and sorrow drenching the question.

"No, not yet," Ren told her. "My friend just woke up. He can't understand what we're saying."

"Perhaps you should go then," Eva protested. "That would be rude to be on the phone with me when he can't even understand you."

"No, Mom," Ren denied, watching Justin close his eyes, not to sleep, just to listen, his hand putting encouraging pressure on Ren's. The corners of his mouth were slightly turned up, the softest smile Ren had ever seen. "I won't get to hear your voice again for a week! Besides, he doesn't mind. I think he likes listening."

"Did you just meet him recently? Is that why you've never talked about him before?"

"You'll probably hear more about him from now on," Ren guessed, though he knew it was too early to really tell her things like that. But right now, sitting here holding hands together as he spoke with his mother, it just felt as though Justin had come into his life to stay. "Want to say hello to him?"

"Oh, I don't know, dear."

Ren understood how self-conscious his mother was about speaking English. But Ren wanted to share his mother with Justin, who had never had a real one. There was no comfort like Eva's voice, no matter what language she was speaking. It was unique in all the world.

"I'll help you," Ren encouraged, switching the call to speaker without waiting for her to consent. "You can speak whatever language you want. Just say hello to him, please; he's having the worst time, and he doesn't have a family."

"What happened to his family?" Eva asked, and Ren heard the compassion in it. Ren looked at Justin, who still had his eyes softly closed even now that Eva could be heard plainly in the room. He knew Justin couldn't understand them, but it still felt odd to say this out loud where he could hear.

"His mom left him when he was a baby," Ren informed her. "And his dad died when he was four."

"Oh, Enzo, the poor boy!" Eva exclaimed, the shock and pity clear enough in her voice that it roused Justin. His face hardened into concern as he opened his eyes, removing his hand from Ren's as he weakly tried to sit up. He looked at Ren, trying to figure out what had happened in the last couple seconds, reading his expression to determine how much he should be worried about what Ren and Eva could be talking about. "How horrible! Who's been taking care of him?"

"Different people," Ren responded, calmly but hearing bitterness in his voice. Eva didn't know the half of it. "It's been me for the last couple days."

"Ren?" Justin whispered as Ren gently pressed against Justin's chest, pushing him back against the bed. "Ok?"

"Everything's fine," Ren answered. "I'm talking to my mom. Tell her hello."

Justin shrank away from the phone, confused and unsure about being thrown into a conversation like this.

"I don't know how," Justin excused himself, while Eva sat quietly on the other end of the line.

"She'll understand you; just speak slowly," Ren instructed.

"Enzo, are you still there?" Eva asked, in Spanish still.

"I'm here, Mom. Justin and I can both hear you now," Ren informed her, then looked at Justin, switching languages again. "Say hi."

"Um, *hola*," Justin said, almost too quietly, glaring at Ren for putting him into weird social situations before he was really awake. "*Señora?*" Ren felt his eyebrow lift without conscious effort. Justin's accent was atrocious, but the words were recognizable.

"Those are the only words I know," Justin answered the question Ren hadn't asked out loud. He looked a little panicked.

"*Hola, cariño,*" Ren's mother responded kindly. "I'm sorry *por,* ah … sorry … Lorenzo, *no puedo hacerlo. No sé que decir.*"

"You can use whatever language you want," Ren reminded her, keeping his hand on Justin's chest. Justin looked afraid, like he'd done something wrong. "I can translate."

Eva muttered something Ren actually couldn't translate because he couldn't hear. But he did hear her take a deep breath, and then they all had a strange, extremely short, conversation where one of them would say something and Ren would repeat it. Polite introductory phrases filtered through Ren as he tried to force a bond that was natural to him but completely alien to them.

"I'm so sorry you're in the hospital," Eva told Justin via Ren. "I hope you feel better soon."

"Thanks? I'll be fine. Ren is helping me."

"How did you meet my son? Do you work together?"

"No, we take a class together. English."

"Ah, I see. Do you like it?"

"Um, it's ok?"

They went back and forth a couple more times. Talking about the blanket Justin was using. Ren putting in a comment here and there when the conversation lagged too long.

"Lorenzo, please, no more," Eva begged suddenly after a very long pause, and he caught himself just before translating it. "I just can't."

"What's wrong?" Ren asked her, oblivious. Justin tensed at the tones he was hearing, but visibly relaxed as Ren turned away from him, as if making the conversation private again.

"It's too much. I know what you're trying to do; it's just like you, but it's not fair to ask this of either of us."

"But Mama," Ren struggled, wondering how she knew what he was doing when he wasn't completely aware of it himself. "I just thought … I wanted to give him." *He's been alone for so long.*

"I know, my love, but I'm your mother, not his. Speaking to him doesn't mean the same thing as me talking with you; we are strangers." What Eva was telling him made perfect sense, but that didn't mean he liked it. "Now, I know you're very busy. We will call you again next Sunday."

"What? Mom, wait. You don't have to go yet," Ren protested, wishing he'd never thought to introduce her to Justin if it meant she was going to stop talking earlier than she ever had before.

"It's all right, *mijo*. I understand. You have things to do over there. It's important." She said she understood, but Ren could hear she was disappointed and sad.

"I don't, though! We're just waiting for the doctor right now; it's still early here."

"I will pray for you, my love. I'll pray for you both."

That's what Eva said at the end of all their conversations. The way she said goodbye. Ren wasn't sure what he'd done; how something so innocent as an introduction could have hurt his mother's feelings to the point where she wanted to cut their conversation so short. And she did sound hurt.

"Mama?" Ren tried one last time to keep her a little longer. But then he heard the click. Ren clung to the phone in both hands, staring at it with his mouth open, as if on the verge of making one more plea to her. What just happened? He tried dialing the number again, but this time no one answered.

"Ren?" Justin said his name tentatively, moving uncomfortably on the bed, but Ren wasn't paying complete attention. He pulled the phone closer to his chest, holding it, feeling disconnected and empty. "Ren, is something wrong?"

"She had to go," Ren murmured, staring at the floor, overwhelmed with a strange kind of grief. A mourning for someone who wasn't actually lost, just missing. It was a feeling he knew well; it happened almost every time he'd finished speaking to his family, but Eva's abruptness sharpened it considerably. Ren squeezed his eyes shut, hating how often he felt like crying lately.

"Ren, seriously," Justin continued as Ren tried to gather his energy to take a walk. If he was going to *feel* this alone, then he wanted to actually *be* alone. "Are you ok? Ugh, I can't ... damn this stupid stuff! Ren, come here."

Ren sniffed without meaning to, risking a side glance at Justin who was straining against all the lines connecting him to machines on the opposite side of the bed, reaching for Ren but not being able to get close enough to touch him.

"What?" he asked Justin, wondering what he needed, what he was trying to do.

"Put down the damn phone and get over here," Justin ordered, voice not quite as strong as his words. Ren let the phone drop gently onto his coat, still plugged in and charging. He didn't know why he was obeying Justin when he'd originally intended on leaving the room. Maybe because Justin made it sound so threatening.

"Do you need something?" Ren asked quietly, hoping he did. *Please send me on a mission, Justin. Give me something else to think about. Make me as busy as my mother seems to think I am.*

"No, you do," Justin told him, frustrated, beckoning with his non-IV hand. "Why are you making this so hard?"

"Maybe if I knew what you wanted," Ren suggested, watching Justin from the chair, feeling as fragile as a soap bubble. Now that his hands were free, he'd curled both arms around his ribs, holding himself tightly.

The phone started ringing again. Ren grabbed it from the floor, recognizing the country code, almost answering it directly before he remembered about the long-distance charges. He let the three rings complete, ignoring Justin's questions in the background about what he was doing staring at a ringing phone.

"Mama?" Ren asked desperately, after he'd called back and someone picked up.

"What did you say to her?" It wasn't Eva. It was Luis.

"Nothing. Why? What's going on?" Ren asked, feeling extremely far away from them.

"She's sobbing in Siara's skirt! What happened?"

"I don't know. She's what? Go get her; put her on," Ren

demanded. Justin's hand appeared in his peripheral vision, still reaching for him as he sat there, furious and miserable, staring at the floor. He needed to talk to her, needed to figure out what he'd done to make her so upset.

"I don't think so," Luis denied his request. "In fact, I don't know if it's a good idea that we keep doing this; Mom's always a mess after she talks to you." This was news to Ren. He'd thought his mother enjoyed their Sunday conversations.

"What are you talking about?" Ren challenged. "Just go get her; I need to ask her something."

"You've done enough already," Luis snapped at him. "She tries so hard to support this … thing you're doing. The least you could do is respect her when she calls. She said you're getting too busy for us. What the hell is that about?"

"I am *not* too busy; I'm right here! I'm begging you to let me talk to her!" Ren had to stand up now; he was too mad and Luis was too far away for Ren to get in his face. The only thing he could do was try and vent the energy, but Justin grabbed his wrist before he could start pacing, tethering him to the bedside. Ren forced himself not to rip his hand from Justin's fingers. He hadn't done anything wrong.

"Ren, what is it?" He heard Justin murmur, his voice also far away. Everyone seemed so distant from Ren right now.

"Did you ever think about what you were doing?" Luis demanded. "Leaving us like you did? You know you're Mom's favorite; after losing Amayah, she can't stand thinking about anything happening to you. She's afraid you'll never come back."

"Luis, please," Ren begged, hearing the tears in his voice before he realized his face was wet with them. "That's not true. Please let me talk to her."

Luis sighed, and Ren could feel his anger dissolving. "Enzo, we miss you," he admitted.

"I didn't mean to hurt anyone," Ren defended himself. "Luis, let me apologize to Mom. Please. I can't go another week leaving it like this. You don't have to protect her from me. Come on."

"Siara," Luis called, his mouth away from the phone receiver, and Ren dropped in an exhausted heap on Justin's bedside as he realized his brother was going to do what he asked. "Enzo wants to apologize."

Justin shifted as close as possible next to Ren, dragging all his cords and tubes with him, breathing hard at the effort. Ren sat with his head hanging, waiting for Siara to bring Eva back into the room, grateful Luis hadn't just hung up on him again.

"What is it, *mijo*?" Eva's voice was sweet, but Ren could hear Luis was right. She had been crying and was doing her best to hide it. Ren knew he wouldn't be able to hide either.

"Mama, I'm sorry," he sobbed remorsefully into the phone. He never wanted to be responsible for his mother's pain; he was devastated to learn he hurt her every time they spoke to each other. He hadn't even known. "I'll never be too busy to talk to you. Don't ever think that."

"I don't want to bother you," she responded.

"You could never! Do you want me to come home?" he asked, surprising himself. He'd never been direct about that before, but if that's what it took, then that's what he would do. He would work in the orchard or in the tobacco fields; whatever she needed.

"Darling, every day. I always want you to come home, but I know what you're doing is the right thing for you, so it can't be about what I want."

"You know it's for you, right?" Ren checked, needing her to understand this. "I'm doing this for you — all of you. I'm going as fast as I can. Mom, if you only knew." *If you only knew what this country could be for us if I can only finish what I started here.*

"I do know that," Eva assured. "But I'm still your mother, and I still miss you. I guess I just wish you missed us too."

"Mom, you have no idea," Ren gushed out the words. "What do you need from me? Should I call more often? Write more? What can I do so you aren't crying after we talk to each other? I don't want that, Mama."

"I told Luis not to tell you."

"Well, he did, and I'm glad he did. So what can I do?"

"I don't think there is anything more you can do. You're already working hard."

"Send us pictures," Siara suggested from the background. "We've forgotten what you look like."

"Mama?" Ren checked.

"That would be lovely, yes," Eva agreed. Ren had yet to send them a picture, but he didn't know why not. It would be something Eva could hold in front of her eyes and clutch to her heart. He hadn't shown her the gothic castle-like campus that was the University of Chicago, the way it looked when covered in autumn or in snow. She had no idea what Denny or Alek looked like. The frozen lake. He should be sending them millions of pictures.

"And when you call, make sure we have your full attention," Luis said, a lecture in his voice. Ren looked down at Justin, feeling guilty. That's what had brought all this out into the open. Ren hadn't been thinking.

"So, we are going to keep up with the calls?" Ren asked, making sure Luis wasn't going to take this away from him.

"Of course," Eva responded readily, and Ren understood she had never thought about discontinuing them, despite how hard they were for her. He knew that feeling. How he could want something so much even though it hurt afterward. "I look forward to this all week."

"I do too," Ren agreed, wishing they could see him, see how he'd practically clawed himself out of bed to get to his phone this morning. "I love you." *If only you knew how much.*

"I love you too, *mijo*. I can't wait to see the photos."

"Are you ok now, Mama? No more crying?" Ren checked.

"I'll be fine. And you?"

"Sure. I'll send you pictures of me in the snow in the next couple days, ok?"

"And photos of your friends?"

"Definitely. And we'll talk next Sunday."

"I'll pray for you."

There came a shuffling on the line. Ren pictured Siara walking with Eva out of the room. Luis must not be finished with him yet; that was the only explanation Ren could think of for why the connection was still active.

"That's better," Luis acknowledged. "She's smiling at least."

"Why didn't you tell me sooner?" Ren accused.

"She asked me not to, of course. Didn't want to bother you. But it was so bad today I had to say something. Probably lit into you harder than I needed to, though."

"That's nothing new," Ren said before he thought too much about it. He heard Luis sigh again.

"Enzo, I'm sorry. I'm just trying to keep us all together now that Dad's gone, you know?"

"You're doing a great job, Luis," Ren consoled him.

"Doesn't feel that way. Hey, listen, do you think you could come back for a visit sometime? How hard would that be to work out?"

"Good question?" It had been so difficult for Ren to get into the US that he was timid about ever leaving it again before he was done. The paperwork and medical examinations had been ruthless for him to get a student visa. The flight had been paid for by a sponsorship connected with his scholarship grant. The process and expense seemed too daunting to even attempt a second time. "I'll ask my friend, Denny, to help me figure out if it's possible."

"That'd be good. I know you're busy, but I think you should try." Ren knew that, but he wondered if a visit would somehow make it worse. Wouldn't it just hurt the entire time, knowing every minute he was with them was one minute closer to when he would have to leave again? "Look, Enzo — Mom won't tell you, and she'd kill me right now if she were here, but there's something else I think you should know."

"Luis?" Ren said his brother's name like a warning, but he wasn't sure what kind. What other secrets could his family be keeping from him? "What is it?" Because it sounded serious.

"You remember before you left, we all had to go in for that TB test?"

"Sure, they needed to clear the household before they'd let me leave the country. We all tested negative, so I got my visa."

"Mom didn't test negative — just latent."

"What?" Ren forced his brother to repeat what he'd just said. Because he remembered the questionnaire, the medical form. The consequential testing after he'd put down that there was a family history of the disease. He tried to remember what they said. He'd been cleared; he assumed since he was allowed to go, everyone had returned a negative result.

"She didn't want to tell you."

"Why are you telling me now? Is she sick?" Ren asked, his mind switching into high gear to hear this. Because no, not now, not yet. He needed more time; he wasn't even close to the point where he could do anything.

"She's fine. Like I said, it's dormant, but I don't know what we're going to do if that changes."

"Is there anyone else?" Ren demanded, angry that Luis would keep something this big from him. "Luis?"

"No, Enzo. I swear. Everyone else is clear. I've been meaning to tell you, but this was the first chance I've ever had to speak to you alone."

"How long have you known?"

"Not very long. I promise. But Enzo? None of the others know; Mom begged me not to say anything. It's our secret for now, ok? I just wanted you to know in case you need to come home quickly."

"Right. Thanks, Luis."

"See what it'll take to come back. I'll keep you informed. Whatever I know, you'll know."

"Ok," Ren responded quietly, overwhelmed by this week's phone call. On top of everything else that was already going on.

"And Enzo? I'm sorry about what I said. I know what you're trying to do, and I'm proud of you for getting so far. It's just weird having my baby brother so far away at college. You know you're the first one to ever do that."

"I know," Ren repeated, a strange, weak calm rendering him almost paralyzed.

"I don't want you to worry," Luis cautioned him, hearing what he'd done to Ren by giving him this information. "It's something we may never have to deal with."

But Ren didn't hear that part. He was already thinking ahead, thinking of what he would do if something happened to his mom. Thinking of how he could get her what she needed if it turned out she did need anything. Tuberculosis infections were curable, but only with almost three years of consistent antibiotics. An expensive treatment that wasn't always available to the regular citizens of the Dominican. The Corderos had already lost two family members to this disease because those treatments were so hard to get. Ren was not willing to lose anyone else.

Ren wasn't sure how much longer he spoke to his brother. He couldn't even recall when Luis hung up. He only noticed because Justin plucked the phone out of his stiff hands for him, dropping it once again onto the soft cushion of Ren's coat on the floor.

"Ren!" Justin grabbed onto his sleeve and shook him back into the present. "What the hell is going on?"

Ren could only shake his head, not sure where to start, not sure how much he wanted to share. It wasn't fair to unburden this onto Justin; he had his own problems.

"Is it like this every time you talk to them?" Justin demanded, unbalanced. "Does it always make you cry?"

"My mom has tuberculosis," Ren heard himself say quietly, way too calmly, without even meaning to say anything. But it felt like he had to repeat it because it didn't feel real. Or maybe it felt too real.

"Oh. That's ... is there a cure for that?" Justin asked, still uncertain. He was sitting up, but now that Ren turned to face him, he could tell it was too much of an effort. Justin was trembling, blinking too often.

"Justin, I'm sorry," Ren apologized for what seemed like the hundredth time that morning. He was letting everyone down today, and the sun was barely up. "I'm not taking very good care of you, am I? Come on, lie back; you're shaking again." And his heart rate was back up to ninety-four.

"No, I'm ok," Justin insisted on continuing an obvious lie. "What about your mom though? Is that why you were yelling?"

"That's not why," Ren returned, still feeling spacey as he replayed the conversation over again. How could his mom think he was getting too busy for her? Did she live in fear that one Sunday morning she would let his phone ring and he wouldn't respond? How? How could she ever think that? How could he prove to her that it wasn't true?

He felt sudden, deep pain on his back and flinched away from it instinctively before realizing it was Justin, awkwardly trying to comfort him by running his hand up and down Ren's spine, not knowing about the bruising. Justin immediately pulled his hand away at Ren's extreme reaction, his expression wounded as he folded his arms over his chest, turning his face to the wall.

"No touching, got it," Justin muttered, shaking his head. Ren didn't know he could feel any more miserable, but somehow seeing Justin misunderstand why he'd shied away from him sank his spirits. Ren scooted closer so he could put a hand on Justin's chest, covering his heart. Justin rolled his eyes over, a defensive film of anger shining across them.

"You didn't do anything wrong," Ren told him, defeated, wishing he could communicate better. "It just ... hurts."

"Hurts?" Justin repeated, then something clicked inside his head. He pushed himself upright again, leaning behind Ren and tugging at his shirt the way he'd tried to lift it yesterday when Alek had asked about it. "Oh shit." Ren heard him hiss, and he gave up. He let his head fall forward into his hands, his elbows resting on his knees as he sat hunched over, allowing Justin to pull his shirt all the way up to his shoulders. "Ren, what did you do?"

"Tried to catch you when you passed out yesterday," Ren answered. "I kept you from cracking your head open, but we crashed into the coffee table. It looks worse than it is."

"How do you know?" Justin accused. "Your whole back is ... it looks awful."

"Better my back than your face," Ren returned. "You could have snapped your neck."

"Ren," Justin began but didn't seem able to say anything else. Ren wriggled until his shirt fell back, covering the damage. He twisted toward Justin, tucking one of his legs up on the bed so he could sit more securely, holding tight to his ankle. Justin was now hunched forward, braced on one hand while the other rested against his chest.

"I'd do it again," Ren promised, not really knowing what to say.

"A couple more days with me and you'll be the one in the hospital," Justin muttered bitterly. Ren tried to smile, tried to make Justin's statement a joke instead of a comment of despair.

"Justin," Ren started, desperately thinking of something else they could talk about that wouldn't be quite so heavy.

"Alek's right," Justin cut him off, lifting his head with effort, a tiny smile quivering at the corners of his mouth as he met Ren's eyes. "You did get your accent back."

Just like the last time Ren tried to laugh about this, he ended up breaking down. He brought both hands up to cover his face, fire flickering into his lungs as he held his breath to keep quiet. He couldn't even hear it, hadn't noticed that he'd changed the way he spoke in automatic imitation of his childhood language.

He felt Justin shift, panting with exertion from trying to move a few inches closer. He felt fingers closing carefully in the fabric near his shoulders, gentle pulling that Ren submitted to. He leaned into Justin, resting his chin over his shoulder, letting his hands fall loose into his lap. Justin's skin was hot, and for the first time, Ren noticed the scent of the fever on him, a distinct musty sort of smell that accompanied illness. Justin was still very sick. Ren shouldn't be falling to pieces on him like this.

"Am I hurting you?" Justin asked softly. Ren couldn't respond vocally. Instead, he slowly reached around Justin's waist, clasping his hands together at the small of Justin's back, clinging to him selfishly for support. He so wanted something to hold onto right now, and Justin was the only one here. "Is your mom going to be ok?"

"I don't know," Ren confessed.

"She sounded ok," Justin said, trying to be reassuring, still holding Ren gently.

"Her infection is dormant," Ren explained, reluctantly pulling back to save Justin the effort of maintaining the position. Justin's expression resembled an abandoned wolf pup, but Ren wanted to get his head down. "I want you to stop shaking," Ren said as he helped Justin lean back against the bed.

"What does that mean?" Justin pressed, ignoring what Ren had just said but allowing Ren to force him down. "Dormant?"

Ren took a deep breath. He was going to talk about this, and he was going to do it like a professional. "It means the bacteria is present, but it's not causing any symptoms and it's not contagious right now. It also means it could wake up at any time and turn into an active infection."

"But there's medicine for it now, right? People don't still die from this anymore."

"No, they do," Ren whispered, voice choking up. "My dad and my twin sister both died from it."

"I'm sorry."

"Do you remember your dad at all, Justin?" Ren asked, wanting to change the subject, even though his question was just shifting potential pain to someone else.

"Not really," Justin answered after a pause. They weren't looking at each other anymore; they were both looking at where Justin's hand covered Ren's. "I can't picture his face, but I remember a little of what his voice sounded like. I remember his smell when I'd sit with him. I always thought he smelled like dusty sunshine, but I know that doesn't make sense. But you know when you can see the dust in a sunbeam? If that had a smell, that was his smell. What about you? How old were you?"

"We lost Dad four years ago, so I have a lot of good memories," Ren said, grateful he could still see his father's face, hear his words of advice, replay the days when he would dance with Eva in the yard.

"And your sister? Your twin?" The way Justin said the word twin reminded Ren of how special that had been to be part of a set. How sometimes it seemed the cells of his body remembered Amayah more than his mind could. He dreamed of her sometimes.

"She died when we were two," Ren heard his own voice from behind a fog of passing years, speaking of a pain that somehow belonged to another person. "I don't remember her, but I've seen a few pictures of us." Ren had no memory, but Eva told him that after Amayah was gone, he had cried for her for weeks, searching the house and the orchards, calling for her, asking for her, screaming for her. After Amayah disappeared, Ren could not tolerate being alone.

"I don't understand," Justin confessed. "How could that happen? I thought there was a cure."

"There is," Ren said. "It just takes a long time. Sometimes, you have to take antibiotics for years, and if you stop, even a dose or two, it can make the bacteria even harder to get rid of. It's expensive. My family couldn't get the medication when they needed it. But that's not going to happen to my mom. I'll figure it out. I'll work harder."

"Wow," Justin said suddenly, and Ren raised his gaze. "Congratulations."

"What?" Ren asked, puzzled.

"Your life is officially more complicated than mine."

"I —" Ren began to protest but discovered he couldn't. There was no way to say anything that wouldn't somehow downplay their challenges.

"I get why you want to be a doctor now," Justin said, as if he were sorry for being flippant about Ren's difficulties. "You're going to be amazing at it, so I'm sure you'll be able to help your mom."

Ren heard himself choke, unexpectedly touched by what Justin was telling him. How Justin sounded as though he truly believed Ren could do anything. Ren wasn't quite so sure, but he had to make it happen. There was no one else.

"And how are you doing?" Ren asked after swallowing, more than ready to talk about something else. "You're still shaking."

"I can't even tell," Justin replied tiredly, not wanting to talk about himself as usual.

"Does anything hurt?" Ren checked, wanting something to do, something to demand his attention. All of it.

"I just feel heavy," Justin tried to explain. Ren nodded, understanding, pulling his quilt higher over Justin. All the movement from this morning had left it in a disheveled heap, almost falling off the side of the bed. Ren took his time adjusting it, brushing it smooth.

"It'll get better," he promised, meeting Justin's eyes, finding them full of pain and sympathy. Seeing in them a longing, a loneliness he recognized. Something he'd seen in his own reflection. He let his hand rest on Justin's chest, bowing his head. "For both of us."

"Ren?" Justin started, and Ren waited expectantly, ready for anything Justin might need.

"Justin?" Ren invited.

"Morning, boys." North's voice at the door, breaking them from each other as he let himself in. Ren smiled one more time at Justin before turning to help North, whose hands were full of Justin's file, coffee, and fast-food bags. "How's everyone?" North asked, monitoring the atmosphere, noticing he'd walked in on something.

Both Ren and Justin shrugged.

17
CIRCUMSTANTIAL EVIDENCE

"**B**ad night?" North questioned, looking between Justin and Ren, pausing just inside the door.

"No," Ren answered at the same time Justin said, "bad morning." They looked at each other, Ren trying to beg without words for Justin not to mention the phone call. There wasn't anything that could be done about what he'd learned this morning, and Ren knew he only had enough energy to deal with one problem at a time. He was going to have to reschedule processing about his mom later. Something Dr. Delacroix had warned him would lead to his eventual nervous breakdown, but seriously? What was he supposed to do? His mom was over a thousand miles away and asymptomatic right now while Justin on the other hand ...

"What's that mean?" North said, studying them, not liking the lack of information. "Justin, you're shaking; why is he shaking?" North put the last question to Ren, turning toward him and handing him the cup carrier, then walking to set down the file and the bags in the empty chair so his hands were free to grasp Justin's shoulders, trying to steady him.

The snarky, exhausted part of Ren wanted to answer this rudely, but North looked almost as tired as Ren felt, worried and desperate. He handled Justin gently, brushing his hair away from his forehead so he could rest the back of his hand there, standing close and help-less. Justin closed his eyes, leaning against North in grateful trust, obviously happy he'd returned. Ren remembered what North had walked into yesterday afternoon, how Justin had collapsed, and he swallowed his sarcasm.

"Good question, but I'm not sure," Ren answered simply. The shaking could be due to a number of things. Exertion from moving around so much this morning trying to comfort Ren. Justin's fever could be rising again, causing chills. Maybe it was low blood sugar from eating almost nothing the past two days. Actually, that one seemed the most likely. "But I bet some calories and rest would take care of it."

"Are you hungry, Justin?" North asked, stepping back, switching the food to the bed and taking over the chair. Ren could smell it now, grease and salt. Justin looked like he wanted to rip the bags apart.

"Yeah," Justin said, sounding hopeless. Just because he was hungry didn't mean he could eat. North started emptying the bags, removing items one by one and setting them in front of Justin.

"I wasn't sure, so I got a little of everything," North explained, then suddenly remembered that Ren was still standing by the door with the coffee. "For you too," he invited. Ren slowly came closer, feeling like an outsider, but not as much as he had yesterday while watching them be together. Justin maneuvered himself cross-legged in the bed so Ren would have space to sit down at the foot of it.

"I got you tea," North half-apologized to Justin. "I didn't think caffeine would be so good for your heart right now." He handed over a cup from the carrier, which Justin accepted, holding it in both hands and staring at it with a concerned expression on his face.

"Let it cool, and I think you can do it," Ren assured him, receiving a look of doubt. "Or maybe we could ice it?"

"Ice?" North repeated, also looking at Justin. "Justin?"

But Justin had returned his focus to the cup, holding its warmth in both hands, breathing shallowly, dedicatedly not looking at anyone.

"Justin's mouth and throat are burned," Ren volunteered for him, not remembering if he'd already mentioned this. A lot had happened; he couldn't keep track of which people had what information. "Fever blisters."

This knowledge raised North's eyebrows, and he redoubled his efforts to find something suitable.

"It doesn't matter, North," Justin dismissed, not wanting North upset that he had gone to the trouble of bringing food for nothing. "You guys go ahead and eat."

Still clutching the cup tenderly, Justin leaned his head back, closing his eyes. Ren checked the stats on his oxygen, thinking it would likely do him good to have the cannula replaced for a while. Ren felt the familiar weight of guilt, seeing how worn out Justin was from supporting Ren this morning, ashamed he'd lost control in front of him.

Meanwhile, Justin's answer wasn't good enough for North, who had pulled a plastic cup full of yogurt and berries from the bag and was now carefully scraping the crunchy granola bits off the top of it.

"You've got to eat something, Justin," North ordered, and Ren could hear the repetition in the phrase. This was not the first time North had coaxed Justin into eating. He took the hot tea, replacing it with the yogurt cup. Justin glanced at Ren, as if asking for assistance, but Ren was back in full doctor mode now, which meant doing what Justin needed instead of what he might want.

"He's right," Ren betrayed him. "I don't have a problem spoon feeding you if I have to either." This was not as gentle as he wanted to be, especially after their morning, but he'd been with Justin long enough now to know his pride would force him into action to prevent Ren from doing anything like that.

Justin huffed as expected, shaking his head, and then obediently tried to take small bites of the yogurt. As he did so, Ren inspected the food, removing the egg from a biscuit sandwich and offering it to Justin.

"Are you kidding?" Justin scoffed.

"Do I look like I'm kidding?" Ren checked. "You need the protein, but if you'd rather, I can get you a can of Ensure that's used for feeding tubes. It tastes like chalk, but you could live off it for years." Justin glared, but Ren put the egg on a napkin anyway, setting it on the blanket next to Justin's side. "It's better than pickle juice," he said, with the tiniest tinge of warning. Justin sighed deeply, and Ren knew he'd gotten his point across.

"Can you just quit looking at me?" Justin requested, eyes downcast, as if he were unable to move if he had an audience for his meal. Ren saw North duck his head to hide a smile, and he relaxed into the idea that if neither of them glanced at Justin, he would eat.

"Ren, here," North drew his attention by handing him his own sandwich, voice full of understanding and gratitude. Ren returned to the bed, also sitting cross-legged, but turned away from Justin, more towards North. "Help yourself; there's plenty," North said, rubbing his robotic hand self-consciously against the back of his head. "I think I went a little overboard."

"I can pay you back for it," Ren suggested, but North shook his head, insulted.

"After all you've done? The least I can do is feed you," North denied, pulling a sandwich for himself out of the pile on the bed. "Has the doctor been in yet?"

"Haven't seen her," Ren answered between bites. As he ate, Ren indulged in surreptitiously watching North since he wasn't allowed to look at Justin. North sat with a structured grace, appearing both at ease and ready to leap up simultaneously, and Ren caught him giving Justin rapid sidelong looks to check on him every so often.

North held his food in his real hand, beginning to sift through Justin's file again, balancing it on his lap and turning the pages deftly with his robotic fingers. Ren forgot to be so guarded and flat out stared.

A balled-up napkin smacked against the side of Ren's face. Realizing what had hit him, Ren turned to Justin, who was watching him disapprovingly.

"Have some respect," Justin muttered, misunderstanding why Ren had been watching North's right hand so closely. North glanced up, noticing immediately that he'd missed something.

"Justin?" he said as a request for an explanation. Justin shrugged, going back to his yogurt. "Ren?" North switched his attention since Justin obviously wasn't going to give him anything. Ren hurled the napkin back at Justin, hitting him lightly on the chest, wanting to point out the double standard. If Justin didn't want anyone looking at him, how come it was ok for him to watch Ren eat?

"I have nothing but respect," Ren defended himself to Justin, though he was still embarrassed at being caught. "It's just impressive, ok?"

"What?" North began, but then he seemed to catch up with the whole thing. "Oh, you mean this." He wiggled his artificial fingers, and Ren couldn't help but be awestruck all over again. Such. Fluid. Natural. Movements.

"Close your mouth," Justin ordered, more used to it than Ren. Plus Justin didn't understand. He'd probably never seen what regular prosthetics were like.

"Sorry," Ren apologized — to North, not Justin. "I've never seen anything like that before. It's ..." he paused, not sure what word he wanted to use that wouldn't sound weird. He decided not to pick one and ask a question instead. "Where did you get it?"

"That's classified," North answered, again with the practiced clip to his tone.

"You didn't tell me that," Justin said, offended. North smiled.

"That's what classified means," he retorted teasingly, and Ren swallowed hard so he wouldn't burst out laughing. "It's a prototype," North said to Ren. "That's all I can say, but you're right, you've never seen anything like it. Yet. Hopefully, they'll be more available in the future."

"Does it have any limitations?" Ren asked, too intrigued not to pry.

"What the —" Justin began, but Ren shushed him.

"You wanted us to ignore you, so fine, I'm ignoring you. Keep eating. I'm really curious about this. You don't have to answer," he added to North in what he hoped would be a respectful tone.

"It's fine," North granted. "Not sure what you mean by limitations."

"Well, like, can you do buttons? Shoelaces? Tie a necktie? Type? Use a pen?" Ren cut himself off before his list got too long, trying to curb his enthusiasm.

"Took some practice, but yes, I can do all those things."

"Wow," Ren breathed, wondering how much of North's capability came from the elegance of the design and what part was because North seemed to be one of those people who always made extremely difficult things appear easy. Like grabbing Justin off the floor, for example. Ren leaned toward Justin now. "Impressive," he repeated, drawing out the word unnecessarily long to make a point. Justin shook his head again.

"I agree," a female voice concurred from the doorway, and all three of them jerked their attention that direction. Dr. Delacroix wore lavender scrubs today under her white lab coat, her multitudes of tiny braids hanging loose for the moment. She leaned against the doorframe, one hand in her pocket while the other held Justin's chart, all his stats from last night dutifully recorded by Abbie for her review.

Ren scrambled to his feet, hoping he didn't have anything on his mouth. He could see North's startled expression about his reaction, but he just didn't understand who this woman was and how much Ren wanted to impress her. Ren still didn't want to be an ER doctor, and he wasn't convinced that what Justin suspected about

Angelique's plans for him could be true, but he still wanted her approval. Or at least not her disapproval.

"Morning, Dr. Delacroix," Ren greeted her. "Sleep well?" For a second, he thought he'd crossed a line and been too familiar as he watched her eyes tighten above the mask she wore.

"Better than you did, I imagine," Angelique answered, coming all the way into the room. "Did you sleep at all, Lorenzo?"

"Sure," Ren said, looking at the floor so she wouldn't see the lie on his face. Well, no, she'd already seen it; he just didn't want to discuss it in front of the others. To his relief, she walked right past him on her way to Justin.

"How about you, darling?" She spoke differently to Justin, her voice warm and judgment-free. It was wasted on Justin, though, who shied away from her, looking at Ren as if he could answer for him. Ren nodded toward the doctor encouragingly. *Come on, Justin, she's not going to bite you.* "You're looking better. Sitting up, talking, eating, very good." Dr. Delacroix continued a visual assessment since Justin wasn't answering. "May I listen to your heart, please?"

She was already putting the stethoscope earbuds in, assuming the affirmative. North took the almost empty yogurt container so Justin could sit up more, allowing Dr. Delacroix access to his chest and back. Ren watched closely, wishing Justin could trust Angelique as much as he did. Maybe he shouldn't have told him all that stuff about how Angelique made students cry, but he'd also told him how good she was at her job. Couldn't Justin tell she was being so gentle with him? Or maybe it had nothing to do with Angelique. Maybe it was just Justin. The way North was also watching, like he suspected Justin to physically push Angelique off him any second, Ren figured that was it.

"Deep breaths, love," Angelique instructed, listening, shifting the stethoscope to various positions to hear different things. Ren couldn't tell what she thought about what she heard since the mask hid so much of her face.

"Ok," she said neutrally, pulling back. "There's definite improvement, but your heart's still beating fast, and your temperature hasn't come down." She spoke as she walked around the bed, opening a drawer by the sink without even looking and pulling out a package. A nasal cannula. Like Ren had wanted to put on less than half an hour ago but hadn't dared. "Let's hook your oxygen back up." Skillfully, she unplugged the mask Justin used in the ambulance yesterday, the one that covered the entirety of his mouth and nose, and replaced it with the less intrusive apparatus, turning the oxygen level to three instead of fifteen. "There. That shouldn't get in your way too much. How does it feel, lamb?" Justin raised an eyebrow without answering. "I know," she acknowledged, but Ren guessed Justin was reacting more to being called a lamb than the actual question.

Angelique gave Justin a reprieve from questions as she gathered the EKG printout, a significant stack by now. "I'll review this as quickly as I can," she promised, and Ren wondered how many uninterrupted minutes she would have consecutively to study it. When you worked in the ER, things could change every second. "Did we ever figure out the question about insurance?"

"We did," North answered. "And, unfortunately, that paperwork was not complete."

"So, no insurance at all?" Dr. Delacroix double checked, though there wasn't a lot of ambiguity about what North just said. Ren felt his shoulders stiffen at the tone. It wasn't going to be like that, was it?

"Seems not," North responded, sounding frustrated.

"Ok," Angelique responded with an efficient little click of her tongue, as if that answer meant nothing. Ren knew better, and it pissed him off. "Then I think that's all for now. Did you need anything, honey?" she asked one last question of Justin, though it seemed he was dead set on never speaking a word to her.

"Can you do something for his back?" Justin asked in a short burst, surprising everyone in the room. He couldn't bring himself to look up from Ren's blanket, but his voice was clear. Dr. Delacroix's gold-tinged eyes flickered over to Ren.

"And here we are," she said softly, almost to herself. Ren had no idea what she meant by that. From the look on his face, neither did Justin.

"Please?" Justin amended his request, raising his head. "He's hurt."

"I know, dear. I saw. How about you take care of him for me?" Dr. Delacroix said, reaching into her pocket and pulling free a brand-new tube of antibiotic ointment. Ren internally startled, knowing Angelique didn't just carry stuff like that around. It wasn't even from the hospital. She'd picked it up on her own, and now she held it out for Ren, who still stood awkwardly between the bed and the door. He reached to take it, but she didn't let go right away, staring at him with her intense tiger eyes. "Since he doesn't seem to be able to take care of himself."

"I got it," Ren whispered to all she meant by that, causing her to tilt her head a fraction and relinquish the ointment into his fingers. Angelique rebalanced the printout and Justin's chart, preparing to leave.

"North?" Ren gave the pilot a split-second of warning before tossing the tube his direction, but he still caught it easily without even appearing surprised. "Thanks; I'll be right back. Let me carry that for you, Dr. Delacroix?" The offer was part politeness and part a desire to speak with her outside of the room. She seemed to know exactly what Ren wanted, and she handed off the stack of paper readily, opening the door for him to leave ahead of her.

"Ren?" He heard Justin call to him on his way out, but he'd talk to him later. He needed to clear something with Angelique first. Except she cut him off before the door had even closed behind them.

"Wait," she ordered, gesturing with her arm where she wanted him to go. Her main office, where she'd taken Ren last night, was not located in the emergency room. Since it would take too much time for her to go back and forth, there was another, smaller office near the ambulance entrance for the ER doctor-on-call to use during their shifts. There was a computer there, several books, random storage supplies, and a desk for just the sort of data review that Angelique would be doing for Justin. Since it didn't belong to any one person, and ER doctors spent more time on their feet in patient rooms than anything else, there wasn't a whole lot to be said for the place except it was private.

"Here will be fine," Dr. Delacroix instructed, clearing away a box of manila folders to make a spot for Justin's printout on the desk. "Thank you, Lorenzo." She took a seat and began rifling through the sheets almost before Ren had removed his hands, scanning for abnormalities. Ren felt as though he were being deliberately ignored. It wasn't as if she didn't already know what he wanted to talk to her about.

"Does anything on that paper even matter at this point?" Ren finally spit out after waiting as long as he could for her to acknowledge he was still standing there. She slowly pulled the mask down, revealing an expression that indicated she'd had enough from him already.

"Of course it does," she answered smoothly, unruffled, but her eyes had begun to heat.

"I thought the ER was required to provide treatment regardless of insurance," Ren shot back. He may not have been there when Justin had transferred to the foster system. He hadn't been able to do anything to prevent Justin from being abused into his teenaged years, hadn't been there to speak for him during the trial, but he was here now and determined that Justin not be written off again.

"That's correct," Angelique agreed with him, but the edge in her voice meant that even though she was telling Ren he was right, she was about to educate him on why he was also wrong. "The ER is required to provide life-saving treatment to the point where a patient is stable regardless of that patient's ability to pay. After that, however —"

"So once he's not dying you kick him out?" Ren returned, disgusted. Not at her, just at the policy. He couldn't believe it.

"Lorenzo, listen to me."

"No! He shouldn't leave! We don't know what his heart will do once he stops receiving the anti-arrhythmic medication. He still has a fever; I don't think he can walk on his own yet. He can barely eat. Just because he's not in active heart failure doesn't mean he's stable." There was a tiny part of Ren that found it odd that he'd tried so hard to keep Justin out of the hospital and now he was arguing to keep him in. But he didn't want to think about taking him home, watching as the medication wore off. What if he crashed again? Or maybe Justin wouldn't come home with Ren at all. Maybe he'd go with North, and then Ren would never see him again.

Angelique leaned back, keeping her delicate fingers wrapped around the printout, pulling it toward her. Her mouth tightened into a flat, frustrated line that accentuated her tone.

"Did you know that the words 'regardless of ability to pay' do not mean 'doesn't have to pay at all'?" she questioned him icily.

"I'm not in the finance program, Dr. Delacroix; I'm in the *medical* program. I thought you were too."

Dr. Delacroix's mouth and hands twitched; she bowed her head as if praying for patience, and Ren wondered if she were reminding herself that "do no harm" had been part of her Hippocratic Oath.

"Lorenzo," Angelique began, but he already knew she'd be telling him more of what he didn't want to hear.

"Heart patients like Justin are monitored for at least three days," Ren steamrolled over what she'd been about to say. "If he had insurance, you would have admitted him already."

"Yes," Angelique sighed, and Ren lost his momentum. "I would have admitted him last night."

"Then why aren't you going to admit him now?" Ren demanded. Keep him here, safe and protected, out of court.

"Because at some point in your medical career, Lorenzo, you'll understand it is about money. And it's just as much for Justin's sake as it is the hospital's."

"That makes no damn sense," Ren pouted.

"That's because you're not giving me a chance to explain," Angelique responded, making Ren feel whiny and childish. And mad. "If I admit him, who is going to pay for it, Lorenzo? Justin can't. I don't think you can. But someone will have to, and it will take one or more forms. The hospital can raise treatment costs for everyone else to make up the difference. They can garnish Justin's wages for years. They can file a claim against him and damage his credit for a significant portion of his life. You see where I'm going with this. Discharging him as soon as possible is the only way to minimize the damage on both sides." Ren looked at the unreadable lines of the EKG printout, knowing he was going to lose this debate and hating it. "The hospital can't deny life-saving treatment, but they can discharge a patient who is no longer experiencing a medical emergency. I cannot keep Justin here because of a fever, even one as high as his, do you understand?"

Even though Ren technically did understand, he couldn't say so. His fists were balled up at his sides, his entire body tight at the predicament. It hurt to hear that yet another system didn't care about Justin, and there was nothing Ren could do about it.

"Lorenzo, please look at me," Angelique requested, her tone not in the least bit softened, but Ren somehow heard a new gentleness in it anyway. "I don't like it either, but at least I know he won't be without all medical care when he leaves," she said, trying to be encouraging. "It feels more like a transfer than an abandonment knowing you'll be with him."

"He almost died in my living room," Ren reminded her, bitter and uncooperative. "And I thought you told me not to perform ahead of my classes, so I don't know what you think I'll be able to do for him?"

"I'm delighted you were listening, but I don't think you'll have to go to such extreme measures to keep Justin alive now that we're raising his iron levels and he's not so severely dehydrated. I'm confident you'll be able to look after him, no special training required, and from what I've observed of you two together, I think he would prefer you helping him to anyone else. You just remember the other things I told you about taking care of yourself, will you?"

"I will," Ren made the promise, but even he thought it sounded empty. "But are you sure there isn't anything more we could do to keep Justin here?" He was doing it again, talking to Angelique like they were partners, speaking to her with far less respect than she deserved. But when he looked at her, she didn't seem to have noticed, or at least she didn't mind.

"I'm going to take my time with this," Angelique went on, patting Justin's report. "I probably won't get to it until this afternoon. I'll be checking it thoroughly, and in the meantime, Justin will continue to receive pain medication and fluids. I'm going to taper off the anti-arrhythmic gradually over the next eight hours so we'll at least get a hint of what might happen to him without it. Neither of us wants him to be in danger or in pain. I need you to believe that."

Ren felt his anger chip away as he realized Dr. Delacroix was on his side, and she was deliberately going to stall her assessment to give Justin more time. What she'd just said soothed Ren. She couldn't break hospital policy, but she could stretch it. He should have known it wasn't her fault. She was a doctor who cared about her patient. He'd been raging at the wrong person.

"Thank you," he whispered, dropping his gaze again, ashamed. It didn't change much about the situation, to be honest, but even just this much was more than Justin had been given before.

"Would you like to go back to your friend now, or is there something else you wanted to tell me?" Her face was calm and knowledgeable, ready, sitting there as though she had all day to talk to him. A question circled into Ren about how some of the more sinister rumors about her had started. He suddenly felt as though she didn't deserve them.

He almost took her up on the invitation, but he caught himself before he unloaded onto her again. Despite how she made it seem, she had so much more going on today than being there for him. She wasn't his mother, or really anything except the ER doctor-on-call who happened to be on duty when Justin showed up yesterday. Ren didn't know why he even felt compelled to speak to her the way he did.

"You can only carry so much, Lorenzo," she prompted when he didn't answer her, as if she knew he was holding back.

"Haven't hit my limit yet," he responded, though there was no humor in his voice as he'd intended.

"That's what I'm afraid of," she said, standing up, looking as though she meant to walk past him to open the door for him to go. She paused on her way by, staring at him so hard he could barely stand it, giving him one last chance to be honest with her. He deliberately looked away.

"Go on," she finally dismissed, much to Ren's relief. "Justin needs you."

Ren nodded, taking this responsibility seriously. He turned to go, but then heard Angelique say one more thing in parting, one last sentence he wasn't sure he was supposed to hear.

"And you need him."

Angelique Delacroix, Ren decided, was the most mysterious person. He couldn't really figure her out. He didn't know how she managed to be so fierce and so gentle at the same time. He also wondered how whenever he spoke to her, she never gave him what he wanted, but he somehow felt more loyal to her after she'd talked to him.

"There you are," North sighed, relieved when Ren let himself back into the triage room a few minutes later, all the fight taken out of him. "Whenever you leave with her, I always worry you won't come back."

"What do you think she's going to do?" Ren asked, half smiling and half apprehensive, curious to hear. How did Dr. Delacroix come across to other people?

"I don't even know," North replied unsatisfactorily as he beckoned Ren over to them. "Come on; let's get this medicine on your back like she said."

"That's all right," Ren began, not wanting North or Justin to be responsible for that. His back was tender, but it wasn't that bad.

"Ren, get over here," Justin snapped, causing Ren to stare at him. "I don't know how, but she'll know if we skip it, and you know *you'll* be the only one in trouble about it, so let's get it over with already."

Ren convinced himself in the next three seconds as he went to sit on Justin's bed that he was cooperating only so Justin wouldn't get all worked up about it, but part of him was moved that Justin had thought to ask Angelique about his wound. He knew it wasn't really appropriate, given their situation, so he tried not to let himself be too pleased.

"Take off your shirt," Justin demanded gruffly. Ren hesitated again. He'd been vulnerable enough already this morning. Justin wasn't having it. "Ren, I'm sitting here two shoelaces away from being completely naked, so you don't get to be worried about taking off your damn *shirt*. Let's go."

Ren watched North struggle with his face, not wanting to upset Ren by laughing about what was going on in front of him. To hide his amusement, North decided to continue talking about Dr. Delacroix.

"You two seem to have an unusual working relationship — you and the doctor," North mused, keeping his eyes carefully away from where Ren was pulling his shirt over his head, too tired to fight about it. Justin put both hands on either side of the worst part of the scrape, and Ren had to hold back a groan. The heat of Justin's palms was surprisingly soothing, though Ren felt guilty enjoying something like that. "Is she always so cold to you?"

"Ren spilled coffee on her," Justin volunteered as he took his time studying Ren's back. He hadn't even started putting the ointment on. Ren kept his gaze on his lap, feeling as though all his control over this conversation had been stripped off him just like his shirt. He heard North chuckle softly.

"Here, Justin, it's open," North said, and Ren could see him pass

Justin the tube of medicine out of the corner of his eye. "She doesn't seem to be the type to hold a grudge about something like that," he continued, talking to himself now.

"And she's testing him," Justin went on. "She wants him to be her ER apprentice or something."

"She does not," Ren protested, unwilling to let this go any further. Why couldn't Justin let that go?

"I think Justin might be right," North agreed. "She does act like she's holding you to a high standard. She must see a lot of potential in you."

"Well, it doesn't matter. I'm not interested in the ER," Ren closed the topic, shuddering as Justin began smearing antibiotic over the broken places in his skin. He heard himself involuntarily grunt.

"Sorry," Justin apologized for hurting him. "I can't believe a *coffee table* did this kind of damage."

"It was more the weight, speed, and angle that we fell on it," Ren responded automatically. He curled his back, leaving his arms in his sleeves so he'd be ready to throw his shirt on again the second Justin finished, though he was becoming less in a hurry about it the longer Justin kept his hands on him, the heat in the touch relaxing all his muscles. After a little while, Ren noticed Justin's hands slow, resting against him for longer and longer stretches. He was getting tired. "That's probably good for now," Ren said, tugging his shirt on and turning to consider Justin behind him.

"Sure?" Justin slurred, exhausted, slumping back against the reclined mattress, his eyes clouded and heavy. Ren smiled kindly at him.

"Thanks for the help, but I think you should try and get some sleep now. Are you still comfortable? Nothing hurts?" At least he wasn't shaking anymore.

"What are you going to do?" Justin asked, not liking the idea of nodding off again while Ren and North were still awake. Though from the looks of it, he probably wouldn't be able to help it.

"Homework," Ren suggested. "You may not be going to English tomorrow, but I probably am."

"Oh," Justin responded, putting energy into sounding surprised. "Right."

"Put your head down," Ren encouraged. *Enjoy the pain medication while you've got it*, he added sadly in his head, wishing there was some way Justin could stay here until his fever broke. Who knew how much longer that would take? Justin submitted easily, closing his eyes.

"North?" Ren questioned quietly after they'd both been silent long enough that Ren was certain Justin was asleep. "Can I ask what happened with the insurance? You sound like Justin was supposed to have some kind of coverage." Who dropped a ball on this? Who had made it so Justin wouldn't be able to get the treatment he should?

Ren was still sitting on Justin's bed, though he'd made room for Justin to stretch out. However, it seemed Justin never slept extended. He curled while he rested. Not quite as tightly as when he'd been in pain, but still a defensive little knot snuggled close against Ren's hip. Ren absentmindedly rested his hand on Justin's ankle, watching him sleep, worried about him in several different ways.

He heard North's hesitation in answering, and Ren knew it was a personal question. Another thing that was none of his business. But he also knew North was going to tell him, that there was some invisible disclosure agreement between them. A trust.

"He is supposed to have coverage," North admitted, sitting in the chair, also watching Justin. "Kasey had the documents all ready, but Justin never turned up to sign them."

"Part of the exit interview?" Ren guessed.

"That's right," North confirmed, sounding disappointedly sad again. Ren was about to follow up with a question about what an exit interview was, but the words must have been too much on his face because North went on without him having to say them. "When someone ages out of the foster system, like Justin did when he turned eighteen last October, there's an exit interview that goes over the changes. What support will stop and what will stay in place and for how long. Basically, everything ends when kids become legal adults, but Justin would have received Medicaid coverage until he turned twenty-five or until he found employment that would provide coverage for him instead. There's paperwork, but without Justin's signature, it's worthless."

"Where was he? Why did he miss the interview?" Ren asked, though he could probably guess what happened.

"I don't know," North said, but Ren could hear he had his opinions. "I lost track of Justin. He disappeared from the group home and quit answering phone calls. He turned up often enough that we didn't have to send the police out looking for him, but that's about it. He avoided me. Kasey said he'd leave messages every few days to let him know what was going on. Then he turned eighteen and disappeared completely."

"North," Ren began, intending on asking why he'd wanted to be transferred. It made no sense. Ren just couldn't figure out why North would do something like that.

"I'm not going to tell you before I tell Justin," North answered before Ren could even ask. "No offense, but that really is personal."

"Right," Ren agreed, knowing he was asking too much to begin with.

"You'll probably be there when I tell him anyway," North followed up, his voice taking on a slightly lighter tone. "Seeing as you're becoming inseparable."

"We'll see if he still feels that way when his fever breaks," Ren said dismissively, because he knew firsthand that being sick made people clingy. He knew better than to expect Justin's feelings about their friendship to remain the same once he recovered. "He may never want to see me again."

"I doubt it. You should have seen him while you were out of the room." That made Ren smile, and he patted Justin's leg as he slept, feeling genuine affection for him.

"He didn't really like it when you left yesterday either," Ren offered. "And I wasn't gone *that* long."

"What did you and the doctor talk about? Did she give you any more information about Justin's condition?"

Ren shook his head, growing serious as he remembered his discussion with Dr. Delacroix outside the room. "North, were you able to get the court to postpone the verdict reading tomorrow? They're not going to make Justin show up to court when he's this sick, right?"

"They don't really care much about that," North revealed carefully, watching Ren as he spoke as if he knew it would make him furious. "If he's still here in the hospital, then yes, I'll provide proof of the stay and they'll reschedule. But if Justin's discharged before tomorrow at ten, he'll have to show up — sick or not."

"That's awful," Ren said softly, once again hating people he didn't know.

"But I thought you said patients like Justin were normally admitted for three days," North clarified. "So it's likely we'll get the extension, and we won't have to worry about that part at least. I can submit the request tomorrow when the office opens."

"I guess I should have said patients with insurance are normally admitted for three days," Ren clipped bitterly. "Unless Dr. Delacroix finds something really terrible in that dataset of Justin's heart, she can only keep him here for twenty-four hours. He'll be discharged this afternoon."

"What? Really?"

"Looks like the hospital and the court have something in common. Neither of them cares that Justin is sick."

North was staring at Justin now, a whole new worry creasing his forehead. Ren could see him planning for this unexpected scenario, how he was going to support Justin from one kind of hell into another. Ren had innocently tricked him into thinking he had more time to prepare.

"North?" Ren called him back. "They can't really send him to prison?" He thought back to the tiny room where he'd found Justin. The cell. Justin alone and sick on the bed. He couldn't go back to that.

"The Hunts can be incredibly persuasive," North replied, his voice far away. "And they have all the resources."

"Can I look at the file?" Ren requested, holding out a hand for the paperwork Justin had hidden in his backpack. That seemed like such a long time ago now when Justin hadn't wanted him to see it. Back when he thought he could keep something like this a secret.

"Guess it won't hurt now," North agreed, passing it over to him.

Ren pressed closer against Justin's legs, leaning into him slightly as he opened the file carefully on his lap. It was hard to tell where to start. He saw copies of the official charges, notes from the defense that he guessed the woman named Kelly had written across some of the pages. He paused to consider her handwriting; she seemed to favor all capital letters and exclamation points. And bold words like fabricated, inconclusive, circumstantial, lies, and privilege. Ren decided he liked her.

"Ms. Kelly seems passionate," Ren murmured as he flipped through the documents, seeing where her red pen had scratched out and rewritten the trial as she thought it should have gone, smiling at some of the more colorful language.

"I haven't heard back from her yet," North said, his voice balanced so Ren couldn't tell his opinion of Justin's lawyer. "I don't even know if she's received my messages updating her about where Justin is. I couldn't find a cell number, so I had to leave them at her office phone. The weekend is really messing with efficient communication."

Ren returned to the papers. He was skimming the details of the original incident now. What the Hunts said about what happened. What Justin said. The testament of the girl Justin rescued. Ren stared at her name before moving on to the pictures.

Most of them were from the first trial, the one for assault when Justin was sixteen. Photos of the victim, David. There were pictures of his injuries. Looks like Justin had given both Ren and David matching bruises under their eyes. David, of course, was much worse. Justin had lacerated his lips, broken one of his cheekbones, his jaw, and his nose. Ren could only study them for a few seconds each before he had to turn them over. He didn't like seeing what Justin could be capable of doing to another human being. Under the photos of the beating were David's death certificate and the autopsy report.

"Ruptured cerebral aneurysm," Ren read quietly from the line of print indicating the cause of death. "Wait. What kind?"

He flipped through more pages, finally finding the photos he suddenly wanted very much to see. There were MRI, MRA, and CT scans of David's postmortem brain, dark patches indicating the rupture, the spread of the blood. Ren read the report, how David woke up with a headache on a Monday morning eight weeks ago. Texts to his friends said he was suffering a hangover, a souvenir of his weekend activities. He told them he'd feel better after lunch. His mother found him unresponsive in bed that evening.

"This can't be right," Ren whispered, continuing to read, looking back every few seconds at the scans. Ren read that the Hunts were convinced David's aneurysm was a direct result of Justin's attack, that Justin had slammed the back of his skull onto the cement. Traumatic subarachnoid hemorrhage. But the force required to do something like that was probably more than sixteen-year-old Justin could have managed. And that wasn't the term listed on the death certificate. There was a definite difference between the two kinds of bleeding. Right? It wasn't clear. Ren sifted through the papers faster, looking for any sort of medical history on David before Justin touched him. Had anyone else in his family suffered an aneurysm? Did he have high blood pressure? Ren already knew he drank; did he also smoke?

"Ren?" North broke into the frenzy of his thoughts, mildly inquisitive but with a hint of concern.

"It's not his fault," Ren said, louder, definitive, looking up to glare at North, not because he was angry with him but because he was the only one in the room Ren could share his anger and confusion with.

"What do you mean?" North asked, resigned.

"If Justin had hit him with a *car* maybe we could say he was responsible, but with his *bare hands* over a year afterward? I don't think it's possible. Oh my *God*; the way you were both talking like there was no doubt. This is completely different."

"Can you slow down a little? How can you tell it wasn't Justin's fault?" North's words were no longer mild; they'd gained intensity, but he still enunciated with a specific grounding clearness. Ren suspected he was starting to get overexcited about this again.

"I ... well, I guess I can't say for sure, but if I can't know from these reports that it wasn't, they sure as hell can't say for sure that it was. Where's the rest of the documents?"

"There aren't any. Whatever I have is in that file," North responded, leaning in, looking down at the papers as though he hadn't checked them before. Like he was trying to read whatever Ren had seen. "What do you think is missing?"

"A lot," Ren hissed. "Where is David's medical history? The notes from the hospital aren't here; I only see the police report. How many checkups did David have in the interim between when Justin hit him and his death? What was his quality of life during that time? Because it seemed pretty normal if he was partying with his friends on the weekends."

"You think his death is unrelated to what Justin did to him?" North checked.

"I think it's completely impossible to *prove* it was Justin's fault, and that's all we really need, right?" Ren was talking over his shoulder now, on his way to the hall, in search of Dr. Delacroix, moving quickly even though rushing wasn't going to get him anywhere.

"I don't know ... Where are you going?" North asked, watching as Ren opened the door, Justin's file in his hand.

"To get an expert's opinion," Ren called, heading out.

He spotted Angelique's braids at the nurse's station where she was speaking with the staff, her back toward him. From the phrases he could hear as he approached, Ren gathered that the ER wasn't too busy at the moment.

"Dr. Delacroix?" Ren broke into the gathering, certain whatever they were discussing was nowhere near as important as the questions he had. Angelique turned with feline fluidity, her hand coming to rest on one hip. "Can I talk to you?"

"That depends on what you'd like to talk about," Angelique warned him. She was not interested in any more discussion about ethics and insurance, though as she studied his face, she softened, recognizing Ren's distress. "Is it Justin?"

"No, well, yes, but he's ok. He's sleeping. Can you take a look at these with me?" Ren opened the file, pulling free the MRA images of the bloodied brain. Angelique took hold of Ren's wrist instead of the papers, steadying him and twisting to get a better look.

"I don't really have time to help you with your homework, Lorenzo," she chided, exhaling now that she knew there wasn't an emergency.

"It's not homework," Ren pressed. "It's way more important. Please?"

"Where did you get these?" Angelique asked, nodding toward the papers. Ren shook his head. He didn't want to tell her that, at least not yet. Not before she gave him her completely uninformed, unbiased opinion on what she was seeing in the scans. She locked eyes with Ren, making assumptions about what was happening here.

"I'll tell you after you give me a diagnosis on what this is," Ren bargained.

The nurses were moving off now, repelled by the intensity of the situation, no longer wanting to be involved. Angelique removed the papers from Ren's hand, holding them up to her face in silent agreement with Ren's request.

"There's no diagnosis necessary," she told him. "With this kind of bleeding, I don't think the patient survived."

"You're right, but what caused the rupture? What sort is it?"

"It's hard to determine. I can tell you this is a saccular aneurysm, sometimes called a berry aneurysm. It's the most common kind. This one is obviously very large. Was it causing symptoms before it burst, do you know?"

"The patient woke up with a headache and thought it was a hangover. By evening, he was dead."

"That's sad," Angelique mused. "It must have been awful for whoever found him, but no, I can't tell what caused the rupture from looking at this. It could have been genetic, or alcohol use can sometimes weaken the artery linings, making them more susceptible to a bleed. Smoking too since it's linked to high blood pressure."

"What about trauma?" Ren guided her, feeling more confident since she hadn't come up with that one on her own. It meant it was one of the least likely culprits.

"Hmm, possibly? But no, I doubt it."

"Why? What makes you say that?"

Angelique looked up from the photos to stare at Ren, the desperation of his questions triggering her suspicion.

"Lorenzo, exactly what am I looking at here?"

"Can you answer my question first?"

She squared her shoulders, then set the pages on the nurses' desk so she could be free to point. "In almost all cases of traumatic aneurysm, there is a skull base fracture present. I don't see one here, or evidence there ever was one. Why would there be suspicion of trauma? Did the patient fall before complaining of head pain?"

"I don't know. He was … in a fight over a year before this happened, though. Could the events be related?" This question caused Angelique to turn all the pages face down on the desk, removing her hands and folding them securely under her arms. As though she had made a mistake in touching them in the first place and wanted to wipe them clean.

"Lorenzo, are these evidence documents?"

"Remember when I told you yesterday Justin was on trial?" Ren began cautiously. He didn't like how Angelique was talking right now. She sounded furious.

"The police officer who showed up with him was a giveaway," Angelique shot back, her lips pursed. "But you neglected to mention he was on trial for killing someone."

"He *didn't!*" Ren insisted, then cringed as Angelique glared at him.

"Keep your voice down," Angelique hissed. "You're getting in over your head, Lorenzo. How many times do I have to say to look out for yourself?"

"I'm doing the right thing," Ren insisted. "I can't let them put him in prison."

"If he's so innocent, then why was he beating someone up in the first place?" Angelique whispered, so close to Ren's ear he could smell her shampoo. "Judging from these photos and your face, this seems to be a habit."

"I already explained my face," Ren dismissed. "And he stopped a kidnapping and probably an assault too. It's *wrong* what they're trying to do to him, and if there is any way I can prove it, then I'm going to try."

He felt Angelique relax. In another moment, her hands rested alongside his as she also leaned over the desk. He turned his head apprehensively to find her staring at him.

"Is this all you have?" she asked, her voice surprisingly rough.

"Yes. Is it enough?" Was she going to help him?

"I'm not sure. I need more time to look."

"Does that mean you'll help?" Ren asked. He took the papers, replacing them in the file, closing it, and holding it out to her hesitantly.

"You have absolutely no idea how to act in your best interests, do you?" she asked, still staring at him, though they were both standing straight once more. "You have no self-preservation instincts at all." But Ren did not understand what she meant. He wasn't on trial. Nothing horrible could happen to him if Justin went to jail, though he didn't think he could live with himself if that happened.

"This isn't about me," Ren tried to explain. This was about Justin. This was about someone looking at the facts instead of making assumptions about him. Angelique reached forward, and Ren thought she was going to take the folder. Instead, she put her hand on his shoulder. She had to reach up to do it; he was several inches taller than she was.

"Draft me a statement," she demanded, regaining her composure, releasing him. "I make no promises."

18

AGAINST MEDICAL ADVICE

"She's going to help us," Ren triumphed as he returned to Justin's room. North had done some cleaning while he'd been away. The food wrappers and napkins were gathered and disposed of; Ren's coat draped over the back of the chair instead of lying in a heap on the floor, and his backpack tucked up against the bed, out of danger of being stepped on or tripped over. Ren smiled as he noticed the differences, his respect for North raising another notch.

"Help us what exactly?" North questioned, not wanting to kill Ren's sudden good mood, but he was confused about it.

"Dr. Delacroix asked me to draft a statement. She's going to sign on as a medical witness."

"Oh, Ren," North slumped, and this time he really was starting to damage Ren's spirits. No, this was a good thing. Ren was going to secure a statement from one of the most respected trauma doctors in the city, possibly the state, and she was going to put in writing either that David's aneurysm occurred outside of anything Justin had done, or that it was impossible to determine what had caused it. Both scenarios were in Justin's favor. What could be wrong with that?

North considered him carefully, and his face softened. His

expression of concerned incredulity shifted to his gentle smile, and he shrugged off whatever he'd been about to say. "That's great," he finished, and Ren nodded with certainty. That was a better attitude, even though Ren knew North was only going along with it to humor him. He would see. This was going to make all the difference.

As Justin slept, Ren threw himself into preparing the statement. He flipped the notebook from his backpack to a clean page then plopped himself right on the triage room floor, spreading David's photos in a semi-circle around him, staring at them from different angles.

North watched him from the chair, sometimes asking questions about what Ren could see in the scans, sometimes being overcome by what they depicted and needing to look away for a while. He made several phone calls, speaking in such low, smooth tones that even if Ren had been giving him his full attention, he probably wouldn't have been able to understand what he was saying. Ren had to admit that the hum of North's voice in the background was quite relaxing, a steady cadence blurring through his mind as he tried to focus on the scans. Despite his initial enthusiasm, it was getting harder to pay attention, to organize his thoughts enough to make a cohesive argument. His long night, and the night before that, was starting to weigh on him. He pressed his hands against his face, shook his shoulders, and kept working.

North called him away for a break to finish the breakfast sand-wiches around lunchtime. They saved one for Justin, just in case. Twice, North tapped Ren on the arm, gently reminding him to eat as Ren kept zoning out, staring at the photos on the floor but not seeing them. The triage room grew increasingly fuzzy, and Ren slowed down in his work as he became unsure how he was going to get his point across, as he noticed that he kept repeating the same not-quite-there statements. He just couldn't pinpoint exactly how to prove Justin's innocence, and it was exhausting and frustrating him.

It didn't help that, as usual, Justin did not rest quietly. Some-times, his voice rose so clearly that Ren was certain he'd woken up.

North stayed near his side, speaking to him, comforting him, allowing Ren to remain on the floor with his report. Justin didn't say much, or at least not much that made sense. He moaned wordlessly. He called their names in that heartbreaking tone that meant he thought he was being abandoned. He apologized for nameless sins. At one point, he cried so hard about Ren's twin sister that Ren had to get up to put a stop to it before it broke him.

"Shh," Ren begged, stroking the side of Justin's face. "That's not your fault, Justin. That happened a long time ago. *Descansa*."

"Who's he talking about?" North asked, standing supportively next to Ren, watching him trying to soothe Justin, curious as to why this particular thing had pulled Ren from the floor in such a hurry. "Someone real?"

"My sister, but she's gone," Ren answered, rubbing calming circles over Justin's chest. "We were talking about her this morning; I guess it got stuck in his head. Justin, come on, you didn't hurt her. *Basta*."

"Ren," North began, the sympathy thick in his voice. Combined with Justin was almost too much; Ren didn't want to listen to either one of them right now.

"I'm all right," Ren protested, though not very convincingly. He didn't know how to explain that Justin's crying somehow hurt worse than what he was crying about, but it *was* bothering him. He felt like lying his head on Justin's chest and sobbing with him even though that was a waste of time. However, he probably wouldn't have much choice if Justin didn't stop soon. "Justin," he pleaded, hearing the break in his voice. "Please."

"Ok, Ren, take a break," North insisted, shouldering between them, forcing Ren away from the bedside. "This is getting to you, and I know you're exhausted. Do you want me to take you home for a while so you can rest?"

"No, one of us needs to be here." Ren shook his head stubbornly, monitoring Justin's face as he also turned his head from side to side. "He can't wake up alone, and I'm not done yet with the statement.

I'll just ... I'll take a quick walk around until he switches to a different horror channel."

"Ren," North said, and Ren knew he'd gone too far. But it'd just been going on so long. How did Justin even have the energy to put into this while he was supposedly sleeping?

"You said he's always been like this?" Ren asked as he cleaned up the mess of documents from the floor. He didn't want them disturbed while he was out of the room. "Even when he's not sick he does this?" Because wow. But even as he said it, Ren knew Justin could rest quietly. It was possible for him to be still, to actually rest. He'd done it last night, curled against Ren's chest. He hadn't moved or made any sound for hours.

"Not every night," North responded, defensive about Justin. "But like I said, trauma has to be processed at some point. Justin won't allow himself to talk about things that bother him, but obviously that doesn't make them go away ... or make them easier to listen to."

Justin continued to apologize for Amayah's death, and Ren stood with his arms full of papers, looking at his suffering.

"Go on, Ren," North prompted. "And ... I'm sorry about your sister."

"We were two," Ren dismissed. His heart ached for other reasons. He struggled to tear his eyes away from Justin. Perhaps he shouldn't leave. Perhaps he should fold himself against Justin again, see if that would quiet him as it had last night. "I don't remember her. North, maybe I should —"

"I've got him," North said firmly, then he turned toward Justin, somehow shutting Ren out before he'd even left the room. "Take a break, Ren." Ren closed his mouth and walked backward out into the hallway, resting his forehead against the door after he pulled it closed, clutching Justin's file under his arm, dazed.

He wasn't sad about Amayah; he had discovered a long time ago that he could no longer summon much grief for her loss. There was no memory; therefore, there could be no real pain. What made him sad was Justin had decided to shoulder that burden for him, a hurt

Ren couldn't force himself to feel, but Justin had not only assimilated it, he'd made himself responsible for it. How many times had he done that? How many times did he blame himself for something he had nothing to do with? Like Amayah. Like David.

And North. Ren liked him, respected him, but maybe he'd thought too soon that he was included in the special tightness North shared with Justin. Of course North could handle Justin right now, quiet him down, help him relax. He didn't need Ren's help; he'd just made that extremely clear. Ren shouldn't really think he was all that special, that he had any more right to be next to Justin than North did. In all honesty, he had less.

"Lorenzo, what is it? What's wrong?" The questions sounded close to his ear, and a gentle hand rested on his shoulder as he stood there thinking, fingers still loose around the doorknob. Ren could smell the increasingly familiar sharp scent of tea tree oil shampoo and knew Dr. Delacroix was standing next to him. He didn't bother opening his eyes. He wondered if he would ever not be tired again. He wondered how time moved so quickly and yet so impossibly slowly. He'd been in that triage room for days, except it hadn't even been one yet. He'd been trying to help Justin for his entire life, but not even a weekend had passed.

"Lorenzo!" Angelique snapped, but not in anger. She shook his shoulder, trying a more invasive method to get him to answer her. "What happened?"

"Justin talks in his sleep," he murmured, still facing the door with his eyes closed, giving the simplest of facts, trying to pretend they weren't slicing into him. "It's hard to listen to sometimes, so North sent me out for a while."

"And how long has it been since you slept?" she asked, and he shrugged. It still wasn't about him. He could sleep later; he had things to do. She sighed, and Ren could tell she was frustrated with him. But he couldn't remember a time when she wasn't frustrated with him, so he wasn't about to conjure any energy to worry about it now.

She physically pried him from the door, turning him toward her, reaching up to place the back of her hand against his forehead. It took all he had not to irritably brush her off.

"I'm fine," he repeated, standing straighter, forcing himself to look at her. "There's nothing wrong with me."

"On the contrary," she returned, voice resolved, but then her expression crumbled as she decided to let it go and change the subject. "Come with me, please."

Ren rubbed his eyes and decided not to fight it. Like yesterday, he blindly submitted to wherever Angelique wanted to take him. She had a hold on his wrist, pulling him through the emergency hallway to the small working office where they'd argued over insurance a few hours ago.

"Let's take a look at those scans again while I have a minute," she offered, closing the door and gesturing toward a chair. Ren had almost forgotten he had taken the file out with him, but it was still there, tucked under his arm. He pulled it out numbly, setting it on the desk in front of her as she moved around him to take the other seat. "Did you have a chance to get started on that draft?"

"Sort of," Ren said, suddenly remembering every poorly made argument in the thing. He'd worked so hard on it, and he'd been sure of every word he'd written down until this moment when she would be looking at it. Now everything seemed rough and inexperienced. Not even good enough to be called a draft.

"If I may?" Dr. Delacroix asked politely, so Ren also passed over the notebook, opened to where he'd started writing down his thoughts on the scans and Justin's lack of responsibility for the damage. Odd that the conviction he'd felt on the floor had turned into an anxious embarrassment. But when had his best effort ever been good enough for Dr. Delacroix? Maybe she was right, maybe he was out of his league on this. But that's why he'd asked for her help in the first place.

Not wanting to watch her read his thoughts, and because his head felt so heavy, Ren crossed his arms on the desk and hid his face in the folds, waiting for Dr. Delacroix's assessment and instruction. It was extremely quiet in this office, far from the main entrance and the nurses' station. Angelique herself sat with an almost unnatural stillness, reading, studying. Ren could hear the tick of a clock on the wall. Every so often there would be a soft whisper of a page being turned over. There were no windows, no pictures on the walls. Nothing but a weighted silence.

No, not quite silence. There was a deepness too. A lull, like a voice, humming in the background without ever focusing into discernible words. Ren hummed a little in response, acknowledging that he heard it, but couldn't bring himself to fully answer. There was the softness of his sleeve against his cheek, the curve of his spine over the desk, the clock. Time moving without him, running slow and yet still running out.

Ren hadn't noticed falling asleep until he was waking up again to the sensation of someone shaking his shoulder. He groaned, coming back slowly to consciousness. His entire body felt stiff from how he sat hunched against the desk. How long had he been here?

He shook off the touch, unlocking his spine and sitting up, opening his eyes to see Angelique pulling backward.

"Dr. Delacroix?" The last time he'd seen her, she'd been sitting across from him, scanning his documents without expression. Now she stood next to him, closer to the door, watching him. "What time is it? Is Justin ok?"

"You two," she murmured, a hesitant smile just touching her lips. "That's almost exactly what he said when he woke up."

"You shouldn't have let me fall asleep," Ren accused groggily.

"You needed it," Angelique defended. "Though it would have been better if you'd been lying down. When you go home, could you please make sure you get a decent amount of rest? Or Justin won't be the only one with a weakened immune system."

"You said he was awake? How long?" Justin was awake and Ren hadn't been there for it. How would Justin take that? Somehow it didn't help that North had probably been with him, sitting in that chair, forever still, patient, and watchful, untouched by fatigue, completely in control of his emotions. It didn't help knowing North had done it first and for longer either. Ren began rearranging his body to stand up.

"He's only been awake a few minutes. That's why I came to get you. There's no need to rush; he understands where you are. Here, this is for you." She held out the familiar file and Ren's notebook. Ren took them with both hands, flipping the folder open automatically. All the papers were present, neatly clipped together in some pattern that must have made sense to Dr. Delacroix. In addition, his notes were there with an official looking document printed on hospital letterhead.

"You made an excellent start," Angelique complimented as he scanned the statement. "You really are quite advanced." Ren barely registered the compliment as he was reading. He was surprised to recognize several phrases, whole paragraphs he'd scribbled onto the notebook, now copied verbatim but organized and flowing into a full cohesive report. It basically read that the cause of the rupture in David's brain was impossible to state for certain; however, the likelihood it had anything to do with Justin's attack was statistically and medically unlikely. It acknowledged the tragic loss of life but denied the evidence was strong enough to make that loss a punishable crime. Angelique had signed it.

"Thank you so much, Dr. Delacroix," Ren exhaled in awed gratitude. "This is perfect."

"I'm not sure what help it will be," Angelique began, then continued apologetically when she saw Ren's face. "But it seems important to you."

"If you only knew," Ren whispered, closing the folder and hugging it to his chest since it wouldn't be appropriate to hug Dr. Delacroix. She stood with her arms crossed, watching him, her face a complicated disarrangement. As though she couldn't decide herself what she was feeling.

"Lorenzo?" she started to ask a question, but just as quickly changed her mind.

"He's worth it," Ren answered her anyway, willing to challenge anyone on that point. Worth the lack of sleep and the worry. Worth the bruises and the time and effort. Because no one should be so surprised by kindness. "He shouldn't have had to go to trial in the first place."

"I agree with you," Angelique said, and Ren didn't know he needed her to say that until the moment it left her mouth. "On this point, at least."

"How is he doing?" Ren asked, wanting to see him. He felt like he'd been away too long; he needed to go to him right now. Make sure Justin understood it wasn't only North who cared about him. Ren hadn't really wanted to leave.

Dr. Delacroix's features settled into the slightly exasperated expression that indicated he wasn't asking the right questions. It wasn't exactly disappointment; it was somewhere between sad and annoyed. But again, as before, Angelique masked it quickly with a professional detachment. She regained her composure in an instant, though she allowed herself a shake of her head.

"Let's go see," she said.

Ren nodded in agreement, following her across the emergency room floor to the triage room that had been Justin's entire world for the last day. When Ren and Angelique came in, North's and Justin's heads lifted together. North had pulled the chair close to the bedside. It looked as though they'd been interrupted during an intense discussion. Ren lowered the file to his side when he saw Justin's eyes fix on it. After the lengths Justin had gone to keep that file a secret, it was probably a shock to discover Ren had it anyway, and Ren didn't want him too angry before he had a chance to explain what he'd done.

"Hi guys," Ren greeted, clearing the sleep from his throat. "Sorry I took so long."

"Are you ok?" Justin questioned him from the bed, melting Ren's insides at the earnestness in his face and voice as he asked. *Damn it, Justin; worry about yourself.*

"That's my line," Ren retorted, not answering. He hadn't paid enough attention to himself to know if he was ok. This was one of the longest days he could remember. They weren't even finished yet.

Ren invited himself to Justin's side, handing the file to North who secured it immediately out of sight. Ren wanted to take Justin's hand, but somehow seeing him with North reminded Ren that they were still practically strangers.

"Now that we're all here," Dr. Delacroix interrupted the strange pause that had settled between Justin, Ren, and North, pulling all their eyes toward her. "I'd like to go over the EKG report with you." Ren prepared to bite his tongue. He was not going to argue with Dr. Delacroix in front of Justin, not when she'd just handed him the piece of paper that could save Justin from going to jail.

Justin took hold of Ren's sleeve, causing him to turn toward him. Justin looked worried, and Ren realized it wasn't because of anything Dr. Delacroix had said, it was because Ren was suddenly tense. He forced himself to relax against the bed.

"For the most part, it's encouraging," Angelique began. "I've been gradually lowering your dose of anti-arrhythmic medication all day, and your heart rate has remained steady. It seems your iron and hydration levels will be the most important factors in keeping stress off your heart. I'll be sending you home with a prescription for Tenormin and a recommendation for an iron supplement."

"We're leaving today?" North inserted into the conversation hopefully, as if there were any chance Justin could remain under the hospital's care. "Ren mentioned there was a possibility that Justin would be admitted for several days of monitoring?" Ren admired his attempt, though Angelique narrowed her eyes at him for forcing her to have to address this outright.

"I did consider that," Angelique admitted, and Justin's hand tightened on Ren's sleeve. He probably didn't want to stay here that long, even if it would be better for him. "But given the circumstances, we will be sending Justin home today."

She wouldn't do that unless she was sure, Ren reminded himself. She said she would check the report carefully; if there had been anything concerning in it, she would have admitted Justin regardless of insurance. Ren had to believe that even though it still felt wrong.

"Home?" Justin whispered, as if the word meant nothing to him. He turned his face toward North, and Ren's skin chilled. Home to Justin did not mean that abandoned apartment. No, when Justin thought of home, he thought of North.

"The hide-a-bed at my place is open," North told him kindly. "You can come home with me, Justin."

Ren felt like something was slipping away from him, that Justin was slipping away. North and Justin were staring at each other, having a silent discussion, so Ren shot a look toward Dr. Delacroix, as if she could or would do anything to stop this. Because he wasn't ready for Justin to go with North. For some reason, he thought he'd be with Justin from now on. But it wasn't like he could say so. It wasn't like it should matter to him.

But then Justin turned to look at Ren, his expression was torn, as though he were waiting for Ren to say something. Ren wasn't sure what that could be; if he wasn't going to stay at the hospital, North's place was obviously better. So then why did it look as though Justin wanted to go with him? Or maybe Ren was seeing things that weren't there because of his own desires.

"Forgive me," Dr. Delacroix broke in with the phrase she used when she felt no forgiveness should be necessary. "I was under the impression that Lorenzo and Justin were roommates and he lived on campus. Is that not correct?"

"Justin's been staying with me since he got sick, but he doesn't live there," Ren clarified, though he felt certain she already knew they didn't live together. So what was she doing?

"Does it matter?" North asked, just as confused as Ren.

"Perhaps not," Dr. Delacroix allowed, though her tone betrayed her words. "But I am discharging Justin with reservations. I thought he would be staying close to the hospital. Can I ask how far away you would be taking him?"

"I live in McKinley Park," North answered, his shoulders squared. "It's a twenty-minute drive, a little more with the roads like they are now."

"Hmm," Angelique hummed disapprovingly, but maybe that was a good thing. Maybe this would tip her into allowing Justin to stay. Maybe North wouldn't be taking him away from Ren. Then they could delay the court hearing too.

"What do you mean reservations?" North prodded, reining in any accusation in his voice. "If that's the case, shouldn't he stay here?"

"He is currently stable," Dr. Delacroix defended her decision. "However, his temperature remains elevated, and he is still exhibiting flu symptoms, including a faster-than-normal heart rate. There is a slight chance he might need to return. Possibly very quickly."

"That ... that could happen again?" North asked, sounding disturbed. North looked across Justin at Ren, as if checking with him about all this, sharing the memory of Justin on the floor between them, hardly able to breathe. Ren found it difficult to meet his eyes and remain calm for Justin at the same time. It still pissed him off. Remembering the frightening circumstances of coming to the emergency room just made it harder to not say anything he'd regret to Dr. Delacroix regarding hospital policy and exactly what he thought about it. That would not help.

"There is a small chance," Dr. Delacroix replied, still calm despite how her explanations were tensing everyone else in the room. "But I believe that was an isolated incident. If Justin has enough fluids and takes the medication I'm prescribing for him, everything should be fine; however, I think it would be safest if he stayed close until he's completely recovered. I had hoped that I'd be sending him home with an EMT who lived within walking distance of the hospital."

"That's fine," Ren offered, maybe too quickly, and there was an edge to his voice he hadn't intended. "Justin's welcome to recover at my place. That was the original plan anyway." Back when he didn't know who North was, when he thought he'd have to protect Justin from him.

"But ... wait," North said, keeping up even though this was not going the direction he thought it would. He sounded exactly as Ren had felt a moment ago — like he thought he was about to lose Justin forever.

"You can come too," Ren invited, though where he was going to put North was a complete mystery. If Justin took Ren's bed, and Ren slept on the couch, then North was ... on the floor somewhere? Under the table? But they'd have to figure that out. He didn't want to keep North away from Justin, that felt cruel for both of them. They still had things to discuss.

"You can decide among yourselves," Dr. Delacroix told them now that her points had been made. "I'll be back in a little while with the discharge papers and prescriptions, and I'll send someone in to disconnect you from the EKG machine and remove your IV."

"You mean now?" North asked her, surprised at the suddenness. They'd been in this room for so long, going hours without anyone coming in to check on them. So much movement all at once was a little disorienting, even to Ren who had expected it.

"Wait," Justin spoke up unexpectedly. The first time he'd said anything since Dr. Delacroix had begun her assessment regarding the EKG data. Angelique paused, a sad compassion in her eyes as she looked at Justin.

"I'm sorry, sweetheart, I should have asked. Do you have any questions or concerns?"

"Can't he do it?" Justin asked, nodding toward Ren.

"Do what, baby?" Dr. Delacroix clarified.

"The IV? He put it in so —" Justin trailed off.

Ren kept very still in the hopes Angelique would be able to tell he had nothing to do with this request and had not put it into Justin's head to even ask.

"I'm not supposed to," Ren told Justin gently. "That's out of my scope of practice, remember? Taking them out isn't a big deal, though. You won't feel it at all."

Justin nodded, as though he had expected that, but he looked uncomfortable. Ren remembered how little Justin liked to be touched by strangers. How he shied away from even Dr. Delacroix when she examined him.

"You want Lorenzo to take out your IV, honey?" Dr. Delacroix questioned him directly. "Would you be most comfortable that way?" Justin nodded, looking ready to have his request denied. Ren glanced at her, wishing she wouldn't lead Justin on this way when he knew she wasn't going to let him so much as pick at the tape.

"All right," Angelique accepted, and Ren clamped his teeth shut so his jaw wouldn't fall into Justin's lap. She'd just … said yes? She hadn't even stopped to really think about it. Ren was never going to figure her out.

"I can?" Ren checked, just to make sure he'd heard right. All that talk about hospital policy and she was going to cave on this?

"Sounded like patient consent to me," Angelique told him, way too casually. As though they had never argued about it. As if she hadn't threatened Ren's EMT status over it. "It's low risk; you're trained, and I wouldn't mind watching your technique."

"Should I … right now?" Ren asked.

"Preferably," Dr. Delacroix told him teasingly. But what was he supposed to think about this? What had changed? Was it something she saw in Ren or something she'd noticed about Justin? Both? Still, Ren supposed it was a whole different game to remove an IV in a motionless and quiet hospital setting with a licensed MD supervising. He probably shouldn't overthink it.

Justin put his hand closer to Ren expectantly, some tension gone from his shoulders.

"Hang on; there's a protocol," Ren told him, wrapping his head around how this was actually happening and walking past Angelique so he could wash his hands and put on some gloves. *I'm not nervous,* he scolded himself, feeling the fluttering of anxiety over being watched while he did this. *I remove needles all the time. **All the time.** I never think twice about it.* But Angelique had never watched him before either. He'd never thought she might be assessing him for something. He monitored his hands for shaking as he assembled what he'd need and noted the location of the biohazard waste receptacle.

But when he returned to the bed, gloves in place and ready to start, he locked eyes with Justin and immediately felt nothing but calm. Justin looked up at him with the same sort of expression Ren had seen him give North. Grateful, comfortable, trust. Like he was certain, more than anything, that Ren wasn't going to hurt him. Ren almost got choked up seeing that. It felt so special to be half of the grand total of humans on earth Justin felt he could trust.

Ren proceeded with refreshed confidence to disconnect the IV line, first discontinuing the drip flow. Justin would be on his own now. The meds would likely wear off sometime in the next four hours, leaving him prone to the pain of the fever again. But Ren would be ready to do what he could to help. Because he was still responsible for Justin. He was taking him home. Another gift Angelique had given him.

He carefully peeled away the medical tape he'd applied in the ambulance, stabilizing the needle with his thumb to make sure it didn't twist under Justin's skin as he did so. It was like there was no one else in the room anymore. He couldn't feel Angelique's eyes on him. Couldn't tell if North were even still there. He concentrated on Justin's wrist, deftly pulling the needle free with one hand and covering the site with a piece of gauze with the other.

"Put pressure on that," he instructed, though it wasn't a vein that would bleed very much. It was more for putting things into the body than getting blood out, the exact opposite of the kinds of veins Ren usually worked with. But having Justin hold onto the gauze allowed Ren to cross the room and properly dispose of the needle into the sharps container. Once it was gone, he put a simple bandage over everything. Nothing to it.

After that, he started disconnecting the EKG wires. First the lines, then the electrode disks sticking across Justin's chest. Surprisingly, this activity was more difficult because Ren had to reach around and inside Justin's hospital gown to get at them all. It made his face feel hot to do something so intimate, and then he felt stupid for thinking this was more intimate than removing the IV. Being with Justin was a complicated thing, especially as he watched Ren the entire time, his eyes focused. Ren looked at Dr. Delacroix as a distraction, finding her impassive, standing in exactly the same place as when he'd started. He wasn't sure if that was good, but he figured if he'd been doing something wrong, she would have said so by now.

"All clear," he said, indicating he was finished. Test complete. If that's what this had been. Why did Justin have to put that idea into his head?

"Very smooth," Angelique acknowledged, though she was careful not to sound too impressed. "Looks like it's true what they say about you." She turned her attention to Justin. "Let your friends help you get dressed, darling. I'll be back in a few minutes with the discharge papers."

With that, she pivoted on her heel and disappeared into the hall. Ren exhaled, then wasn't sure if he'd been breathing that entire time.

"All right, Justin?" Ren asked, slightly winded.

"Told you," was all he said, and if he didn't look so fragile there in the bed with the hospital gown dangling off one shoulder, Ren would have shoved him against the mattress.

"Would you stop it? I'm going to be a pediatrician, ok? With a nine-to-five practice, a gorgeous wife, a white-picket fence, and ten kids waiting for me to come home to dinner every night, got it?"

"Very American," Justin returned, though the humor was gone from his voice. He was suddenly staring at Ren's blanket, rubbing his fingers thoughtfully across the cotton patch that had been part of one of Eva's dresses. "Ten kids?" he double checked quietly.

"Or more," Ren shot back with conviction. "Now where did we put your clothes?" Ren found it easier to go forward now, preparing to leave the hospital, to return to his own place. It still made him mad, but at least Justin was coming home with him and not leaving with North.

"I can't even remember how they got taken off," Justin admitted, and Ren looked at North, suddenly drowning in that dark memory. Ren would have to try his absolute best to make sure Justin didn't relapse to that point again. Just because Angelique had suggested staying close to the hospital didn't mean Ren wanted it to be necessary.

"They're here," North offered helpfully, handing over the white and blue plastic bag labeled "Personal Items" that had been tucked on the corner of the counter near the sink. Ren didn't remember how they'd gotten there, nor could he remember ever seeing the bag even while he'd been standing near the sink. He'd been thinking about other things.

Justin began pulling the contents out — his charcoal and maroon striped sweater that he'd worn to class on Friday, Ren's pajama pants, and his socks and underwear. He moved slowly until he was sitting sideways on the bed, bare legs hanging over the edge, holding on to the mattress, reorienting himself to being upright, his bandaged hand immediately going to his head. Discharged with reservations indeed.

"Let me help," Ren said, unable to watch. He reached to undo the first knot of the hospital gown at Justin's shoulder but paused when Justin cringed.

"It doesn't make sense for me to feel weird about this, huh?" Justin said, not looking at Ren. "I mean, I just let you take a needle out of my hand."

"It's not the same thing," Ren comforted him, even though he'd been in the room when the hospital staff had stripped Justin the first time. Still, if their positions had been reversed, he wouldn't want Justin to dress him either. "I can leave if you want me to?" Ren looked over at North again but saw on his face that Justin probably wouldn't want him to do this either. But neither of them trusted Justin's strength enough to leave him to dress all on his own.

"Let me show you how we did it in boot camp," North came to the rescue.

"You had to change out of medical gowns at boot camp?" Ren asked without pausing to consider if it were a good idea to challenge the validity of anything North wanted to say right now that might be helpful. Especially since Justin looked more interested than timid now.

"Well, not every day, but yes, there were med checks where the whole squad would have to strip down into gowns and back again. I can probably get you into these clothes with my eyes shut, Justin."

"Let's just get it over with before she gets back," Justin requested, sounding horrified at the idea of having Angelique in the room again.

"She doesn't hate you, you know," Ren defended Dr. Delacroix.

"I don't care what she thinks of me," Justin dismissed. "I want her to be fair to *you*."

"We're fine," Ren assured, wishing Justin could understand why Angelique behaved the way she did toward him. But he'd been asleep or just not there for Ren's quiet moments with Angelique — her hand on his head in the hallway, working on Justin's medical statement while Ren slept on her desk, buying antibiotic ointment for his back, and then manipulating the situation to make sure Ren wasn't separated from Justin. Now that Ren was thinking about it, Angelique probably had to force herself to keep her distance to make sure she wasn't favoring Ren too much. That was so weird. "But you're right; let's get this done."

In the end, North did the hard parts — lifting Justin when necessary, keeping him steadily upright, while Ren did the finessing bits like socks and fitting legs through the appropriate holes in pants. The second time Ren reached over to undo the gown's tie string, Justin didn't move away. Ren noticed North gazing sorrowfully at the burn scars on Justin's upper back, so he hurriedly tugged the sweater over them. They'd barely finished when Dr. Delacroix reappeared with the discharge papers.

"That will be all from me," she said in parting, clutching the papers in both hands after securing her pen into her breast pocket. "When you get wherever you've all decided you're going to go, I want you to relax, darling. If you do what Lorenzo tells you, then I likely won't see you again. Is there anything else before I go?"

"Thank you," Justin told her, only a hint of reluctance in the gesture, sitting once again cross-legged on the bed, this time dressed and with Ren's blanket folded in his lap. "No offense, but I don't want to see you again."

"I get that a lot," she replied, chuckling, still as affectionate to Justin as she left as she had been when she'd first come to his side. Then she looked at Ren and immediately hardened, though not very much. "You, on the other hand," she said to Ren. "I would like to see more of. I'll be in touch with Dr. Taneja. I want to discuss your training plan with the two of you." Ren felt Justin's knuckles press against his hip, but he forced himself to look only at Dr. Delacroix. He wanted to tell her, without a shred of doubt, that he knew what she was doing, and he just wasn't interested. But then he remembered the things he'd heard about past students she'd mentored — how successful they turned out to be. How they could get a job anywhere and there were only a handful of them. It'd be stupid if he didn't at least listen to what she had to say.

"Sounds good," he said instead.

"I agree. All right then. Whomever is driving can bring your car around to the main entrance. One of the techs will be bringing a wheelchair."

Her flurry of last-minute directions complete, Angelique gave them all one final nod and disappeared to the hallway. North left next, zipping up his coat with his remarkable prosthetic with the same grace as if it had been his real hand. Ren began gathering his coat and backpack, looking about the room to make sure they weren't forgetting anything.

When the tech came with the wheelchair, both he and Ren helped Justin pivot into it, holding on to his arms carefully and then covering him with the quilt. Justin didn't look too happy about all the assistance, but he didn't say anything. In fact, he sort of shut down, concentrating silently on transport. He submitted tensely to whatever hands were on him as he transitioned from the wheelchair into North's white Nissan Altima, a tricky maneuver considering there was so much disgusting slush at the entrance and Justin's boots were still sitting next to Ren's couch. As soon as the tech closed the car door, Justin lowered down to rest his head on Ren's lap.

Justin also allowed North to carry him, one last time, just from the car to the carpeted entrance of Ren's apartment building. Ren helped him into one of the random chairs stashed around the study area near the front door while they waited for North to park somewhere legal, monitoring his breathing, which was shallow and quick thanks to the effort of moving. Wanting to do something and not liking how quiet Justin was, Ren adjusted the quilt around Justin's shoulders, giving in to the desire to rub his back a little, feeling the tautness of his muscles even underneath the blanket. This was taking a lot out of him, mentally and physically.

"Almost there," Ren encouraged, though as expected Justin didn't answer him. He was breathing hard, but he kept his mouth tightly closed after North returned, and they both supported him quietly to the elevator and down the hall to the apartment, obviously despising every second of it. Like he'd forgotten during his time in the hospital just how weak he truly was, and now he was seething about how he couldn't even walk on his own. Ren did his best to not make it a big deal, and he knew North was doing the same. Every little shift and catch happened with each of them vigilantly keeping their eyes averted, pretending they were alone even though they were all quite focused on forward movement.

Alek broke through all of that in half a second. They stood in the hall, Ren searching one handed for where he might have put his keys, when the door was almost ripped off instead of open and Alek pounced on them. Ren watched, astonished, as Alek grabbed for Justin, who half-collapsed against him, all the tension in his body breaking in an instant as he leaned against Ren's roommate.

"Justin!" Alek boomed so loudly Ren wondered if their neighbors were going to start poking their heads out. "Welcome back, man! We were so worried. Dude, you ok? For sure, you look better than when you left, but you still look awful. Ren, why does he still look awful?"

"How about we get him inside and then ask questions?" Ren reminded him, not quite successful at keeping the anger out of his voice. He wasn't angry at Alek; he was still mad at the hospital for kicking Justin out.

Fortunately, Alek was caught up in getting Justin into the apartment and onto the couch, so he didn't seem to notice the edge in Ren's tone. He chattered at Justin as he guided him inside, North and Ren following more slowly. As Alek took charge of Justin, Ren checked the place over, reacclimatizing himself. The scent of Alek's baking extravaganza yesterday was still thick in the heat of the place, and there were still several loaves of bread and plates of cookies on the kitchen counter. Denny was in the kitchen too, watching Alek with concern.

"Hey Denny," Ren greeted her, happy to see her despite their recent differences of opinion. He had a lot he wanted to explain to her.

"Hey Ren," she returned, emotionless, and she hid her face by taking a sip of something from a tea mug. "And North."

"Hello," North said pleasantly, standing near the door he'd just closed, also looking around. Like the first time he'd stood in that exact spot, he seemed to fill the whole space, appearing too large, too mature, and honestly, too sophisticated to truly feel at home here.

"This is Denny," Ren introduced her, trying to ease the awkwardness of their homecoming. "Our pet genius. And that's Alek." He knew North had already seen them before, and they'd spoken together on the phone last night, but this situation was new and different. North would be joining them, possibly for a long while. Ren thought he should tighten up the relationships.

"Nice to formally meet you," North said, smiling that gentle smile of his.

"Sure. Can I interest you in a cookie?" Denny asked politely, snatching up one of the plates and coming toward them. Ren grabbed one, and after a moment of thought, North took one too. Then Denny looked over to where Alek was fussing over Justin, getting him settled under the blanket at the corner of the couch and seemed to lose all her hospitality. Yeah, Ren had to talk to her very soon. She was still coldly glaring at Justin like he was the Zodiac Killer.

"Justin wants to try one," Ren prompted her, giving her a little push toward the couch. She spun around and actually dropped the plate into his hands, barely giving him enough time to catch it without all the cookies spilling onto the floor. Ren glared at her, but she simply gave him an innocent little head tilt and returned to her mug in the kitchen.

"So, what are you guys doing back?" Alek questioned them, somehow missing the whole thing with the plate. North hadn't, though, if his raised eyebrows were a clue. "I thought you'd be staying at least one more night."

"Justin's heart is steady," Ren tried to explain without sounding pissed. It was harder now that Denny was acting the way she was. "They don't keep people in the hospital for fevers, so they said we could go."

It seemed they all turned to look at Justin then, as if they could determine everything about him by staring. Justin bowed under all the scrutiny, intensely uncomfortable. He tugged the quilt tighter around him like a shield, curling up as much as he could.

"So what'd we miss?" Ren invited, hoping they would start some sort of complicated explanation about something. Meanwhile, Ren brought the plate over to Justin, sitting next to him, gently putting his fingertips on his leg.

"It's been boring," Alek shrugged. "It snowed, then it snowed some more. Um, did some baking. Watched like thirteen movies. Got the mail — oh, there's a package for you, Ren. From your family."

"You didn't open it, right?" Ren checked sharply. If it was what he thought it was, Alek's birthday present was inside.

"Where's the faith?"

"Good." Ren felt Justin relaxing in tiny fractions, easing himself into the couch, into the conversation going on around him. *That's better, Justin. You were here before. You're welcome here.* Ren wasn't so sure what to do with North, though. He still stood near the door, eating his cookie more slowly than Ren thought was humanly possible, quietly observing.

"North, you can come sit here," Ren offered, though he didn't want to leave Justin's side. But he didn't want to be rude either. North's eyes fluttered shut in momentary relief as Ren prepared to trade him places. "Justin, did you want one of these?" Ren offered the cookie plate before he got up, though maybe he shouldn't have. Justin looked tortured about it.

"Maybe later," he said quietly.

"How are you feeling, Justin?" North asked him, perching with characteristic military stiffness next to him on the couch. Ren stayed nearby to hear the answer.

"Disgusting," Justin answered.

"You want a shower?" Ren offered, knowing exactly how nasty he would feel almost three days into an illness and after a hospital stay. He also figured they should make the most of the time they had left before Justin's medication wore off.

"Hell yes," Justin emphasized his consent, his desire to get clean overcoming any awkwardness he might feel about using Ren's bathroom.

"Ok," Ren said as he started thinking through the logistics. "Let's get that started then."

19
MATTER OF PERSPECTIVE

Getting Justin showered and dressed turned into the main event of Stony Island with everyone participating in some fashion. Alek prepped the room with fresh towels and washcloths. Ren went through Justin's duffel bag for clean clothes, though he ended up donating his own University of Chicago hoodie and another set of cozy pajama pants since apparently all Justin owned were three pairs of identical black jeans. Ren was taller than Justin, but not enough for it to matter when it came to comfortable, warm clothes that were supposed to be on the loose side. North helped Justin off the couch while Denny grudgingly pulled a cardboard box full of electrical debris closer to the wall to make space for both of them to walk back to the bathroom.

Which is where Justin decided he would rather die than have a single person help him any farther than the doorway.

"Justin, we've been over this," Ren lectured, already standing in the bathroom so he could assist with the finicky old plumbing and get the water a decent temperature. "Or don't you remember what happened the last time you were in here by yourself?"

"I got it," Justin snipped, pulling away from North and leaning against the door frame. Ren took a second to be impressed. Justin presented a credible posture, tolerably solid, extremely determined. "I'm not going to stand up," he continued, gesturing toward the bathtub. Despite what he said and how he looked, Ren was worried. Justin had almost passed out in here. Justin had almost died yesterday.

"I'll be in the hallway," Ren agreed, his teeth clenched. But there wasn't much else he could do. "Stay on your knees; everything's here for you, and you should be able to reach it all from the floor." Which Alek had practically carpeted in towels. "Don't get the water too hot, and put your hands in first before you douse your head, that'll help adjust your body so you don't get too dizzy. Take your time, and if you need anything, just say so."

Ren could feel he was being stared at, and he glanced away from Justin, who was smirking at the floor, to notice that it was North, again with his eyebrows raised and one corner of his mouth twitching up. Yeah, whatever. Ren didn't care if they thought he was nuts. Justin had enough going on already, and Ren was unwilling to go through the ordeal of getting Justin back to the ER where Ren would certainly have to endure Angelique lecturing him over any kind of head wound when it could have been completely preventable if Justin weren't such an ass about privacy.

"Why don't you just stay with him and keep your eyes closed?" North suggested, meticulously pulling his features back to neutral when he saw Ren had noticed his staring. "You can do that, right?"

"Of course *I* can," Ren quipped, but he knew it was useless. "But I don't think Justin trusts me enough." He layered the challenge on thick. He understood, though. It wasn't so much about Justin trusting him; it was just embarrassing. And there was no way for Ren to make the point clear that being with Justin while he showered was more about keeping him safe than anything else.

"Ok," Justin burst out, frustrated. "If it'll make you stop freaking out, you can stay. You are the worst mother hen ever."

"Think you mean the best," Ren corrected, suddenly triumphant, refusing to be offended.

"Ugh," Justin humphed, letting go of the door and kneeling on the towels. To Ren, who was watching closely, there seemed to be control in the movement. Justin had meant to do that; he hadn't collapsed.

"All right then. Justin, if you're ok, I'm going to see if I can find somewhere that will fill these prescriptions," North told him, watching their interaction carefully, no longer quite so amused but also not appearing very worried.

"There's a Walgreens up the street that would probably work," Ren volunteered, liking this plan.

"Thanks. I'll be back soon. Justin?"

"Yeah?"

"Cooperate. Ren is trying to look out for you."

Justin waved him off, though Ren saw him lift his head to watch as North retreated down the hallway. There was a hint of fear in his eyes every time North went out of his sight. Terrified that it might be the last time he ever saw him. Even though their conversation here had been casual and friendly, there was still that momentary panic. Justin repressed it, visibly turning away, his hands curling into fists on his thighs. Ren closed the bathroom door.

"How much of my help do you want?" Ren offered. "Can I start the shower for you? The water's kind of weird."

"Fine," Justin acquiesced, again in a huff. Ren slipped past him in the tight space in order to flip on the faucets. Behind him, he heard Justin struggling out of his clothes.

"Justin?" he checked. "Can I do something?"

"Just sit down and shut up. I've got it," Justin hissed. Keeping his back turned, Ren made his way around to the toilet, taking a seat and firmly closing his eyes. He settled in, folding his arms and focusing on what he could hear over the pelting noise of the shower. He wished Justin would narrate what he was doing, but that seemed a bit much to ask of him since he should save his energy for movement.

"I'm ... sorry," Justin broke their silence after several long minutes.

"We're good," Ren told him.

"No, this really sucks," Justin insisted. Ren supposed real apologies were not something Justin did often, so maybe he should treat it with more solemnity. "You've got better things to do with your weekend than babysitting me."

Ren thought about that but came up short. He honestly couldn't think of anything else he'd rather be doing right now. Justin needed him, and that was kind of his favorite thing.

"Nothing comes to mind," Ren denied mildly, not wanting to upset Justin anymore. It was like he wanted Ren to tell him he was right, that Ren was wasting his time, and he desperately wished he'd never decided to check on Justin. That was completely untrue, though. Ren didn't even want to think about what might have happened if he hadn't spent his time worrying about Justin.

"But ... Denny," Justin went on, and now Ren really did have to get serious. Because Ren didn't think Justin had noticed Denny's attitude, and he hadn't had a chance to explain to her that all her hostility toward Justin was unfounded and unnecessary. "I don't know what I did, but she's really mad at me. She doesn't want me here."

"Ok," Ren put the brakes on Justin's spiral into rejection. "Stop right there. First of all, Denny always looks like she's mad. Second, she doesn't live here. She's a guest just like you, so she doesn't get a say about who stays with us. If she doesn't like it, she can leave. Meanwhile, Alek *does* live here, and he's pretty much adopted you. He's in the kitchen right now trying to figure out something you can eat. And lastly, none of that matters because Dr. Delacroix said you should stick close to the hospital. I promised you I'd look after you, and I don't know why we're even talking about this."

Ren's little tirade silenced Justin. Ren waited for any kind of contestation from him about anything Ren had just said, but nothing came. It went on for so long that Ren got worried.

"Justin?" he checked, though he hadn't heard anything disconcerting. It was so tempting to open his eyes, but not breaking Justin's trust was more important. "I need you to say something; you're kind of scaring me. You all right?"

"Y-yes," Justin answered, sounding overwhelmed again. Ren wondered how long it would take before Justin really understood that Ren was his friend. Sometimes, it seemed he got it — teasing Ren in the hospital, putting medication on his back, asking for Ren to remove his IV, leaning trustingly against him. Then all of a sudden it would get to be too much, as if he just couldn't believe it, so he'd push at the boundaries to see if they would break. Had he done this with North too? Yeah, probably more violently too since he'd been younger. There was still a little of it going on even now. But if North could be patient for years, then Ren could do it too.

"We want to help you, Justin," Ren assured him again. "You're not bothering anyone; we just want you to be ok. But, um, I do need to talk to you about Denny." Because that had to be resolved. Especially if Justin could tell that Denny was being deliberately hostile toward him.

"Ok," Justin allowed, sounding uncertain, like something was about to be broken between them. "What's her deal?"

"So, she's the one who told me about, you know, the whole court thing, but she got it all wrong. I don't know what she was looking at or where she got her information, but it's just twisted and one-sided. She knows what you did, but she doesn't know why, and ... yeah, it's messing with her opinion of you."

"I hear there's a club," Justin tossed out, but Ren could decipher the hurt. He moved on without acknowledgment.

"I wanted to ask if you'd be ok if I told them the truth?" Ren requested. "You don't have to agree," he added quickly. "But I don't like how Denny is treating you, that's not fair, and I also don't like how that makes her mad at me because she thinks I'm ignoring her advice, and honestly, that's going to end up hurting Alek's feelings because he hates it when we disagree about something. So I thought, since we are all friends and we care about you, I could let them know what really happened? Set the record straight?"

Again Justin paused, silent and brooding. Again Ren wished desperately that he could get some kind of visual feedback since Justin wasn't saying anything. But all he heard was the faucet turning off, and then even the shower was quiet.

"Justin?" he prompted.

"How is that going to make her not mad at me?" Justin questioned bitterly.

"What?" Ren squawked, unable to comprehend Justin's thought process. "How can you say that? It'll make all the difference in the world!" By the time Ren finished explaining, he was certain Denny would change her mind. And everyone would be a lot better off if Denny were content with the ethics of the situation.

"It might be different in the Dominican," Justin droned, voice still tainted with that defensive bitterness. "But around here, the truth doesn't count for a whole lot, you know?"

"You don't know her," Ren said quietly, sadly. "But I do. She's like my sister. And I can tell you that if anything matters to Denny, it's the truth."

"Tell them whatever you want," Justin conceded, his voice sounding as though he were hanging his head in exhaustion or defeat. "I just don't want to be there for it, all right?"

"Deal," Ren agreed, keeping his tone flat. He stood up, groping around the room until his hand found the towel Alek had left for Justin. "Here," he offered, not wanting to attempt draping it over Justin's shoulders since he still had no real idea where Justin was in actual space, though he knew he was still somewhere in the bathtub. Then he once again moved out of the way to allow Justin the room to get up, get dry, and get into his clean clothes. He listened to Justin panting at the exertion of these activities, and once Justin grabbed on to Ren's shoulder. Ren automatically lifted his elbow on that side, feeling Justin's weight half falling into him, preparing to somehow catch him even though he was blind.

"I got you," he assured, even though he didn't know if that were at all accurate. Turned out he didn't have to do much but sit still as a brace. Justin balanced himself; the weight on Ren's shoulder lifting but not leaving. Justin kept his hold, breathing hard.

"Trade me places?" Justin requested, and Ren used the hand on his shoulder as a guide to find Justin's other arm, taking his opposite elbow as he stood, pivoting them around each other and easing Justin onto the toilet lid. "You can open your eyes now," Justin allowed.

Relieved, Ren took visual stock of Justin, now sitting down with his elbows on his knees, his head resting in his hands, spent. He wore Ren's pants but had to take a break before he finished dressing. Ren took the towel from Justin's shoulders to help him finish drying his hair, which was a dripping, shiny-black mess. Justin let him do what he wanted as he recovered.

"How are you doing?" Ren checked as he let go of the towel. "Are you just tired or are you having trouble breathing?"

"Tired," Justin answered, for which Ren was grateful.

"Back to the couch?" Ren offered.

"In a minute," Justin said, eyeing the floor as though he wanted to skip the couch and just curl up on all the towels.

"I can call Alek in to help," Ren suggested, half teasing, remembering the last time Justin had been transported from the bathroom to the couch. What an ordeal it had been. "Or we can wait for North to get back."

"You're enough," Justin insisted, in that strange way he had of making Ren feel somehow complimented in a less-than-ideal circumstance. He shouldn't feel good about Justin saying that, but he couldn't help but be pleased anyway. To make it impossible for Justin to read anything in his face, Ren gathered up Justin's stuff to take it out of the room.

"I'll be right back, but there's no rush," Ren said in parting. He replaced everything into Justin's duffel, then did a quick check of the rest of the apartment. Alek was in the kitchen, of course, a few experimental dishes surrounding him with Denny close by. She'd dragged one of the chairs into the kitchen and now sat on it backwards and cross-legged, resting her arms and chin on the backrest, trying to appear at ease, but Ren could tell she was tense. Alek had picked up on it too and was trying to coax her into telling him what was wrong.

"Everything good in here?" Ren tested the conversational waters.

"It was," Denny clipped, glaring at Ren behind Alek's back. Ren reined in the desire to roll his eyes, knowing it would be the lit match to gunpowder.

"Hey Ren," Alek greeted, looking grateful to be interrupted from what Ren could only guess was a difficult one-sided conversation. "Where's Justin?"

"Resting in the bathroom. He needs a few minutes before moving again."

"Cool. I'm making him some saltless mashed potatoes," Alek volunteered. "And maybe an omelet? I don't know; it's killing me to not use any spices. We'll have to invite him back for dinner another night when he's better so I can cook him something real, ok?"

"Sure, Alek," Ren gave in readily, ignoring the pang in his chest about how they might not see Justin again depending on what happened in the morning. It was so much easier pretending that future was never coming.

"Is North coming back for dinner too? Should I make something different?" Alek went on, stressed over the menu. And probably the static charge coming off Denny, which grew worse the longer they continued to talk without her.

"He's coming back; he just went to fill Justin's prescriptions, but don't worry about making us all different stuff, Alek. We can eat mashed potatoes and omelets too," Ren comforted, his voice friendly even though he was locked in a stare down with Denny.

"Are you staying the night, Denny?" he asked her, figuring he should start planning now for how the sleeping arrangements were going to go.

"I don't know," she returned slowly, a sharpening knife. "I was planning on it, but I thought you had already given away my spot?" Her face. Her voice. She was slicing his heart open.

"No, Denny; you're always welcome," Ren assured, trying to put something more to the tone. Try to make her understand that everything was fine. He didn't think he was coming across very well, though, if her tight expression were any clue. "But there is a chance North will be staying here too, so I need to figure out where we're putting everyone. I wouldn't dream of giving away your spot; you're the only one who can sleep on the couch comfortably anyway."

"North can have my bed," Alek offered immediately. "It won't kill me to sleep on the floor a night or two."

"Anyway, we'll work it out," Ren said, suddenly wanting to put off making decisions even though he was the one who had brought it up. He didn't want Alek sleeping on the floor, even though he seemed more than willing to do so. But obviously the mattress-to-person ratio was terribly skewed, so there wasn't a good way out of it. "One thing at a time, I guess."

"I have a suggestion," Denny spoke up, and Ren knew what she would say. Why doesn't Justin go home with North? Why do they both have to stay here? Why do you feel so obligated to house and feed these people, especially when one of them is a complete stranger and the other a murderer?

"North lives too far from the hospital," Ren shut her down before she could go any further. "Dr. Delacroix said Justin should stay close in case he has another cardiac emergency."

"Well, isn't that just ... What the hell is wrong with you?" Denny snapped.

"Whoa, Denny, what's up?" Alek turned from whisking eggs.

"I can't believe you brought him back with you," Denny went on, ignoring Alek, piercing Ren with both her words and the anger in her face, apparently deciding there was no point holding back anymore.

"When is it going to be enough, Ren? How bad does it have to get? When are you going to listen to me?"

"Maybe you should listen to me," Ren returned. Somewhere in the corner of his mind, he remembered Justin was still waiting for him in the bathroom, that he didn't really have time for this, but in the very next second, he'd decided that since this was broken open now with Denny, he should take care of her first. "He's not what you think he is."

"Whatever," Denny denied with an annoying shrug.

"What's with you guys?" Alek broke between them, putting a hand on Ren's chest but wisely not touching Denny. "Why are we arguing about Justin staying here when we all know this is something Ren does all the time and it's never a big deal?"

"Because Ren has never brought home a violent criminal before," Denny said coldly.

"He's not," Ren began, but he was drowned out by Denny. She growled wordlessly, allowing the sound to escalate into a frustrated scream. Now she wasn't even going to let him explain?

"I would really like to know what's going on here," Alek interjected, the calmest in the room, looking worriedly at Denny.

"We weren't going to tell you," Ren said, putting emphasis on each word, reminding Denny about their agreement. She folded her arms, twisting away from them on the chair, unimpressed.

"But we changed our minds," she quipped. "When a police officer showed up talking about a verdict hearing; you went off to the hospital and had *every opportunity* to leave Justin there and *no one* would have said you didn't do more than enough for him. You ignored everything I told you and brought him back here anyway. So yeah, deal's off. Alek should know when you bring murderers home, Ren. But hey, if you don't want to tell him things like that, here's a clue — *maybe you shouldn't do it!*"

"M-murder?" Alek repeated, wobbly. "Justin?"

"No," Ren denied.

"Lorenzo!" Denny shrieked.

"You need to check your facts!" he yelled back at her, surprised at himself. "And accept that it's possible for you to be wrong about something for once!"

"I did my research; all I have to do is look at your face!"

"You guys!"

Ren could barely register Alek between them, keeping them apart, making sensible pleas for them to chill out so they could talk this over. But Ren was already furious at people he didn't know, who he would never see, situations he couldn't control, and suddenly it was all coming out at Denny.

"My face is my fault," Ren insisted, leaning against Alek's hands on him, talking around his roommate like he wasn't even there. "It's because I did what you're doing now, Kayden — making assumptions and thinking I knew everything that was going on. Well, newsflash, you have no idea. Justin didn't kill anyone, got it?"

"Then why'd he confess, you moron?" Denny retaliated, half standing from the chair.

"Because he doesn't know how traumatic subarachnoid hemorrhages work and apparently neither did anyone at the trial!" Ren shouted.

"All right, House, and what's on next week's episode?" Denny scoffed, which just infuriated Ren, even more so when he didn't understand what random television series she seemed to be referencing. Denny took the pause to wedge her insult in deeper. "You think you know more than the *medical professional* they called in to witness at that trial?"

"Hey Denny," Alek tried to cut in, though he seemed to not know what his role should be here. He appeared torn between trying to stop them or allowing them to get it all out of their systems while acting as a referee.

"No," Ren felt himself spiritually stepping down, not knowing how to quickly get across the messiness of the situation. It was getting out of control in the wrong direction again. No wonder Justin's first instinct was to hit people — Ren was starting to see the appeal. "It shouldn't even matter; this should have never been taken to trial."

Denny almost slammed her hands against her face in frustration, groaning at Ren's dedication to being ignorant. "How?" she pleaded to the ceiling, her fingers trailing down her face as though she were trying to peel her cheeks off. She looked ready to either scream or cry, maybe both. Her apoplectic fit forced Alek to chance it touching her, resting one of his hands gently on her arm. She shook her head while Alek turned to Ren, frightened in his worry.

"Ren?" he timidly begged. Ren knew this was the only chance he was going to get. He needed to speak fast and very clear.

"Justin stopped a kidnapping almost two years ago," Ren dove into the shouting reprieve, no longer talking to Denny, who was now staring furiously at the floor. He didn't want to talk to her anymore anyway. But he could talk to Alek, who had no previous knowledge of any of this, and no pre-formed opinions. "This guy, David, had grabbed a girl, his ex, in a parking lot and was trying to force her into his car. Justin was the only one who saw it. He ran out to help, and they got into a fight. David went to the hospital, and Justin went to a juvenile correctional facility for six months. Which also shouldn't have happened, but apparently David's family has a lot of power in Chicago, so they got their way about it."

Denny's posture changed. She'd folded her arms tightly around herself again, turning her face even further away from Ren, as though she didn't want to hear this. Meanwhile, Alek's eyes grew larger with almost every word. He shifted closer to Denny, as if to protect her.

"Fast-forward to eight weeks ago," Ren continued when no one said anything to challenge him on any point thus far. "David wakes up thinking he's hungover, but what's actually happened is a ruptured brain aneurysm. His mom finds him dead that night in his room. The family is grieving; they want an explanation. They want someone to blame. Justin's the perfect target; the death does seem to be a consequence of the fight. They go after him again, this time for manslaughter and as an adult. Justin confesses to beating him up, everyone already knew that, but Justin hasn't even seen David for over a year, never touched him or went near him again. He may have messed him up, but he didn't kill him. But even if he had beaten him to death on the spot, that wasn't what he was trying to do. He only wanted to save that girl. He's been dragged through hell for trying to do the right thing, and I'll be damned if he has to put up with it here too. He doesn't deserve it, so lay off him."

"Um, ok, wow," Alek breathed, his face all twisted up. "That's ... a lot. That's heavy stuff, man."

"That's the truth, Kayden," Ren could feel the sneer in his voice and didn't like it, but he wasn't ready to let go of being mad yet. "And I will go against anyone who tries to say it's Justin's fault. That may make me look stupid to you, but no one has ever doubted which one of us is smarter."

Denny glared at him, eyes surprisingly full of tears, and Ren felt himself soften immediately, realizing in that moment how harsh he'd just been. With Denny.

"What happened to the girl?" she asked, her tone flat, as though she didn't really care.

"She's fine," Ren said, wondering why that would be the question Denny would ask first. "She's a student here."

"It didn't mention her anywhere in what I read," Denny mused to herself, and Ren almost asked her exactly what she had read and where she'd found it before deciding it didn't matter as much as smoothing the raw edges of their argument. "How can that be true?"

"Your information wasn't wrong," Ren told her, quieter, gentler, ready to start making it up to her, ready to get back in sync. It should be easy now that everything was out in the open. Now that Denny had all the facts. "Just incomplete and probably biased. It's like they're trying to set Justin up —"

"Stop talking," Denny whispered and without a moment's notice she was headed stiffly toward the door, ripping through the coats on the chair to find hers, stepping quickly into her boots. "Just shut up; I don't want to hear anymore."

"Denny," Alek entreated, going after her as soon as it was clear she was preparing to leave. "What are you doing? Come on; don't be like that."

"Don't," Denny told him, ducking out from the hand Alek tried to put on her, unable to look at either of them.

"Denny, you don't have to go," Ren told her. He also reached out to try and take her coat away, to grab onto her to keep her with them if he had to. She slapped at his hands, not making contact, but forcing him to draw back. "Denny, let's talk."

"No, I'm out," she returned, doing her laces up with shaking fingers. "I can't do this right now." That statement was so cryptic; Ren couldn't even guess what she meant. She didn't bother with her zipper or putting on her hat or mittens. Instead she bundled them all against her chest, holding them tight against her with one arm so she had a hand free to open the door. Ren and Alek both stood helplessly watching her. Ren had been so sure she would understand.

Ren let himself hope when she paused in the doorway, looking back over her shoulder with her hand clasped tightly on the knob. She'd changed her mind. He almost took a step toward her until he saw the expression on her face. Somewhere between fury and shame.

"You really believe that?" Denny asked, not skeptically. There was too much sadness in her tone. "That Justin risked himself to save a girl he didn't know?"

Denny asked him things like this often, more to gauge his sense of naiveté than because she thought he was lying to her. It was how she determined his grasp on culture, science, and human nature. It was her way of placing him into an emotional and psychological category.

"It wasn't supposed to hurt you, but yes, I do," Ren tried one last time to get her to come back in. "Please don't go yet, Denny." He was about to apologize, but she cut him off.

"I'll call you later," she gave the emptiest-sounding promise Ren had ever heard, gullible or not. Denny closed the door behind her.

Ren looked at Alek, who stood there stunned with his mouth half open. "You gonna go after her?" Ren asked, figuring that between the two of them, Alek had better odds on getting through to her.

"No point," Alek explained, resigned, though it was obvious he wasn't happy. "She'll figure it out eventually."

"And what about you?" Ren asked. "What do you think about all this?"

"I think I'm opting out of thinking about it," Alek allowed, still staring forlornly at the closed door, a puppy who had been abandoned. "This is what you and Denny took a walk for yesterday, isn't it? She wanted to tell you about Justin without me finding out."

"Sorry, big guy, we didn't want you to worry. We probably shouldn't have kept it a secret."

"No, it's cool. To be honest, I kind of wish it was still a secret."

"I know what you mean," Ren agreed miserably.

"But you trust him, right?" Alek checked, meaning it when he'd said he wasn't deciding a stance on Justin. He would blindly accept Ren's take on the situation.

"Yeah," Ren said without reluctance, remembering how Justin looked as he spoke, how his eyes were far away in memory, reliving the night in the bookstore parking lot where he had saved a girl but ruined his life. "He told me the truth."

"Ok then," Alek said, as if that were all that needed to be said, heading back to the kitchen where he'd left his bowl of half-whisked eggs. Ren knew him well, so despite his casualness he could see how hurt he was that Denny had gone. How it was bothering him not to take her side on something. Alek had just touched the whisk again when something struck him, and he turned toward Ren quizzically. "But ... did he actually hit you? Because I thought you ran into a door."

"No," Ren sighed, knowing this moment had to come eventually. "He punched me."

"Um, why though?"

"Because I didn't listen to you," Ren said. "When you were telling me Justin probably had a good reason for missing all our homework appointments. He was sleeping in class, and that made me so mad at him, I just didn't even think about figuring out why. I shocked him awake, and he's one of those people who do the fight thing over flight when they're surprised. He wasn't even thinking about what he was doing. It was my fault. How long do you think it'll take Denny to come back? Do you think she'll forgive me?" Because Ren would rather talk about that than the bruise on his cheek. And Alek knew her better, could make the best guess.

"Dude, it's going to take a while. This is kind of more serious than the day you beat her at chess. I've never seen you yell at anyone like that, and … well, this whole situation is crazy, isn't it?"

"Sorry I dragged it home with me, Alek," Ren apologized. He didn't think he would have done anything different, even knowing everything he knew right now, but it still felt wrong to involve Alek without his permission. "I didn't mean to ruin everything."

"I wouldn't say everything's ruined. At least not forever. We'll be ok," Alek promised. "Hopefully Justin will be too. Maybe you should go check on him? He's been back there by himself for a while."

"Uh, yeah," Ren acknowledged as Alek released him. He hadn't meant to leave Justin stranded in the bathroom for so long. Hadn't intended to have a shouting match with his friend either.

As Ren stepped away from Alek, he felt Denny slip painfully out of his soul. A piece of a connection lost or broken. Because there was nothing he could do now except wait for her to decide what her next move would be. Whether she could forgive Ren and believe Justin or if she wouldn't be able to accept anything Ren had told her. Ren paused to look over his shoulder at Alek in the kitchen, noticing the absence of the tiniest person with the biggest personality he had ever seen, marveling at the massive hole she had torn into the feel of the place.

Ren just couldn't believe she'd run away. He thought he knew her.

He flipped on all the lights as he made his way back to the bathroom. The kitchen light was already on, but the rest of the apartment seemed relentlessly dark here in the aftermath. Ren switched on the living room light, then the one in the hall ... which is where he almost tripped on Justin, who was sitting braced against the wall just out of sight of the living room.

"Jeez, Justin!" Ren yelped, shocked to find him there on the floor. How had he gotten there? Had he been listening? How long? Ren went to his knees beside him, checking him over for physical and emotional damage. "What are you doing? You were supposed to wait for me."

Justin lifted his head slowly, his expression a variety of pain. Yeah, he'd definitely heard everything.

"Still think the truth matters to anyone?" he asked morosely. *You think I matter to anyone?* Ren heard the inaudible question twisted up hard in Justin's words and something inside him ripped a little more. He leaned in, cupping a hand against Justin's face and touching foreheads, trying to force it closed again. Justin didn't move.

"It matters to me," Ren said firmly. How could Justin not see that? Hadn't he heard Ren losing his friend out there defending him? Ren sat back, shifting his hand from Justin's face to his knee. "Are you ok?" Ren checked.

"No," Justin answered, quick, sharp, and honest.

Alek's shadow appeared next to them; Ren's shout pulling him over to see what was going on. "Oh," was all he said, seeing Justin and Ren together on the floor.

"I should leave," Justin abruptly volunteered. "I'm messing everything up. You didn't sign on for this."

"It sounds like you didn't sign on for it either, buddy," Alek told him, leaning against the wall across from them after stepping lightly over the tangle of their legs to get to Justin's other side, gazing benevolently down at them. "And my vote is no on leaving, but I think we should get you off the floor. Come on."

Justin looked up at Alek as though he hadn't understood a word he just said. Or maybe that Alek had no idea what he was offering. Ren was struggling to get his emotions under control. There were so many, and they were all powerful.

"Not going to pick you up this time," Alek said as he took hold of Justin's wrist and began pulling him forward so he could slide his other arm behind his back. "Ren?"

"Oh, right." Ren realized Alek would need him on Justin's other side. Most of Justin's strength seemed to be gone, but Ren couldn't tell if it was because he'd used it all in getting down the hallway on his own, or if it had drained him to hear Ren and Denny fight about him, or if he were just too overwhelmed by Alek's unexpected kindness. Probably some combination of everything. He shook under their hands.

"Man, you really are burning up," Alek said piteously as they clumsily made their way the few steps over to the couch. "How long is it going to take for him to feel better, Ren?"

"Shouldn't be much longer," Ren answered, more than half guessing, wishing he could make that the truth just by saying it. He no longer sounded very convincing. "But Justin's immune system was damaged by anemia before he even got sick, so it's moving slower than normal. I can't say for sure how much longer." He was doing it again. Talking about Justin like he wasn't there. Like he wasn't physically shuffling toward the couch between them, like they weren't the only things holding him upright. But Ren figured Justin would like to disappear right now. He wanted to be ignored. At least for a little while.

Alek sensed it too, sitting Justin down and disappearing back into the kitchen without another word. Meanwhile, Ren made himself busy finding where his quilt had disappeared to, wanting to bring it to cover Justin. Now that the lights were on indoors, he also went to the sliding glass balcony door to draw the curtains closed, noticing the snow had picked up again, heavy flakes not so much drifting as hurtling to the ground. He tried to remember how far away Denny lived, how far she'd have to walk in this before she was warm and safe again.

"Five minutes," Alek broke into his thoughts, jerking him into finishing with the curtains, hiding the storm from view.

"What's that?" Ren questioned, not following what Alek meant, looking quickly at Justin, who was huddled in a little ball at the end of the couch closest to the hallway and the kitchen, face hidden in his arms.

"Her place is a five-minute walk from here," Alek explained. "She'll be fine."

Ren nodded numbly, taking that in, then started wondering how long he should let Justin sulk like that on the couch before he started trying to comfort him somehow. He'd only taken one step toward him before needing to switch directions toward the door. Someone was knocking on it. Someone who couldn't be Denny because she never knocked.

"I made it," North said in greeting as Ren opened the door to him. He was soaking wet with melting snow, pushing his dripping hair backward from his face with one hand. In his other, he carried a Walgreens bag. "Thought I'd have to call you to get in the building, but someone let me in."

"Sorry! I should have let you take my key card. Come in," Ren invited, hoping North's powerful figure would somehow make up for what was suddenly missing.

"It turned out fine. Here, you probably know what to do with these better than I do," North offered the handles, unconsciously looking around the apartment. Ren accepted the bag, stripping off the multiple layers of packing to reach the prescription bottle of heart medication and the iron supplement so he could check the timing and the dosage requirements. Meanwhile, North made a beeline for Justin, who had timidly raised his head when he heard him at the door.

"Dinner will be ready in a few minutes," Alek called out from the kitchen. Only Ren heard him mutter under his breath, "such as it is." He knew it was going to bother Alek that North's first sampling of his cooking would be so simple.

"What'd I miss?" North asked, not in the casual tone of a passing remark either. Even North, who was new here, noticed something was going on. "Justin, you're shaking again, what's wrong?"

Ren turned from where he'd been making a new home for Justin's medicine on the kitchen counter to see what was going on in the other room. North's dark head had joined Justin's on the couch, but it seemed as though Justin really didn't want anyone to look at him. He curled away from North, hiding his face again.

"What happened?" North demanded, this time from Ren, who was mostly focused on Justin. He must be feeling so trapped right now. Out of place, out of options, and unwanted. Like he didn't belong anywhere. "Where's ... um," North seemed to forget Denny's name, so he held out a hand at about her height instead.

"Denny had to go home," Alek said, dedicatedly calm about it, dishing food onto plates. Ren watched Justin wince but wasn't sure if it was the name or Alek talking about going home that did it.

"She couldn't stand to be in the same room with me," Justin murmured darkly, the statement dramatically narrowing North's eyes as he leaned in closer to Justin.

"It's not like that," Ren protested weakly, but he didn't have another explanation. Alek gave him a moment's respite by handing him plates for North and Justin. "Here, guys, it's kind of a weird dinner, but you should be able to eat it, Justin."

Justin didn't look like he wanted to eat anything. He uncurled enough to take the plate, but sat there with it on his lap, his hand holding it just enough to make sure it didn't fall to the floor. North took his own portion but placed it immediately on the coffee table. He went to put an arm around Justin's shoulders, but Justin flinched away from him.

"You don't have to," Justin told him. "You can go; I've wasted enough of your time."

"You have never been a waste of my time, Justin," North assured him, resting his arm around Justin despite his words and actions. Ren found he couldn't step away from them, even though he knew he should for privacy's sake. He didn't want to leave Justin's side. Instead, he tucked himself onto the floor beside them, also putting a reassuring hand on Justin.

"Then why did you transfer?" Justin begged, months of hurt attaching to the brand-new wound Denny had caused. How it all seemed to culminate into one dominating trend of pushing Justin to the side. Of leaving him behind.

North looked uncomfortable, as though he didn't want to answer the question. "This isn't where I wanted to talk about that either," he confessed, then hurried to explain as Justin tightened up again. "I mean, I wanted to take you out for dinner ... this isn't how I pictured it. But you've got the wrong idea, so maybe now should be the time."

Justin looked at him, utterly confused.

"Just remember — I wanted to tell you this months ago," North reminded him. "I asked to be transferred so I could start the adoption process for you, Justin. I wanted us to be family — legally."

"W-what?" Justin almost gasped.

"A social worker isn't allowed to adopt a minor they are directly working with; it's a conflict of interest. I had to transfer if I even wanted to start the paperwork, and I couldn't have been working with you for at least three months before I could submit anything. I picked Kasey because I thought he'd be the only one in the office besides me that you could put up with."

"You're kidding," Justin struggled. Ren tightened his hold on his hand, wondering if he was going to fall apart. "Why didn't you just tell me?"

"Because we ... had to try and find your mom," North admitted. "I didn't want to make you any promises I couldn't keep or get your hopes up about something I couldn't follow through on. You've had way too much of that."

Ren took Justin's plate for him, knowing he was two seconds from losing his hold on it. Once it was off his knees, Justin drew them up again, turning toward North, who readily wrapped him in both arms and pulled him in close, protected. Ren could hear Justin sobbing into North's sweater.

"I withdrew the submission last October after your birthday," North went on. "It was taking so long, and we never did find her. But now that you're an adult, we just have to fill out a simple form and turn it in at the county clerk's office. I've got it at home; it just needs your signature."

"And I can come stay with you?" Justin managed, breathing hard, almost too overcome to speak.

"I really hope you do," North answered genuinely. "I've missed you, and no one can say we can't anymore."

"I want to go home," Justin whispered, wrenching Ren's heart.

"I'll get you there," North promised, though Ren noticed he was careful not to say when. He looked at Ren over Justin's head, his expression tight with worry. He ran his hand up and down Justin's back. "Easy now, Justin, calm down. Maybe I should have waited a little longer to tell you."

Because Justin was still shaking, hard, tucked up against North's chest, looking small and breathing raggedly. He looked like he needed a distraction, something to take his mind off everything for a little while until he could go through it more slowly. Or at least he needed everyone to stop paying so much attention to him.

"Hey Alek," Ren called to his roommate. "Put on that annoyingly cheerful playlist."

"Wha ... oh, yeah, sure, good idea," Alek caught on almost instantly, synching his phone to the Bluetooth speaker in the kitchen and letting his cleaning music fill the apartment. Fill the corners and drown out the wind, cover Justin's crying, and replace the pieces of conversation Denny would have contributed if she were still here.

"Congratulations, Justin," Ren said softly, patting him on the knee. "It's going to be ok."

He kept watch out of the corner of his eye as he ate with Alek, watching as the tension left Justin. Watched as North spoke to him softly, too low to hear over the music, coaxing his plate back into his hands. He ate less than half, but at least he ate something. North didn't seem to notice anything he put into his mouth; he was completely focused on his newly adopted son. Or at least he would be as soon as they could get that form signed and filed.

They stayed tight like that until it became obvious that Justin was fading. The shivering became less an emotional problem and more of a physical one. North pulled the quilt tighter around him as the evening went on, and Justin squirmed ever closer to North in an effort to get warm.

"Ren?" North eventually called him over, after the dishes were cleared, washed, and dried. After Alek had excused himself to his bedroom for a while. Ren suspected he went to call Denny in private. Hopefully, Alek could talk some sense into her. Ren paused in the homework he'd brought to the table to see what was going on, ready to be of service. "I don't know what's wrong; he won't tell me."

"My guess is the pain meds are wearing off," Ren explained, watching Justin, who was barely awake. "Huh, Justin?"

The frustrated half-glare was more than an answer for Ren. He returned to the kitchen to get Justin a glass of water, the heart meds, and something for whatever pain he was in. North helped him take it while Ren went to his bedroom for the familiar notebook, the stethoscope, thermometer, and everything else he'd been using for Justin before they went to the hospital. It was time to start keeping track of those things again.

"Temperature 103.1," Ren said out loud as he documented it. "Heart rate is ninety. Blood pressure is ... not too low, and your oxygen is good. But I think we should get you in bed, Justin. Are you staying, North? The couch is kind of small, but you're welcome to it."

"No, thank you, but I can't stay," North declined again. And again Justin reanimated immediately at the news.

"North?" he said his name more as a request.

"I need to get ready for tomorrow," North said gently. "I need to find your suit for one thing, but I'll be here to pick you up around eight-thirty, ok? Ren will call me if you need anything."

Ren nodded, accepting the plan, preparing himself for the last night Justin would be with him.

"M-my suit?" Justin seemed confused, which made Ren worried. North and Ren exchanged glances.

"For court," North explained. "Remember? Your verdict hearing is tomorrow at ten?"

"*Tomorrow!?*" Justin rasped, alarmed, and Ren realized their mistake. It seemed everyone knew about the court date and time. Officer Geisler, Alek, Denny, Ren, North. Hell, even Dr. Delacroix knew. But it seemed that every time this information had been shared out loud Justin had been either out of the room or asleep.

They'd all forgotten to tell Justin.

20

ESCAPE VELOCITY

In less than thirty seconds, the atmosphere of the apartment shook itself of all calm. The revelation to Justin that his hearing was in the morning had struck him like a gunshot, leaving North and Ren both sputtering apologies.

"Justin, I'm so sorry," North began at the same time Ren said, "I can't believe we all thought you knew."

North kept a tight hold on Justin, who seemed to want to leap from the couch and bolt for the door.

"Settle down, Justin; there's no point getting all frantic about it. You'll end up hurting yourself," North advised, just a hint of exertion in his voice as he tried to calm Justin down. Justin obviously disagreed with all of North's logic and continued to struggle. Ren took pity on him, snagging his hands and pulling him upright off the couch, though North shot him a look of confused exasperation for enabling Justin's panic. But Ren understood. If Justin wanted to stand up to feel as though he had the tiniest bit of control here, then Ren wasn't going to deny him.

Though he allowed him to stand, Ren kept close to Justin, pulling him tight against his side as Justin began to realize that his body just wasn't able to keep up with his flight response. He groaned, miserable and angry, shivering with uncontrollable fever chills and shaking with exertion simultaneously. It was all Ren could do to hold him, and he wondered if he hadn't made a mistake helping him upright. He almost set Justin back on the couch, worried about what all of this was going to do to his heart, but Justin determinedly dragged them over to the table, reaching out for one of the chairs and taking a seat there as if that were some sort of compromise. North stood near the couch still, his face full of Justin's pain.

"North, how?" Justin begged, though the question was so unclear. He could hardly get the words out, his throat sounded constricted, as though he were being strangled. Ren pulled up another chair so he could sit knee-to-knee with Justin next to the table, reaching out to steady him. Justin grabbed on to Ren's wrists, frantically hard, as though Ren were the only thing stopping Justin from falling off a cliff. "I can't. I just ... I can't go back. Tomorrow?"

Ren didn't mean to wince, but Justin's fingers dug into the pressure points against his pulse; Justin's voice stabbed him deep in the chest. He wanted to make this better for him, but he didn't know how.

"Easy, Justin," North calmed uselessly. "Come on, let go. You're hurting Ren."

North's words caused Justin to rip his hands away, horrified, and he immediately turned sideways, cowering against the backrest, folding his arms across his own chest and grabbing on to the extra fabric in the sleeves of Ren's hoodie so he could continue to hold tight to something. His breathing rattled away from any kind of normal pattern; he'd returned to quick gasps followed by long, disturbing pauses. Ren leaned closer, wanting to comfort him but suddenly being too afraid to touch him. He'd become so breakable in the last minute.

"Justin," Ren tried instead to reach him with words alone. "Please don't hold your breath like that; give your heart the oxygen it needs. It's still working extra hard, ok?"

When Ren mentioned Justin's heart, Justin reached over to him again, this time slower, obviously trying to be gentle but needing help. He put his trembling hand against Ren's chest, panting. Ren supported Justin's arm, held it upright to allow Justin to keep his palm against Ren's steadier heartbeat, understanding that Justin was trying to do the same synchronization technique Ren had explained in the hospital. Though he still felt that hadn't worked as well as everyone seemed to think it did, Ren mirrored Justin's movement and put his own hand against Justin's chest, unable to feel anything under the bulk of the sweatshirt.

"That's right," Ren encouraged softly, calmly even though he found it difficult not to match Justin's stress.

"Ren," Justin gulped, completely undone, sounding as though he were hoping Ren could help somehow. But Ren couldn't do anything about this, couldn't stop time, couldn't change events that had started before he'd even met Justin. The only thing he could do was stay with Justin until it was over.

"Shh, it's going to be ok. Come here; put your head down," Ren commanded, shifting even closer to Justin, forcing Justin to back up as Ren slid their chairs together. Ren tucked his legs underneath the table so he also sat sideways, hips touching Justin's, facing opposite directions. Justin folded against him as Ren pulled him over, guiding his head to his chest, allowing him to rest his ear against Ren's heart. "Don't think."

"I can't," Justin repeated into Ren's shirt.

An unfamiliar tone broke the scene, causing Ren to look around to determine the source of the noise, but went back to Justin when he saw North pulling his phone out to answer it.

"It's ok," Ren continued to murmur reassuringly, folding Justin in the cadence of it. "One breath at a time for now."

"Yes, speaking," North was saying into the receiver. Ren held tight to Justin, both of them quiet enough that North's phone conversation became the dominant focus. "Yes, thanks for returning my call." The voice on the other end of the line suddenly shredded into the room, just loud enough that the tone was clear but the words were not. Whoever had called North sounded extremely pissed off. Not shouting into the phone, but racing through ... what? A lecture? Questions maybe? Yes, shooting off questions to North at a rapid pace. North stood next to Justin, hand rubbing up and down his back as he listened to whoever it was run out of steam, the action appearing more as if North were doing it to keep himself calm rather than Justin. Ren wasn't sure how he would take standing there listening to someone shouting at him like that. North always seemed the very picture of patience.

"There was no way for him to contact you," North cut in, excusing Justin. "Like I said in the message, he was in the emergency room. Yes, he's with me now, but I don't think he can talk. He certainly can't be screamed at."

Justin tried to sit up, but Ren wouldn't let him. He didn't want him to have to deal with anything or anyone else. Not one thing more if he didn't absolutely have to.

"North's got it," Ren whispered, wanting to join North in protecting Justin from the fury on the phone. "Hold still."

But Justin paid no attention. He seemed to have recognized the intense voice. As North made protests, Justin reached up to tug on his sleeve, using that and a few gestures to indicate that North could put the call on speaker. That Justin was going to try and participate in whatever was going on.

"All right," North sharply broke into what seemed to be a rather long, exhaustive tirade of threats on not being able to speak to Justin. "Justin's agreed to talk to you, but please keep in mind that he's ... yes, thank you." Hesitantly, as though he were questioning himself on whether this was a good idea, North pushed a button and knelt into the tangle of Justin and Ren to allow them better access.

"Kelly?" Justin asked in a broken, exhausted voice. Ren stared at the phone as if that would give him some kind of clue about her. That voice belonged to Kelly? Justin's lawyer? She sounded absolutely terrifying.

"Kit?" Ren wasn't sure at first if Kelly had said "kit" or "kid," but as she began repeating it in the conversation that followed, he decided for sure the end consonant was a T. He did notice she had lowered the volume and the violence from when she'd crashed into North. The intensity was still there, just shifted, barely contained, a simmer rather than a boil. "For fuck's sake, Kit, why didn't you contact me? It's been a complete disaster. You missed the check-ins; I called and called. No one could find you. I've been putting out fires since Friday. They all thought you ran, hell, even I was starting to believe it — that bastard Rozensweig was just having a field day with *that*. I think he already put your name and face out to the TSA, the rotten little prick. How *could* you?"

"Tone it down," North threatened in the background, a warning that if this continued, he was going to hang up. Ren nodded to himself in total agreement. He thought he heard Kelly growl, but she did let up enough to let Justin respond.

"I'm sorry," Justin apologized weakly. He had a hand against his forehead, leaning against Ren's chest as Ren twisted awkwardly in his seat so he could support Justin and see the phone, as if that would let him hear better. Ren was completely astonished by Kelly, by her dark, murderous voice. He thought the phone might melt from the venom in her tone. "I didn't mean to disappear, Kelly; I just ... I ..."

"God, you really are sick, aren't you?" Kelly asked, suddenly gentle after she heard Justin speak. "Where are you now? Still in the hospital? Have you been there this whole time?" Ren had never heard anyone talk as quickly as Kelly, the waves of her questions crashing against each other, the next already started nearly before the last one had finished as if that were even possible.

"I ..." Justin started to explain but couldn't manage it. His voice broke, and he buried his face into Ren's shirt, which caused Ren to instinctively pull him closer. "I'm sorry."

"All right, Kit, stop, never mind. Elias was right; you shouldn't be talking. Go ahead and let him answer for you now. Is he still around?"

"I'm still here," North volunteered, ready to speak for Justin. He shifted as though preparing to stand up, take the phone away, perhaps into another room, but Justin put a hand on his wrist to keep him there. He might not be able to say much, but apparently he did want to hear the conversation. Ren didn't blame him. After they'd screwed up in not telling him when the hearing was, it made sense that Justin didn't want to potentially miss out on any more information.

"Elias, what the hell happened to my boy?" Kelly addressed him again, voice stripped of any tenderness, but North stopped her before she got started.

"Justin's still listening," he warned to prevent her disclosing anything she may not want Justin to hear. "And he's been through a lot, so I'm glad we're in agreement about it now."

"So, are you still in the hospital?" Kelly began. "Because I know Justin isn't at home."

"No, Justin was discharged today. We're staying with one of Justin's friends since he lives nearby. There's a chance Justin will have to be readmitted; we have to watch his heart rate closely right now. I was hoping to talk to you about postponing tomorrow's hearing until Justin is stronger. Do you think there's any chance of that?"

"Eh, maybe, but I don't know. They normally don't allow that unless someone actually *is* in the hospital, and Rozensweig — the little weasel representing the Hunts — anyway he's being such a jerk about the whole disappearing thing I don't think we can get away with any sort of exception at this point. I believe they'll see it as a delay because no one's found Kit yet." Kelly paused, as if thinking of all possible angles. "How bad is he? You said his heart?"

"He can't even stand up," North easily said the words that always caught in Justin's throat. "His heart's beating too fast and irregularly; it dropped his blood pressure so far yesterday we almost lost him."

North no longer spoke quite so easily telling Kelly that. Those memories still haunted him. "He was treated for anemia at the hospital, but he's still running a serious fever. He's very weak."

"Why the hell did they let him leave?" Kelly interjected, her anger rising again but at least directed at the right target this time. They shouldn't have let him leave. Ren felt his hands involuntarily clench, which caused Justin to twitch in his arms. Ren had to force his muscles to relax, unconsciously shushing Justin into stillness, reminding himself of his role in all this; he was only here to support Justin, that was his only purpose. And right now that meant keeping him calm.

"Well ... I guess because they figured he was stable enough to recover at home from now on, but really his condition is not good," North tried to make sense of the hospital's policy without downplaying Justin's symptoms. "Do you think anything can be done?"

Justin's hand could not grip any tighter to Ren's sleeve, and he pressed as close as possible against him. Every muscle taut in agony as though he were trying to shrink himself into invisibility. Ren looked at North, hoping he could see it too. They were going to have to take the conversation away from Justin; he couldn't stand listening to it anymore despite how he'd wanted to. North nodded, understanding, and patted Justin's knee before getting up. Justin's head was tucked so close to his chest, he didn't seem to notice the change.

"Listen, can I meet you somewhere to talk more about our options?" North requested.

"It's so cute how you think we have options," Kelly droned sarcastically.

"There has to be a solution," North remained steadfastly hopeful. "But I think this conversation is getting too much for the phone, and Justin needs to get some rest."

"If Kit gives you a written statement that he gives me permission to talk with you, then, sure. We can meet."

"Great. Is now ok?" North made a writing motion to Ren as he continued with the particulars of where and when with Kelly. Ren tipped his chin toward the kitchen counter where they kept a notepad and a pen, unwilling to leave Justin to get it for him and figuring North would understand. North scribbled a few lines about granting clearance to discuss everything about Justin, the case, and the trial. Justin had to be prodded to sign it, but both the form and the phone conversation were finished almost at the same time.

"We'll do what we can," North promised, kneeling in front of Justin again, obviously conflicted about leaving him. "Justin, I'll call Ren with updates. I'm not leaving you, do you understand? I'm coming back."

But Justin seemed broken inside, reminding Ren of a bicycle chain that had slipped from its gears. You could turn the pedals all you wanted, but there would be no forward progress.

"Justin?" North asked again, disturbed and worried, then switched direction when Justin didn't respond. "Ren?"

"It's shock," Ren named what was happening to Justin, still holding on to him, holding him together. Justin's mind was processing what had happened tonight, all the life altering and shattering details dumped on him all at once. He'd hit the point where he had to shut down in self-defense. "He's overwhelmed."

"Should I stay?" North asked, torn about which action would be in Justin's best interests.

"No," Ren determined, hoping it was the right answer. "See if you can get this thing pushed back a few more days."

North nodded agreement, putting a hand on Justin's head in parting. "We're going to get through this," he said determinedly. His voice was strong, but his face was full of doubt and question. "Get some rest, Justin. Ren is here watching over you, ok?"

Painfully resolved, North gathered up Justin's note and his file and hurried into his coat. Ren remembered just in time to have him grab the key card so he could let himself back in. North looked at them hard, as if he'd never see them again, eyes brimming sympathy for Justin, and a shared sense of responsibility with Ren.

"I've got him," Ren promised, which allowed North to tear himself away, heading off into the snow again, a warrior on a mission. "Good luck," Ren wished after him, wondering which one of them had the harder job.

He continued to sit with Justin on the dining room chairs until it simply became too uncomfortable to hold him that way anymore. Justin's full weight was on him now, and Ren wasn't sure if Justin was even still awake. Ren didn't want to move, but he could feel a spasm starting in his lower back and thought it would be a good time to relocate Justin to his bedroom.

"Justin?" Ren called him gently, beginning to shift them apart without causing Justin to fall. "You awake?"

Justin nodded but made no sound. Ren kept his hands on his shoulders, holding him as he stood up. "Let's get more comfortable. Come on. Can you move, or should I call Alek to help us?"

Still silent, Justin dragged himself to his feet, using both the table and Ren as support. Just looking at his posture made Ren weary all through his own body, as though Justin's physical and emotional exhaustion were bleeding into him through contact. Alek heard their movements and came to help, but Justin waved him off, never even raising his head to look at him.

"Ren? Where's North?" Alek entreated, also thrown off balance by Justin's weird, almost oppressive silence.

"He had a meeting with Justin's lawyer," Ren answered. "He'll be back later, probably tomorrow morning."

"You guys good?" Alek went on, watching them with a distressed expression on his face.

"We're tired."

"I'll make you some tea," Alek stated more than offered, watching them cross the hallway into Ren's room, his voice betraying how unsettled he felt. There was such a heaviness in the apartment now, the combined effect of the snow, Denny and Ren's falling out, the dread of the hearing, and Justin's unrelenting fever. It cast a tangible shadow over their once cozy and warm threshold. Alek making tea seemed an almost religious gesture, a ceremony to cleanse the air of the harsh darkness that weighed them down.

"That would be nice," Ren accepted readily, relieved Alek had stayed. That he was continually helpful. "Thanks, Alek." He almost asked about Denny, but he knew it was too soon.

Justin unexpectedly reached out to Alek as he slipped past them at the junction where the hallway, living room, and tiny walkway to Ren's door all met together. It made Alek pause, looking first to where Justin's hand barely touched his arm, then up to meet his gaze.

"What's up, buddy?" Alek asked him, trying to keep his voice light, though Ren could see that Justin's behavior was freaking him out. "Change your mind? I can still carry you the rest of the way if you want."

"No," Justin denied the offer, the first word he'd spoken in what seemed like hours, and Alek tried hard not to show rejection in his face. "But ... thank you. Ren's right; you really are amazing." Again, Alek restrained himself, this time from grabbing Justin too tight. Instead, he patted him gently on the shoulder, smiling warmly at him.

"Whatever, man," Alek joked, though Ren could see how touched he was at the compliment. Ren was pleased at Justin's expression of gratitude, but it also worried him. It felt too much like a goodbye, like Justin was trying to set his affairs in order. As if he truly believed this would be his last night.

Alek separated from them into the kitchen while Ren half-carried Justin the remaining steps into his room where he helped him under the covers.

"It's so dark in here," Justin observed, voice quiet, almost mournful. Ren switched on his lamp, giving a dull illumination to the small space, understanding Justin's need for it to not be completely black, but not wanting so much light that it would hurt Justin's chances for resting.

"You should try and get some sleep," Ren recommended, stretching his back now that Justin's weight was off him.

"I don't think I can," Justin responded, sounding like a man already condemned. Unwilling to waste any of his final hours of freedom on something so trivial as sleep. Ren understood the motive, even though he disagreed about its practicality.

"That's why I said try to sleep instead of go to sleep," Ren reiterated, still trying to lighten the mood. "It makes your success based on attempt not outcome."

Justin almost smiled before being dragged back down by despair. Ren pulled out his desk chair, pushing the power button on his computer so he could restart his soothing piano soundtrack. Maybe that would help.

"It's always about the outcome," Justin pointed out miserably. "No one cares about the attempt."

"You did the right thing, Justin," Ren assured him, perhaps harshly, but he was convinced on this point and needed Justin to understand. "The jury will see it too."

"No," Justin replied, sounding on the verge of a final confession. "That's the worst part, you know? It might have been the right thing, but I didn't do it for the right reason, and that's why ... that's why I should go to prison for it." Ren turned from his start up screen to give Justin his full attention, sensing that this was important for Justin to say. That it was hurting him somehow to hold this information secret. It also sounded like something else Ren wasn't certain he wanted the responsibility of knowing. And yet, Ren could see it in Justin's face, an undisclosed memory, an overpowering feeling. Guilt that was eating into him like poison.

"Ok," Ren invited, preparing himself for yet another mental shock, getting closer to Justin, going down on his knees by the bed. "I'm hanging on to my right to disagree with that, but do you want to tell me?"

"You looked at the file, right?" Justin checked, lying on his back on Ren's bed, one of his arms draped over his eyes, blocking his sight as though he needed to be blind to be able to speak.

"I … did," Ren said slowly, wondering what Justin was getting at, hoping he wasn't upset about Ren looking at the file when he'd said he wouldn't. "I was trying to help; I'm sorry."

"You don't have to apologize," Justin said shortly, then appeared to force himself to relax, to speak calmly again even though it was obviously hard for him. "But you saw the photos? You saw what I did to him?"

Ren didn't want to remember, but the images came back to him immediately as Justin referenced them. David's swollen, bloodied face. The broken nose, the fractured jaw, the badly bruised eye. Why did Justin want to talk about this now?

"You did what you had to, Justin," Ren told him neutrally, trying to keep any judgment or horror out of his voice. "I know that."

"No," Justin denied, gathering courage and strength to sit up, eyes fever-bright and burning into Ren. "It wasn't like that. I didn't have to do all that; I wanted to hurt him."

Ren involuntarily cleared his throat, holding himself motionless by the bed, trying not to cower under Justin's sudden intensity.

"Why are you telling me this?" Ren asked. Was this another assault test on the boundaries of Ren's offered friendship? What kind of assurance was Justin after by giving Ren this information?

"Because you need to understand. You and North … you keep trying to see something good in me. God, sometimes you try so hard, I almost believe there might be something there to find. But that just makes it harder."

"So, what, you want me to treat you the way everyone else does?" Ren asked, surprised how disinterested his voice sounded, how far away. "Like you can't do anything right; you're just a waste of time? Like I'm afraid of you?"

"But you are afraid of me," Justin pointed out.

"I was," Ren admitted. "Now I'm just afraid for you."

Justin broke eye contact, overcome, while Ren pushed himself up onto the edge of the bed. He might not be doing Justin any favors here, but he just couldn't stand for him to think he deserved how he'd been treated. Not just for the trial, but by all the people in his past who had failed him, hurt him, judged him, made assumptions about him. They were all wrong, and Ren hated that he used to be one of them.

"How can you be like that?" Justin demanded, not the first time he'd asked Ren this question, as if he just couldn't wrap his head around how different Ren behaved toward him. "I'm not a good person. I hurt people, Ren, and … I like doing it."

"Of course you do," Ren accepted without hesitation. "You specialize in pain; that's mostly all that anyone has ever given you, but that doesn't mean you're a bad person. It means you weren't given much of a choice about what kind of a person you could be."

"They had to drag me off him, Ren. I couldn't even see him anymore; I'd forgotten how it even started. It just felt so good to keep going."

Ren could only smile sadly at Justin's continued protests about how terrible he was. It hurt too much not to. He opened his mouth to say something but was having a hard time figuring out how to express his thoughts into words, or at least into words Justin would accept. He was too thoroughly injured by his previous experiences, and it seemed all Ren had were tiny bandages and too little time to apply them. Justin behaved exactly how everyone believed he would. He'd been told he was no good so much that he couldn't see himself any other way.

"*Todos sueñan lo que son*," Ren recited from the monologue in a whisper as he slowly tipped his head to study Justin. "*Aunque ninguno lo entiende.*"

"What are you saying?" Justin asked, tired and frustrated, but Ren shook his head. He'd just gained a sudden clarity about that line, but it was too abstract to try and translate the meaning.

"You couldn't see him because you weren't hitting him," Ren tried to explain. "It had nothing to do with him anymore; it was all about transferring pain. Yours. I'm sure it did feel good to let that go, to finally have a reason to get it out of you. You're not a bad person, Justin. He hit you first."

"But I killed him."

"No, Justin, you didn't. I looked at the scans; Dr. Delacroix looked at the scans. Trying to pin this on you is the biggest stretch in medical history. Statistically, the chances that his death had anything to do with you are less than two percent."

"But," Justin continued to protest, beginning to crumble in front of Ren. "Two percent. Then what —"

"Genetics, probably," Ren almost shrugged but remembered this was very important for Justin; they were still talking about someone's life. "Combined with his own poor health choices. Reasons that can't be seen, can't be fought or punished. And just like you were transferring your pain to him, his parents are transferring theirs to you. It's not right, in either case, what you all actually need is a lot of therapy, but you didn't take David's life ... so they shouldn't be allowed to ruin yours."

"Dr. Delacroix looked at the scans?" Justin didn't seem to know what to think or say, his face full of questions, a wreck of disbelief.

"Yes, Justin, the most respected trauma doctor in the city looked at the scans," Ren emphasized. "We went over them together this morning while you were asleep. And we both agree. Not only should you not be put in prison for this, but you should have never been brought to trial in the first place."

Alek entered quietly as Justin was processing this information, tiptoeing into the room as though he could come in, hand them mugs, and then back out without them knowing he was there.

"Sorry, guys, not interrupting," Alek said as he bent over Ren. "Pretend I'm not here ... but I am, you know, here ... in the other room if you need anything."

Ren smiled gently at Alek as he closed the door softly behind him, then returned his attention to Justin, who was staring, bewildered and lost, at the drink Alek had handed him.

"He iced it," Justin murmured.

"There are more people on your side than you think," Ren told Justin, leaning over to set his steaming mug safely on his desk to cool before he tried to drink it.

"Stop," Justin begged, and Ren nodded. Some truths were hard to hear, even when they were good; he should give him a break. "This isn't helping."

Again, Justin had a point. Like with Denny, sometimes the truth didn't matter. Sometimes innocent people did go to jail. Sometimes innocent children were molded into criminals and taught to believe they deserved to be hurt for it.

"You don't make any sense," Justin said. Ren forced himself to take a sip of tea so he wouldn't comment on that. He knew he was making almost too much sense. Justin took a drink too, his eyes closing as he swallowed, shuddering. Ren watched him, aching to fix it. All of it. Hating that he couldn't.

"Why couldn't I have met you a long time ago?" Justin wished, again almost too quietly to hear. That thought almost doubled him over, something hitting him hard, causing him to physically cringe. "North," Justin muttered, and Ren understood.

"Do you really think it wasn't my fault?" Justin asked Ren, as if he needed to hear it one more time. Or a hundred more times.

"It's almost impossible for it to have been your fault," Ren assured him, wishing this truth didn't cause Justin to look even more hopeless.

"They made it sound ... they were so sure," Justin whispered, shivering, very far away. He looked as though all his memories were rearranging themselves as everything that he'd believed for the last few weeks flipped. He'd thought he had killed someone, but he hadn't. He'd thought North didn't want anything to do with him, but he'd been trying to adopt him. He looked ready to shut down again like he had at the table.

"You're going to have a future, Justin," Ren promised him, hoping to keep him from sinking too far, from some sort of mental snap.

"After tomorrow, or whenever this hearing thing is over, it's going to get better for you. I know it. You have a family now. You and North — you can be together. You'll be free."

"I can't afford to think like that," Justin admitted, sounding as though he were drowning. "You wouldn't even be saying it if you'd been there. If you heard what they said."

"You're right," Ren allowed while still trying to stop Justin from despair. "I didn't hear what they said, but I did hear your lawyer, and I can't imagine anyone getting the better of her. She's pretty badass."

Justin smiled in spite of himself. "You should see her in person," he said.

"Yeah?" Ren followed this topic of conversation eagerly. "What's she like?" he encouraged more description, partially to distract Justin and partially because he was insanely curious. He shifted his hand from Justin's arm to gently push his mug toward his mouth again, hinting Justin should drink some more.

"Tall," Justin said, before taking another few swallows. "Taller than you, and slim, like really thin."

"Is she always so intense like that? Or was that just because she was worried about you?"

"No, she's always like that. The first time I met her, she came to get me from … from jail." Justin almost cracked under this detail, but glossed over it quickly and Ren let him, though he was curious about that too. "She picked me up in her Mazda like we were in some kind of action movie — shifting gears, talking on the phone, and eating a cheeseburger at the same time." The way Justin spoke of Kelly, Ren wondered if he'd put her at the same level of respect where he held North. Or at least very close. "I thought we were going to her office or something, but she drove us to this gym, and we did a couple games of racquetball. She talked nonstop, never broke a sweat, and never missed a shot."

"Wow," Ren complimented. "And I bet I'd be even more impressed if I knew what racquetball was."

"Oh," Justin paused in his memories. "You guys don't do … it's kind of like tennis?" Ren must have looked clueless, because Justin cut off, taking another drink. "I'll teach you; it's fun."

Ren felt some tension leave him as he heard Justin expressing that something could be fun. Also that he had just unconsciously made a plan for the future. It didn't last long because Justin immediately realized what he'd said, and he darkened again, staring off at nothing.

"You know what my dad used to say?" Ren offered. Justin looked at him but seemed to have exhausted all his words. "He would tell me that worrying about problems before they were problems only made it so I had more problems."

"That is such a dad thing to say," Justin murmured.

"Yeah, but he was right," Ren acknowledged. "I know it's awful, waiting to see what will happen, but it's not helping you to worry about it." In fact, Ren suspected it was part of the reason it was taking Justin so long to get better.

"It's so hard not to," Justin admitted. "Ren, it was so bad."

"No, stop, don't think about that," Ren interrupted, not wanting to lose all the progress they'd made. "Take another drink; pay attention to the taste. I'm going to turn on some music for you. Tell me some more about racquetball or Kelly or ... anything."

Justin took a deep breath, and Ren could see the mental struggle as he tried to do what Ren instructed. He could see how tired he was, how completely drained. How was Ren supposed to calm him down enough to sleep? He really needed it.

"It's going to be ok," Ren assured him again, convinced he couldn't say it too often.

"At least one of us thinks so," Justin said, gratitude mixed with the worry and weariness in his eyes.

"I'm pretty sure North thinks so too," Ren told him. Justin had a tired, bittersweet smile just touching the corners of his mouth, as though he were humoring Ren in his fantasy about how the world worked. He surprised Ren by lifting his hand, barely brushing the back of it against the bruise on Ren's cheek.

"I don't understand," Justin thought out loud. "How can you believe in me after I did this to you?"

"It's simple," Ren explained, trying to channel some of North's patience, reminding himself that one conversation, however earnest, wasn't going to erase all the years of negative conditioning Justin had already been through. "It's called a startle reflex, and you can't control it. I'm glad about it, honestly, because if it hadn't happened, I probably wouldn't have thought to check on you. We wouldn't be friends now."

"That's a real shitty way of making friends," Justin maintained, still gloomy. "And I'm not being a very good one. I've ... never really had one before. I don't think I know how."

"I thought you were going to teach me how to play racquetball; that's friendly," Ren tossed out, desperate to keep this light, but then decided to be honest and vulnerable again. "And you are a good friend, Justin. I've been feeling selfish about it, really."

"What? Why?" Justin demanded, incredulous. "I haven't done anything but ruin your life. I cost you a date, almost your place in the med program ... and Denny. Your face ... your back."

"Justin, stop; you've got to quit doing this to yourself. It wasn't that solid of a date, to tell you the truth. Nothing bad happened with the med program; you said yourself it might lead to a mentorship position under Dr. Delacroix, so hey, that's a huge benefit if I wanted to take it. Denny just needs some time; it's more because she hates being wrong than anything to do with me or you. You haven't ruined my life, Justin."

"Ren," Justin began to protest, but Ren didn't want to hear it.

"You realize I basically kidnapped you," Ren told him. "Just came and scooped you up, and you just went with that like it wasn't the weirdest thing in the world to do. The entire time we've known each other, you've been extremely sick, literally fighting for your life and freedom, but the only things you're worried about are my career and a scratch on my back? You could barely move, but you were trying to make me feel better about the bad news I heard from my family. And

I've never told anyone those things I told you about my family, never told anyone about Amayah before. Just you and North. And I wouldn't have told North if you hadn't been trying to comfort me about her even *in your sleep*. You've been worrying about me, putting your trust in me, trying to help me feel better, and my God, Justin, I can't imagine the amazing person you are when you're strong and healthy if this is what you're like when you are suffering so much. I don't know how I got so damn lucky."

"Would you shut up?" Justin begged, and Ren obeyed, letting him breathe. "You talk more than Kelly."

Ren decided to give him some space for a few minutes, so he busied himself with gathering their empty dishes and taking them to the kitchen, noticing how Alek had put the apartment to bed for the night. Door locked, counters wiped, thermostat turned down. Everything familiar, but at the same time not. Like this weekend had been the beginning of a huge shift in all of their lives, something they would never come back from. Ren didn't like it. It felt uneasy and distressing to him. He'd gotten used to his life as it was, the rhythm. He felt secure in the routine. He didn't like standing here in the dark, forced to wait and see what would happen. See if Denny and Alek were moving to California or if Denny would forgive him. See if Dr. Delacroix truly wanted to apprentice him in the ER. See if he would see Celeste on Wednesday and have another chance with her. See if his mother would be ok, or at least ok long enough for him to be able to put himself into a better position to help her. See if Justin would be found guilty in the morning, or maybe not because he also had to wait and see if North and Kelly had been able to move that meeting.

So much uncertainty. So much waiting. He could hardly stand it. He gave himself a minute more, looking around the front part of the apartment at the things that didn't change. The crocheted afghan on the back of the couch. The boxes of electronic pieces under the partial wall between the kitchen and living room. The camp chair drowning in coats and hats. But even those things weren't truly permanent. Ren felt a hazy, exhausted slipperiness shiver into his soul, icy as the draft from the balcony door, and just like that, he'd hit his limit on how long he could be alone. He took long strides toward the light shining weakly from his bedroom, taking his bag with him to get one last set of stats before Justin fell asleep.

Justin was curled on his side, but when he heard Ren coming in, he tried to straighten and began moving to sit up again.

"Stay down, Justin; I know you're worn out," Ren advised, knowing they'd been talking for probably too long, gone over too many emotionally exhausting topics. "We're just going to do a quick stat check, and then it's bedtime."

"Has North called yet?" Justin asked, relaxing as much as it was possible for him to relax onto the mattress again. Which wasn't much.

"No, not yet," Ren replied. "They probably have a lot to talk about, though."

"I don't want to go back to jail," Justin admitted, sounding frightened.

"Kelly won't let it happen," Ren assured, checking Justin's temperature, relieved to see it was 102.5, even with the sun down. "Now get some rest, ok?"

"Ren?"

"Yeah, *querido*?" He didn't know why he called Justin that; it had just sort of slipped out. He hoped Justin didn't know what it meant, or that Justin was too caught up in whatever he was thinking about to really notice. Ren hid his embarrassment by taking Justin's wrist, noticing the spike in heart rate, Justin's slight gasp at being touched. Still so fast. "What is it?"

"I really don't feel good."

It was such an obvious statement, but Ren knew how hard it had been for Justin to say it. Ren shifted his hand from Justin's wrist to his palm, holding onto him comfortingly, though he sensed it wasn't quite enough.

"You know," Ren said, not sure what he was offering or really who it was truly for. "When Denny was sick, all she wanted was for

Alek to hold her. I don't know if it was the position or just having him there or what, but it really seemed to help. I'm not as soft as Alek is, but ... maybe we could try?"

There was resistance in Justin's expression about this plan, but it crumpled quickly into a sort of desperation. He was at the point where he'd try just about anything to get some relief, no matter how embarrassing or strange it may be. Ren didn't wait for him to agree; he'd already seen his answer.

"Come here," Ren invited, first assisting Justin in sitting up so he could slide onto the bed with him, pushing himself tightly into the corner, bracing himself so he could maintain whatever position they ended in, forcing himself not to wince as the wall pushed against his wounded back. He settled at an angle in the bed, bringing Justin backward, not in his lap, but draped over it. Justin readily rested his head against Ren's chest again, reclined against him, hot, trembling, and scared. Though he did seem to be breathing easier now. "How's this?" Ren asked him. "Ok?"

"Thank you," was the answer. Ren pulled the blanket over them both, though he knew he'd be suffocating in a few minutes between the quilt and Justin's extreme heat.

"Sure. Is there anything else I can do?"

"Could you ... say that poem again?"

"Easy enough," Ren agreed. Everything seemed to slow, the way it does in the dark, and this time Ren was happy about that. Because tomorrow could take Justin away from him, in a variety of ways. And he wasn't ready.

"*Sueña el rey que es rey*," Ren began, the soft and steady rhythm he wanted Justin to breathe in, reciting the revelation of a fictional prince kept prisoner that nothing in life is truly real, that everything is just a dream — all fortune, good and bad, simply shadows of thought, created subconsciously by the dreamer. He knew Justin didn't understand a word of it, though he found it appropriate that he seemed to be drawn to it. Justin and Segismundo — both wrongfully incarcerated. Both their personalities forcibly molded by the incorrect assumptions of those around them. Both lashing out in pain.

Segismundo's story ends with him gaining his freedom and becoming the king of Poland. For Justin, Ren would settle for keeping him in his life long enough to make good on his racquetball promise.

21

NEUROSCIENCE

Ren found himself admiring Alek as he sat pinned to the corner by Justin. Once situated in Ren's arms, it had taken Justin less than five minutes to fall asleep, all his weight leaning into Ren, who tried not to fidget underneath him. Alek had been able to sit motionless with Denny for hours, all his muscles trained on the effort to make her comfortable. Ren felt disappointed in himself that this was so difficult. His back hurt — a deep ache from the position, the weight, and the aggravation of the wound from the coffee table; it kept him anything but motionless. Justin was unbearably hot under the quilt, stifling Ren, dragging the minutes as Ren desperately tried to find something to focus on. He looked around his bedroom, the med bag on the floor, the screensaver on his computer. The piano music he'd selected to be soothing did nothing to distract him, though intimately studying Justin as he slept seemed to do the trick ... at least for a while.

Ren looked carefully at Justin's hands, noticing each tiny scar, the length of the fingers, the minute bruise at the wrist from the IV. He watched what the dim light did to Justin's hair as he stroked it, curling his fingers through and around the strands in a method he would have never tried if Justin had been awake. He pulled everything off the back of Justin's neck so he could look at the burn scars.

Through it all, Justin rested still and silent, reminding Ren there was a purpose to the discomfort of the position. Despite knowing this, Ren wished he could move. A guilty, almost constant thought that made him cling to Justin every few moments as he remembered, again, that this may be the last night Justin would be with him. He should enjoy this while it lasted because everything could change tomorrow. Justin could be gone.

Ren didn't know why that hurt so much. The few days of his life where Justin had been present had been so tumultuous that he was surprised how he didn't want them to end. He tried to tell himself it was only because Justin needed him, more than any of Ren's other patients. Once that aspect of their relationship was removed, Ren hoped it wouldn't be quite so hard to think of Justin being somewhere else. Provided that somewhere else wasn't prison. But even thinking of Justin being completely happy in his new life with North didn't sit well with Ren either. He couldn't really be jealous of North? That would just be wrong. But then again, so was the reason Ren didn't want Justin to leave.

He didn't want to admit Denny might have been right, and he hated that she had put the thought into his head. Or that she'd brought it more to his attention; he was no longer sure what had come first, the emotion or the suggestion it was present. How it started wasn't as important as how much he couldn't keep it out of his mind that he might be falling in love with Justin. He didn't want to think about it, but Ren indulgently pressed a small kiss on one of the burn scars, forced himself to be still a few more agonizing minutes, and couldn't help but think about it. He shouldn't do things like that, though. Even though he no longer had to worry about starting a relationship with a murderer, there were several other huge and heavy obstacles to this. There was no happy future here. He couldn't do that to his mother, for one thing. His sweet, sacrificing, devoutly Catholic, widowed mother who expected him to find an equally sweet, devoutly Catholic girl to marry and give her those ten grandchildren he'd been promising her his entire life. What would that do to her if he told her that he was ... Ren was fortunate enough he didn't have to pretend to be attracted to girls for his mother's sake ... but he'd known for a long time now that he was just as attracted to ...

But even if he were attracted to Justin and this wasn't some weird symptom of Justin's illness all on its own, and even if his family would be perfectly all right with it, how likely was it that Justin could even return his feelings? It was a bad idea, such a self-destructive bad idea; he should try and talk himself out of it. What would be the point of falling in love with someone who probably couldn't love him back? It was a huge disaster in the making. Ren was just asking to be emotionally shattered if he dropped his guard too much, allowed himself to consider the possibility. And yet ... he held Justin closer. He smelled like Ren's soap, and heat, and misery.

Ren sat there conflicted in the lamplight of his room, worried about the morning, listening to the wind blowing outside, listening to Denny in his mind as she teased and chastised then screamed and pleaded about Justin. He held Justin tightly, nuzzling his chin over the nape of his neck, rubbing his back and pretending it had everything to do with keeping Justin comfortable and nothing to do with how much Ren wanted to touch him ... even at the same time it tormented him on a variety of levels, physical and otherwise.

"*Mi vida era tan fácil antes de que vinieras,*" Ren sighed at Justin. Well, maybe that wasn't quite fair. His life wasn't easy, but it had made more sense before Justin. He'd been accustomed to its challenges and moved easily within them. "*Pero no quiero que me dejes.*"

Through it all, the back-and-forth frenzy of Ren's thoughts, the uncomfortable twitching and shifting underneath him, Justin remained peacefully unaware. Ren figured he should be grateful at least one of them could rest, but he was even more grateful when his phone rang, giving him the excuse of finally disengaging from Justin and the bed to answer it. Justin groaned as Ren carefully settled him on the pillow, but he surprisingly didn't wake. Ren congratulated himself on improving his new sneaking-out-from-under-sleeping-Justin skill, surprised how often the need for it was coming up. It took a while, though, so by the time Ren was free to pick up the phone he'd left charging on his desk, he'd missed the call. Predictably from North — who had sent Ren a series of text messages when Ren didn't answer.

I hope you guys are sleeping, the first text read.

Call me if you need to. Hearing is still on; no way to change it. I'll be there around 8 to pick Justin up. Get some rest. Thanks.

Ren noted the time. He checked Justin, pleased he still seemed peaceful lying there without Ren holding him. He thought he'd take advantage of that and started moving. First, he replied to North to let him know everything was fine at the apartment, Justin was resting at least, and Ren promised to keep North updated. Then he took a shower, a very quick one since he didn't want to leave Justin alone too long, but he wanted to clean the hospital off him too. He knew he should probably get some sleep, but it just seemed like such a waste of the time he had remaining. He didn't want to sleep. And as much as he wanted a future, the uncertainty of what it would bring made him wish the night would never end.

When he returned to his room, it seemed Justin had somehow subconsciously noticed he was alone. He'd curled up again, tight, his features no longer quite so calm. Ren dressed, wrapped himself in the couch afghan, and sat at his desk, keeping an eye on Justin as he started typing. Because as much as he wished, the morning was coming, and he needed to prepare for it.

The first time he'd attempted the biography assignment, he'd been forced to make up everything about Justin. He didn't know a single thing about him apart from his name. Now he knew so much more, but the information felt too special to share. Still, Ren felt he should turn something in, so he typed a new, crisply-MLA-formatted version of Justin's life, still almost completely fabricated, though much softer in tone than the first rage-filled draft. Ren barely made the word count but felt satisfied by his attempt.

He attached the document to an email, indicating he probably wouldn't be attending class in the morning. He'd be helping North get Justin ready for court somehow, but he didn't say that either. He went on lying to all his Monday class instructors and his supervisor at the donation center; he told them all he wasn't feeling well. *Please find attached the assignment. Can I please reschedule my oral presentation? I hope to be back to normal by Tuesday; sorry for leaving you short-handed.* He wondered if his dance teacher would even notice he was missing, but he sent the email anyway.

Because he knew he'd be absolutely worthless tomorrow. He may not be coming down with anything, but the part where he didn't feel well was not a lie. His emotions were twisted around Justin and what would happen to him.

He finished the emails and was just beginning to wonder what he should do now to distract himself from his own exhaustion when his phone chirped again, another text message. It was after midnight now, closer to one, so Ren was surprised North would still be awake and sending him messages. But this text wasn't from North.

Can I come up?

"Denny," Ren breathed, and tossed the afghan aside to hurry down the stairs to the front entrance, not bothering to take the time for a reply or to even put on any shoes. She'd come back, though she'd picked an unpromising time for it. How had she known anyone would even be awake to let her in?

Or maybe she had just taken a chance. Maybe she thought she'd come to the door and then have to go back home anyway. It seemed that was the case, since she had already started walking away by the time he got down to her. He threw the door open, leaning out into the cold, the snow still falling.

"Denny!" he yelled after her, not being able to chase her down. She paused hesitantly, as though she didn't believe she'd heard anything over the wind, but she did check over her shoulder, and he waved wildly at her, beckoning her inside. Her face crumpled into pained relief as she returned to the entrance, though she walked as though forcing herself forward.

"Hey," she greeted, dedicatedly nonchalant, as though this were normal, just another day. "I saw your light on. Everything ok up there?"

"It's better now," he said, physically pulling her into the lobby, sealing them from the snow outside. It seemed she'd been out so long she didn't notice the cold anymore, didn't notice how it had stiffened all her limbs. Or maybe that had nothing to do with the cold. "Denny, what the hell are you doing wandering around in the snow at one in the morning? I thought you'd gone home a long time ago." Ren couldn't bring himself to be angry at her; she looked too forlorn, cold, and lost.

"I did go home, but I couldn't sleep, and I couldn't sit still. I figured if anyone was still awake, it'd be you," she said, unable to look at him, seeming frozen to the spot where he'd left her, as if blocked by some barrier between them only she could see.

"Yeah, I ... I've got stuff to do," Ren excused himself, knowing no matter where they were, opposite sides of a debate, she would understand what he meant and how it had more to do with how he felt than what needed to get done. "Did you want company? Because I could use some, if it's ok."

For the first time since they'd started talking, Denny looked up into his face, eyes large and hurt.

"Ren, I'm sorry," she apologized in a rush, lowering her head. Her next sentence garbled up in her mouth, which meant she was probably trying to tell him either he'd been right or she'd been wrong. Both versions were difficult for her.

"Come on," he told her, taking her hand, ignoring her apology. Because it wasn't necessary. "Come upstairs; the couch is free for you."

"Ren, I —" she tried again, but he shook his head, pulling her toward the elevator. He didn't need her to say it, not even the first time.

"We'll talk inside," he half-promised. "After you warm up. How long were you outside looking at my light anyway?"

"I don't know," she confessed, having a hard time looking at him again. "An hour? Maybe a little more."

"You were outside my window for an hour? Why didn't you call me sooner?" Ren chastised gently, pushing the elevator button and tugging Denny close to his side, forcing them to behave as they normally did. Because it seemed she needed physical permission at every step to be next to him, to go to the apartment where she practically lived. She had an extra toothbrush there; a section of Alek's closet held her clothes. But now she was acting like they were strangers. All because of what? Guilt? Rage?

"I needed to sort some things out first," she told him, her voice edgy. Not mad, or at least not at him. Yet. "I guess I'm so used to things being a certain way, and you being a certain way, but then nothing was like that, and it was this huge shift, and I needed to wrap my head around it." She shrugged while Ren tried to figure out what she meant. "I didn't really notice what I was doing or where I was, but when I snapped out of it, I was standing under your window. Guess your apartment is my default setting."

"You didn't have to leave," Ren reminded her, opening the door to the dark apartment and dragging her back into the warmth.

"No, I did," she denied, though there was no longer any heat to her contradiction.

"Well, I'm glad you came back then," he said, unzipping her coat as she looked around the quiet living room, as though it had changed somehow during her absence. She seemed so delicate all of a sudden, which was strange because Denny was not fragile; she was fierce and determined and set.

"I did some more research, Ren," Denny started talking, not even noticing he was taking her coat off for her. She stood rigidly right where he'd let go of her hand, just inside the door, her eyes downcast.

"It doesn't matter, Denny," he told her firmly. And he meant it; he didn't care what new details she may have uncovered. He was staying loyal to Justin, so there was no point in talking about it, getting frustrated with each other again. Not now. He was so tired, and so was she, and if neither of them could bend on their stances, they needed to just avoid the issue. At least for tonight. *Please, just for tonight.*

"Let me get you something warm," he continued as he set her coat on the camp chair, turning to light the stove under the kettle and then get the afghan for her, but she grabbed onto his arm, her fingers still icy through his sleeve.

"No, Ren, it does matter, and I don't want a drink," she contradicted emphatically. He opened his mouth to stop her, but she shook her head at him. "I looked up the assault instead of the murder case, and there was a girl Justin was protecting. The guy had a knife and everything; he sliced open Justin's arm, cracked one of his ribs too. This isn't murder; it's a justifiable homicide. Justin's being profiled; it's the only explanation about why this has been taken so far. You ... you were right, Ren."

"I know," he said, sad even though she was now agreeing with him, removing her hand so he could at least get her a blanket if she didn't want a warm drink. He decided not to go into how it wasn't really either, not murder or homicide, just an extremely unfortunate coincidental death. Because again, it just didn't matter at this point. "Hopefully the jury knows it too."

"I don't know about that; that's the worst place where it doesn't seem to matter," Denny murmured, her eyes scanning the floor as if she were rereading something she'd found and not liking it.

"How is he doing?" she asked, changing the subject. "You know, apart from being wrongfully accused, almost dying, and me being a bitch."

"His fever came down a little bit," Ren reported the small pieces of good news, deciding not to acknowledge most of the self-degrada-tion she'd slid into the conversation. "And his heart is steady, but he's obviously worried about the hearing tomorrow. It's taking a lot out of him."

"It shouldn't even be like that!" She sounded close to tears. "If their positions had been reversed ..." she cut off, too mad to speak.

But Ren knew. If it had been Justin trying to force a girl into a car with a knife and David had stepped in and sent him to the hospital, David would have been called a hero. He'd be interviewed by the news, celebrated, congratulated. Because David's upbringing made everyone think the best of him. And Justin's upbringing did the exact opposite.

"Ren?" He heard his name faintly from his bedroom, and he winced. He'd left Justin too long. He'd woken up alone, perhaps dragged from sleep by Denny's emphatic outburst. Denny stared down the hall like the apartment was suddenly haunted.

"Come on," Ren invited, wanting to reintroduce them to each other now that Denny could see Justin for what he was instead of what had been presented to her.

"Wouldn't it be better if just you go?" She hesitated as he stood near the couch, hand out to her as if he would help her cross some emotional bridge into his room.

"I figured we'd take advantage of your apologetic mood while it lasts," Ren said casually. "But for your information, he's angrier with himself than with you."

Denny closed her eyes as the tragedy of that comment struck her psyche. But she did take Ren's offered hand and allowed him to pull her. Though she paused at the doorway, unable to cross the threshold into Ren's room ahead of him, needing him to go first. Ren allowed this, one thing at a time, letting go of Denny and leaving her in the shadowed hall.

"It's all right, Justin," Ren assured, coming to his side, ready to assess the damage he'd done in leaving him by himself. "Sorry I had to leave you for a minute."

"What's going on? Is it time to go?" Justin asked the questions in rapid succession, looking around worriedly. He was sitting on the edge of the bed as though he were in the process of trying to get up, eyes wild, and panting with effort and fear.

"It's nowhere near time to go; it's the middle of the night," Ren told him gently, even though he could feel the minutes slipping away from them. "Lie down now. You should be sleeping."

"But where were you?"

"Oh, you know," Ren said lightly, trying to calm the souls on both sides of his door. "Just making sure all my strays are safe and warm for the night." For a second, Justin looked confused, but his face softened into partial relief and understanding.

"Denny," he said to confirm. "Did you talk to her? She's ok?"

"I think she's ok," Ren said, unwilling to answer for Denny. He looked pointedly at her, again reaching out a hand to bring her closer. She narrowed her eyes at him, guilty tears all over her face, clearly visible even in the dark. "Denny?"

"She's here?" Justin asked. Ren watched as Denny jerked herself forward, almost as if the shadows had pushed her from behind. He stood to assist, throwing the afghan around her shoulders and using it to swing her around into his desk chair.

"Presto," Ren said, as though he'd conjured Denny from the snowstorm. They stared at each other in silent discomfort. Both looking hurt. Both looking guilty. Ren was at a loss for what to say to break the pained stalemate. He thought perhaps the best way was to help Justin get his head down, though like before, Justin seemed set on staying upright in Denny's presence, forcing an appearance of strength that made no sense to Ren.

"Hi Justin," Denny was the first to speak, as Ren expected. He stood a little apart from them, retreating to bystander status, or referee status? He leaned against his doorframe, wondering if this was how Alek felt all the time. He could almost see the unspoken emotions in the room, the broken trust, the silent accusations, the burning apologies, rippling back and forth between Denny and

Justin, hesitant but rapid, a strange and wobbly weaving.

"Hi Denny," Justin returned, hand on his heart, entering a verbal chess match — pawn meets pawn and suddenly neither can move anymore unless another piece comes from the side. Something Ren wasn't sure about doing yet. Denny clung to the afghan, holding it tight against her chest.

"You look terrible," Denny commented, and Ren prepared to intervene. Or translate? Justin didn't know how Denny communicated friendship — how most times it sounded like the exact opposite.

"Strays usually do," Justin returned capably, impressing Ren and making Denny smile, though her lips trembled alarmingly.

"I don't know who I hate most," Denny confessed, speaking faster as though it would steady her voice. It didn't. Justin struggled to pay attention, to remain sitting up and facing her, understanding that this was important. "I hate that jerk for trying to force himself on that girl, and I hate his parents for trying to blame you for him being an asshole. I especially hate her for just living her spoiled, simple, little life unbroken and carefree without ever thinking about what happened to you for stepping in and fighting her fight for her, and I hate … I hate myself for hating you."

"Maybe that's too much hate," Justin suggested wearily after it became obvious that Denny had run out of things to list, giving Ren the fastest side look, as though he were checking for his approval on how he was handling the conversation. Or maybe he wanted Ren to help him end it? The glance was over before Ren could give him any sort of silent feedback, though Ren wished he could let him know that he was doing very well.

"Maybe," Denny agreed quietly, fizzled out. "But there are some things I don't hate."

"Hopefully Alek made the list," Justin supplied her helpfully, and Ren watched her slump, though not in sadness.

"It's not possible to hate Alek," Denny admitted. "Or Ren, even though he's a frustrating piece of work most of the time," she continued, twisting her head toward him with one of her normal expressions just under the surface of worn-out pain. "And I don't hate you either," she finished, addressing Justin again, somber. "Not anymore."

"Same," Justin accepted, gracious and breathless, hand still covering his heart. Denny's smile lingered as she gazed on Justin with new affection tinged with concern, but then she toughened up unexpectedly.

"But if you ever mess up Renzo's pretty face like that again, or hurt him in any other way, at all, I will eviscerate you, got it?" Denny slammed the threat between them like flipping on a switch to an electric chair.

"You won't have to; I'll do it myself," Justin promised calmly, solemnly, as though he were making an actual vow of some sort. He settled his mystery eyes on Ren, startling him with their sincerity. Ren shrugged to hide a shudder, though it wasn't a cold feeling that trembled down his neck.

"All right, that's enough," Ren stepped in, hands lifted to push through the abrupt heaviness of the conversation. He drew the line when people started laying down their life for his sake. Particularly since it wasn't clear if Justin hadn't already done that for a girl he didn't even know in a parking lot. Ren half glared at Denny for even bringing it up. "And you say I'm dramatic. Justin, lie down; this isn't helping."

"You are dramatic," she said, though she was smiling at him again, their friendship a disconnected joint snapped back to its correct place. Something that would ache for a while and would need to be treated tenderly, but it worked properly, almost as good as new. "Better do as he says," she instructed Justin as she stood up, leaving the afghan on the desk chair.

"Where are you going?" Ren asked cautiously before he allowed her to trade places with him in the room. He didn't want her to think she had to leave again.

"To see Alek," Denny answered, though the way she said it made

Ren wonder why he'd even thought to ask. Before she left, she gently pushed Justin into the bed and pulled the quilt over him. They didn't say anything else to each other, but Ren knew just how good Denny was at letting her eyes and face speak for her. For all he knew, she could be reading Justin a silent, encouraging bedtime story in the last few seconds before she left him. Justin looked at her with undisguised relief.

She didn't touch Ren on her way out, but that made it feel more normal. Ren sighed as his world came together again, a little closer though it was slightly larger.

"I guess the truth does matter," Ren emphasized to Justin, kneeling on the floor next to him on the bed, reaching out to cover his shoulder with his hand and allowing Justin to run his fingers along Ren's sleeve cuff. "Now sleep."

"You too," Justin ordered.

"Soon," Ren promised.

Similar to the last time Justin and Ren had spent the night together in this bedroom, Ren found himself waking in a befuddled heap on his floor, half covered in the afghan, not knowing what was going on. Again like last time, he hadn't meant to fall asleep and couldn't pinpoint exactly when or how it had happened. He remembered Justin drifting off not too long after Denny left, his arms folded across his stomach rather than his chest this time. Ren had heard Alek's deep rumble through the walls as Denny joined him in his room. They'd talked in a hum that grew quieter and quieter, like the wind outside. Justin remained silent, maybe, for a while, though now Ren was trying hard to think about what had happened in those strange hours of the very early morning. He seemed to remember comforting Justin, that he'd been whimpering, his muscles tight and trembling in the low light of the faithful lamp, murmuring frightened phrases about his frightening future. Then simply moaning — a painful, lonely sound, twisting in distress on the bed. In fact, Ren was shocked he'd been able to fall asleep with Justin moving so much.

Ren pushed himself up so he could orient himself to his surroundings. Figure out the time. See how Justin was doing; he couldn't hear him right now. He hadn't made it very far before he paused, shifting his attention instead to the door, which was being opened in a soft and careful way. Come to think of it, the knob being turned might have been what had woken him up to begin with.

"Great, you're already awake," Denny greeted him, moving faster now that she'd confirmed she wouldn't be startling him by coming into his room. But why would she be doing that? Why was she happy he was awake?

"Something going on?" Ren whispered, hoping Denny would lower her voice when she responded. He didn't want to wake Justin.

"Yeah, I need to go get something, but someone needs to help Justin, and Alek can't do it, so that leaves you." She spoke quickly, tugging at Ren, trying to get him on his feet. "We didn't want to wake you, but," she finally paused, which was good since Ren was in no way keeping up with her. He looked behind him at the bed, amazed to find it empty. Justin wasn't there? How had he gotten up and out of the room without Ren waking up?

"Where is Justin?" Ren asked, untangling himself from the afghan in a rushed attempt to stand up, confused and inexplicably alarmed. What kind of help did Justin need and how long had he needed it before they'd decided it was something that required Ren?

"He's in the bathroom puking his guts out," Denny responded with simple efficiency, though it rearranged everything in Ren's brain. Now he knew why Alek couldn't help.

"What?" he hissed, though he did it in motion, taking long strides down the hallway, on his way to assess the situation. "How long?"

"He just started," Denny answered, half explanation and half excuse for not coming to get him sooner. "I heard him moving in the hall so I got up to check on him, and he said he needed to use the bathroom but he didn't want to wake you, so I helped him get in there, but then he started throwing up, and I think there's blood in it, so I figured I'd better come get you anyway." Denny also spoke as she moved, rapidly filling in the details in the couple of steps. Ren could hear loud music from Alek's room, his friend's attempt to drown out any noise from the nearby bathroom. Alek couldn't handle blood or vomit, so Ren was glad that he knew enough to keep out of the way of this one. Denny seemed to be doing ok, though her face was startlingly white.

"I'll be back," she said in parting, retreating down the hall, but this time she turned toward the front door. Ren didn't have time to even ask her where she was going, but he couldn't blame her for wanting to scram. She obviously wasn't as bad as Alek, but most people experienced some degree of sympathy nausea in the presence of someone being sick. Even Ren wasn't completely immune, though he could suppress it enough to be helpful. It did mean that despite being in a hurry, he took one last deep breath for himself in preparation for what was waiting for him on the other side of the closed bathroom door.

He came in as Justin was wiping his mouth on a wad of toilet paper, and Ren noticed immediately that there was indeed blood. Justin dropped it in with last night's dinner and then dropped himself, helpless and limp, on the towels still covering the floor, panting with his eyes squeezed shut.

"Hey," Ren alerted him of his presence as he dampened a washcloth for him, kneeling down next to him on the towels, ignoring for the moment what was in the toilet basin, though it was impossible to ignore the scent of it, heavy in the room.

"Just let me die," Justin begged, a plea that staked Ren through the chest as it was so pitifully adamant. He hadn't been sure what Justin would sound like when he'd finally hit the end of his endurance, but now that they seemed to be there, he wasn't surprised.

"Sorry, already too invested in not letting that happen," Ren told him, as undramatically as possible while pressing his washcloth on the back of Justin's neck.

"Ren, I can't —" Justin gulped, and then desperately hauled himself over the bowl again. Ren kept his cloth carefully in place and added a supportive hand to Justin's bicep, staying close to him despite how he'd really like to follow Denny out of the apartment. Something with a ton of bass started thundering in Alek's room to the point that Ren wondered if their downstairs neighbors were going to start pounding on the ceiling in a minute. As if being woken up early on a Monday morning was the worst thing that could happen to a person.

Justin's dedication to not making a mess on the bathroom floor seemed to be unnecessary; there wasn't much left in his stomach to come up, just some blood-tinged bile. Ren squinted at it, puzzling out its source. He knew Justin didn't have any internal bleeding because that would have come up looking like coffee grounds while this seemed to be a tiny amount, brighter in color, pinkish. Ren realized it was probably coming from the blisters in Justin's mouth.

"I can't go back," Justin panted, hanging his head over the toilet, the most pathetic posture Ren had yet seen in him, worse than curled up in the hospital bed, worse than unconscious on his living room floor. Worse because he had no solution for this, no medication, no training for how to get Justin's fear under control. No way to reassure him it would be all right. But he did have to figure out something because this was going to mess everything up. All the progress they'd made to get Justin rehydrated was going to be for nothing. Ren could almost see his racing heartbeat in his neck and the vein in his forehead, but how to get his heart medication into him if he couldn't keep it down? Ren figured just telling him to calm down wasn't going to work, but what was he going to do? And how much time did he have left to do it?

Ren pulled slightly on Justin's clothes when he was certain he was finished for a minute, offering Justin whatever solace he could find in his arms, and Justin collapsed into him with absolutely zero resistance, twitching and distressed.

Ren didn't know what to say, so he communicated in touch only.

Justin felt different this morning, still hot, but also a weird sort of clammy that happens when you're throwing up. Ren relocated the cloth from Justin's neck to his forehead, pulling him down so his head rested heavily on Ren's lap. Justin kept his eyes closed, his breathing feathered, groaning every so often.

"Please," Justin pleaded, though Ren was unable to give him anything he needed or wanted, despite every wish he had that he could. "I can't." Ren opened his mouth to say something but stopped. There were no words. There was no time.

The morning dissolved out from under them, new but softer songs beginning and ending on the other side of Alek's closed door. Ren helped prop Justin up several more times, though he was only dry heaving at this point. Between episodes, Ren moved his hands over Justin, up and down his arms, down the side of his face, somehow treasuring and abhorring these moments. How they were so special. How they were so awful.

"Ren," Justin whispered, on his side on Ren's thighs, weak. Ren didn't trust himself to answer, so he squeezed Justin's shoulder in response instead. *Still here, Justin. As long as I can. It's going to be ok.* He wiped Justin's mouth and ran his fingers through his hair and thought desperately hard on how he was going to fix this, keep Justin safe, how he was going to keep him from being taken away.

Ren heard the knock on his front door, but he didn't move right away to answer it, though he knew Alek wouldn't hear anything over his music and wouldn't come out until Ren gave him the all clear it was safe. The knock came again.

"There's someone at the door," Ren notified Justin, knowing he wouldn't care much. "I'll be right back. I'll bring some water for you."

"No," Justin answered, though Ren wasn't sure what he was saying no to. He smoothed his hair back one more time before sliding out from underneath him, leaving him broken and crumpled on the floor to go and see the culprit who had forced time to start again in the apartment.

It was North, and Ren almost slammed the door closed on him in frustrated protest. If North was here, it meant it was eight in the morning already. Ren stared at North, at the suit he was already wearing — all completely black, even the dress shirt and the tie he wore underneath the coat. Everything such a deep black that North stood an astrophysical marvel in the hallway; he had his own gravity, dragging Justin out the door.

As Ren stood there, blocking the way in, staring and motionless, North reached forward with his artificial hand, circling it around the back of Ren's neck and pulling them together as though they were comrades rejoined after a long night battling a separate, yet common, enemy.

"It's almost over," North spoke the comforting things Ren hadn't been able to say, holding him secure, powerful and patient, and somehow getting through this so much better than Ren was. "I'm sorry this has been so hard on you; I can't thank you enough."

"North," Ren began, his voice croaky and wet with tears he'd swallowed instead of shed. He didn't know what else to say, though. *Don't take Justin away from me. Don't let anyone hurt him anymore. Say we don't have to go, that the whole thing's been called off. There's too much snow. There's too much pain.*

North let him go, checking his face for the report of how the night had gone and seeing it had been more rough than restful, the faintest wonder in one of his eyebrows about how it could have gone so poorly and Ren had not thought to call him.

"How's Justin?" North asked, a pointed, should-be-easy-to-answer question. And as though Justin had decided to answer for himself, Ren could hear the familiar half-cough, half-retching noise starting again from the bathroom. North's head jerked that direction, something in his shoulders collapsing.

"Bad," Ren said, but North was already moving. He tossed the garment bag containing Justin's suit over the armrest of the couch and followed the gut-wrenching sound through the apartment. Ren gave him a few seconds head start as he filled a glass with more Gatorade from the fridge.

North stood helplessly watching in the doorway as Justin finished. Justin had one of his hands up, blocking North from coming in, as though he wanted to spare him from seeing this. Ren ignored the hand, slipping tidily past North to join Justin on the floor, waiting with the glass for Justin to stop gasping, to stop spitting ineffectually, for the moments of calm on the other side of this, however few they may be.

"Ren, can you tell me what's happening," North requested, voice gentle, mild as always.

"Probably the medication," Ren answered, understanding what North wanted to know. "Iron infusions sometimes cause nausea. Anxiety isn't helping either. Or stress."

"Please shut up," Justin requested, moving to return his head to the towels, but Ren prevented him, catching him one-handed to keep him semi-upright, handing him the glass.

"Sip it," Ren ordered.

"No point," Justin shot back, miserable.

"I don't care if you swallow it. Use it as a mouthwash if you want, just take a damn sip," Ren returned, suddenly angry, but not at Justin, who looked wide-eyed at Ren's abrupt break in attitude, though he took the glass, suddenly meek. Ren sighed, knowing he'd have to do something else with his anger, so he turned on North instead.

"Does he have to do this?" Ren said snappishly to North, who he also wasn't angry with, but he figured he could handle Ren's fury better. "Isn't there something we can do? I mean, look at him!" He was so sick, so weak, so emotionally battered. To force him up, into a suit, and out into the weather to the courthouse seemed unnaturally cruel.

"He just has to sit there," North returned, infuriatingly calm. "And then it will be over."

But what if it wasn't? Or what if over meant Justin would be taken into custody? What would they do to him? Ren tried to remember Kelly's voice on the phone yesterday, tried to imagine her standing in the courtroom fighting for Justin, wishing he could have heard what she'd said. Wishing he had a better guess as to what the jury had decided.

Ren continued to glare at North, though it wasn't his fault. In his peripheral vision, he saw Justin take extremely slow and tiny amounts of Gatorade into his mouth, though he was right, he didn't keep them down. Ren took the glass for him so he would have his hands free, one to support himself on the rim as he leaned over, and the other pressed tight against his churning stomach. It was such a hopeless place.

That's where Denny joined them, returned from wherever she'd had to go and letting herself into the apartment. She took in the scene instantaneously, giving Ren an exasperated look that he couldn't figure out.

"Ren, what are you doing?" she barked, her hands emphasizing her question. "Where's your rubbing alcohol? I thought you would have taken care of this already."

"My what?" Ren asked her, confused, another avalanche of weird and terrible closing in on him. Taken care of what? And how exactly? He kept one hand on Justin's back, on his knees on the floor, switching his gaze from North to Denny as she started dismantling the tiny hall closet where they kept their extra bedding and some cleaning supplies.

"Don't tell me you don't know this trick," Denny continued, successfully pulling a small bottle of clear liquid away from the dusting stuff, the hydrogen peroxide, and an extra container of dish soap. "Excuse me," she said politely to North, stepping past him into the crowded bathroom.

Ren tried to think of something snippy to say to her, but he was at a loss. His head was too full of other things, bigger things. He exchanged a final look with North, who was watching Denny with baffled interest.

"Here, Justin," Denny instructed gently, leaning down with the open alcohol bottle since there wasn't any more room for her to get properly on the floor. "Deep breaths; it should help. I brought you something that'll help even more, but it's something you have to swallow so we need to get this under control first. I thought Ren knew about this, but I guess not, so I'm sorry it took me so long to get back."

At first, Justin tilted his head back, as though he thought she meant for him to drink it or something. But as Denny held it close to his nose, swirling the contents so the scent would waft up, he stopped trying to lean away. He lifted a hand to hold Denny's wrist, looking ready to just douse himself. Apparently, it was doing something helpful.

"How does that work?" Ren asked in spite of himself.

"I don't know; that's neuroscience," Denny dismissed, still leaning over Justin, who was now breathing heavily in and out of her offered bottle. "I just know the scent somehow shuts off that need-to-puke reflex. It doesn't work if you have food poisoning or something, but for anxiety stuff, it's instantaneously effective. Huh, Justin?"

Justin only moaned in relief, and Ren felt guilty. If he'd known that, as Denny seemed to think he should, he could have spared Justin a lot of painful heaving. He was also curious. How did Denny know about it? But when he looked at her to ask, she just shook her head.

"How's it going out there, guys?" came Alek's sudden question from behind his door. Ren hadn't noticed the music had stopped. He'd almost forgotten Alek was still trapped in self-quarantine in his room.

"Better give us a few more minutes, Alek," Ren called to him, considering Denny and Justin. It wasn't clear yet if Denny's alcohol thing was working or if it was just because Justin was between bouts. "Can you try another drink?" Ren asked Justin.

"That's a good idea," Denny agreed encouragingly. Ren noticed

North checking his watch and realized that no matter what, Justin was leaving soon.

"Denny, you got this?" Ren checked as he stood up, eyes still on North.

"If you aren't going far," she allowed, taking his place on the floor, helping Justin alternate between sips of Gatorade and deep inhales of alcohol. Ren nodded, pulling North down the hallway, out of earshot so they could talk without Justin hearing them.

"I'm sorry, Ren," North apologized again. "We just don't have a choice."

"I know," Ren acknowledged, contrite. "Sorry I snapped at you. I just wish he didn't have to do this."

"Hopefully, it won't take long."

"I'll give you some of the bags they use in the hospital, in case he gets sick again." Ren began planning for the rapidly-approaching separation, giving North as many details as possible for taking care of Justin when Ren couldn't be with him anymore. "And some alcohol pads since that seems to be working pretty well. Please make sure they let him have water; he really needs to be drinking. His meds are in the kitchen; he hasn't had any yet this morning, obviously, but he will need to —"

"You know I was planning on you coming with us, right?" North interrupted. Ren swallowed his next instruction.

"Really?" he double-checked; this was news to him. "But I thought they wouldn't let me?"

"I really think Justin needs an EMT escort. You have a uniform, don't you?"

"I ... sure, of course, I do," Ren stammered, rearranging his day.

"Go put it on," North said, pushing him toward his room.

22

CLOSED COURT

After more pushing and persuasion, North returned to the bathroom to help with Justin, and Ren hurried to his room to change, grateful he'd already cleared his schedule for the day, though he went back and forth on whether it was a good idea for him to go. On one hand, he was relieved to not be separated from Justin yet, but another part of him worried about what he might be forced to helplessly watch after the verdict was read. He pushed past those dark thoughts and the hanging sets of scrubs in his closet to access the uniform pieces he kept pressed and ready for his monthly ambulance runs and certain certification trainings.

EMTs in this area of Chicago wore sky blue button-downs tucked into navy pants so dark that they looked black from a short distance. Ren chose his long-sleeved version of the shirt, his last name stitched above the left breast pocket in navy thread, and his hard-earned blue first responder patch likewise secured to his sleeve over his left bicep. Another patch indicating his volunteer connection with the Chicago Police Department was sewn on his right.

Once he was dressed down to the heavy black boots, he quickly put together a kit, not in his monstrous medical bag, but in his backpack, which he first emptied for the occasion. He wanted his stats notebook, two pens, his phone and charger, the blood pressure cuff, thermometer, stethoscope, pulse oximeter, some emesis bags in case Denny's weird aromatherapy mind trick didn't work for long, plus all of his individually wrapped packages of alcohol pads to make sure it could work as long as possible.

Satisfied he'd taken all he'd need from his room, Ren went to continue packing in the kitchen, where he unexpectedly ran into Alek, who was staring blearily at their current bag of coffee, still pale from all the commotion this morning.

"Doing ok, Alek?" Ren asked him kindly, receiving a slack-jawed, disoriented stare in response.

"I need coffee," Alek droned, rubbing his hands over his face, looking Ren up and down between his fingers. "What's with the uniform?"

"Apparently, I am going with Justin and need to look official," Ren answered, securing Justin's medication and two unopened water bottles into the backpack. He wondered how long they'd be gone. Maybe he should pack more?

"Dude, no, to *court*?" Alek sputtered, sounding maybe a little too worried. Or surprised? Skeptical? Whatever the emotion, there was too much of it. "What about your classes? What about work?"

"Hey, chill," Ren tried to calm his friend. "I took care of all that already; they all know I'm not coming. You shouldn't be more worried about it than I am; what's going on?"

"I don't know, man; this is not really your area. And what if Justin ends up ... you know, not coming back ... you can't unsee stuff like that." Alek answered while messing around with the coffeemaker, though he was not doing a very good job of it. Normally Ren made the coffee since he was almost always up first. Alek didn't seem to even know how to do it. Either that or he'd finally hit his last nerve on this whole Justin situation, and it was rendering him incapable of functioning. You could only push roommates so far. Ren decided to intervene before Alek dumped in the grounds before he put in a filter.

"Knowing you," Alek continued, staring into the bag as though someone else were holding it. "You'd probably blame yourself. It would haunt you forever."

"Alek, bro, go sit down," Ren instructed since he was acting like a person in shock, or maybe he was just sleepy, but either way Ren elbowed him away from the counter and physically removed the scoop from his hand before he ruined their coffeemaker. This wasn't really a morning either of them could go without coffee. "I'll be fine; it's Justin I'm worried about. I can't let him go alone."

"Um, technically North's going with him, so he won't be alone," Alek pointed out, not leaving the kitchen to sit as Ren had told him, but his speech was speeding up slowly, not sounding quite so spacey and strange. "I think it's really that you can't stand waiting here at home with the rest of us to find out what's going to happen."

Ren tightened up slightly at Alek's uncomfortably accurate observation. No, he couldn't stand staying at the apartment while North took Justin away, where Ren may never see him again. And honestly, he didn't think Alek and Denny could stand him if he were to stay behind anyway. He knew he'd be a pacing, fidgety wreck until North could give them an outcome. It was for everyone's sake that he was tagging along, really.

"I'm going anyway," Ren decided, silently congratulating himself on sounding calm and resolved, steadily pouring water into the machine and starting it up.

"And I knew you were going to say that," Alek sighed, leaning tiredly against the sink, closing his eyes.

"Alek, seriously, you ok?" Ren pressed, getting truly worried about him.

"It's just been a little roller coaster-ish this weekend," Alek admitted, though he pulled himself together enough to stand straight, opening his eyes to consider Ren again. "You ever feel like you're living the moments where everything you were used to is going to just be, like, gone forever? Do you think you can notice things like that when they're happening, or do you think that's something you can only tell after the fact?"

"Is this astro or metaphysics?" Ren asked, slightly teasing though he knew exactly what Alek meant, but he was surprised Alek had noticed and could express it so easily. That tangled, slippery weirdness that was making the apartment feel like a place Ren had never been before — all the familiarity just suddenly vanished, a door closing, a shrinking, a change in the wind. Nothing had actually changed, but it felt like it was going to. He'd thought it was just his own life that was at worst falling apart and at best rearranging. Or maybe it *was* just Ren's life, and Alek's empathy was locked in high gear so he was feeling it too.

Whatever the case, Alek gave him a flat, unimpressed stare, and Ren was reminded that Alek hardly ever got up this early. He was never awakened by vomiting strangers in his bathroom. He'd never had to watch Ren and Denny argue to the point where she'd left in a huff. He'd never brought police officers into the apartment or stayed up all night packing snow into freezer bags while unknowingly listening to an unconscious person repeatedly apologize for murder. Alek was such a rock of support for Ren, over and over, that he'd grown too accustomed to him adapting endlessly to the variety of chaos that seemed to follow Justin.

"I think every moment changes something," Ren told him, not teasing him anymore. "Most of them are so small and insignificant you don't notice, but I guess every so often, choices make big enough changes that you can feel it. You know you're making an altering decision. Or that the next decision you make will mean you can't go back to where you were before."

"Definitely meta," Alek said, and Ren wasn't sure if he were teasing him. He also wasn't sure what life-altering choices Alek might be talking about. What there was in either of their lives that made him think it would never be the same again. He wondered if he should ask.

Ren started slicing one of Alek's remaining loaves of bread from

Saturday night, dropping two pieces into their toaster. North came into the living room briefly to retrieve the garment bag from the couch.

"Need any help?" Ren asked him, ready to assist though he wasn't sure if Alek were ok to be left alone yet either.

"Not yet," North said. "It's pretty slow going in there."

"Denny's thing still working?"

"So far so good," North answered, sounding relieved. "I'll call for you if we need you; finish what you're doing."

"Do you think," Alek began as North disappeared down the hall again. "Will it be like this all the time with Justin, or will things calm way down after today?"

"It'll settle," Ren immediately stated. Justin's whole life seemed to be tainted with intensity, but it was quickly moving away from them. A storm crossing to the other side of the lake. "One way or another," he murmured almost to himself. Though things would slow down, going back to the old, but different, normal — none of the future scenarios were appealing to Ren. They all seemed empty.

"That's good," Alek sighed, not understanding. "I mean, don't get me wrong, I wanted you to find someone, but I always figured it'd be some cute and quiet nursing student who would be cool with you making all the plans. Someone a little more predictable and ... less intense, you know?"

"I don't know," Ren played dumb, his voice cooling as he transferred the finished toast to plates and began frosting them with butter and Alek's homemade strawberry freezer jam. He added two more slices of bread to the toaster and checked the level on the coffee, then the time, which was maddeningly moving closer to ten. He wasn't even sure how far of a drive the courthouse was, but he figured they would have to leave very soon now.

"Except you do," Alek said, not allowing Ren to be vague. "And hey, it's not my place to judge or anything, but it would be nice if things could just settle around here for half a minute."

"I thought you said we should get ourselves an A, complete our

STAR set?" Ren poked, a defensive technique because he didn't want to get into it yet. Didn't want to tell Alek that he was right or wrong, didn't think he'd get very far convincing him. Probably because he didn't know which way to convince him. And it didn't matter.

"That was before I knew how *exhausting* it was going to be to have one," Alek returned.

"It'll be over soon, Alek; he's not staying," Ren said, handing him a plate full of toast. "I'm not even sure he's coming back here after today. He'll either be going with North or —" Ren stopped himself before saying it out loud.

"That's the other part I'm worried about," Alek said, as though glad it was Ren who had brought it up, though Ren wasn't sure what he'd done. "Since Justin doesn't seem to be the type to stay in one spot or with one person for very long ... are you going to be all right with that?"

"Dude, I've only known him for one weekend," Ren answered glibly, hoping his voice would hide how not ok he would be with that.

"Yeah, I know, but you just said yourself there are some choices you don't come back from."

Ren heard himself growl, though Alek didn't deserve it. He poured his friend a cup of coffee, adding sugar and cream the way he liked. "Some choices aren't ours to make," he told him, raising his own mug and heading toward the bathroom. Alek was too on point, reading Ren's emotions better than Ren could himself, as usual, and Ren wasn't ready to have a therapy session about this. "I'd stay here if I were you," Ren recommended as he walked away, more than ready to escape, even though he might be walking into something even worse than what he was leaving. "And sit down."

The bathroom remained crowded when Ren returned to it. Justin was perched wearily on the edge of the bathtub now with his shirt off, but no other progress had been made into getting him into the suit. Denny had kept Ren's wet washcloth on the back of his neck, but Justin was holding the alcohol bottle himself now. North kept anxiously checking his watch while Denny seemed to be coaxing Justin into taking something she had in her hand.

"Wait a second," Ren paused them as he entered the scene. "What is that, Denny?"

"Something you wouldn't have even known about if you'd finished your coffee in the kitchen and waited two more minutes," she said tersely. He pushed into her with a glare, demanding an answer. Medications, though plentiful, didn't get dispensed lightly around here. "But it's Xanax if you must know."

"Xanax?" Ren was surprised. Is that what she'd gone out to get this morning? But where? "What's the dosage?"

"Point five milligrams," Denny answered. "It'll get him through the day, I figure. Or at least the next four hours."

"But where did you get it?" Ren asked, worried about the answer. Denny rolled her eyes.

"This is why I was rushing you," she said to Justin before returning to Ren's question. "It's not mine, it's not expired, and I didn't steal it, but that's all you need to know." Ren wasn't sure he could accept that as an answer, though he also didn't think he could approve of any method of acquisition. What did it mean that Denny knew exactly how to get her hands on a dose of Xanax within thirty minutes before nine am on a Monday morning?

"Is it safe?" North asked, watching the exchange, and Ren thought about that. Went through what he could remember about the effects, and side effects, of that particular drug and also what it might do when taken with Justin's other, legally prescribed, medication. Then he thought of all Justin might have to do today starting with just getting him into the car and realized that if the pill Denny held in her hand could ease any of that for him, Ren would be more grateful for it than anything else.

"Yes," Ren relented, though his jaw wouldn't unclench very well for him to say it. "But we're not done talking about this," he warned Denny, wanting to know what sort of campus black market existed for this type of thing and how she'd found out about it. "Go ahead and take it, Justin, if you think you can keep it down."

For the first time since Ren had come back, Justin lifted his head to look at him, reacting to Ren speaking to him specifically. He peeled his eyes off the floor in slow motion, as though he were already drugged, but he did a much faster double take when he saw Ren in the doorway, then checked him up and down much like he'd done the very first time Ren had met him in his room — though without the hostility. It made Ren want to fiddle with his uniform buttons to make sure they were done up correctly.

"Holy shit," Justin muttered, averting his gaze, inhaling deeply from the alcohol bottle. Ren didn't know what to make of that, but it made Denny smile.

"Cleans up nice, doesn't he?" she said as she handed over the small white pill and reached backward toward the sink for Justin's Gatorade cup. Justin had to gag the pill down, keeping his hand over his mouth and his eyes tightly closed in concentration.

"Your turn to get dressed now, Justin," North instructed gently, coming closer to assist. "Sorry, but we only have a few more minutes. We'll have to drive slow as it is; the roads aren't great today."

"Could you check on Alek for me?" Ren asked Denny, partly because he knew Justin wouldn't want her to watch him getting dressed. "Make sure he's eating and not still staring at nothing in the kitchen?"

"When did I become a physician's assistant?" Denny quipped, though she gently patted Justin on the shoulder as she made her way out of the room, not minding the task Ren had given her in the least, and they both knew it. Ren switched out the alcohol bottle clenched tight in Justin's hand for a sterile wipe to make it easier to do things like put arms in sleeves and to test the effectiveness of the smaller wipe against the more concentrated solution in the container. North and Ren teamed up practically silently to get Justin dressed, with Justin doing his best to not be dead weight between them. Ren noticed that he could almost stand on his own power today, thank you iron infusion, though did not have the balance to put on pants yet. Throughout the process of dressing, Justin's body loosened, his fingers relaxing, the tightness leaving his shoulders as the quick-acting Xanax shut down the panic in his brain. He raised his eyes to Ren, watching him brazenly as North knelt in front of him to knot the tie, something Ren had wanted to witness, but found himself instead staring back at Justin.

He was used to it now, how Justin stared at things, hard and unflinching. When Denny stared at Ren like this, they could communicate. But Justin was closed. Ren could see pain and desperation, though it dulled almost as he watched due to the drug. He could see Justin hadn't been joking when he'd asked Ren to let him die, that he wished so hard that he didn't have to go do this terribly hard thing that was his only reward for trying to do something good. And then there was something mysterious, like the color, emotions plainly visible but untranslatable for Ren.

"Aren't you late for class?" Justin finally asked as North finished the tie but left it hanging loose around Justin's neck, presumably waiting until the last minute to discomfort Justin in any way by tightening it.

"I'm not going to classes today," Ren confessed, surprising himself by how embarrassed he was about admitting it. All the work that had brought him to this campus to allow him the privilege of attending classes, even semi-stupid ones like their English 101, and he was wasting it. "Or work. I'm taking the whole day off."

"Ren is coming with us," North answered for him. Justin's eyes widened, his chin coming up in pride even as his expression softened into relief, and any guilt Ren felt about skipping his classes and calling in sick to work disappeared. This was undoubtedly the best use of his time.

Justin didn't say thanks in words, but his whole body communicated gratitude. North took hold of his arm and helped him stand up, allowing Ren to study the effect of Justin in a suit, though it fit him rather poorly. It was too loose, for starters, as though someone had purchased it for him with the idea that he would grow into it. It made him look small and extremely vulnerable. He was gaining a little color into his face, the fever flush was back now the Xanax was taming the nausea, but Justin still had deep shadows under his eyes, which were also off, too bright.

"Come here," Ren begged more than directed, suddenly wanting to take Justin from North, wanting his weight on his arm, his heat against his side. Still here. Still with him. North gave Ren a look of surprised compassion, but he did transfer Justin to his arms.

"I'll go get the car," North offered once he was satisfied that Justin only needed one of them to help him walk this morning.

"Next time we get dressed up," Ren said lightly, trying to hide how deep and hard his emotions were cutting into him. "Let's make sure we're going to a better party." Justin leaned heavily, used to walking next to him this way now, his hand across Ren's back, holding to his shoulder right above the patch. Ren's arm draped across the back of Justin's waist, though with the suit he found it impossible to tuck his thumb through Justin's belt loop. He settled for grabbing onto the fabric of his pocket.

"Deal," Justin panted as they made their way through the narrow hallway and into the living room. Denny helpfully brought Ren his backpack, which he slipped over the shoulder that Justin wasn't holding on to. Alek looked up from the table, his face crashing into compassion immediately on seeing Justin.

"Thank you," Justin paused to say to them. Ren held on to him tighter, sensing a sudden weakness in him, as though he'd buckle any second from either strain or sentiment.

"We'll be back," Ren heard himself promise.

"Dinner's at six," Alek said. "Don't be late."

"We won't," Ren agreed solemnly and began walking slowly away from them. Out the door, down the hall, into the elevator.

North met them at the door, giving Ren back his keycard and taking up guard on Justin's opposite side. Which was good as the cold always beat into Justin the hardest, and he reacted to it as though he'd been punched in the stomach. Ren eased him into the backseat and hurried in next to him so he could secure them into the warmth of the car.

Without invitation, Justin immediately put his head down on Ren's thigh, breathing hard after all the movement, the alcohol-drenched wipe held tight against his face. North looked over his shoulder to check on them, his eyes worried and hopeful at the same time, before he pulled the car away from Stony Island and into a world that was covered in snow, hard edges, and incorrect assumptions.

Ren hadn't been paying much attention outside of the apartment, there hadn't been much reason, but now that North was taking them off campus, Ren found himself staring. They quickly were past Hyde Park and the shopping center where Ren sometimes went with Alek. North was driving them north along Lake Shore Drive, and Ren watched the sunlight on the water intently. It didn't compare to the beaches he'd grown up on. It made Ren cold just to look at it. The shoreline was frozen over, giving way to broken gashes of icy waves, and then further out was the black-ish choppiness that refused to reflect the sun's brightness properly.

And it was bright. Not snowing for the moment, and the blue of the sky seemed to promise that the storm, at least this one, was over. Not that it hadn't left the city anything to remember it by. The plows were still out, doing their best to clear the side streets. Along the lake's path, there were hardly any joggers or dog walkers, and those who had decided to brave the outdoors did so in layers of scarves, ponchos, and thick hats. And while North never faltered in his perfect control of his vehicle, Ren could see the roads were covered in patches of ice.

All the while they drove, Ren stared at the water that wasn't at all like the ocean and tried to think of something comforting to say to Justin. He came up short each time; nothing seemed appropriate. Every few seconds, Ren was aware of North's soft black eyes glancing at them in the mirror.

"So, Ren?" North began, apparently deciding that since neither of them could think of anything to say to Justin, the next best thing would be to talk to each other. "You and your friends are quite the talented group. How did you all come to know each other?"

"I got lucky," Ren answered without hesitation. "Alek and I were assigned to the same apartment."

"Oh, so it wasn't your decision. Good thing you ended up getting along so well."

"Alek gets along with everyone," Ren pointed out. "Well, no, I guess that's not quite true. He's friendly to just about everyone, but if he ever doesn't like someone, you don't ask why, you just keep away from them. But yeah, he and I synched up quick; it felt like we'd been friends for a long time before we met. It's hard not to like someone when you walk into an apartment, fresh from customs at the airport and scared to death, and the first thing you see is a huge smile and a cup of chocolate. I'm just glad he puts up with me."

Justin squeezed his knee at that comment.

"And your other roommate? Denny? Is that her name?"

"No." Ren smiled, watching as the lake disappeared when North pulled onto the Stephenson Expressway and started heading west. "And Alek's name isn't Alek either, but honestly, I think I've forgotten Alek's actual name. It's long and has, like, two apostrophes in it. But Denny's real name is Kayden, and she's a friend, not a roommate. Alek started bringing her home sometimes to work on physics stuff and robotics. Then the sometimes turned into all the time, and now it's weird when she's not there."

"Are they together?" North asked, not to be nosy, but in an attempt to continue to fill the oppressive silence of the drive. Ren tried to laugh.

"If you ask them, no, but if you asked literally any other person who has seen them together for longer than five minutes, it's a definite yes," Ren said, watching the businesses along the streets pass, reading the signs, missing the lake. It might have been disappointing, but at least it was familiar.

"What about you?" North continued. "Are you with anyone?"

Ren's soul snapped shut like blinds being pulled over a window. Justin tightened against his leg, and his mouth felt dry. He knew North was still just trying to make conversation, to keep Justin's thoughts off where they were going, but this innocent question seemed too personal, somehow invasive.

"No," Ren answered, staring intently out the window, the light extinguished from his voice, Justin's fevered body heavy and twitching on his lap. "I don't have time for that kind of thing." He offered the statement as an excuse as to why he was alone, effectively killing the mood and allowing the cold to rush back into the car. North gave him a quick, repentant look through the mirror, and Ren could tell he was sorry he'd asked, that he hadn't meant for it to be a touchy subject.

"You had a date on Friday," Justin offered helpfully, his voice quiet and breathy from Ren's knees. He shifted against the seat, twisting off Ren's lap.

"Yeah, that's true," Ren admitted, watching Justin with increasing concern.

"That you canceled because of me," Justin went on, ashamed of costing Ren his social life even though Ren had already tried to absolve him from any guilt about that.

"Don't be sorry about that because I'm not," Ren told him. "It would have been our first date, and I probably would have made a fool of myself. She's way out of my league, so maybe it's better to not know how it would have gone."

"You sound like you're never going to see her again," North pointed out, his tone careful now. "Couldn't you reschedule?"

"I'm not sure," Ren answered, wishing they could talk about something else. "It was kind of a miracle I got the first one, and she ... well, to say she was disappointed would be an understatement. She's not the sort of girl you cancel a date with and then get another chance. Justin, what's going on with you? Need us to stop for a minute?"

Because Justin had not stopped fidgeting ever since their discussion had centered around Ren's romantic endeavors. He'd pulled his legs up on to the seat, tucking into a smaller ball, then tried to stretch in the tight space, and now he was trying to sit up, but not straight, in obvious distress.

"Are you feeling sick?" Ren asked, reaching for his backpack so he could retrieve one of the blue emesis bags in case North couldn't get stopped in time. There wasn't a good place to pull off the expressway, and even if they'd been on a side street, the piles of snow everywhere blocked most of the parking.

"Justin?" North questioned from the front, unable to give them his full attention as he frantically searched for somewhere he could stop.

"It's not that," Justin answered, and Ren could see now that he was sitting up that he was more flushed than pale. He lifted the saddest puppy eyes to Ren, turning to him again in search of relief. "It's my back," he admitted. "It feels like it's going to snap in half."

"Oh!" Ren exclaimed, relieved despite the circumstances. "Jeez, that's bad timing. You can't ever catch a break, can you?"

"It means something?" North asked, his driving calming again.

"It's the last stage of this version of the flu," Ren answered them both, though he was looking directly at Justin, his face and voice both calm. "It hurts like hell, but it means the fever will break soon." He reached for Justin, helping him turn on the seat, helping him curl tight against Ren's hip and chest, as though cradling an infant. The only position of comfort he'd found was consistent with each patient. At least for a while, but with this kind of unrelenting pain, even ten minutes was a blessing. With one arm he reached around Justin, holding him close and with his other, he slipped under Justin's suit coat and untucked his shirt, palming the place on Justin's lower back where he knew it would be the most painful, knowing from past experience that there wasn't much that would soothe this, but the heat from a hand would do at least something. Justin whimpered, resting his head trustingly against Ren's chest.

"How soon?" Justin grunted with his teeth clenched.

"I shouldn't have said soon," Ren backtracked. "We're talking several hours. In your case, it could be more than twelve." Another whimper. Ren pulled him as close as possible in the strange position in the backseat. *He just has to sit there*, North had said. Except just sitting had now become excruciating for Justin. "It doesn't feel like it, I know, but it means you're getting better." Justin twisted to give him an uncertain look, and Ren didn't blame him.

All too soon, North was pulling off California Ave, and Ren was looking up at a concrete block of a building with eight intimidating columns stretched evenly across its face. The courthouse even looked like it was covered in prison bars, all the windows slit with stone. Ren involuntarily swallowed.

"Ok, you two," North instructed. "I'm dropping you off here because the parking lot is up past 26th Street. There's a reception area in the front entrance, just past the metal detectors. Wait for me there."

"Right," Ren whispered, wishing his voice sounded stronger for Justin's sake. "Here, Justin, before we go in." Justin twisted agonizingly from his lap as Ren reached for his bag again, pulling out an emesis bag, more alcohol wipes, and his most comfortable, reusable black face mask. He took it upon himself to stuff the bag and wipes into the inside pocket of the suit jacket and then tucked the loops of the mask over Justin's ears, slipping his fingers around the edges to adjust the fit. He didn't want Justin to have to wear it, but he was likely still contagious, and they were entering a public place.

Then with his bag on one shoulder and Justin clinging to the other, Ren steeled himself and helped Justin out of the car. Justin walked hunched at his side with an almost limp from the pain in his back, from the debilitating weakness of the past few days, with the dread of what was waiting for him that the Xanax could dull but not fully remove. Together, they staggered up the three steps and across the icy entryway to the glass front doors, covered in official postings and notices with the words George N. Leighton Criminal Court Building arched over the two central entrances.

As North had warned, each entrance had its own metal detector and a security officer in full uniform to man them. Ren prepared himself for a rough procedure, but the entrance guards were amazingly accommodating. They expectantly stopped them to ask for names and what business brought them to court, but they quickly noticed that Justin needed extra help. Within minutes, someone had brought a wheelchair, and they gently patted Justin down. They inspected the contents of his pockets but replaced everything when none of it was of particular concern, speaking to him with calm reassurance through the whole thing.

Ren had a slightly harder time — he was covered in gear. He had to remove his belt. They had him take off the black boots, and the contents of his backpack was carefully scrutinized. Ren suspected they were going to confiscate the water bottles and the peanut butter and jelly sandwiches Alek had apparently packed in secret. But in the end, they allowed everything through once Ren had shown them his ID and his volunteer EMT card.

Justin laughed uneasily as Ren came away, pushing the chair with one hand and carrying his boots with the other toward the waiting area North had mentioned.

"You'd think *you* were the criminal," Justin told him as he sat uncomfortably in the chair watching Ren retie his laces.

"That was actually a lot better than I thought it was going to be," Ren returned, finishing up and looking toward the doors for North. "How are you doing?"

"Just don't ask."

Ren reached over to pat Justin's knee, appreciating the wheelchair at the same time he hated how it was keeping him so distant. Justin put his hand over Ren's, needing the contact, unable to sit upright. They sat silently together this way for several more minutes, waiting. There weren't many people in this area of the courthouse, but the ones who did move past them did so with nervous glances at

Justin, who bowed his head so he wouldn't see how everyone was avoiding him. Ren hated them for it but understood. Justin looked terrible, part plague victim and part Hannibal Lecter.

"There's North," Ren told him comfortingly as he spotted the entirely black suit coming past the brightness of the doors. There was expectedly an issue with the metal detectors and North's prosthetic. He had to remove his suit coat and roll back his sleeve so he could be examined, though he took it all with the familiar grace of someone who is asked to do this sort of thing all the time.

He spotted them quickly after he was cleared to enter, and Ren watched him stare at Justin as he crossed the polished floor to where they waited. Without a bit of a pause, he went down to one knee in front of the wheelchair to make eye contact with his adopted son, reaching up to place a hand at the back of Justin's neck. He wisely did not ask Justin how he was doing, taking all his answers from just studying him this way.

"We're on the fourth floor," North told them, standing to take custody of Justin's wheelchair, pushing it with certainty towards the elevators. Justin shrank into the seat, curling miserably to one side, ashamed and terrified. Ren flanked the chair, keeping an eye on Justin even as he took in the building.

For some reason, he'd expected it to be covered in dark wood paneling, but it was much more modern than that. The walls were painted a light dove gray, the tile almost the same color as the hospital. Instead of wood trim, there was galvanized metal, and it seemed as though all of the doors, at least on the main level, were made of glass. The outside of the courthouse looked as old as the city itself, but the inside had been updated.

The fourth floor was nearly identical to the first, though the doors up here were much more solid, because up here was where the secrets were. Where trials happened. Pictures of past judges, administrators, and donors lined the walls at regular intervals, along with several pictures of what Chicago looked like when this place had been built. The hallway eventually transitioned to another waiting area, but Ren knew they were close because he could hear Kelly long before they got there.

She didn't see them; her entire focus was on her phone as she paced in a frenzy along the far wall. They all stopped just a few steps away from blocking the hallway, though Ren was the only one who did so in shock and not out of respect for the privacy of her conversation. However, at her volume level there was nothing private about it.

"Justin, that's your lawyer?" Ren gasped the question.

"Yeah," Justin confirmed, not near as emotional, but he'd spent more time with her and had built up some immunity to her presence.

"Dude, you have nothing to worry about," Ren breathed, watching Kelly. What Justin had mentioned was true; she was taller than Ren, but not by very much. Still, she seemed taller because she was indeed an extreme kind of thin. But there was no weakness to her figure; she was as strong as a slim steel rod, and as she paced there in her blood red heels, Ren had an abrupt revelation as to what people meant when they were said to be dressed *sharp*.

Kelly wore a pale gray pantsuit with claret pinstripes that had been pressed immaculately smooth and fit her so perfectly there was no way it had not been made for her. As she cut an angry turn, he got a glimpse of a rather stunning pendant of an eclipsing moon on a thick silver chain. Her hair was dyed — again the deep red color she seemed to favor, and cut short, the kind of style that seemed post-apocalyptic in its chaos. She'd gelled it so it stood out from her face in wavy sorts of spikes that would have looked more goth than professional on anyone other than her, but which cooperated well with the sharp features of her face and gave a vampiric, ageless, paleness to her skin tone.

"I don't care about the snow," she was yelling into the phone. "We all live here; we all know about the snow! I got here early — my client is here from the fucking hospital, so bad roads are hardly an excuse, Phillip. Everyone's here, so you get your asses down here too. Now!"

So it seemed she had noticed them after all, though she'd made no acknowledgement until after she hung up, looking unsatisfied that all she could do was click a button instead of slamming a receiver into a wall.

"The Hunts are having trouble getting through the snow," Kelly sneered distastefully in greeting as she stalked the waiting area toward them. "They would like to postpone until this afternoon so the plows have more time to clear things." She had her lips curled in a predatory way, and she moved with sinister intensity. God, she was glorious. Ren felt his heart speed up, amazed that he could be both terrified and partially aroused at the same time.

Like North, Kelly went immediately to her knees in front of Justin, though she did not soften. If anything, she tensed at the sight of him, her fury almost visibly steaming off her clothes. From his position behind Justin, Ren could now see that Kelly had gray eyes that were just like the rest of her — sharp.

"Oh my God, Kit, look at you," she exclaimed, a wild, affectionate worry in the words, reaching out to touch him, cupping her hands around each of Justin's elbows. "I'll make them hurry, ok?"

Justin nodded, and Kelly pulled a handkerchief from her sleeve to efficiently wipe Justin's eyes for him. Her motions were sure, but as Ren studied her closely — honestly he couldn't keep his eyes off her — he could tell she was uneasy with this. Nurturing was not her strong suit, and she would much rather cage-fight someone than deal with anything emotional.

"Why the hell are you muzzled like a dog?" Kelly asked fiercely, taking it upon herself to start removing the black mask, and Ren moved before he thought about it, putting a hand around her wrist to stop her. And though he knew she was moving slowly, her attention snapped onto him with a ferocity that made it seem far too quick and hard. Ren found he could no longer speak.

"Justin's still contagious," North spoke up, not seeming intimidated in the least by Kelly's presence. "We're trying to minimize the risk."

"Damn the risk," she said to North. "I hope he infects everyone in that room, and they'd deserve it for forcing him into this freak show."

"It's ok, Kelly," Justin's words were hard to hear, but they were all close enough that he was understandable. "The mask is to protect you. You're the one who will be closest to me in there, and I really don't want anyone to catch this, least of all you."

"That's sweet, Kit, but I don't mind if you want to take it off. You look so miserable."

"Taking the mask off isn't going to help with that," Justin informed her, and Ren watched her jaw clench as she realized Justin was suffering and there was absolutely nothing she could do, no one she could fight, that would make it any better for him. The tension in her arm changed, causing Ren to release her — intimidated by what she might do. She stood with a controlled slow elegance that trembled into Ren's stomach. Holy shit, this woman was scary.

"I'm going to rip their throats out," she promised with a cruel smile, and Ren swore that her canines were longer than normal. She looked like she actually might have fangs. "You see if I don't. If they don't let you off today, I'm going to descend on them with so many appeals and mistrial accusations it will rival the plagues of Egypt."

Ren felt an unhinged giggling threatening to burst out of him, so he bit his tongue hard to prevent it, clinging to Justin's shoulder. He'd heard violence as a form of affection before, from Denny, but she was nowhere near Kelly's level. When Denny said she would murder you, it was cute. When Kelly said the same thing, it was terrifying.

"So, what are the chances of this being postponed?" North cut in with the most practical of questions. Ren would like that answered too. Would it mean they could take Justin home and wait another day? Another week? He wasn't sure if that would be a good thing to have this continue to hang over Justin that long. On the other hand, he wouldn't mind if it could be pushed back until the snow completely melted.

"Zero," Kelly assured. "If the Hunts can't make it, we'll proceed without them. Just because they want to watch doesn't mean their presence is required. All the main cast is accounted for." She turned her harsh gaze onto Ren again. "Plus an unexpected extra. Elias, who is this? I told you the courtroom is closed. It was already a hassle to get you allowed inside."

Ren did his best to stand straight and look professional, like he had every reason to be here, though he was so far out of his element.

"This is Lorenzo Cordero," North made the simplest of introductions. "He's an EMT from the hospital, training under the doctor who treated Justin. And if I get to pick which one of us goes in, it will be him over me. Though I thought if anyone could get us both in, it'd be you."

Kelly smiled again, this time sly, her eyes narrowing at North, knowing exactly what he was trying to do in order to get something from her. However, Ren could see North had played his hand correctly. He'd touched something in Kelly by challenging her, though she wasn't ready to give in just yet. Instead, she walked around Justin, staring hard at Ren, who didn't have to look up very often to meet someone's gaze and found it extremely intimidating. Kelly smelled like very fancy soap and whiskey, a mixture that was intoxicatingly attractive to Ren, and he felt that if this woman had only come this close to strangle him, he'd likely submit without hesitation.

"The doctor, you say," Kelly spoke low, the growl still there. "And is this the EMT who helped her prepare the testimonial in Kit's file?"

"That's right," North confirmed, not sounding very sure all of a sudden. As though they'd discussed that piece of paper at length last night in a not-so-positive way.

"In that case, he's waiting for us right here," Kelly decided in an unpredictable flash. And Ren suddenly found he could speak after all.

"What?" he said, confused. "Why?"

"Because you're the sort of person who causes trouble," she told him dangerously. "The kind who doesn't understand how things should be handled via proper channels, who isn't going to sit still and keep his mouth shut. And that's the last thing I need when we're in there. What were you thinking, taking confidential evidence from a closed court case and displaying it in the ER? Asking for unsanctioned medical testimony? I shredded it."

"You ... shredded it?" Ren choked out. All that hard work, all he'd asked of Dr. Delacroix, all for nothing.

"You're welcome," she hissed.

"Kelly, please," Justin interrupted, grabbing on to Ren's arm and using it to get himself out of the wheelchair, in preparation to stand between them. But the pain in his back was too much for him to stand straight, or on his own. He winced, folding alarmingly forward, and Ren braced him while Kelly again took hold of his elbows, scrutinizing the situation. North hurried to Justin's other side to help keep him from falling, and he sagged between them all, but stared strong at Kelly. "We didn't know; he was just trying to help me."

"You of all people should know that intent doesn't always justify the crime," Kelly said, as if unable to yield on any point.

"Please, Kelly," Justin begged a second time, but for a different thing. "He's my friend."

"Please, yourself," Kelly shot back. "Enough of this; Kit, sit down."

As North and Ren helped Justin return to the wheelchair, Kelly sighed, watching Justin's pain as though it belonged to her, then turned her burning gaze back to Ren. "If I do this," she began her conditions. "You sit in the back and do not move or speak. You call absolutely no attention to yourself; do you understand me?"

Ren's instinct was to return with a "*Sí, Doña,*" since she was so formidable, but he switched it to a simple, "Yes, ma'am," that didn't seem to pacify her in the least.

"No guarantees either," she gave a final caveat. "But I'll see what I can do. In the meantime, wait here."

23
BREAKING POINT

The moment Kelly's powerful form disappeared down a different hallway, Ren's brain suddenly supplied him with everything he should have said to her. *Too late*, he internally growled at himself, hating how it was always like that. His spirit retreated, sulking, coiling around one of the last things Kelly said that Ren couldn't shake.

"She shredded it," he whispered to himself, still staring after her, still paralyzed in the aftermath of her presence. But saying those words out loud clicked his neurons functional again, and he whirled on North. "She *shredded* it?" he repeated, this time with high-pitched accusation.

"Ren?" Justin questioned, still tapped into Ren's emotions. Meanwhile, North raised his hands in good-natured defense.

"I'm sorry, Ren," he apologized immediately. "I know how hard you worked on it, but it can't be used, and it's better if no one knows it ever existed. I was certainly going to tell you, though not quite like that. I should have never let you see what was in the file to begin with; she's right, it was confidential."

And not only had all that work been for nothing, but now the fact that he'd even tried had biased Kelly against allowing Ren into the courtroom. Ren folded his arms, forcing himself to stand still for Justin's sake, though he wanted to storm after Kelly. Wanted to start throwing chairs.

"If it helps at all," North continued, but Ren had very little hope of anything he was about to say being actually helpful. "Ms. Kelly did say it was an elegant and impressive argument." Ren exhaled so hard through his nose it came out as an angry snort. No, that did not help. At least, he didn't want it to help.

"It wasn't homework; I don't need a grade," Ren snapped, turning away, hoping any blush on his face would be read as anger and nothing more.

"She also said," North went on, voice slower as though he were weighing his words carefully. "Well, she mentioned that should we need to go any farther with this than today, she'd be interested in contacting Dr. Delacroix to ask for her analysis in a more official capacity. However," here North looked very pointedly at Justin, "no one thinks that will be necessary."

Ren found himself almost overpowered with the need to move, quickly and furiously, though he knew Justin hated it when he did things like that. It was probably driving Justin crazy enough already with Ren standing here drumming his fingers against his arms, eyes scanning over the room, counting the chairs instead of throwing them to try and get a hold on himself. Would Kelly even try to get him in at this point? It'd be so easy for her to return and shrug and pretend she'd done her best.

And where did she get off insinuating that he was a person who caused trouble? She was the one who yelled obscenities into phones and threatened death for minor infractions, terror clinging to her like a perfume. And *he* was the one she was worried about in the court-room? She was worried that *he* wasn't going to be able to control himself? She'd seen him for less than five minutes; they'd barely spoken to each other, and he'd been nothing but the picture of calm cooperation. Ren heard himself make that furious exhale again at the sheer hypocrisy of it.

"Ren, hey," Justin was calling him, making him shake his hands loose, getting ready to refocus. Justin reached out to him, his eyes enormous over the mask, his other hand pressed against his chest. "Why don't you take my blood pressure or something?" Ren blinked, confused at the odd request. "You know, before we have to do something about yours."

Ren's lips jerked upward in a worried smirk, not wanting to admit how witty that comment had been, nor how much he'd needed it.

"I suppose you think you're funny," Ren responded, pulling all the emotion out of his voice. He took a step toward Justin and took hold of his hand for no other reason than he wanted to touch him, noticing the tremor still shuddering down his arm. Then Ren too went to his knees on the floor in front of the wheelchair. Justin might have been joking, but it did seem that now would be the perfect time to get some stats and finally have Justin take his heart medication. "But that is a good idea."

"Wait, you actually brought — of course you did," Justin sighed as Ren pulled the blood pressure cuff free of his backpack. Justin winced as he moved, his eyes closing involuntarily against the deep ache in his lower back, but he put his arm forward so Ren could strap the cuff to it. Ren didn't comment as he watched Justin deal with the pain. He pulled his stethoscope out instead, pushing himself into what he knew best. It wasn't exactly helpful, but it was comforting. For him, at least. Meanwhile, North pulled up one of the chairs, sitting close to them and watching.

"Why is it whenever I get mad, *your* heart is the one that acts up?" Ren asked quietly as he listened to Justin's pulse via the stethoscope.

Justin appeared startled at the question, stiffening in the chair enough that North put a hand on his arm. Ren listened to his heart shudder.

"I ... don't know?" Justin answered hesitantly. "Should I know?"

"No," Ren assured, concerned. "Don't look so scared; I'm messing with you." He'd thought they were both using humor as defense today, but judging from Justin's reaction to what he'd just said, apparently, he'd been wrong. "Your heart is definitely getting better. It's still jumpy, though not as extreme as it was, but to keep it tamed down, let's get some medicine into you. Here," Ren handed Justin a water bottle he'd opened for him and his first dose of Tenormin for the day. "We'll wait on the iron, but do you think you can keep this down for now?"

Justin nodded, accepted everything Ren gave him, and dutifully did as he was told. He seemed to swallow much easier than the last time Ren had watched him take a pill, so he pulled one of Alek's sandwiches out too on the off chance he could get Justin to eat.

"No," Justin protested before Ren had even mentioned taking a bite.

"You sure?" Ren encouraged, not wanting to push too hard, but who knew how long they were going to be stuck here today. This might be Justin's only chance for calories for hours. "Alek made it."

Justin stared at him, unimpressed, and Ren knew why. There wasn't a whole lot that could be done with a simple peanut butter and jelly sandwich.

"And by made it, I mean the bread and the jam, and I think he might have grown the strawberries himself — he's got a little plant on the counter next to all the herbs. This isn't just a sandwich anymore. This? This is —"

"Would you shut up?" Justin blurted, and for a second Ren thought he had indeed pushed too hard, but then he saw Justin's open hand. He smiled in relieved triumph and passed over the sandwich, watching as Justin tore it in two heavily unequal halves. "Here." Justin gave back the much bigger piece. "Since you probably didn't have breakfast either."

Ren pulled the second sandwich from the bag to offer to North, who declined with a polite shake of his head. Ren ate only so Justin didn't have to eat alone. Justin took extremely slow and small bites, pulling them from the sandwich with his fingers instead of his teeth. And all throughout, he shifted in continuous and increasing discomfort until he had to give up on the sandwich, rewrapping it so his hands would be free to shift him from the wheelchair, heading for the floor.

"Justin?" Ren checked him, preparing to catch him if necessary.

"I can't sit like that anymore," Justin explained, joining Ren on his knees, trying to find some relief for the cramping ache in his back. Ren knew it was futile. Since the cause of the pain wasn't due to position or muscle strain, there wasn't really a good way to move or sit that would improve it. But Justin still curled over, again resting his head against Ren's knee, not knowing any of that, trying to find some position of comfort. Ren put his hand on Justin's back, hoping the heat would help.

"Where did Kelly go?" Ren murmured, wondering why she'd been gone so long when she seemed to be made of rush and movement. He wasn't certain what time it was; the lack of clocks in this space seemed to be a deliberate choice to keep those waiting disoriented and frustrated. But Ren was certain it had to be past ten.

The irony of Ren's impatience wasn't lost on him. He'd wanted to push this back as long as possible, but now that they were actually in the building and ready, he wanted to get it over with immediately. What was taking everyone so long? What had to get done and finished for them to sit in a room and hear a verdict being read? Not that he knew much about it, but it seemed a simple enough thing. Something that could be done and dusted in half an hour.

Ren knelt on the floor with his hands pushed against Justin's back long enough that his own back was starting to ache from maintaining the position. He forced himself not to shift and give Justin any reason to think he had to move. In the end, it wasn't his own discomfort that forced him to his feet. It was Justin's.

Justin had started the gasped-loop breathing again, holding his breath as if that complete stillness would do something, twitching and trembling until Ren just couldn't take it anymore. This was stupid; if no one was coming back, then why didn't they just walk out?

"Ren?" Justin croaked, shuddering as Ren removed his hands from him to stand up. "What?"

"Breathe deeper, Justin; I'm going to find Kelly," Ren decided affirmatively. "It's crazy the way they're treating you. They were so insistent you be here on time and now they're going to ignore you? Not on my watch."

"Ren, stay here," North intervened.

"Relax," Ren assured, or maybe warned; he didn't want to upset Justin. "I'm just —"

"Intending on proving my point, *Pana*?"

Ren's spine straightened without any prompting from his consciousness, hating how he couldn't ever feel just one sensation at a time when it came to Kelly. This particular emotional cocktail was one part guilt that she'd caught him doing exactly what she'd told him not to do, one part fury for making them wait so long he'd thought it necessary to defy her, and one part impressed confusion as to how she'd correctly addressed him in Dominican slang. The one thing he wasn't feeling this time around was frightened or intimidated. Watching Justin suffer had removed both of those.

"What point?" he challenged her with his back still turned. "What about the part where you said you were going to hurry? What happened to that?"

"Ren," North warned quietly as he helped Justin into the wheelchair.

"I know it's not your fault," Ren backtracked, but only slightly, finally shifting to turn and face her. "But waiting around like this isn't good for him, so what the hell is taking so long?"

Kelly met his gaze with an intense calmness that almost buckled Ren's resolve, almost made him apologize for his outburst, but then he saw she wasn't alone. There was a man. He stood a few paces back, watching the proceedings with a critical purse to his lips. He wore a tan suit with a blue paisley tie, and he stood with impatience in the tilt of his hips and in the hand that he lifted to adjust his glasses. The immediate disgust that flooded Ren just from looking at him kept him standing straight against them both, a demand for an answer in the strength of his posture. Kelly's head tipped at Ren as he let the silence draw out, a tiny smile just touching her mouth — not quite the reaction Ren had expected for his behavior.

"Ok, I see why you like him now, Kit," Kelly said to Justin, who was pulling his mask securely in place. "And to answer your question, we're waiting for the judge now as well as the Hunts. This storm has pushed more sessions back than just ours. However, now that Mr. Rozensweig has finally arrived, he's insisting it's time for Kit to come with us."

Ren glanced backward at Justin, meeting his eyes for a moment. There was a drugged calmness to them, a weariness that was beyond emotion, as though Justin was too tired for even fear at this point.

"Tamsyn, what is this?" the man, the Hunts' lawyer, said to Kelly, his voice higher than Ren expected considering the darkness of his expression. It made Ren dislike him even more. Ren took a deep breath to tell him off, forgetting that he didn't really have to do that himself seeing as Kelly was standing with them and was much more capable.

"I've already explained, Phillip," Kelly responded coldly, deciding to also address him by his first name in return for him using hers. "He's been in the hospital all weekend and still needs medical attention. I told you there was an EMT assigned in case of an emergency."

"Who? This kid?" Phillip snorted, gesturing vaguely at Ren, who felt his chin jerk upwards. He was getting tired of being dismissed this way because of his age and appearance. "Looks more like he's going trick-or-treating to me; Tamsyn, you could have tried harder."

"I *am* an EMT," Ren protested forcefully, but Kelly glared him into silence.

"If you say so," Phillip gave in condescendingly. "But you can do your job from here. We'll know where to find you if we need you."

There was so much wrong with that Ren didn't know where to start.

"I recommend keeping them together," North cut in on Ren's behalf. Or maybe Justin's. Maybe both; it was hard to tell. Ren didn't like how the conversation was going, didn't like anything about the room, or the atmosphere, or Phillip.

"Phillip," Kelly began.

"Enough, Tamsyn," he bravely cut her off. "Quit stalling. Or should I go get the deputy sheriff to speed this up?"

Kelly looked down on Phillip as though she'd love nothing more than to get him alone in a dark alley somewhere. She had her mouth slightly open, her lips curled back, reminding Ren of a wolf when it's about to tear out a throat. He waited expectantly for her to do just that, some verbal attack that would cut Phillip down and bring him around to her way of thinking. *Go on, Kelly*, Ren mentally encouraged her, excited to watch. *Tear him to pieces.*

"That won't be necessary," Kelly snarled, and Ren felt completely betrayed. Where was the fight in her? Why had she given in so quickly? Watching her back down here also made Ren wonder what the trial had been like. Had she truly fought as hard as she could for Justin's freedom?

"Then let's go," Phillip droned, motioning for them to head down the hall to some mysterious destination.

"Give us a minute; you know they aren't here yet," Kelly shot at him with such fierceness that for a half a second, he looked properly afraid. When she turned back to Justin, she was gentle again.

"Since the Hunts could enter the building at any moment, it's time for Kit to go into protective custody," Kelly explained quickly. "Both parties need to be kept in separate locations for their own safety until the judge arrives. For your information," she looked pointedly at Ren, who knew he was glaring at her, but he couldn't seem to stop. "It's a much more comfortable room than this one. I've got you a couch and everything, Kit, since apparently no one knows how long we're going to be stuck here."

"But there really is no way to allow Ren to stay with us?" North double checked. "I'd feel more comfortable with him around; Justin's not as stable as he looks. If something happens, it will be unexpected and fast."

"Unfortunately, I can't even let you go with him," Kelly informed them, which made Justin seem to wake up between them.

"Not even North?" he asked, a little bubbled question of fear. "I thought you said he had permission. He's family."

"Sorry, Kit." Kelly really did seem to mean it. "That's not legally recognized yet, and those are the court rules. Elias will be waiting for you in the courtroom when the time comes. The only person who can stay with you right now is me."

Justin looked again at Ren, then at North, a desperate sort of study, like he wanted to remember what they looked like because he expected to never see either of them again. And even though Ren was furious and frightened, he forced himself to smile supportively.

"It's ok, Justin; I'll just wait for you here," Ren said, as though it wasn't a big deal. "They'll come get me if you need me. Right?" he asked Kelly, trying to keep the bite out of his voice. She looked at him with an amused sort of pride.

"Certainly," she confirmed.

"I'll see you soon," Ren told Justin with as much conviction as he could. He wanted to say something else, wanted to stroke the side of Justin's face, put his hand behind his neck and kiss him. But he didn't want to say goodbye, didn't want to put any hint into the universe that he thought Justin might not come back. So he grasped his hand in parting, a good luck instead of a goodbye, and then watched helplessly as Kelly bent down over the handles of the chair and wheeled Justin away.

Justin turned, twisted to look back at Ren and North, keeping them within his sight until Kelly turned him down a different hallway, completely out of their view, possibly the last they would see each other. It was only when he was fully gone that Ren slumped, giving in to his own pain and anxiety. North noticed immediately and gently put his arms around him, allowing him to seek comfort against him as if they were old friends.

"She didn't even try," Ren accused against North's black suit.

"We don't know that for sure." North somehow remained free of judgment on the subject. "This place doesn't allow for much flexibility."

"If that were true, we would have been done and on our way home by now," Ren returned, exceptionally bitter.

Ren stepped backward, and North released him. They stood together in silence, in a strange place with an uncertain future. How long would it take? Would Justin be ok without them? Questions Ren wanted to ask out loud but didn't because he knew North didn't know anything more than he did. And the only people who did know weren't around to ask and probably wouldn't answer even if they could.

"There you are," a familiar voice broke into the moody standoff. Ren raised his eyes from the floor to see Officer Geisler joining them, his uniform slightly different from the security guards at the entrance, an actual revolver holstered on his belt. "Oh," he continued as he recognized Ren. "And you're still around too, huh?"

"Hey, Fritz," North greeted, glancing out of the corner of his eye at Ren even as he took a step forward to shake hands with the officer. "You're assigned to us or are you on your way to something else?"

"I'm with you, have been from the beginning," Geisler answered. "Kelly said you were here, asked me to take you into the courtroom to wait. Most of the jury is already there, so once the judge arrives, the doors will be locked right away."

"She didn't say anything about Ren coming too?" North checked.

"Sorry, no, just you," Geisler returned, looking apologetically at Ren, who tried not to wilt like a teenager. He was in uniform. He was a professional. He was going to act like it even if no one was going to treat him with any sort of dignity or respect. Except he couldn't stop himself from commenting.

"That's so stupid," Ren judged but switched topics rapidly when both the older men gave him dark looks. "Watch him for me," Ren advised North, feeling slighted, ignored, and helpless. "Make sure they let him have water and they don't make him stand up too long. Don't let them hurt him."

Officer Geisler watched Ren solemnly as he spoke, his gaze shifting every so often to North as if to check that Ren wasn't being overly protective or dramatic about this. But North was every bit as serious in accepting any advice Ren had to offer.

"If you can, tell Kelly to pay attention to his breathing," Ren finished. "Make sure he's not holding it like he keeps doing. Have her speed the meeting up as much as she can; he really shouldn't even be here, and they've already kept him waiting so long."

"He's still that bad?" Officer Geisler asked, breaking hesitantly into the exchange. "I mean, they let him out of the hospital, right?"

"He's getting better," Ren acknowledged. "But he's a long way from recovered. I have his medication if, you know, if he … if they decide … he'll need it. Maybe you should take it?" Ren offered his backpack to North.

"No, you hold onto it," Geisler told him, putting a hand over Ren's to gently push the bag back toward him. "We'll come find you if we need to get it."

"But —" Ren wanted to beg to be allowed to come with them, furious that no one seemed to be taking this with the seriousness it required.

"I'll make sure to bring you to him for anything he might need," Geisler said again, this time weighing his tone with a meaning Ren understood. He was trying to do Ren a favor. It was such an unexpected kindness that Ren wasn't sure how to acknowledge it. In the end, all he could do was sigh, holding his backpack to his chest with both hands.

"Ok," he gave in for the second time in the past twenty minutes, realizing he was going to be left alone in this waiting room. He'd canceled all his plans for the day knowing he wouldn't be able to concentrate on classes or work, but he'd never expected he'd spend his time waiting to learn about Justin's future all alone in this place.

"Thank you, Ren," North told him, putting a hand on his shoulder, not like an adult comforting a child, more like a soldier extending respect for Ren's different, but not any less difficult, part in all this.

"Take care of him," Ren responded, rooting himself to the spot and focusing his gaze on the legs of the nearest chair so he wouldn't have to watch North leave with Geisler to a place he was not welcome. He wanted to be worthy of the gesture North had just given him, to prove he could be whatever kind of brave was required.

"Hang in there, kid," Geisler said before he left. And Ren did. He hung in there, motionless, as he listened to their footsteps fade around the corner. He hung in there as the silence of the clockless waiting room closed in around him, as though this place existed outside of time. When he finally did move again, it was to cast a scowl at the portrait of George Leighton, the person responsible for the construction of this building. Then Ren finally gave up and tossed his backpack into a chair to indulge himself in pacing. Hell, he was alone; no one was going to get annoyed watching him if there was literally no one but a portrait on the wall to see.

He counted steps as he stalked around the waiting area, punctuating the numbers with furious little pangs of indignation. They were all taking so long to get things going; why the hell were they taking so long? But then again, he had no way of knowing exactly how long he'd been here. There was nothing but gray walls and stiff plastic chairs and solitary waiting as far as he could see.

So he paced, changing direction through the chairs at random, like someone trying to dodge a bullet, worrying even though he knew it would do nothing except make him tired and frustrated. What was he doing here? Not helping, that's for sure.

"Wow, kid."

Ren's body responded to the voice before his brain recognized who it was, tightening and twisting toward it, raising a hand as though he expected someone to hit him. Because he *was* waiting for a blow, just not a physical one. Geisler took a step backward, checking Ren up and down, noting the tenseness in him. "You're worse than the one on trial."

"Yeah, well, he has chemicals to keep him calm," Ren grumbled, not backing down much, though he did lower his arm. No sense in looking ridiculous, except it was probably too late.

"You really hate being away from him, don't you?" Geisler drawled, as though he were bored, as if he had all the time in the world.

"It sort of defeats the purpose of why I came," Ren returned, reminding himself that it wasn't Geisler's fault; he was just doing his job. Like last time.

"Yeah, I was thinking about that. Why'd they release him from the hospital anyway?"

"Long story," Ren dismissed, still feeling uncooperative and mad. It wasn't any of Geisler's business anyway. "Though a big part of it was because Dr. Delacroix thought I'd be *watching him*."

"Dr. Delacroix? She's the one I spoke to, right? The one in purple with all the braids?" Geisler's gaze shifted away. "You know her first name?"

"Angelique," Ren supplied, studying Geisler. What was he really doing here? Ren wasn't even supposed to be here, so why send Geisler to babysit him?

"She's something," Geisler continued, staring at the portrait across the room, putting a nonchalant hand against the top of one of the chairs. And just like that, it clicked in Ren's head. Geisler was interested in Angelique.

"She's a force of nature," Ren corrected.

"I can tell. Do you know if she's, um," Geisler faltered, shrugging as though he had changed his mind about asking that question.

"Single?" Ren gave him the word he hadn't been able to say, feeling as though he'd been handed a bit of control. He wondered if he could use this. Maybe exchange information about Angelique for

... what? Getting into the courtroom? Sneaking in to check on Justin wherever he was right now? He wasn't even sure Geisler could do either of those things; they could both be against the law. But then again, Ren couldn't give Geisler what he really wanted either since he couldn't speak for Angelique. Maybe they were both coming to this table with no cards.

"Yeah," Geisler brought him back to the conversation. "Is she?"

"As far as I know, the tiger is a solitary creature," Ren said. Geisler stared at him, puzzling him out, probably trying to figure if Ren were making fun of him. "Yes, she's single. Never married," Ren amended. "The emergency room keeps her busy, you know."

"I bet. You got her number?" Geisler asked, his voice strong but his posture humiliated. He'd probably never had to ask a teenaged boy for a woman's number before.

"You got a death wish?" Ren returned.

"You'd know all about that, wouldn't you, boy?" Geisler shot back, voice not quite as smooth and calm as before, enough of a stab that Ren could feel the wound. He took a step backward, remembering what Geisler had told him in the hospital a couple days ago. How he should go home, get away from Justin if he knew what was good for him. How Justin would bring him nothing but trouble. How he'd been right, but probably not the way he thought he would be. A soft shine of regret instantly went over Geisler's blue eyes.

"Look, kid," Officer Geisler began, obviously intending to repair what he'd just done to their dynamic. "No, sorry, it's Ren, isn't it? I got to admit, you don't look much like a kid today." Ren gave in to Geisler's attempt at repentance by meeting his gaze, waiting to hear what he had to say. "That was out of line; you're right. It's not like I know him."

"You know he's innocent, right?" Ren demanded. "If you were there for the whole trial, then you have to know that."

"Innocent isn't the word I'd use," Geisler said softly, reluctantly, as though he knew that by sharing his real thoughts with Ren, he'd be removing any shot he had of getting Dr. Delacroix's number. "He made some bad choices. Nothing I'd throw him in jail for, but still — there's a lot of anger in him."

"There's a lot of kindness in him too," Ren returned, though he couldn't look at Geisler anymore when he said it. "It'd probably be easier to notice if anyone could ever believe it was there."

"I do believe it," Geisler allowed. "And I did notice, now you've brought it out in the open for everyone to see."

"What are you talking about?" Ren asked, tired, staring at the floor. "It was always there; I had nothing to do with it."

"I was just with him," Geisler shared, and now he had all of Ren's attention.

"How is he?" Ren interrupted to ask. Geisler smiled softly, shaking his head.

"He looks awful; he's in a lot of pain, you can tell in a second. But all he wanted was to know about you. Before, during the trial, he never said a word, wouldn't look at anyone. He'd just sit there with his arms folded, glaring at the world, and barely answering questions. When he did say anything, it was quick and hard. And he never asked for anything, not once before today. And yeah, I think that has everything to do with you. That's why I came to get you."

"What?" Ren checked, not allowing himself to hope too hard.

"I say, he looks awful. And my first aid training doesn't hold a candle to yours, for sure. I know the lawyers are fighting about you, and they're never going to get anywhere with Judge Bruin with it. He can't give in to either of their requests to keep you in or out without some sort of time-wasting backlash, so I'm going to make the call instead. Because in my completely unbiased opinion, he needs medical assistance, which means he needs you. So get your supplies and come with me."

"Why are you doing this?" Ren had to ask, taken completely by surprise. He'd thought maybe Kelly would ask for him, but Officer Geisler?

"You know," Geisler said, closing his eyes and turning his head away. "Despite your first impression, I'm not actually a jerk. I have a son of my own — a little older than you two. He lives in New York now, but I remember what it's like."

"I'm sorry," Ren apologized for the harsh and hurtful things he'd ever thought about Officer Geisler, feeling the need to do that even though he'd never said any of them out loud.

"Me too," Geisler returned. "So, are you coming, or what?"

"Y-yes, of course." Ren began rushing, but then thought of something and took out his notebook first. "I don't have Dr. Delacroix's number," he confessed. "But I do have her email address if you want it."

"I'll take what I can get," Geisler said, smiling at Ren, who wrote down the address as quickly and neatly as possible, tearing out the entire sheet and beginning to hand it over. Though he stopped with his arm half extended, which made the officer also pause questioningly in the act of accepting it.

"This wouldn't be considered some kind of bribe, would it?" Ren asked, not wanting to get anyone in trouble for what was going on here. Geisler burst out laughing, reaching forward to snatch the paper out of Ren's fingers.

"No, considering I was going to do this anyway," he answered when he could talk again. He started walking, and Ren fell into step beside him, both of their boots sounding hard and heavy in the empty hallway. "Though if you wanted to chat me up with the doctor, I wouldn't say no to that."

"What should I tell her?" Ren asked, ready to agree to anything Officer Geisler wanted now that he'd made it possible for Ren to stay with Justin.

"I don't know, kid — Ren — you don't have to tell her anything," Geisler backtracked. "If I can't get a woman on my own then I don't deserve her."

Ren was starting to be of the opinion that if anyone might deserve Dr. Delacroix, it could be Frederick Geisler.

"Now," Geisler shifted as he took Ren's arm, not a rough grip, but definitely a firm one, the kind of hold he used to bring defendants into and out of courtrooms. Walking this way was probably instinctual to him in this place. Geisler started talking before Ren could ask anything.

"We're going to speak to the judge. He just finished, and Justin's case is next. I've told him a little about what's been going on, but I want you to explain the medical situation in detail as well as give an account as to where Justin's been since Thursday. Don't be afraid, but do be respectful."

Ren swallowed, not sure he could help being afraid. The gray walls seemed more like concrete to him now as he walked. The lights were dimmer, at least in his imagination. It was a good thing Geisler kept hold of Ren's arm. He was so overwhelmed by what was going on and what was about to happen that it was difficult to pay attention to something like watching where he was going. Not that he knew where they were going, but it seemed they'd walked the entire length of the building before Geisler tugged him to a stop in front of an office door. Judge R. J. Bruin was embossed on a placard inserted into a slide on the wall. Ren wanted to pause here, catch his breath even though he wasn't out of breath, but he definitely wanted to collect himself somehow. He hadn't prepared to meet with the judge.

Geisler needed no recuperative moment and simply knocked with familiarity, beginning to open the door before the deep call came for them to enter, dragging Ren in behind him.

For a moment, Ren was stunned. Everything in this office seemed enormous. The desk, the two oversized armchairs in front of it, the massive high-backed burgundy seat behind it. Monstrous paintings of wildlife were displayed on two of the walls — moose in the snow and a couple of bears fishing for salmon in a river. Twin, gargoyle-sized bookcases stood guard in the back corners, bearing the weight of hundreds of thick, hard-bound books.

"Judge Bruin," Officer Geisler broke the pressed quiet. "This is Lorenzo Cordero, the EMT escorting Mr. Kittrick."

"Thank you, Officer. Please stay with us," said the judge in the deepest voice Ren had ever heard. He decided to channel North and stood in his best imitation of parade rest, trying not to stare too hard at the man behind the desk, a file open in front of him and a pen at the ready for notes. Like the rest of the office, the judge himself was an enormous man. Big enough that he didn't really look like a judge. He looked more like an Olympic wrestler. He had a broad nose which fit well against his broad, squarish face, and coal-black skin. The only thing light about the judge was his graying hair.

"Thank you for your time, Mr. Cordero. I have some questions for you, if you're willing?"

Ren swallowed again, trying to coat his dry throat as he stood in the judge's deep brown gaze. His eyes were not fierce like Kelly's nor soft like North's. They were somewhere between — completely impartial. Ren found all he could do was nod.

Judge Bruin offered them seats in the large chairs and began asking his questions. How long had Ren been an EMT? How long and in what capacity did he know Justin? What exactly happened after Justin left the courthouse on Thursday evening? What medical limitations was Justin struggling with currently, and what were the risks involved in keeping him from resting at home? Was there anything else Ren thought the judge needed to know?

Ren gave the most thorough answers possible without babbling. He told the judge he hadn't known Justin when he tracked him down on Friday morning after class, but now that he'd spent practically every moment since then with him, they had become good friends. He wanted to explain what he and Dr. Delacroix had discovered about the scans, plead Justin's innocence, but decided he'd better not. He also did not ask to be allowed into the courtroom; Officer Geisler did it for him.

Geisler confirmed what he could about Ren's story. How he had witnessed Justin collapse himself on Saturday afternoon. Had seen Ren take him away to the hospital in an ambulance and spoken with the ER doctor there regarding the severity of his condition. He closed with his opinion that Ren be allowed admittance to the courtroom despite the Hunts' insistence to the contrary.

"I see," Judge Bruin toned thoughtfully over the fingers he'd pressed together at his chin. "Very well. Officer Geisler, if you could please have Mr. Cordero assist you in escorting the defendant into the courtroom and then finding him a seat where he can monitor? We will keep the proceedings as brief as possible."

"Your honor?" Ren practically squeaked, so grateful this had been granted to him that he was surprised he was taking a chance in asking this question.

"Yes, Mr. Cordero, what is it?" the judge asked quietly, though he was now looking down at the file.

"If Justin is ... if the jury says he's guilty, what happens to him?"

"Ah," Judge Bruin breathed, and raised his head again to look at Ren, not unkindly. "He won't be thrown into a cell if that's what's worrying you. There is a medical wing at the prison where he will receive any and all necessary treatments. He won't be transferred into the facility until he's fully recovered."

"Oh," Ren exhaled, though this answer didn't really make him feel any better. He thought it was odd that the prison would be prepared to offer Justin more thorough treatment than the hospital.

Officer Geisler was standing now, reaching down to also pull Ren to his feet. Because it seemed now was really time to get started. The waiting over. All the movement back and forth to this room and that room and who goes where all sifting down to this one last walk to pick Justin up and take him into the courtroom.

"Thank you, Officer," Judge Bruin said. "I'll meet you there in fifteen minutes."

24
VERDICT

R en followed Officer Geisler to where Justin and Kelly waited, noticing his senses dulling one by one until all he could see was a fuzzy black movement ahead of him that was Geisler's boots, and all he could hear was a pulsing hum. His emotions had tightened so hard it seemed they'd given way like a stripped screw, and he could no longer feel himself moving forward.

He thought Officer Geisler said something to him as they walked, maybe asked a few questions, but he hadn't answered with more than an ambiguous grunt, and now if Geisler was still talking, Ren couldn't hear it. Nor did he notice when they arrived at a partially hidden door. He only stopped because Geisler suddenly gripped his arms and squeezed hard.

"Get it together," Geisler told him, shaking him slightly. "We need the other Ren; the one barking orders at me and taking charge and being *sure*. You figure out where he is in that head of yours and get him out here."

"You're right," Ren acknowledged, wishing the Ren that Geisler was talking about was the only one available ever. Geisler knocked his fist against Ren's chest, not hard enough to hurt, just enough to jostle him.

"That boy needs you," Geisler said, though Ren struggled accepting that. Justin needed a lot of things, mostly North. Need was a strong word. "Now go bring him out to me."

"Can you give us a few minutes?" Ren requested, not knowing exactly what he would do in those last moments, just knowing he wanted to have them.

"Five," Geisler allowed. Not near enough, though Ren knew Geisler was being generous. He reached up and removed Geisler's fist from his chest with both hands, releasing him just as Kelly opened the door, her face hard and ready.

"Judge Bruin has asked us to escort Mr. Kittrick into the courtroom," Geisler said smoothly as Kelly studied Ren carefully.

"No kidding," she said, the growl tamed but still present, staring Ren down. He discovered it was easier to look her in the eye now that he had formal permission from the judge to be here. Her eyes took on an amused shine that put him off guard. "Aren't you a lucky bastard? Congratulations."

"How's Justin?" Ren cut in, not wanting to hear how lucky he was or any other lecture about how much of a liability he was going to be in the courtroom. He wasn't going to do anything crazy, and he didn't need a lawyer who hadn't vouched for him to give him any advice about it.

"Pretending to sleep," Kelly said, looking over her shoulder. "The poor kid — dragged through this circus."

Officer Geisler cleared his throat, a physical testament that time was running out while they were standing here in the doorway. Kelly glared, her eyes weapons all by themselves, renewing Ren's respect for her slightly.

"Knock it off," she almost spat at Geisler. "This whole thing is nothing but profiling and you know it."

"It's not up to me," Geisler absolved himself. "I'll escort the Hunts in first to give you some time." He nodded to Ren, tapping his own chest with his fist as a reminder that Ren needed to get it together and keep it together. Ren nodded in acknowledgement, then turned to go in, finding Kelly still guarding the doorway, watching Geisler leave.

"Ms. Kelly?" Ren nudged her with her name. Kelly set her shoulders, shaking her head and closing her eyes, making an obvious mental pivot.

"Never mind," she said to herself. The cold smile was back on her face, as if she had a secret she wasn't sharing, the same sort of smile villains have in movies as they watch a victim drink from a poisoned glass. "It'll all be different after today. Go on in, *Pana*; I'll wait for you here."

She shifted slightly to let Ren pass, and he shot through the doorway, knowing that five minutes would blur past too quickly. He saw Justin half lying down on a blue plaid couch, in a similar position to when he would rest his head on Ren's lap in the back seat of cars. Though Kelly was right; he was not actually sleeping. Ren could see that from across the room. He'd spent so much time this weekend monitoring Justin as he slept.

"Justin," Ren called to him. "You can open your eyes; it's just me."

"Ren?" Justin's voice wrapped his name in several layers of disbelief. "What are you doing here?"

"Surprise," Ren said, smiling even though he didn't feel like it. Forcing himself to be the version of Ren that Geisler had asked for. Support, strength, and sureness. "The judge said I could stay with you. Courtroom and all."

"Oh," Justin returned, unenthusiastic. He was sitting up now, at least partially. He had his head bowed, his back curved over as though he were incapable of straightening it, looking as alone as he had when Ren first joined him in his room. "I don't ... You probably shouldn't."

Ren sat down next to Justin on the couch, their shoulders touching, wondering what sort of emotional mess was forcing Justin into partial sentences.

"Justin, what?" Ren checked, unsettled by what Justin seemed to be saying. Ren had worked so hard to be here, he'd jumped so many hoops to be allowed in that room, and now Justin didn't want him there? Why not?

"It's just," Justin said, speaking extremely slowly, staring hard at the table, at the carpet, at anything that wasn't Ren. "If they take me away ..."

"They won't," Ren countered with so much force that Justin flinched.

"I don't want that to be the last thing you see," he finished after a pause. "How you remember me."

Ren slipped off the couch and onto his knees next to Justin, dipping his head so he could force Justin to make eye contact with him. Justin kept his gaze for less than two seconds.

"If that's what you really want," Ren managed, though it was far from what he wanted. "I'll wait outside, but Justin, it's not going to happen like that. Today is not the last time I'm going to see you, but even if it was, that's not how I'd remember you at all." Ren was about to describe his favorite memories of Justin and their strange weekend together, but his voice deserted him. He'd remember Justin on the couch in his apartment, amazed at the taste of his soup. He'd remember the ice pack on his cheek, the way Justin had comforted him about his family. He'd remember the feel of his head on his lap, running his fingers through his hair. There were so many, in fact, that Ren knew none of them would be the last, and none of them would be forgotten either.

"I'd like to come with you," Ren said when he trusted himself to talk. Justin had his face turned away and his eyes closed. "I came here to support you, but that's hard to do behind a locked door."

"Are we ready to go, gentlemen?" Kelly joined them, slicing into the room, apologetic and rushing. There before Justin could even think about giving an answer.

"Almost," Ren answered without taking his eyes off Justin,

amazed that the hardest permission to receive for entering the court-room would come from him.

"I wish there was some way out of this," Ren continued. "I wish I could do it for you, and I wish I'd met you sooner. I hate that they're making you do this, but I promise you it will be better on the other side of it."

"You can't make promises like that," Justin muttered.

"Too late," Ren challenged.

"Kelly," Officer Geisler called as let himself in. Not all the way, he hovered close to the door as though he weren't allowed to enter this room. Ren wondered if that were the legal truth, or if it was just because he was trying to allow them a safe space, or maybe Ren was overthinking everything. "Ren, I'm sorry, but we really have to go. Come on now."

"Coming," Ren said before he could force himself to move. He took hold of Justin, who was struggling to get up, pulling him to his feet and holding him ready to pivot into the seat of the wheelchair. But Justin forced himself as straight as possible, holding tight to Ren's sleeves.

"Here, Kit," Kelly invited, bringing the chair closer.

"I don't want that," Justin denied, shaking his head. "I can walk."

Kelly tilted her head, unconvinced, making eye contact with Ren to check about allowing this. Ren nodded; he could keep Justin upright for however many hallway steps were between here and the courtroom. He wanted to give Justin whatever control was possible.

With Ren's agreement, Kelly moved the chair out of the way so Ren and Justin could walk side-by-side toward the door. She plucked her briefcase off the table and smoothed a hand down her already perfect blazer. Then she fell into position behind them, following them out, switching the light off as she exited.

Ren walked Justin out to the waiting Geisler, who also took a place on Justin's other side, automatically encasing Justin's elbow in a deputy sheriff's escort grip. Justin stopped breathing when Officer Geisler touched him, so Ren put more pressure into his arm. Justin turned to look at Ren, deliberately inhaling deeply in acknowledgement.

"Let's go," Geisler gave the signal to start walking forward, but then remained silent even though he looked at Justin and Ren as though there was plenty he wanted to say.

Before, when Ren followed Geisler away from the judge, everything had gone fuzzy. On this walk, it was the opposite. He could see and hear everything in sharp, clear detail. The fleur-de-lis pattern on the buttons of Justin's suit, the flint-hard strike of Kelly's heels against the floor, the scars along Officer Geisler's knuckles. The way the light touched the photos along the walls, the portraits, the trim. The unsteady rhythm of Justin's walking, the weight and heat of him on Ren's arm. Time may have started again, but it wasn't up to normal speed yet. Ren wondered if it would catch up, or maybe it would surge forward faster than he wanted it to.

The courthouse was designed with the smaller waiting rooms and offices along the outer walls, building the perimeter for the central expanse of the courtrooms. Ren wasn't sure; he'd turned around so many corners in this place already, but he thought the double doors ahead of them and to the right faced the same direction as the main entrance four floors below. But there was no glass here. Here, the old dark wood had been preserved. No attempt had been made to modernize the feel of this place. Ren could even smell the age of it — a mixture of damp, dust, and wood polish. It sucked in the light, dimming the entire corridor.

Two security guards stood on either side of the doors, but they opened them readily for Officer Geisler. The one closest to Ren looked at him for maybe a hint too long, but no one said a word.

It all changed on the other side of the doors, enough that Ren was temporarily overwhelmed. They were inside the courtroom now, actually here. Ren tightened his grip on Justin, feeling him beginning to sag not just from the exertion of getting here but from the sudden weight of judgment that had been thrown over him from the front of the room.

Ren could see them long before he could hear the low murmurings. The Hunts stood from their table at the front, watching Justin as Ren and Geisler brought him down the center aisle. William Hunt was much taller than Ren had expected him to be. Tall and trim, clean-shaven and crisp, brownish red hair styled professionally to complement his age and the shape of his face. He leaned down, as graceful as water, to speak to Mr. Rozensweig. His presence was so commanding that Ren almost missed his wife, who stood so close to his side wearing so much black she might have been his shadow. If it hadn't been for her shining golden hair, Ren would have never seen her.

On the other hand, now that he could see her face, he wished he hadn't noticed her. She stared at Justin with an intense sort of loathing, a very clear disgust that Justin was alive and allowed to walk on the earth when her son could not. She gripped her husband's arm much tighter than Ren held onto Justin, so hard that Ren marveled that Mr. Hunt could just stand there calmly and quickly whispering to his lawyer as though he felt nothing. Rozensweig had his hands out in patient supplication, also whispering.

"I wish —" Justin whispered as they came closer to the front, shrinking unconsciously closer to Ren, as far as possible from the Hunts.

Officer Geisler gave Justin a tiny shake, warning him against talking anymore, not allowing him to complete his wish, especially now they were at the half-gate separating the front of the courtroom from the benches where spectators and witnesses sat at the back. Ren didn't want to shake Justin; he wanted to help him stand straighter. Justin had done nothing wrong; he had nothing to be ashamed of. He also wanted to put his arm around Justin to shield him from the tangible feeling of hatred that radiated from that side of the room. It took all he had not to glare at Mrs. Hunt.

Since Justin couldn't, Ren pulled his shoulders back, drawing himself to his full height. He lifted his chin, which was as defiant as he was going to get in here. He didn't even dare whisper any words of encouragement. Geisler had told him to keep his mouth shut. He didn't want to give anyone any reason to kick him out.

But there was one thing he needed clarification on. He remembered just as he helped Justin sit down at the defense table, before they had removed their hands from each other's sleeves. Kelly took her place at Justin's side, though she remained on her feet, placing her briefcase with a sure calm in front of her. Officer Geisler had his hand on Ren's shoulder, intending on pulling him back, separating him from Justin. Before he could, Ren bent down close to look Justin in the eye.

"Do you want me to leave?" Ren whispered, not because he wanted to but because he wanted Justin to have a choice about something. Even if it meant he'd have to pace outside with the security guards, he wanted Justin to be able to choose. Justin's eyes flickered to the Hunts before resting again on Ren.

"Ren," Justin said, breaking eye contact, throwing his gaze to the floor at Ren's feet. He hadn't let go of Ren's sleeves.

"That's not an answer," Ren breathed. "Do you want me to leave?"

"Damn it, Ren," Justin burst out, though quietly. "No," he finally confessed, though he sounded as though he'd clenched his teeth around the word.

"Ok," Ren said, relieved. "I'll be in the back." He gave a final look to Kelly before submitting to Officer Geisler. There was only so much he could see from a distance, looking at Justin's back. Kelly would be closest; she'd be the one to notice something first. It would be mostly up to her to call Ren if it became necessary. Kelly tipped her head at Ren before he turned away, which Ren supposed meant that she understood.

Officer Geisler took Ren by the shoulder to the half-gate, turning him as he pushed him through the opening to give him some last-minute advice.

"Stay back there unless you're called forward," Geisler reminded him. "You stay still and keep quiet. Go sit next to Elias now."

Elias. Elias? The gate closed between Ren and Justin, and for the first time Ren looked at the back of the room instead of the front, searching for North. He was surprised to see him seated close to the center aisle, the very back set of benches, the closest to the big double doors. He'd been so focused on the Hunts and Justin's walking that Ren hadn't even seen North. Now he made a beeline for him.

North sat stiff and rigid in the pew-like seat, his back barely touching the rest. His hands were positioned carefully on his knees. Looking at him from a distance would give the indication that he was at ease, calmly and peacefully waiting. But when Ren got close enough to sit next to him, he could tell it was all a façade. North's stillness was the same in intensity as Ren's stress-pacing. Where Ren felt the need to move, North drove all his nerves into carefully sitting motionless, the only hint of his inner turmoil visible in the clench of his jaw and the unnatural stillness of his posture. His eyes moved, though. They shifted continuously from Justin to the Hunts and back again.

North also looked at Ren, carefully and slowly turning his head toward him. He kept his mouth tightly closed, but he asked Ren a question as loudly as if he'd spoken it. Ren gave him a quick thumbs-up in answer. Yes, he was allowed to be here. Yes, Justin was sort of ok. He'd be a lot better once this was over.

Justin sat hunched at the table, a broken crumple next to Kelly's strong posture. The Hunts and their lawyer continued to whisper amongst themselves while Officer Geisler went to his post near what Ren supposed was the judge's entrance. This was also the first time Ren saw the jury box, filled with people. Ren nervously tapped his fingers along his leg as he looked at the mix of men and women who would be responsible for what happened to Justin today.

They looked so ordinary. All of them. A plump older black woman wearing a dark green sweater and a long swath of cream-colored fabric, looped several times around her neck and cascading down her shoulders. A young man who wore ebony plugs in both earlobes and had a tattoo just barely peeking out of his shirt. Another man with white hair wearing a vest and spectacles. A petite lady in a black and white striped dress and jean jacket who didn't look old enough to even be here absently playing with a thick brown braid pulled over her shoulder. Who were these people? Why would they care one way or another about Justin? How could Ren trust them to have made the right choice? His fingers sped up so much that North reached over to still them. Ren guiltily tucked his hands tightly under his arms.

He was grateful when Officer Geisler finally announced the arrival of the judge. First because it broke open the anticipation of waiting, and second because Geisler commanded that everyone in the room get to their feet to show respect for the judge's position of authority. Ren sprang up, trying to scan everything at once. He looked to Justin first, who used the table and never took his hands off it in order to stand. He didn't lift his head. Kelly stood as straight as a flagpole, but only until she realized that Justin wasn't standing at his normal height, then she leaned over him to make sure he was all right. Good. She was paying attention.

Judge Bruin marched into the room like a threatening thundercloud, all billowing robes and broad shoulders. He looked purposeful, but not in a hurry, moving quickly without rushing, a man not willing to waste time but who was willing to take as much time as necessary. His face was perfectly blank as he placed himself with monumental solemnity at the front of the courtroom. The gesture stilled the already silent air. He bid them all to be seated. Ren found himself impressed, wishing it had been only the judge's decision about what should be done with Justin.

The judge announced the title and number of the court case, thanked the members of the jury for their service to the county and for appearing today despite adverse weather. Ren noticed that he looked at each of the members, one at a time, personalizing his gratitude.

"I have been informed," Judge Bruin said, gazing quickly at Rozensweig before returning his attention to the jury. "That the defendant was released from the hospital yesterday and remains under medical care. For this reason, I will be giving my decision on the civil case attached to this verdict directly afterward instead of the previously scheduled separate hearing later this afternoon. I ask for the jury's understanding in this matter and promise to be as brief as possible."

Ren leaned into North questioningly but remembered at the last second that he couldn't whisper anything to him. There were so few people in this room, anything he did would be noticed. But what was the judge talking about? What civil case? And this afternoon? They were thinking of doing two cases today? What was the other one for? He didn't have long to speculate; Judge Bruin was being true to his promise on brevity and had already moved on.

"Are there any concluding statements from either party before we proceed?" Bruin inquired, turning toward each council table, giving only a few moments for a response. Rozensweig looked like he wanted to protest something but didn't say anything. Kelly also had nothing else to add.

"Seeing as there are no closing statements, I believe the jury has reached a verdict?" Bruin continued, the cadence of routine in his voice, but surprisingly no boredom. Though he'd probably said these words hundreds of thousands of times, knew the protocol and the order for these sessions as well as signing his own name, Ren could tell he was mentally present here. These ceremonial proceedings had his complete attention. Ren admired his discipline.

All eyes in the room centered on the young woman in the jean jacket as she stood up, no taller than Denny, a sealed envelope in her hand. Officer Geisler acted as mediator, retrieving the small packet from her and crossing the floor to hand it to the judge. That was it. The verdict. In that envelope. Ren swallowed hard. He forced himself not to squeeze the bench seat in front of him. Time was doing weird things again. Not stopping; it couldn't be stopping because there was still movement. The shuffling of the jury members who probably just wanted to be done with their duty, who wanted to go home or to other jobs. Judge Bruin carefully opening the verdict envelope. Time hadn't stopped, but this process was driving Ren crazy with how serious everyone was taking everything.

"If possible, will the defense please rise?" Judge Bruin addressed Justin, the jury's response to the trial now open in front of him.

Justin once again pushed against the table to get up, and Ren couldn't stop looking at him, marveling at his attempt to stand with the sheer weight of the situation and his condition bearing down on him. He had to keep his hands planted as before, but this time he did his best to raise his head, attempting to make eye contact with the judge. Kelly stood at his side, completely serene, one of her hands resting lightly on Justin's back. For an instant, Judge Bruin allowed something that looked like approval cross the neutral expression of his face.

"Mr. Justin Kittrick, for all charges of voluntary and involuntary manslaughter that have been brought against you for the death of David Hunt, the members of the jury of Cook County have unanimously declared you not guilty."

Ren felt as though all the wind had been knocked out of him. He didn't mean to, but he heard himself exhale an enormous breath of relief. No one heard him, however, because his reaction was practically invisible compared to Justin's.

Perhaps he meant to sit down and missed, or maybe his knees just buckled on him. Ren couldn't tell from where he sat, but he did hear Justin give the strangest sounding cry, like a gasp, a moan, and a sob all tangled up together, like something broken and ugly had just torn free from his soul, and then he just dropped onto the floor.

"Justin," North said, torn between following orders to stay where he was and rushing to the front. Ren felt no such restraint. He was already running for Justin, tearing down the center aisle. When Ren reached the bar, he barely noticed. He simply planted his hand on the wood and jumped, vaulting over it without bothering to mess with the latch of the gate. There were glimmers of movement in his side vision, and he could hear grunts and statements of surprise. But he didn't care about anything that might be going on around him in the room. Ren was here for one thing.

Kelly was bending over Justin by the time Ren reached them a few seconds after he'd gone down. She had her palms on Justin's back, her brow furrowed in worry and frustrated helplessness, looking at Justin, then the judge, then the Hunts, then at Justin again in a rapid rotation. Ren skidded to his knees in front of Justin, ignoring everything else. The last time Justin had received an emotional shock like this one, it almost put him in cardiac arrest.

Justin was curled over, one hand covering his mouth while the other pushed tight over his heart. At least he was conscious; he hadn't passed out this time. Ren grabbed at Justin's clenched fingers, dragging his hand off his chest so he could put his own there, monitoring the heavy, rapid thud of Justin's heartbeat. Too strong for this to be a hypotension relapse.

"Justin," Ren called, shifting closer to him on the floor. The buzzing in the background was growing louder. Angrier? "What happened?"

Justin shook his head, removing the hand from the mask over his mouth so he could frustratingly drag his arm across his eyes. When he finally looked at Ren, they were still full of tears.

"When is this weepy emotional bullshit going to be over?" Justin asked Ren, his voice cracking in tense, embarrassed fury. Ren fought not to laugh, listening to the voices droning all around them, as though the very walls of the room were vibrating.

"Did you hurt yourself?" Ren asked instead of trying to answer Justin's question.

"No," Justin answered, annoyed with himself, frustrated that he'd become the epicenter of all the motion and muttering around them. Ren removed his hand from Justin's chest so he could squeeze his shoulder, relief pushing into his own heart and lungs so hard it almost hurt. Justin was ok, just weak. They'd said not guilty. Even though Ren had spent so long convincing himself and Justin that this was the only possible outcome of the trial, that anyone with sense would not send Justin to prison for what he'd done, he still could hardly believe it.

The sound of the gavel penetrated Ren's focus, bursting apart the beehive hum that Justin's collapse had started. Now that Ren was satisfied Justin wasn't in danger, the rest of the courtroom was becoming clear to him again. Though he stayed on the floor with Justin, Ren lifted his head to Judge Bruin, who stood halfway out of his seat, powerfully hammering for order.

"That's enough," Judge Bruin demanded. "Everyone please be seated."

Ren took a second to glance around, wondering how much real time had passed while he'd been talking with Justin on the floor. Probably less than it seemed. North had come to the bar, leaning over it as far as he could right behind the defense table, hands curled hard around the railing. The Hunts and Mr. Rozensweig had taken several steps toward Justin as well, and more than one member of the jury had risen to their feet to better see what was going on. Officer Geisler was crouched just behind Ren's shoulder, his radio in hand in case he once again had to call an ambulance.

"Take your seats," Judge Bruin said a second time. Ren felt he was excluded from this request, but second guessed that when the judge's attention fell on him. "Young man, is everything all right?"

Ren took an extra second to be sure in his answer. Justin's eyes were focused, his heart rate not any more extreme than it had been before. He thought Justin had just been overcome with relief in that moment, that all the tension he'd carried in his body, all the unspoken worry and fear and stress, everything he'd been dragging around since the start of this nightmare had snapped away from him all at once.

"Yes," Ren answered. "Your honor."

His response calmed the entire room. Judge Bruin lowered into his seat once more, leaning back and squaring his wide shoulders, settling his body into place with the same care as he would organize his paperwork.

"Mr. Kittrick," the judge addressed Justin, his deep voice peaceful again as he rested the gavel on the desk in front of him. "Do you feel well enough to continue, or should we adjourn until this afternoon?"

"I'm fine," Justin panted, rather unconvincingly from the floor with Ren, Geisler, and Kelly hovering over him. "We can keep going."

The judge nodded — another quick glimpse of impressed respect just barely visible in his expression.

"In that case, Officer Geisler, could you please assist Mr. Kittrick to his chair?" Judge Bruin requested. But Justin was already moving on his own now, ungracefully pulling himself back into the wooden seat, looking as though he wanted to drop his head on his arms and hide his face, still trembling in shock. Ren stood protectively next to him.

"We're ready, your honor," Kelly prompted, her hand still on Justin's shoulder as he composed himself at the table.

"Very well," Judge Bruin acknowledged. Ren wondered if he should go back with North. Now that the emergency was over, he realized he hadn't followed Geisler's directions at all. Though he was finding it difficult to be ashamed. Not guilty. They'd voted not guilty. Unanimously. Justin wasn't going to prison. "We will continue with the ruling on the civil suit. Perhaps you should remain seated this time, Mr. Kittrick." The judge made eye contact with Ren. "And to be safe, please stay where you are."

Ren nodded, standing straight next to Justin while Officer Geisler stepped back, returning to his position near the jury box. Ren didn't dare glance at the Hunts. He wondered again what more legal business they could possibly have left now that the verdict had been read. Now Justin was free.

"Now," Judge Bruin began, shaking off the last few minutes of uproar that had disturbed the process of his court, his voice calm and quiet and yet stretching to all corners of the room. "In regard to the civil suit of Kittrick vs. Hunt. In accordance with the verdict and the agreement previously signed by both parties, I hereby rule in favor of Mr. Justin Kittrick." Justin raised his head, looking confused. Ren was too. He risked stealing a look at Kelly, only to find her smiling smugly, eyes narrowed in self-congratulatory satisfaction.

"Mr. Kittrick," the judge continued. "This ruling will clear your file of all charges associated with David Hunt, including the assault charges on your juvenile record." What? Cleared? Ren kept his hands to himself, held as still as possible despite how all his nerves were jarred. Kelly had arranged this; she'd prepared a suit against the Hunts in retaliation for dragging Justin into this a second time. Judge Bruin turned his attention to the Hunts.

"Mr. and Mrs. Hunt," the judge addressed them, and Ren risked looking at them out of the corner of his eye. They sat with sorrowful expressions. "As you know, this ruling requires you to pay $650,000 in damages to Mr. Kittrick within ten days, and you are prohibited from pressing any further charges against him regarding the death of your son. Failure to adhere to these terms will result in an additional fine of $100,000 and or imprisonment of up to twelve months. Do you understand this ruling as I have explained it to you?"

"Understood, your honor," Mr. Rozensweig answered on behalf of the Hunts, who sat rigid and white, unprepared for having things turn out this way.

"Good. Then that will be all. Court adjourned." Judge Bruin smacked down his gavel one final time to signal they were done.

Ren blinked, amazed and shocked on many levels. That's it? All that waiting and it was already over? And what had he just said? Did he really just award Justin six hundred and fifty *thousand* dollars? Over half a million dollars? Ren looked at Justin, who sat in stunned silence, just staring straight ahead at nothing. For someone who expected to go to prison today, Ren couldn't imagine what was going on in his head right now.

The room was beginning to clear out, the judge leading, disappearing out the same door he used to enter, on his way to the next meeting. Officer Geisler began ushering the members of the jury out the same door, single file from the jury box. Ren made eye contact with the young woman in the striped dress, the one who had handed over the envelope. She smiled kindly at him, and Ren wished he could run over there and shake her hand. Shake all their hands. Tell them thank you a million times for making the right choice, for giving Justin his life back. He knew he couldn't get close to them, though, so he simply mouthed his thanks from across the room. The woman's long braid swooshed away from her as she bowed slightly in acknowledgement. Then she disappeared behind Geisler's guiding arm and out the door. Ren would never know anything about her.

A jostling closer to Ren demanded his focus. Mrs. Hunt had ripped free of her husband and her lawyer and was striding forcefully over to them, eyes shining and wild. It was the first time Ren really noticed the grief in her, how much she was hurting over the loss of her son. It was the first time he'd ever considered that she was David's mother, that she'd been the one to find him, that she loved him. Though the love she had for him looked like it burned bright enough to hurt someone. She looked like she wanted it to.

Ren took a step forward, placing an arm to block her from Justin, though he wasn't sure what she was really planning on doing. She might not know what she was coming over for either. Officer Geisler was still across the room, closing the door after the last of the jury members, but North was suddenly there. Ren hadn't seen him pass the gate, but he was here now, standing solidly between the Hunts and Justin, staring them down.

"I don't think you're allowed to come any closer," North warned, the words very strangely threatening when spoken in his mild voice. The gentle tone contradicted strongly with his defensive stance.

"Don't you talk to me about what is and isn't allowed. It's not *right*," Mrs. Hunt hissed through clenched teeth, squaring off with North when she realized there was no going past him. Mr. Hunt was right behind her, hands coming to rest on her shoulders, though he didn't look as though he was trying to pull her back. "What he did to David."

Ren glanced over his shoulder at Justin, who sat motionless, staring at the floor. He didn't even look like he had noticed what was going on yet, like he wasn't even listening. Kelly, on the other hand, was extremely tuned in to the situation.

"Phillip, you'd better take them out of here," Kelly suggested, coming to join the human barricade shielding Justin. Her words drew Mrs. Hunt's attention and anger, though Kelly couldn't look any more disinterested at the small, fancy woman jerking her chin up at her. It was wrong, and Ren knew it, but it looked to him like a chicken puffing up at a hawk.

"How could you," Mrs. Hunt said insultingly to Kelly. "You know he should be locked up. *You* are responsible for allowing a murderer to walk out of here. He killed my son!"

"I don't take cases I don't believe in," Kelly snarled, her lips pulled back to show those unnaturally long canines, her arms folded. "And the jury made the decision. Unanimously. My client didn't kill anyone."

"How can you say that?" Mr. Hunt challenged when Kelly's words flustered Mrs. Hunt speechless. Now he did pull his wife backward, tucking her neatly behind him. North tightened the line, touching shoulders with Ren even though Ren had no idea what he was going to do if someone started forcing themselves past him. He didn't do confrontation; he was trained for different emergencies. He wasn't prepared for this; everything was supposed to be over.

"Phillip," Kelly addressed Mr. Rozensweig again, her tone sharp, leaning forward, infuriating the Hunts even more by pretending they were no longer there.

"Clear the room, everyone," Officer Geisler ordered, finally noticing something was going on and coming to the rescue. "Court's adjourned." As he spoke, he spread his arms like a plow, herding the Hunts and their lawyer away from Justin. Except they didn't really move. Mr. Hunt stood resilient against Officer Geisler, making it seem as though Fritz would have to get physical to make him leave.

"And what are you going to say the next time he brutalizes someone?" Mr. Hunt asked Kelly, though he stared down his nose at Officer Geisler, much cooler and even than his wife. "When the death is immediate instead of delayed, hmm? Is that what it's going to take? Boys like him just grow into worse men. David was worth fifty of him."

That was the last straw for North, who lunged forward, surprising everyone. Officer Geisler shouted at him to stop, but North moved too quickly for anyone to prevent him from anything he wanted to do. He struck like a cobra, and Ren felt Justin grab on to his wrist from behind, just now seeming to catch up to what was going on. He was trying to get up, but Ren wouldn't allow it, blocking the area with his hip until Justin had no choice but to stay in his chair. The last thing Ren wanted was for Justin to get into another fistfight. If that's what was going to happen. Geisler wouldn't let it happen, right? Not here in the courtroom.

But no, North stopped himself, his hands clenching, lowering to his sides, though he kept his fierce gaze fixed on Mr. Hunt.

"Get out," North growled to the Hunts at the same time Officer Geisler shoved his way forcefully between them.

"Let's go," Geisler backed up North, somehow pushing the Hunts toward the exit without touching anyone.

Ren let out a breath and sagged onto the defense table, head close to Justin's, inexplicably exhausted. He heard North heave a sigh behind him. It had to be over now, right? Ren didn't think he could handle any more surprises in this building today. He glanced at Justin, who still looked stunned.

"Well," Kelly quipped, the least affected member of the party, inspecting her nails. "That's that. All right, Kit?"

At the sound of his nickname, Justin shook himself, blinking up first at Ren, who was closest to him, then at Kelly.

"What just happened?" he asked innocently. Kelly shrugged nonchalantly.

"You've been acquitted," Kelly told him warmly, on the verge of being self-congratulatory. "Or did you mean the part where Elias almost knocked William Hunt to the floor in front of half a dozen witnesses?"

Ren smiled shakily at North, who looked ashamed of himself. But Ren couldn't fault him on his momentary lack of discipline. North had been through a lot the past couple of days, and he'd been defending Justin much longer than that. Ren was more surprised that he'd been able to stop himself than that he'd gone after Mr. Hunt in the first place.

"I didn't touch him," North said quietly, as though he were giving himself the information, as though the desire to hit Mr. Hunt had been so strong it was messing with his memory of the event.

"Thank God," Kelly replied.

North muttered something unintelligible, casting a dark glare toward the courtroom doors. Kelly barely glanced; she was more focused on Justin.

"Can you stand up, Kit?" she asked him, still looking worried, and Ren suddenly realized that every concerned look and hesitation he'd seen in Kelly today had nothing to do with the case. She'd known Justin would be let off. All of her worry was about Justin's health. Justin stared at her, not moving.

"Did he say six hundred and fifty thousand dollars?" Justin asked, processing everything slowly. "Did I hear him say that?"

"You did, and you're welcome," Kelly answered. "Now, really, can you stand up, or should I go hunt down that wheelchair?"

"Most of it is yours," Justin immediately offered, nodding at her.

"No," Kelly denied as North walked around the defense table to take up position on Justin's other side. Ren hadn't moved, content to stand here and go through it all over again at Justin's pace. He wanted to be sure everything happened the way he'd thought it did too. "I'm a public defendant, Kit. That means you pay me nothing."

"But you —" Justin challenged, looking confused. Like things were too good to be true.

"I do have some suggestions on what you can do with it, however," Kelly went on, steamrolling over whatever Justin had been trying to say. "I know a guy; he'd be happy to set it up for you. I'll put you in touch with him, ok?"

"Thank you," Justin said gratefully, thanking Kelly for more than her financial advice. She shook her head, looking toward the exit.

"You're a good kid," Kelly said dismissively. "Just be careful on that vigilante stuff in the future, you get me?"

Justin nodded, eyes full of memory, and Ren wondered if he'd ever try to help anyone like that again. He hoped he'd never be put in the position where he'd have to decide.

Officer Geisler returned, looking flustered.

"Kid," he said, exasperated, speaking to Justin. "You can go. In fact, I never want to see you in here again, understand?"

"Yes, sir," Justin toned, his voice very much separated from his thoughts.

"It's over, Kit," Kelly explained. "Now go home and get some rest, will you?"

Finally, Justin moved to get to his feet. Ren and North took his arms on either side, but Justin spread his hands to prevent them. He held on to the table, making his way over to shake hands with Officer Geisler. Then he shook hands with Kelly, who could hardly look at him. Only afterward would he allow Ren and North to touch him.

Kelly started fussing with her briefcase, assembling her files, packing it carefully. Officer Geisler followed them to the door, opening it for them, but then he too fell back, remaining in the courtroom. Justin looked over his shoulder when he heard the heavy doors thud closed behind him, then he looked sideways at Ren.

"Told you," Ren said, forced to say something so he wouldn't get choked up. Justin's eyes were still enormous, full of relief and the worry that he was dreaming. He walked between them, shaky, staring at the walls, the windows, the passing security guards. He looked as though he expected someone to stop him, like he couldn't believe he was actually free to leave.

"Ren," Justin began after they were outside, waiting for North to bring the car. Ren had wanted to rest again on the bench where they'd first waited for North this morning, but Justin asked to go outside, so they stood at the curb in the wind, freezing.

"Yeah?" Ren asked, shoulders hunched against the cold, trying to keep still so he could support Justin. "You want to go back inside?" he suggested hopefully.

"No," Justin denied quickly. "I just wanted to tell you thanks for coming with me. For everything, really."

There was something final about what Justin said, and it made Ren worried.

"No problem," he dismissed. "So, where are you going now that you're free?"

North pulled up then, and their half-started conversation paused as Ren helped settle Justin into the backseat, folding himself in beside him. Justin ripped off the mask almost before Ren closed the door, leaning forward and resting his head on the back of North's seat.

"Sorry, Justin," North apologized from behind the wheel. "I tried to hurry. How are you doing?"

"I don't know," Justin answered, like he was answering both North's question and Ren's at the same time.

"Your back still hurt?" Ren asked an easier question.

"Yeah," Justin acknowledged, sounding drained. "Hey North?"

"What is it, Justin?" North asked, pulling away from the court-house, heading back to the Stephenson Expressway.

"Were you going to hit him?"

"It would have been a mistake if I had," North responded coolly, controlled. "I went farther than I should have as it is."

"But were you?"

"I wanted to," North confessed, in a voice that suggested he wished Justin hadn't asked him. "It wouldn't have solved anything, though. I would have ended up facing assault charges if I had. But I couldn't stand listening to him talk like that about you anymore. He was wrong; you know that, don't you?"

Justin didn't answer; he was fidgeting in the seat again, trying to get comfortable.

"So, Ren, I guess we're dropping you off?" North said, changing the subject when Justin went silent. Ren watched Justin, drinking in the sight of him, feeling as though something were being torn away.

"That'd be great," he said, somehow keeping his voice calm. "But I thought Justin would be staying with me again tonight?" Ren met North's gaze in the rearview mirror and felt conflicted about what he saw there. He knew North wanted to take Justin home with him, start their new life. But they both remembered what Dr. Delacroix had said about staying close to the hospital. Justin's fever hadn't broken, meaning her stipulations remained in place even though the trial was over. Ren watched North force patience onto himself, watched him nod to Ren. He'd waited this long, that nod seemed to say. He would wait as long as he needed to.

"I want to try one of Alek's cookies," Justin whispered, though he pierced Ren with a look of intense gratitude.

"We've got plenty," Ren responded, smiling.

Justin stayed quiet all the drive back to Stony Island. No one really had much to say. Ren texted ahead to let Alek and Denny know that Justin was coming back with him. It was not quiet when they returned to the apartment. Alek was blaring Queen's "We Are the Champions," and it seemed every light had been turned on, making the apartment as bright as possible. They cheered for Justin and Ren as they walked through the door, but things settled down once they saw how tiredly out of it Justin still was. Ren felt that way too. The emotional strain of the day was catching up to them all. Ren felt as though he hadn't slept properly for years, though it had only been a few days.

Ren stationed Justin on the couch again, North taking his place beside him. He forced Justin to take yet another cup of Gatorade while North absently held the cocoa Alek had prepared. Justin tried to eat a cookie, but only managed a couple bites. Alek kept the music playing while he and Denny prepared a celebratory, though still bland, dinner. Which Justin didn't seem to be able to eat.

Alek and Denny demanded a play-by-play of the day, what had happened, what had been said. They wanted all the details. Ren had some of them, but he faltered when it came to the part where he'd jumped over the bar to get to Justin. North wouldn't let him leave it out.

"You should have seen him," North reminisced, shaking his head. "He'd been so mad at Ms. Kelly for saying he'd be an unpredictable liability in the courtroom, and then he goes and just *vaults over the bar*. Like it wasn't even there."

"I had a job to do," Ren muttered, not wanting to go too far into it. He caught Justin looking at him strangely as North retold that part.

North allowed the conversation to move on. Alek told the story of the day from the apartment side, what they'd done while they waited. They spoke about the future, but they noticed abruptly that Justin had fallen asleep somewhere in the middle of it.

"Ren?" North once again called him over to the couch where he hovered worriedly over Justin. "Can you come check him?"

Ren obeyed readily, coming to kneel at Justin's side, noticing a difference in his color, in his breathing.

"He's soaking wet," North observed, but Ren could see that for himself. Justin's black hair hung around his face in damp waves, his white suit shirt sticking to him. Ren smiled, relieved all over again because Justin had been released.

"It's a good sign," Ren said. "His fever's broken."

"Ren?" Justin murmured, not fully awake, but starting to squirm. "Why's it so hot in here?"

"Because you're getting better," Ren told him. "Come on, let's get you out of that suit and into bed."

With North's help, Ren guided a half-asleep Justin into his room, changing him from the suit to Ren's pajamas. They tucked him under the quilt, but he just as quickly kicked it off, muttering about heat. North promised to come and check on him the next morning, gripping hands with Ren before heading out.

Ren stayed next to Justin's side for a long while, enjoying the peace on his face. He looked as though he were sleeping comfortably for the first time since he'd been there, and for once he didn't talk in his sleep. He allowed Ren to set cool cloths on his forehead without protest now. Ren continued watching him long after Denny said goodbye, long after Alek had gone to bed. He just wanted to look at him, happy he was still here. He wasn't sure at what point he fell asleep himself, though he didn't see Justin up and awake again until Wednesday.

ABOUT THE AUTHOR

Karin Mallard has loved writing since the second grade when she would race through her schoolwork so she could ask her teacher for a piece of paper with a sticker on it as a writing prompt. These "sticker stories" were later replaced with random paragraphs woven into her math and Spanish notes, whole notebooks full of terrible poetry, and a run in the early 2000s dedicated to fan fiction.

Karin earned a bachelor's degree in English with an emphasis in creative writing from Brigham Young University - Idaho. Currently, she lives in Utah with her husband, Richard, and their three children.

In addition to writing, Karin also enjoys reading, knitting, freelance editing, and rewatching movies.